The Heart of Hearts

Sword/Eye, Book 1

William F. Burk

ISBN: 978-1-7355287-0-0

ISBN-13: 978-1-7355287-0-0

To Richard,
for showing that delinquent in your office that he could create anything
with words.

The Continent of Lythia

Hawkhaven

Ildar

Crown City

Aestriana

Avelle's Brook

Zerlina

The Church of Mhyrmr

The Folke Lands

Dhul

Abdiah

Mirea

The Miljinn Desert

I

The End of the World

The King of Aestriana, Ahmaal zel Reethkilt, awoke from his sleep in a frigid sweat.

So. You're awake.

The voice caused him to jump abruptly. The king frantically raised up and retreated to the headboard.

"Who's there?!" he yelled in ghastly terror.

It is only me.

King Reethkilt shifted his eyes around the room. In the vague moonbeams that dared peer in through the window, he saw the silhouette of a man sitting in the far corner of the room.

"How did you get in here?!" he yelled once more.

There is no need for yelling, Your Majesty. The guards cannot hear you.

The figure extended a hand to the open window.

The wind brought me here. He paused. *You know all about it, don't you, Your Majesty? You hear the Voice of the Winds, after all.*

The man dropped his hand to his lap, or so it seemed in the pervasive veil of blackness.

Do you hear that distant breeze? That faint elegy?

The king's bed was soaked in his sweat; his old heart beat in his ears.

"Who—? Who are you?"

The figure remained still, its posture reclined and comfortable.

Your Majesty, I am, the voice paused, *the End of the World.*

II

The Girl With The Red Eye

Rain gently caressed the gray stones of the Zerlina monastery. Brother Claus strode frantically down the halls, holding his long robe away from his feet as if it were a dress.

"Nox! Where are you, you devil of a girl!" he raged so loudly he could be heard through the thick, wooden walls.

"He's at it again." One nun smiled at another.

"That orphan girl is going to be the death of him," the other sighed in reply.

"Brother Claus," said the withered Bishop as he held out a hand to stop the outburst, "what is all of this shouting about? You're making everyone worry about you."

"Where," he gasped as he doubled over, "is Nox?"

The Bishop scratched his chin with his long, bony fingers.

"I believe I saw her with Lukas this morning." He snapped his fingers. "Yes, that's right! Why? What is the yelling about?"

Brother Claus contorted his face into a sour frown.

"I have *specifically* told her *not* to associate with him!" he said through gritted teeth as he stormed off.

He could feel the jeering glances of the other clergy as they pierced his skin.

That girl is always getting into trouble, he thought, *why couldn't she just do as she was told. She's always with that boy— that...that fool! They were probably playing knights again. He's a bad influence, that Lukas! And she's probably wearing her new dress, too!*

The rain pattered against the stained-glass windows; Claus whispered curses as he opened his umbrella to step outside.

"Those words don't suit a holy man, Brother Claus," a soft voice caught him as he passed by.

"Hello, Sister Helga..." he groaned.

"Nox again?" she said.

Claus rolled his eyes. "What do you think?"

"She's off playing with Lukas, but I'm sure you already knew that."

"I can't believe she's off playing with that ruffian!" Claus fumed.

"Oh, he's a good young man." The nun smiled. "And who knows, maybe one day they'll even fall in love."

Claus' eyes grew wide.

"Nox!?" he called frantically as he rushed out the door and away from the soft laughter of the nun.

Lukas watched as an airship flew overhead. He marveled at its sleek, metallic hull. It was a majestic sight, even in the rain.

"Yo!" Nox said as she waved her hands in front of his face. "Are we gonna fight or are you gonna spend all day in Lukas-Land?"

"Lukas-Land, probably," he smiled as he looked into her mismatched stare.

Her left eye was a bright crimson color—a stark contrast from her right eye, which was an icy blue. The other orphans certainly kept their distance, blinded by whatever superstitions they had about it—but, to Lukas, the vividness of the red was rather...pretty.

"You're such a ditz, Lukas!" Nox laughed as she pointed her stick at him.

"Ready?" he said.

Without another word, Nox rushed forward. Lukas prepared his stance as she suddenly closed in, swinging wildly. Quickly, he blocked her attack, keeping his eyes on her feet.

Any second now...

With one giant swoop, she jumped as high as she could in the air, bringing her wooden blade down like a great hammer.

Now!

Lukas quickly sidestepped without blocking, causing her sword to drop lower than she had expected.

"No—!" she exclaimed vehemently.

Lukas pushed her lightly on the back with his free hand. Nox swung her arms frantically to regain balance. Mud splashed on the tips of Lukas' shoes as Nox hit the soggy ground.

"How do you do that so easily?" she griped as she shook the mud off of her hands.

"It's all in the footwork." Lukas held out his hand to help her up. "Balance, Nox. If you're unbalanced, even if it's slight, you can lose your footing. Like a tree. If your roots aren't sturdy, you can be pushed over."

"LiKe A TrEe," Nox said derisively, a grin across her face. "Know-it-all."

"Am not!"

She took his hand, then tried to rake the mud from her long, pitch-black hair.

"Again!" she said as she pointed her pretend sword at his face.

"Only if you wanna lose again!" Lukas pointed his sword at her in return. "This time, think about your footwork!"

"I'll make you eat *all* of that advice," she smiled darkly.

"Sure you will!" Lukas said sarcastically.

"I will!" Nox said as she charged forward.

"Nox!" a voice thundered. Nox stamped her foot into the ground in a vain attempt to stop and slammed into Lukas.

"You get over here this *instant!*" Brother Claus demanded, as he stormed toward her. *"What* in the *world* are you doing?!"

Nox smiled nervously.

"M-me and Lukas were sword fighting."

"S-sword fighting?!" A ghastly expression cast over the monk's face.

"Y-yeah, and I almost got him, too!"

"Ladies do *not* sword fight!" Brother Claus said as he shook his finger. "And just *look* at what you've done to your white dress! It's covered in mud!"

Nox hung her head.

"I'm sorry, Brother Claus."

The monk took firm hold of her arm.

"Come with me *right now,* young lady!" the monk glared at Lukas. "And what of you, boy? Are your chores done?"

Lukas suddenly turned pale under the monk's frigid glare.

"I thought as much," he snapped, "get to it!"

"I'll get you tomorrow!" Nox called back to Lukas as she was dragged away to the cathedral.

Brother Claus pulled her arm tighter.

"When I'm through with you, you'll be lucky if you even *have* a tomorrow!"

Lukas sighed, watching the two bicker back and forth as they disappeared into the monastery.

He picked up Nox's stick and decided to walk back as well.

The sanctuary was spacious and ornate. Lukas lazily swept the stone floor, his eyes drifting towards the altar. There, in the center of the shrine, was the fabled blade—the Sword Durandal—lodged in a giant stone.

There's no telling how old the thing is, he thought as he stared at the tarnished, chipped blade. *Looks like it would turn to dust if anyone even touched it.*

Sweeping the sanctuary had been his chore ever since he was a child, and now a teen, he had grown accustomed to doing so. The space wasn't *as* vast as it seemed when he was a child—but it might have been that he was smaller then.

He stretched his arms and looked upward to the ceiling of the cathedral. The glossy wooden buttresses arched to uphold the artwork that depicted the Legend of the Sword in the Stone. He had always been told that the cathedral was built around the rusted relic in ancient times, but he knew vaguely of the myth behind the artifact.

It was something about a philosopher king, who was some big-time churchy-Inquisitor-guy..

...or something like that.

Lukas only knew of the Inquisition from the conversations between the monks and nuns, most of which he had vaguely overheard.

They're like, wizards, right...?

Or, are they more like priests...?

And they live on a mountain or something...?

He really didn't know for sure.

Maybe one day I'll meet one. At least then I could ask.

The sounds of the rain created a white noise as it hit the grass outside—a siren's song that beckoned the orphan to shirk his duties and step outside.

The overcast sky accentuated the flora into a vivid green. Lukas looked out into the forest that surrounded the monastery. It was like an encompassing wall save the small road that supposedly led to the city below. He'd never seen anything outside of this little area. Surely, he thought, he would be able to leave one day. He *must* leave! He *and* Nox. She always said she wanted to become a knight, and the thought of her small frame in an overgrown suit of armor always gave him a laugh.

But. What if not? What if I'm stuck here forever? Then what? Would I just be a monk or something?

Lukas shivered at the thought.

"Daydreaming again?" A soft voice startled him. "Is that what she means by 'Lukas-Land?'"

The orphan turned to see Sister Helga, her lively smile betraying her worn features.

"I guess so," Lukas said, scratching his head. "I'll get back to work."

"Who won today?"

"W-who won?"

"Yes. In the sword fight?" the nun laughed, "Who won?"

"No one, really." Lukas scratched his head bashfully. "We were just playing."

The nun chortled.

"You two like being with each other, don't you?"

Lukas turned his face to the rain; he felt the chill of the small droplets on his skin.

"Yeah," he said softly. "She's my best friend."

The nun smiled.

Lukas stepped back through the doorway and ran his hands through his long, wet hair to keep the water from his face.

"But Brother Claus isn't really a fan..."

The nun put her hand on his shoulder.

"It is not that he dislikes you, young man," she began, "he's just austere. Ever since he found Nox in the woods, he's been a bit...overprotective of her."

Lukas nodded at the nun's attempt to console him, but he knew that what she said wasn't true. Claus *did* dislike him. He could feel it.

"You'd best get back to cleaning again." She said as she walked away. "I don't want you to get scolded on my account."

Lukas watched the frail nun slowly approach the doorway.

"Sister Helga!"

She turned.

"Thank you!"

Her soft grin illuminated her face.

"No problem, Lukas."

Brother Claus rubbed a soapy rag on the white dress to no avail as Nox sat on her bed in a fresh change of clothes.

"What have I told you about associating yourself with that boy?" Claus said, his anger now subsided.

Nox looked at the floor solemnly. "I like playing with Lukas. He's my best friend."

Brother Claus let out an exasperated sigh.

"You're already fifteen years old. I am supposed to raise you to become a proper lady, and I can't do that if you're always running around doing such—" he paused for a moment and shook his head, "not-ladylike things."

"I don't like ladylike things," Nox retorted. "They're boring."

Brother Claus inhaled sharply and then exhaled slowly, calming himself.

"You are an orphan of this monastery," he started, "and under *my* guardianship, you *will* be a lady."

Nox thought of living the rest of her life acting all proper in dresses and gagged.

A silence hung between them.

"Brother Claus?" she asked softly.

"Nox?"

"Is it true?" she paused. "Is it true that I fell from the sky? Is that why the others won't talk to me?"

"It is true," the monk nodded, "you *did* fall from the sky; I found you in the woods and brought you here to raise you as my own. You're my miracle child, Nox—you're my gift from the Aeons above."

"It's because one of my eyes is red, isn't it? It scares the other orphans, doesn't it?"

"I'm sure some might find it curious, but there's nothing wrong with you."

"Lukas doesn't mind my eye. He's never seemed to be scared of it. All the others say mean things. They've always said that I'm a witch, or that I came from witches." Claus could see a faint despair in her eyes, the slight glimpse of a hopeless girl. "But Lukas, he's never said anything mean."

"Now, now," Brother Claus said as he stood, "don't think too hard on it, and make sure you get your chores done."

"Brother Claus?" she said. "Why don't you like me playing with Lukas?"

"Because—" he stopped to find the words, "because he plays rough. I want you to grow to be gentle and elegant, not some knight or sword-wielder. I want you to be proper and refined."

Nox imagined her life as a knight or sword-wielder and smiled. She could only imagine the excitement—much more than being all fragile and proper all the time.

But.

She sighed, realizing that the monk's opinions were absolute.

"Yes, Brother Claus..."

"It's almost supper time. I want you to clean this dress until it is *spotless*." He opened the door, then paused. "Now, I need to return to my duties. Be good, Nox."

Claus closed the door behind him.

Nox fell backward onto her bed. She watched outside of her window as airships zipped through the air, going and coming from the city of Zerlina, the city beyond the walls of the monastery— the city she'd never seen.

The one she felt she'd *never* see.

She could hear their faint hums vibrate through the window pane.

A bird in a cage...

...and she knew it was true.

The dull stones of the monastery floor were cold to Nox's bare feet. Several of the other monks and nuns passed her in the hallway, some of them leading other orphans to their classrooms. She could always hear their whispers as they turned their eyes away.

Nox knew she was different; she had *always* known.

The washing room was more a courtyard with a roof and a large water fountain in the middle. Nox wet a towel and began to scrub the white dress. The mud stains that were splotched all over the white laces were stalwart, and, eventually, she got the hint.

The white dress was ruined.

"Returning from mischief again?" a soft voice spoke from the doorway.

Nox turned around to see Sister Helga.

"I guess I am." She shrugged her shoulders. "Brother Claus sure seemed to think so."

"Off sword fighting with Lukas again?" the old nun chuckled.

"Yeah. Brother Claus says he's a bad influence."

"Claus is just a bit high-strung. He overreacts too often."

Nox sighed.

Sister Helga sat beside her and soaked her own towel in the

water.

"He just wants to raise you to be a good person. That's why he's so hard on you. You're like a daughter to him. You're his miracle child, he says. He simply wants what he thinks is best."

Nox gritted her teeth as she began to dig the cloth into the soiled dress. The room was quiet all but the sounds of swishing water and faint birdsong.

"You and Lukas are close, aren't you?"

Nox stopped.

"Yeah. Lukas is my best friend. He's the only one that will talk to me. Because..." she trailed off.

The nun smiled.

"Because of your eye?"

Nox turned her eyes to the old nun. Sister Helga's face was soft despite her old age.

"Well," the nun said and began cleaning her own clothes, "sometimes the world is cruel to those who are different. In those times, we must stick to the ones who accept us. I understand why Claus is so hard on you. He merely wants you to end up well in the long run."

Nox hung her head as she slowly stopped scrubbing. She placed the dress in her lap.

"But," the nun said, "a true friend is a most valuable thing."

She reached over and took the dress.

"I'll clean this for you. You run along."

Nox looked up at the nun. She could see a grace in her worn brown eyes.

"You...will?"

"Of course!" she winked. "But it has to be our secret!"

Nox smiled stupidly.

"Thank you, Sister Helga!"

III

The Master Inquisitor

Morning light filtered through the tall windows of the Church of Mhyrmr, the headquarters of the Inquisition. Stained-glass colored the rays, which blossomed onto the stone tile.

Underneath the high buttresses, a crimson-robed Inquisitor with a cane casually limped across the mosaic. He made his way to the door beside the altar and began to ascend the spiral stairs, holding his arm against the cold walls to help balance himself.

The corridor at the top of the stairs was lit with etherlamps of blue flame. The Inquisitor hobbled down the hall until he had reached the ornate door at the end.

"Master Inquisitor, requesting entry," he laughed as he knocked.

There was a moment of silence.

"Oh, Eldric," someone replied. "Come in! Come in!"

Eldric smiled and opened the door, which he always considered much lighter than it appeared.

"I do wish you would take your position more seriously," said the Archbishop as he sat at his desk amid a forest of papers.

"Don't be so austere, Marven." The Inquisitor smirked as he hobbled over to the chair and sat down carefully.

Marven scratched his head of graying hair.

"I assume you know why I summoned you?"

"No clue, as always."

"Well." Marven took a sip of his drink. "It's because of a special request."

Eldric reached into the pocket of his crimson robe and pulled out an ivory tobacco pipe with a bear engraved upon it.

"It's a bit of a long story," Marven said, "but I'll keep it quick."

Eldric lit the pipe, puffed, then blew out a perfect ring of smoke.

"Eizen Zilheim, Mirea's current Prime Minister, has asked us to seek out a certain fugitive that he believes has escaped to Aestriana—heading to the town of Zerlina, we believe."

Eldric coughed as he ran his fingers through the smoke.

"And what does King Reethkilt think of the venture?"

"Well," Marven said, handing Eldric a folder thick with papers, "I think he wants the criminal to disappear just as much Zilheim does."

Eldric opened the file and perused through the reports.

"'Iago of the Thousand Swords...'" he mumbled to himself. "He looks awfully young. What would you guess?" He scratched the side of his face. "Twenty years old?"

"He *is* rather young," Marven concurred. "However, I wouldn't underestimate him. He's an adept mage—a prodigy even. Probably why Zilheim came to *us*."

"So young to be an international threat," Eldric mumbled as he puffed his pipe.

"Well," Marven began, "from what I gather, he's a revolutionary in the civil war taking place between the Elves of Mirea and the Beastfolk of the Folke Lands."

"But, he's not of the Beast Tribe?" Eldric raised his brow, smoke spilling from his mouth.

"No," Marven yawned. "He's definitely an Elf, which is even more the reason to be extra careful."

"What exactly," Eldric yawned as well, "did he do? This is the first I've ever even heard of him."

"Well," Marven sipped his drink, "according to Elven authorities, he murdered the Prince of Mirea in cold blood."

"Mirea..." Eldric paused, "had a prince...?"

"It's the first I'd heard of it as well. The Elven King of Mirea is a rather..." Marven tapped his fingers on his desk. "Anti-social and...eccentric man. Not only that, but the Elves of Mirea have long dissociated from the Church. That said, I wouldn't put it past King Mirea to have an heir and not tell us about it."

"The mystery intensifies..." Eldric said with a chuckle.

"Indeed." Marven shrugged. "How he even escaped his captivity is also an enigma. According to witnesses of several guards, the door to his underground cell was still locked even after his escape. It was as if he simply..." the Archbishop said as he waved his hands in the air, "disappeared."

"What an interesting place to go, too." Eldric concurred.

"I sense that there is more to this than we can perceive."

Eldric stroked his white beard as if distracted. "Isn't that the location of the Sword Durandal?"

Archbishop Marven swished his hand dismissively.

"So, you wish me to *inquire* about the situation?" Eldric asked as he blew another ring of smoke.

"I would send another, but the whole thing seems shady. That is why I am sending *you*, the Master Inquisitor himself. I will be sending your knight along with you," he added. "The half-Elf, Snow."

"I would take no other," Eldric chuckled nonchalantly.

"Very well. I've already arranged your airship. Check in with the Bishop of the Zerlina Monastery—see what he knows. It is about a day's journey to Zerlina." The Archbishop sipped his wine. "That is all."

"Well." Eldric slowly lifted himself from his chair and limped to the door. "I'll be off."

Eldric made his way down the stairs and out of the sanctuary. He slowly limped down the breezeway. The mountain air blew the flowers that decorated the courtyard, carrying their aroma with it. He stopped and stared out into the sea of clouds. It was a sight he loved, a perk of being positioned on the highest mountain in all of the continent of Lythia. When he was a child, he might have thought it peculiar to see clouds below him rather than above. But now, as an old man, not much surprised him anymore. He breathed in a deep breath as he leaned upon his sturdy cane. He never worried about the dangers of his position. The Inquisitors were a sect of the Church charged with the protection of the common world from the terrors of the supernatural, but, honestly, the thrill of danger had grown old to him.

"Master Inquisitor." A voice from behind pierced his thoughts.

Eldric exhaled and turned to see a tall, blue-haired, young woman in armor standing at salute.

"Snow!" he chuckled with a smile. "Just out of the training yard, I suppose?

"I was ordered by the Archbishop to accompany you to Zerlina," she said, smiling, "as always."

"Of course!" Eldric laughed. "There's no finer knight in all of Lythia."

She sighed at his praises, but she knew at least *he* believed them. She knew he respected her, and she knew that she respected him. She had been his knight for as long as she had worked in the field, and, the more she had thought about it, the more she realized that his unspoken bond with her was more paternal than professional.

The two walked at Eldric's limping pace down the breezeway and into the airship hangar. Many were coming and going in the aerodock, which filled the air with unintelligible noise. Eldric nodded to his fellow Inquisitors who responded by frantic salute. The two passed several docks until they reached one with a large airship. Eldric slowly approached the gargantuan vessel and breathed in the misty air.

"Ah! The Airship *Orca*!" he said as he beheld the metallic gears and steaming pipes, "I never get tired of looking at her."

"Yes, sir," Snow agreed. "She *is* a wonderful sight."

"Master Inquisitor!" a voice called out from among the surrounding noise.

A man hurried over to them, his solid black uniform decorated with medals.

"Hello, captain," the Master Inquisitor said casually.

The captain stood at salute. "It appears I will have the honor of piloting her once again. The travel to Zerlina will be a day and about a half in duration. Archbishop Marven has already prepared your things and all other arrangements. We are ready to disembark when you give the signal."

"Well, let us begin." Eldric shrugged.

The captain turned promptly and motioned to the crew standing behind him. Once inside, Eldric, trailed by Snow, followed the Captain to the cockpit.

"Zerlina is a large trading town in southern Aestriana. It has never in its history been graced with the presence of one of your status."

Snow helped Eldric to his seat.

"Southern Aestriana, you say?" he smiled. "I hear it's quite beautiful there this time of year."

The city of Zerlina was loud with the sounds of commerce as a hooded man slithered within their midst. No one noticed as the figure slipped past the crowded market stalls and into a garden in the back alleys. Concealed by the hood of his cloak, the slim man stopped.

Now prowling the solitary garden, he removed his hood to reveal his youthful face and Elven features.

"You called?" he said into the air.

Suddenly, a black cloud formed in front of him. The cloud lingered for a few seconds, then, out of it walked a large, muscular man. The Elf took a moment and studied him. He was gargantuan, his skin a deep blue. It was obvious he was one of the desert people, a Darkling from the country of Abdiah.

"Iago of the Thousand Swords," the large man said in a deep voice, "you have arrived."

"The one and only," Iago said with a theatrical bow. "What do you want, Agnon? Why did you bring me to this dump?"

Agnon turned his piercing green eyes to the sky and took a breath as if he perceived something no one else could.

Iago watched him impatiently.

"What—?" Iago began.

Agnon held up his large hand to silence the other. "She is here."

"I see," Iago concurred. "Then when must we go retrieve her?"

"Not yet," Agnon paused, "but in short time."

"What are we waiting on? Hasn't your 'Master' grown impatient?"

Agnon waved his hand to calm the young man. "The Master Inquisitor has not yet arrived. You are the bait. We must wait for the fish to bite."

"Very well," Iago shrugged dismissively, "I await your orders."

Iago hooded himself, left the garden, and was soon nameless among the crowd of faces.

IV

The Inquisitor, the Knight, and the Orphans

Steam billowed from the Airship *Orca* as it landed in the Zerlina aerodock. The vessel's gears clanked loudly as the landing ramp descended onto the floor. Once cleared, Eldric limped down the walkway, followed closely by Snow.

At the bottom of the ramp, two monks stood to greet them.

"Master Inquisitor!" the monks praised and bowed in unison. "It is an astounding honor!"

Without a word, Eldric reached into his cloak and pulled out his ivory pipe.

Then, abruptly, he paused.

The monks watched as the Master Inquisitor frantically patted his cloak with his free hand, then looked upward and laughed.

"You two gentlemen wouldn't happen to have a match, would you?"

The monks looked at each other for a moment.

"Master Inquisitor Eldric, right?" one said pointedly.

"You *are* Eldric of the Black Flame, yes?" the other questioned, reinforcing the inquiry of the first.

"Indeed!" Eldric chuckled.

The two monks looked at one another once more, confounded, then turned and bowed again.

"Y-your transportation to the monastery is waiting!" said one.

"We are *humbly* your guides," added the other.

"Then, by all means," Eldric replied with a motion of his hand, "lead on."

The two turned and began walking; however, their paces soon slowed as they recognized the speed of their guest.

"What are your names?" Eldric asked casually.

"I am Grego," spoke one.

"I am Lee," said the other.

"Good to know," Eldric said as he stroked his thin white beard.

The aerodock was filled with steam and smoke; merchants of all different races lined the walls with exotic goods from far away. Sounds of engines and voices filled the air in a droning cacophony.

The monks steered through the crowd carefully with the Inquisitor's limp in mind.

Snow held her hand on the hilt of *Silversong,* the short sword at her belt. She'd come prepared, with her favorite blade, *Silvershear,* strapped to her back; however, in such crowded areas, the shorter blade was more practical than the claymore.

The knight's ever-watchful eyes were set on the movement of her surroundings, watching the bodily movements of the people passing by. Her Elven blood gave her a sensitivity not known to those without, and, combined with her training, she could see almost everything at once.

She was looking for anything sudden.

It was her sworn duty to protect Eldric, and so she diligently scanned the hangar as the two monks guided them out of the aerodock.

"The transportation is right this way, Master Inquisitor," Lee informed as he led them out of the gates and into the city.

They walked for a small time, then Gregor pointed to a shiny black automobile with open windows.

"How quaint," Eldric said.

Lee turned and bowed. "It will be a twenty-minute drive to the monastery.

Eldric looked around at the animated town before him, then nudged Snow.

"See? I told you it was pretty this time of year."

"What do you think he was like?" Lukas' voice echoed throughout the empty cathedral.

"In Lukas-Land again, are we?" Nox smirked as she sprawled out longways on a pew.

Lukas smiled, looking at the art on the ceiling. It had somewhat faded from time, but he could still make out most of its features.

"Who are you even talking about?"

Lukas pointed at the depiction of a man in armor. "Him."

"That Philosopher King dude?" Nox said as she looked upward also. "I dunno. Maybe he was all noble and stuff. Maybe *you* should try to take the Sword."

"Ha-ha," Lukas replied dryly. "Aren't we clever today?"

She raised up, a foxy grin across her face, "Have you ever tried? C'mon, be honest! You sweep the sanctuary *every day!* You really mean to tell me you've never even considered trying it?"

"Not really." Lukas said blankly. "Should I have?"

"I woulda tried it."

There was a moment of silence; Lukas began sweeping once more. The swish of the straw scuffing the ancient stone sounded like whispers in the spacious cathedral.

"Hey, Nox?" Lukas said finally. "Why do you want to be a knight so bad?"

Nox giggled.

"Do you really not know? C'mon! Guess!"

Nox felt Lukas sit beside her. She looked up at him from where she lay. His long, white-blond hair had fallen over his shoulder.

"I really don't know."

"Well," she said, "it's so I can protect *you*."

Lukas looked down at Nox; her red eye and her blue eye seemed so bright.

"Isn't it supposed to be the other way around?" Lukas raised an eyebrow.

Nox squinted her eyes.

"There's no rule!"

"You can't even beat me in a sword fight," he jeered. "How can you plan to protect me if I'm stronger than you?"

"Yeah—! But, that's just right now! Just wait until I get trained!"

Lukas laughed.

The two fell quiet. Nox reclined in the pew; Lukas' eyes were drawn to the Sword in the stone.

"Nox." He finally said.

She looked up at his face as he continued staring forward.

"Let's protect each other. I'll protect you; you'll protect me. Right?"

Nox smiled as she stared into his hazel eyes.

She held up her little finger. "Promise?"

"A pinkie promise?" Lukas said. "You gotta be kidding me, right?"

Nox contorted her face. "What's so wrong with it?"

"You're silly, Nox."

"Well, do you promise or not?!"

Lukas gave in to the gesture.

"I promise."

The large wooden doors to the sanctuary squeaked as they slowly opened.

Lee held the door open for the crippled Inquisitor, who was followed by Snow, then Gregor. Once inside, Eldric took a moment to look around.

"Quite a place you have here," he chuckled.

"This is a place rich with history!" Gregor said as if announcing to a crowd.

"The final resting place of the Sword Durandal!" Lee added.

Lukas stared at the curious new guests as they walked by, specifically the Inquisitor. There was an air about him; he was unlike anyone else the orphan had ever seen before. He watched the old man's eyes—white irises surrounded by black, as if the colors were inverted.

Lukas shivered.

"And who do we have here?" Eldric said as he bit down on his empty tobacco pipe.

The orphan gulped.

"I-I'm Lukas."

Nox raised up momentarily, her eyes instantly gravitating to Snow. She had never seen a knight before, much less a *female* knight. For a moment, Nox stared intently at the soldier, who was lost in gazing at her surroundings.

"Nox!" Lukas nudged her.

"Oh, yeah!" She fell back onto the pew once more. "I'm Nox!"

"Bow, you brats!" Lee commanded as he stomped his foot on the ground.

"Show some respect! This is the Master of the Inquisition!" Gregor fumed.

Eldric held up his hand.

"That is fine." He turned to the orphans and smiled. "Lukas. Nox. I am glad to make your acquaintances."

He turned to the two monks.

"Gentlemen, let us carry on. Perhaps the Bishop will have a match for my pipe."

"Of course!" the monks said in unison once again, bowing. "Right this way, sir!"

Lukas picked up his broom once again. Nox rose from the pew, watching Snow walk away.

"Nox?" Lukas waved his hand in front of her face. "What's up with you?"

"Did you see them?"

"Yeah. He must be some big guy from the Church."

"Did you see *her?*"

Lukas stopped and smiled.

"She was carrying swords, wasn't she?"

"Yeah!" Nox exclaimed with wide eyes. "She was a knight! She was a *girl*, too!"

Lukas smirked.

"What? You gonna run off with them and become a knight?"

"Maybe! So what?"

"You can't even beat *me!*" Lukas ruffled her hair. "You'd be a *terrible* knight!"

Nox slapped his hand away. "You're mean, Lukas!"

Lukas laughed. "I'm just joking!"

Nox stood up straight as she combed her fingers through her raven hair.

"You'll see! One day, I'll be a knight!"

Lukas smiled at her determination.

She never relented; she always persevered. He liked that about her.

"I gotta get back to work."

The room quieted. He could feel her staring at him.

"And," he began, "I'll meet you in the courtyard in an hour."

"I'll beat you this time, Lukas!" she exclaimed as she rushed off, her hands still in her hair. "Payback for tangling my hair!"

Lukas smiled as he watched her scurry off.

Nox skipped down the hall, playfully trying to fit her feet on the tiles and avoid the cracks. It reminded her of when she and Lukas would race from one end of the hall to the other, hopping on the cool stones.

Thoughts of fighting Lukas filled her mind. He had always won —but not today! She would make sure of it!

Halfway down the hall, Nox abandoned her gleeful tile-stepping and proceeded to walk slowly, looking at the stained-glass windows. The rays of the afternoon sun were transformed into bright greens, blues, and yellows, which came to life upon the mundane gray floors. Nox held her hand in front of the light and watched it turn into different colors.

But, soon, that was abandoned, as well.

Her eyes wandered. She could see scattered monks and nuns hurrying to do this or that.

She thought of the female knight.

Nox pondered for a moment as she made her way sluggishly down the corridor.

Where had she gone?

That question, however, was short-lived.

The office of the Bishop! she thought. *That Inquisitor guy was really important, right? He must've had something to talk to the old man about!*

Nox felt a sudden excitement rush through her. The thought of talking to a real, *girl* knight was exhilarating. Maybe she would let her see the swords she carried?

Visions of running off and becoming a knight swirled in Nox's mind. She swiftly turned around and sped off to the Bishop's office. Nox swept past the clergy and down the halls, making her way to the corner leading to the office.

Once there, she placed her hands on the wall and peeked around sheepishly, hoping that the knight was there.

And, she was.

One hundred butterflies fluttered inside of her.

What do I say?

She was so adamant about rushing to see the knight that she hadn't thought about what she would say to her.

Nox took a deep breath.

Here we go!

Snow stood outside of the Bishop's door, listening to the conversation inside. Her pointed ears couldn't make out every distinct word, but she could hear the tone and rhythm of the conversation. She closed her eyes. In her mind, she could make out the lining of the small, lightly-colored desk. She could almost imagine where everyone stood in the room, and she considered what she would do if something went wrong—thinking mainly about how quickly she could draw her sword.

Multiple scenarios ran through her mind.

"M-miss." A small voice broke her concentration. "Are you a knight?"

Snow opened her eyes to see Nox standing in front of her. She surveyed the petite girl and soon determined her to be non-threatening.

"I," Snow hesitated, caught off guard, "I am. Why?"

Excitement suddenly ignited in Nox's eyes.

"And you're a *girl,* too?!"

Snow pushed back her short azure hair, slightly taken aback by the ecstatic teen.

"I am. I am indeed a girl."

Nox grinned widely.

"I didn't know that girls could be knights, too!"

"O-of course they can. Why couldn't they be?"

"Well," Nox sighed, "Brother Claus always told me they couldn't." She mocked the monk's voice. "Ladies *do not* sword fight!"

Snow laughed modestly with her hand to her mouth.

"Someone gets in trouble a lot, don't they?"

Nox could feel her cheeks turning red.

"Well, I mean—" She shook her head. "What's it like? Y'know, being a knight?"

Snow smiled at Nox's curiosity.

"Well, it is different than anything else. It takes hard training."

"What do you do?"

Snow looked at the wooden door behind her.

"I am a knight to the Church of Mhyrmr. That means that I live every day to protect someone." Their eyes met, Snow's were suddenly frigid. "Even if it means death."

The sincerity in the young woman's inflection gave Nox a chill. "D-death?"

"Indeed. I live every moment knowing it could be my last. But, this is the life that I have chosen."

Nox looked at the woman in awe.

"Why did you become a knight?"

Snow looked up at the window. The dim light that filtered through shone upon her azure eyes.

"Someone saved my life once. He raised me as his own. So," she looked as if she were lost in thought, "I owe him my life, at the very least. *That* is why I became a knight. To protect those I love."

Nox couldn't help but smile.

"Now, if you don't mind," Snow began, "I must listen in silence."

"Okay!" Nox nodded and turned to leave, her focus shifting to fighting Lukas.

"Young lady!" Snow called as Nox scurried away. "What is your name again?"

"Nox!"

Snow waved her hand.

"I am Snow. It is a pleasure."

Nox waved and ran off.

Snow stood, questioning what she had just seen. She was sure she saw it, even in the dim light.

Nox had a *red eye.*

V

The Message

The woods around the Zerlina Monastery were dense, an advantageous feature for the two figures hidden within the foliage.

"What now, Agnon?"

"Now," the Darkling's deep voice growled, "we take the target and deliver the message."

Agnon pulled two etherbombs from his cloak and handed them to Iago.

The large man waved his hand and said something under his breath. A black cloud appeared; he stepped into it and was gone.

Iago pushed through the thick vines and thorns, raised his hood, and groaned.

"Here we go..."

As Nox rushed away, the door to the Bishop's office opened and out limped Eldric. Seeing him, Snow began to salute, but he waved his hand dismissively without a glance, scratching his balding head.

"Master Inquisitor?"

"They know nothing. There have been no reports. No occurrences. No signs."

"Perhaps we should inquire with the town guard?"

"Perhaps so," he said as he stroked his beard, "but I don't understand why an escaped convict would come to a town like Zerlina. There are plenty of smaller, more...remote places to hide. Coming to a large town like this one is like asking to be arrested."

He sighed.

"I think there is more at work here."

He looked longingly at the empty pipe in his hand.

"I saw you made a friend," he chuckled.

Snow looked confused.

"The orphan girl, I mean," he corrected himself. "Did she ask you about your service?"

"Indeed, sir." Snow nodded.

Eldric smiled.

"I see! Perhaps someone has a fan now."

The knight blushed.

"Master Inquisitor," she said pointedly, "I missed a detail when we arrived, but I just took note of it," Snow calmed herself. "That girl," she paused. "That orphan girl had a crimson eye."

Eldric's visage turned grim.

"How could I have missed that?" he mumbled. "Maybe, then...I wonder..."

Nox made her way to meet Lukas in the courtyard, which was a small garden outside of the cathedral.

Lukas was standing in the middle of the yard, warming up as he swung his practice sword at nothing.

"Lukas," Nox called as she walked toward him, "you ready to lose?"

"Says the girl who's never won!" Lukas scoffed, unaffected.

"I'll beat you today!"

"Suuuure you will!"

Lukas tossed her the other wooden sword.

Nox picked it up and readied her stance.

"Go!" he exclaimed.

Nox rushed toward him.

She swung downward, but Lukas evaded by sidestepping. Quickly, she shifted her weight to avoid falling, then straightened her back and attacked with a horizontal slice. Lukas blocked and parried, his sword fast approaching. Seeing her doom, Nox dropped her knees and eluded the strike. Surprised, Lukas barely avoided by stepping backward as Nox launched her counterattack. She swung with such force that she put her weight in her swing. Seeing an opening, Lukas put his hand on her shoulder lightly, and the unbalanced girl fell to the ground.

Nox looked up to see his sword at her throat.

"You have to distribute your weight evenly," he said. "If this were a real fight, you'd be dead."

Nox frowned.

"Look who's such an expert all of a sudden."

Lukas smiled gently and held out his hand.

"You *did* give me a challenge this time, though."

As she took his hand, a sudden blast knocked him to the ground beside her.

The blast resounded through the halls. Eldric felt the shock push him over, but, thinking quickly, Snow grabbed him just before the elderly man hit the stone floor.

"An explosion?!" Eldric exclaimed.

He pointed down the hall.

"Snow! Get the clergy to safety."

Eldric looked at the cathedral.

"I'm going to the sanctuary. I have a strange feeling about this."

Snow nodded, then bolted down the hall.

A bomb? She thought as she rushed down the hallway. She had been prepared for the worst, but *this* did nothing but perplex her. She lined up the monks and nuns, along with the other panicked orphans, and directed them outside. The crowd scurried, but she was in armor, so it wasn't hard to make them listen to her.

Brother Claus ran around in a crazed fashion, asking the others something in a frantic tone.

"Where is Nox?!" he screeched.

Snow grabbed him by the arm.

"Get out of here," she commanded, her azure eyes piercing him. *"I'll find her!"*

Honestly, she didn't know where Nox was. She just ran. Snow's long legs covered small distances quickly. She would find Nox soon enough, but she still knew she needed to be careful.

Who would blow up a church? Was it Iago?

If so, why would an escapee risk going back to prison by attacking a monastery? It didn't make sense. If caught, his sentence would be doubled—no, tripled!

There must be more, she thought.

He's after something.

Nox and Lukas recovered from the shock to find fire rising from the cathedral beside them.

"Nox!" Lukas took her hand. "Are you alright?

Nox nodded, coming back to reality.

"Look what we have here!" A voice struck surprise into the two orphans.

They quickly turned to see a cloaked figure standing in front of them.

"So," the stranger held his arms out as if addressing a crowd. "The girl who fell from the sky was raised in a monastery!"

He removed his hood to reveal his young, Elven face.

"Is that how the story goes?"

Lukas stepped in front of Nox, holding his arm in front of her.

"Who are you?"

The Elf bowed theatrically.

"Name's Iago. It's a pleasure." He pointed a finger at Nox. "And, I'm here to take her away from here. I know someone who's absolutely *dying* to meet her!"

Lukas grabbed his wooden sword and pointed it at the intruder. He had never been in a real fight, and he knew what was in his hands wasn't much of a weapon.

"W-what do you want with Nox?!" Lukas' voice trembled.

"Nox, huh?" Iago sneered as he spoke. "Is that the name you go by these days?"

A shiver shot up Nox's spine.

"What do you mean?" she yelled. "I've always been Nox."

Iago smiled and waved his hand.

"Forget it."

Lukas gripped his wooden stick.

"I won't let you take her!"

Iago sighed and extended one arm outward.

"I'd think you'd be smarter than that."

Fear stunned the orphans.

They watched as a gray aura engulfed Iago, his cloak blowing about as if touched by a light breeze.

"*Gladyus Millenio*," he called into the air.

Lukas and Nox watched in horror as ten phantom swords materialized in the air and danced around the criminal.

The truth of the situation suddenly dawned upon them.

Chills trickled through Lukas' skin.

"You're...a mage?!"

Lukas stood between Iago and Nox, a weak buffer in the way of the Elf's plan of taking her with him. The translucent blades danced in Lukas' eyes.

"Scared, kid?" the other taunted.

The truth was that he *was* scared; he was *extremely* scared.

Lukas could feel his legs going numb.

No! He would stand and fight! He wouldn't let this man—or anyone, for that matter—hurt Nox.

He held the wooden sword in both hands.

"What an idiot!" Iago pointed his finger forward.

One of the blades followed its master's command, shooting toward the orphan with blinding speed.

Time stopped, or at least it seemed so to Lukas. Death flashed in his mind for that split second. Nox was calling his name in shrill panic, but he couldn't hear her. He knew she was, though; he knew she was crying for him. How could he have been so dumb? Why didn't he just take her and run? Lukas felt his legs drop.

He flinched.

Then, there was the sound of scraping metal.

For a moment, Lukas felt himself breathing. It felt surreal; it felt...unnatural.

He opened his eyes.

Standing in front of him was the knight he had seen before, a long silver claymore in her hand. Lukas saw her short blue hair and pale skin. Her tall, lithe body was covered in light, silver armor.

"You're definitely courageous," she said looking over her shoulder, "or just plain stupid. I'm not sure which."

Her azure eyes were like frigid stilettos; he felt as if they could spear him through.

Still weak, he nodded as he tried to stand.

"Get away from here!" the knight commanded. "I'll deal with this one."

Lukas pushed himself up, despite his weak legs.

"Nox!" he called as he grabbed her hand. "We have to get out of here!"

Nox nodded in agreement, her eyes filled with uncertainty. But, she followed his lead, just as she had always done.

"What a bother..." Iago groaned.

Snow straightened and pointed her blade at her opponent.

"Iago of the Thousand Swords, I assume?"

Iago bowed theatrically once again. "Yours truly!"

Snow's face hardened.

"As a knight of the Church of Mhyrmr, you are under arrest!"

Sorry, honey," he raised his hand, "I'm not going anywhere."

Ten more lucid blades appeared and orbited around him. At his beckon, three blades sped toward her in quick succession, whistling as they coursed through the air.

With one hand, Snow swung the great *Silvershear,* slicing the phantasms, and watched them explode into bright grayish fragments.

"So," she smiled, "that's twice I've destroyed them. It seems your swords are physical objects."

"Is that so?" the Elf chuckled. "You wield that giant sword with one hand. I guess that explains the blue hair, which makes you a...half-Elf?" he laughed. "Man, do I pity you."

Snow was well practiced in the art of combat, even against those who used the magical arts. She dashed toward the attacker in hopes of closing the distance between them. She had observed all she needed to. His powers worked best at long range.

Iago waved his hand once more and four blades surrounded the knight.

"I wouldn't move if I were you," he said in a grim tone. "We're here for the girl. I don't *have* to spill your blood, but I won't mind doing so. You pick."

Without a word, several silver streaks crossed the phantom swords as Snow sliced through them with *Silversong's* nimble blade, causing them to burst into bright gray dust.

Iago raised his fingers to summon more blades, but Snow was already upon him, swinging horizontally at his throat. His Elven instincts kicked in, and Iago felt the air of the swing over his head as he ducked.

Swiftly, he pointed two fingers upward, and two blades appeared—one above and one below.

"You don't have to die here, knight!"

The blades shot straight for their target, but Snow spun with inhuman speed, her swords creating bright flashes, destroying the illusions once more.

With tempered training mixed with Elven instinct, Snow quickly faced her opponent and rushed forward. Iago quickly stepped backwards, but it was too late. Snow cried out as she moved in with her short sword, thrusting it straight toward the unarmored Elf's heart.

Iago fell to the ground, panting heavily.

Snow felt a terrible pain in her stomach. She looked down to see her own sword lodged in her armor. The hilt of *Silversong* was enveloped by a black cloud and the blade protruded from another cloud just below the first.

"If it weren't for the quality of your scale mail, you'd be dead," a deep voice whispered in her ear. Snow looked up to see a large Darkling. His pale green eyes were locked on the cathedral.

"Thanks, Agnon," Iago said through heavy breaths, "I thought I was dead for sure."

"Stand." He commanded harshly. "It is time we retrieved the

girl, and it is time to deliver the message."

He nodded as they walked past Snow. Agnon lightly pushed her over.

Snow fell to the ground and all went black.

Lukas held Nox's hand tightly as they ran through the rubble of the monastery's halls. Smoke filled the corridors with charcoal-colored fumes, causing them to cough. Still, they sprinted through, the visceral instinct to escape overpowering their numbing bodies.

The orphans entered the cathedral and ran toward the stone door of the back exit.

Then, they stopped, their heart's sinking to their stomachs.

The walls around the door had caved in.

"Lukas," Nox said as she gasped in the thick haze, "we have to go the other way."

Lukas nodded.

The orphans retraced their steps to try one of the other doors. Nox felt as if her legs would give out at any moment, and she knew it was the same for Lukas.

Each door left them with less and less hope for escape, until they found themselves in the cathedral. Lukas and Nox quickly rushed past the Sword Durandal and froze.

Their eyes widened.

Iago stood at the entrance, staring directly at them.

"Let's make this as painless as possible. What do you say?" He gestured with his hands open.

"Let go of me!"

Lukas suddenly felt Nox tighten her grip around his arm. He turned to see a large, blue-skinned man pulling her into a dark cloud.

"Do not resist," the hulking man's voice grated.

"Nox!" Lukas pulled back, but the muscular man slammed his fist into the young man's face.

Lukas felt his head hit the stone floor. He could hear his ears ringing; he could hear Nox screaming in horror. The cloud disappeared and reappeared beside Iago. A beaten boy watched as the grim man emerged from the mist, holding Nox by the throat.

Lukas felt his heart scream.

No...

    Stand...

        You must...

            ...stand!

He could hear Nox choking as she fought back against the large Abdian's raw strength. Lukas rolled onto his chest and put his wearied hands on the floor.

Rise...

    RISE!

With the sheer force of will left within his tattered body, Lukas mustered a stand.

"Looks like we got what we came for," Iago yawned.

"Let go of me!" Nox managed to gasp as she beat on the Darkling's thick arms, her tiny fists weak against the other's massive size.

Nox felt his large hand wrap tighter around her neck.

"You will be quiet!" his voice thundered.

Lukas was barely on his feet.

But at least I'm on my feet.

He watched Nox choke helplessly.

This wasn't happening. This isn't *happening!*

Memories of hours before this event flashed through his mind as if they were memories of bygone days. Lukas stood on weak and trembling legs. He coughed and wiped the tears and blood from his eyes.

It stung.

What do I do? What do I do?

His mind raced in a manic blitz of adrenaline. There *had* to be an answer here; there *had* to be a solution.

I won't let this happen!

He looked to his right...

The Sword Durandal!

He knew it was crazy; he knew the sword wouldn't budge—or

that maybe it was just a legend, all of that about the Philosopher King and whatnot. It would probably just fall apart when he drew it. He knew it was a gamble...

He knew he needed a *miracle.*

"You're going for that old thing?" Iago taunted as he watched Lukas wobble dazedly toward the Sword in the stone.

"Pay him no mind," the other said. "We need to deliver the message to the Inquisitor."

Lukas reached for the hilt and took hold of it. He pressed downward on it, raising his battle-worn, smoke-stricken, body to a proper stand.

This is crazy! Am I crazy? Am I really *relying on a stupid legend—a fairy tale?!*

He felt tears coming to him. He wouldn't let them take her— *NO WAY!*

Lukas roared with all of the strength left in his spirit. At a stand, he gripped both hands tightly around the hilt and pulled upward. Suddenly, a bright light shot from the blade and ascended as a pillar into the sky.

Lukas fell backward onto the ground. He looked at his hand through blood-blurred eyes.

No, it wasn't a dream. He held it...

In his hands, he was holding the Sword Durandal.

Eldric looked into the sky as the illuminating pillar of light shot into the clouds.

"By Empyria..." he mumbled to himself.

Could it be possible? The Sword was truly drawn? Could a Heart of Hearts truly appear in a time like this?

Eldric combed his beard as he limped toward the cathedral, confusion enveloping him.

Whatever was happening in that sanctuary, he needed to be present.

He knew that much.

Iago beheld the orphan, who now held a sterling and exquisite

Durandal. He could see that the young man was on the last of his sudden second wind.

"You've got a sword now, big deal," the ruffian laughed with a wave of his hand. "I've got a hundred!"

Lukas watched in terror as a multitude of phantom swords materialized, lining the ceiling above him.

"You didn't have to get hurt, y'know," Iago said as he waved his hand once more. "You could've just handed over the girl and been on your merry way."

Lukas gulped and held the Sword with both hands.

"Nox." he muttered faintly. "Give me back Nox!"

"You've only hurt yourself." Iago shrugged as he pointed a finger directly at the orphan boy.

Transparent blades swiftly rained downward, one by one. Lukas felt his legs buckle and he hit the ground. He was at the end of his strength. Durandal was heavy in his hands.

Was this it?

He closed his eyes...

"Rex Ynfernim!" a voice thundered throughout the room, shaking the very foundation of the building and all who were in it.

Lukas opened his eyes to see the old, crippled Inquisitor standing before him. He looked upward. The translucent blades above were consumed in a great, brilliant black flame.

Eldric turned to the orphan.

"Lukas, was it?"

Lukas nodded. He stared curiously at the old man. The figure that stood before him was no longer the careless elder. In that moment, Lukas had never seen *anyone* stand more firmly.

"Very well!" Eldric smiled.

Something in that smile caught the young man by surprise— that smile that seemed to spite the hell that was taking place around them.

"Stay by me, Lukas. I will lead you to victory."

"So, the great Master Inquisitor finally appears, huh?" Iago taunted. He waved his hands and a hundred blades appeared once more.

"We cannot kill him, you fool!" Agnon said. "He must be alive to receive the message."

"Well, I'm not gonna let him kill *us!*"

Nox's struggle grew slower and slower against the muscular man's grip until she eventually went limp.

Agnon threw the unconscious Nox over his shoulder.

"Make this quick."

"I shall." Eldric broke into their words.

The old man raised his finger and pointed it straight at his targets. Lukas watched as a bright, black aura swallowed him. For a moment, a gust surrounded them, extinguishing the fires around the sanctuary. His cloak ruffled as if in a great wind. Lukas felt as if his breath was being taken from his lungs; he felt as if he were suffocating.

This old man? Could he really hold such daunting power?

The room was blackened, enveloped in a dark void.

Iago looked upward frantically. "The sun is gone?!"

"Of course it is." Agnon said calmly. "Eldric has the Devil's Blood."

"Devil's Blood, huh?" Iago pointed forward and the phantom swords shot forward, howling as they cut the air.

Eldric stood stalwart, two fingers unhindered.

"*Rex Ynfernim!*" he thundered.

Suddenly, a blast of brilliant black flame shot from his fingertips, shaking the walls of the cathedral under its great might. Windows shattered as it coursed toward its target. The flame exploded into the ghost-like blades, incinerating them into luminescent dust.

Iago was suddenly stricken with fear and horror.

"You *burned* them?!"

"You're a fool," Agnon said. "The black flames do not burn the flesh, they burn the very *spirit* itself."

Agnon whispered to himself, and a large black cloud appeared beside him.

"It is time," he said to the other, "we must go."

Iago nodded, grabbed Nox, and disappeared into the cloud.

Agnon turned in the direction of Eldric.

"I have a message."

Eldric raised his fingers once more. Agnon stuck his hand inside of another black cloud. Suddenly, a portal appeared beside Eldric and a disembodied hand extended and grabbed his arm with great strength. The old Inquisitor cringed.

"I wouldn't do that," Agnon stated. "Heed, for I have a message for the Church of Mhyrmr."

The large man released his hand from Eldric's arm and the small cloud disappeared.

"My Master says: 'Behold, O mankind, for the Black Star's dance shall judge the world.'" He paused. "That is my message."

Agnon stepped into the large cloud and vanished.

"Black Star...?" Eldric repeated under his breath.

He turned to Lukas; the young man had long fainted.

VI

Finding the Monastery

As children, Nox and Lukas sat on the ground across from each other, eye-to-eye. In the dense forest, faint strands of the midday sun pierced the canopies above, creating thin ribbons of golden light between the shadowy branches.

"I don't know why," Nox said as a mere whisper, "but I wanted to give you something."

Lukas tilted his head.

"W-what do you mean?"

"You're the only one who will talk to me, so I wanted to give it to you."

"I still don't understand?"

Quietly, Nox extended her arm and placed it lightly upon his chest. Her touch was soft, and Lukas couldn't help but wrap his hand around hers. As he looked up to meet her gaze, eerie tingles bubbled underneath his skin. Nox was staring directly at him, her crimson eye glowing brightly, illuminating the ground around them in a vivid, scarlet light.

She pressed firmly upon Lukas' chest.

"I wanted to give it to you," she said.

Lukas watched as the glow faded from her eyes...

Then, her body went limp.

"Nox?! Nox, are you okay?!" He cried as she fell into his arms.

Silence.

Lukas could feel a pulsing in his chest—a random, sharp pain.

What is happening? *He thought, his mind suddenly beginning to fade.*

With Nox in his arms, he fell to the ground, and darkness took him...

Eldric sat in one of the phone booths outside of the Zerlina clinic, the phone to his ear.

"'Black Star?'" the voice of Marven mumbled from the other end. "What on Lythia could *that* mean?"

"Indeed." Eldric replied. "The meaning of the message, and its intent, is quizzical to me as well. As a matter of fact, the whole occurrence seemed...premeditated, as if the freeing of Iago was just a ploy to draw out a high-ranking Inquisitor."

Eldric paused.

"Archbishop," he said finally, "the man who spoke those words to me, well...he was a Darkling, a man from the deserts of Abdiah, no doubt."

Archbishop Marven clicked a pen as he listened.

"Abdian?" he said, raising an eyebrow. "Are you certain?"

"Yes, I'm positive. He was a man of dark-blue complexion with pale green eyes."

"Is that so...?" Marven dropped the pen on his desk and reclined in his chair. "But the magical arts are strictly forbidden in Abdiah..."

"Indeed." The Inquisitor began. "He's definitely a wild card—a user of spatial magic, too." Eldric thought for a moment. "He could summon a black cloud that allowed him to move freely, like a...portal, I guess. Even in that explanation, I am unsure; however, it *was* quite...bizarre.

"Also, the girl that was abducted was reported to have a crimson eye."

Archbishop Marven scratched the stubble on his chin.

"Crimson, eh?"

"I confirmed it with Snow and also with the clergy on site. They all indicated to me that the girl, in fact, has a red eye."

"By One..." the Archbishop exhaled as he spoke.

There was a brief pause. Both men awaited the other's words.

"Well," Marven finally said, "return to Mhyrmr. I will speak with you some more upon your return."

"One last thing..." the Inquisitor said a bit slower. "It's...about the Sword."

The Archbishop stopped.

"What...what about it?"

"A young man, an orphan of the monastery...well...you see...he pulled it from its stone in the midst of the chaos."

"Eldric..." Marven sighed, "I am *very* busy today, and I have *no* time for games."

"No jokes here."

The Master Inquisitor's sudden grimness caught Marven by surprise.

What?

"You mean..." the Archbishop drew out his words, "at a time like this...the Heart of Hearts appears once again?"

Eldric bit down on his pipe.

"Maybe. Maybe not."

"I see." Marven said. "Bring him here, as well."

"Very well."

Eldric ended the call, then rose from his seat.

Lukas opened his eyes as rays of evening light poured into his room. He looked up at the ceiling from his small hospital bed.

Was it all a dream?

Or did that time in the forest really happen?

"You were talking in your sleep." A soft, female voice startled him.

Lukas turned his head to see the old nun sitting at his bedside.

"Sister Helga?"

"Yes." She smiled. "Let me raise you up."

Lukas was sore. Everywhere. And, he could feel his muscles scream as he moved them.

"Why are you here?"

"Lukas, how could I *not* come here?!" she sighed. "When I heard what had happened, I hurried here as quickly as I could."

Lukas stared at the old clergywoman in slight disbelief. Truly, he had all but assumed that the monastery would be *glad* to see him gone.

"Sister Helga..."

As she stared back, she could see the youthful uncertainty in his eyes, the eyes of a boy who had collided with a world he had not known even existed.

"Where is Nox?"

The old nun breathed in slowly, then sighed. Lukas could hear a faint shakiness in her breath.

"Well," she began, "she was...taken away by the ones who attacked the monastery."

What...? A wintry cold rippled throughout his body. Lukas looked out the window. He could feel his heart banging against his chest, beating in his eardrums.

She can't be gone! She just—she just can't!

Lukas looked down at his shaking hands; they were covered in cold sweat.

This is a dream! It has to be! This didn't happen! It can't *happen!*

"Sister Helga." A man's voice suddenly entered the room. "If you do not mind, I would wish to speak to the boy alone for a moment."

As the nun made her exit, Lukas turned to see the Master Inquisitor and the blue-haired knight standing at the doorway.

"You?" Lukas became suddenly alert. "You're still here?"

"Please, call me Eldric." He laughed as he pulled out his pipe and began to fill it with tobacco. "Did you sleep well, lad?"

"Why are you still here?"

"Why wouldn't I be?" he replied as he lit the pipe. "You drew the Sword Durandal from it's stone. You know, *that* is something that can only be done by the *Heart of Hearts*."

"So it really did happen, didn't it?" Lukas looked down at his trembling hands, opened them, then closed them.

"It did. You wielded the Sword Durandal." The Inquisitor chuckled as he limped to a chair and slowly sat down. "What *that* means is...well...I have no clue."

Eldric leaned on his cane with both hands.

"Nevertheless, I have received an order from the Archbishop to carry you back to the Church of Mhyrmr with me. That, however, is to be expected, as we haven't heard of anyone wielding the Sword for at least..." he stroked his beard. "I'd say...one thousand years?"

Lukas continued staring at his hands. They were still raw from crawling on the stones.

"Where is my friend?" he said in a low whimper. "Where is Nox?"

"She was taken." Eldric replied blankly.

Lukas winced. He had heard the news only seconds before, but hearing it from the *Inquisitor*—it made his stomach writhe.

"Lukas of Zerlina," Eldric finally said, "your life is about to change quite radically. We do not know what it means for you to wield that Sword, and I know much has happened in a very short time. You are probably still processing all that you have seen..." he paused. "But, I want to make you a *deal*."

The old wizard blew out another ring of smoke.

"Coming with me is supposed to be non-negotiable. However, I will not make you my prisoner. So, listen to me, young man. I do not wish to be a villain in your eyes. I know that you care for your friend, and I know that you probably want to locate her whereabouts. That said, *here* is my proposition."

Lukas looked at the old man in the chair. The dying light of the sun illuminated the Inquisitor's white eyes into a bright golden.

"The clinic has informed me that you have healed at a rather...*unnatural* pace. This, of course, works for our agreement, because it means you will be clear to leave by tomorrow morning. That said, I will give you until *tomorrow afternoon* to decide. Will you come with me to the Church, *or* will you go your own way?"

Eldric ran his fingers through a ring of smoke. Lukas could make out faint black sparks, flickering like static from the

Inquisitor's fingertips.

"I will wait at the Zerlina Monastery until noon tomorrow. If you do not arrive by that time, I will simply tell the church that you've escaped, and you'll then be free to do what you will.

He puffed his pipe.

"In this moment, young man, you will decide your future."

Lukas watched the old man as he raised from the chair and staggered to the door.

"I will end with this, young Lukas..."

The Inquisitor smiled that *same* smile as before, that grin that seemed to spite the problems of the world.

"If you wish to find your friend, you'd do a hell of a lot better if you came with me."

Eldric left as mysteriously as he had come. It had all seemed so sudden, and Lukas watched the empty doorway for some time after the mage exited.

Soon, it was morning. Lukas stared through the window, watching as the light of dawn enveloped the world outside.

Could he trust the Master Inquisitor? What kind of man was the Archbishop?

The old man's words had reverberated throughout his mind all night, and he knew what he had said was true: Going to Mhyrmr was his best chance to find Nox—whether he liked it or not.

But what about the Sword?

The thought quickly flashed through his mind.

Well, what about it?

He thought back to those strange words:

Heart of Hearts.

He called me that. That's the whole reason he wants to take me with him...something to do with that Sword.

At that moment, Lukas knew what he had to do. He *must* find the monastery, and fast!

He's waiting for me there—the Inquisitor and the Sword.

He looked over at one of the chairs in his room to see the fresh set of clothes that Sister Helga had brought him. Lukas moved his legs to rise from the bed. It was odd, but he noticed his body no longer hurt.

I can do this.

Once Lukas had managed to put on his new clothing, he left his room and made his way down the hall. The lobby was spacious with a high ceiling. In the middle of the floor was an elegant fountain, which made trickling noises that echoed inside the hollow room as if it were an amphitheater. Lukas stopped for a moment and looked at the flowing water before opening the door to the outside.

The rush of springtime breezes caressed his face as he exited the clinic and walked out onto the streets. Large buildings of wood and white brick seemed to tower above him. Lukas quickly decided that he had never seen so many people in his entire life. He watched the bustling marketplace with wide-eyed awe. This city was gargantuan, and all he could do was wish that Nox was there to see it, as well.

Don't you worry, Nox.

His heart filled with despair and fire, but, suddenly, it dawned on him...

He had absolutely no idea where he was.

Actually, he had spent so much time worrying about the deal with Eldric that he had completely forgotten about the fact that he'd never been to the city before.

"Okay..." he sighed as he looked around.

He saw the smooth stones, specked in different colors, that made up the streets; he marveled at the high walls and cottages. The streets were busy and crowded, and Lukas had to be wary of where he stepped. The noises of people going about their business conglomerated and became a loud nothingness. The sun was rising in the distance, and the clouds were pink as the steam of airships filled the sky, leaving streaks of fume that lingered momentarily before dissipating.

Lukas walked with his destination in mind. That said, he had no direction in which would lead him there.

I'll ask someone, I suppose, the teen thought in almost an epiphany, and the simplicity of the idea made him laugh at himself.

He saw one of the men selling newspapers, and decided that *this* would be the man he would ask. Lukas meandered through the sea of faces, almost tripping at one point, but, finally, he made his way to the booth.

"Excuse me, sir," he asked politely, "may I ask you how to get to the Zerlina Monastery?"

"Yes, you may ask!" the large, hairy man, thundered with laughter.

Lukas looked at him for a moment with a lost expression.

"Did I lose you, kid? You asked if may *ask* me where it is. So go on, ask!"

"O-okay, how do you get to the monastery?" Lukas asked in a startled tone.

"Easy!" he exclaimed sarcastically. "Take a right at the end of this street. Then a left. Go straight for a bit, then take the third left. You'll be on the main road at that point. Then just follow it to the end and you'll be at the trail to the cathedral!" he laughed. "What? You don't have eyes in your head?"

"It's not that," Lukas said in an attempt to shake off the embarrassment, "I've never been to the city before. I've lived in the monastery my entire life."

"Tough luck, man!" the salesman said as he waved his hand to drive the orphan away, "Now leave me alone! I've got customers!"

"T-thanks..." Lukas waved as he disappeared back into the crowd.

"Okay. Left here?" Lukas whispered the newspaper-seller's convoluted directions to himself.

He wound his way through the maze-like alleyways of the city until, at last, he admitted it.

He was lost.

"Now what...?" Lukas groaned, his mind racing with anxiety, "I only have until noon..."

Lukas looked around for a clock, but there was none.

He's probably already gone.

"Young man!" a lively voice called from behind him. "Are you lost?"

Lukas turned to see a tall man. His icy blue eyes met with Lukas'. Lukas saw the man's large build. His long black hair was streaked with silver strands, which fell onto a coat of silver fur.

"I s-suppose so," Lukas sighed, "I had directions, but...they weren't very helpful."

"Perhaps *I* can be of assistance?" the man said, his face filled with a strange youthfulness.

Lukas paused for a moment and tilted his head.

"W-who are you?"

"Oh, foolish me!" he laughed a hearty laugh. "Let me introduce myself." He held out his hands as if addressing a crowd. "My name is Zurriel, and I am a traveling storyteller! I scour all of Lythia in search of grand tales and myths that I might enlighten the world by telling the public!" he smiled. "What is yours, young man?"

Lukas couldn't help but laugh at the eccentric storyteller.

"I'm Lukas."

"Well, Lukas, where are you looking to go?"

"The monastery!"

"Ah!" Zurriel replied, holding up one finger. "But of course!"

Lukas lit up. "You know how to get there?"

"Absolutely! I know this city like the back of my hand!" the storyteller exclaimed with a wave.

"Then, you'll help me get there?"

"Verily so!" Zurriel motioned his hands. "Right this way."

Lukas followed the curious man as he walked slowly, yet, with a strange vitality. Lukas studied him. He had only just met this man—and Lukas didn't know many people—but, he decided that Zurriel was the strangest man he'd met so far.

I wonder if he's the strangest man?

They came to an open space then stopped.

"Plant your feet, Lukas." Zurriel commanded in a serious tone.

"You don't want you to lose your footing."

"Why would I——?"

Before Lukas could finish his question, Zurriel held out his hand and whispered something. At that moment, green flames flickered upon his fingertips. Suddenly, the walls of the town warped and contorted. Buildings flew over Lukas' head, twisting and turning until, abruptly, he and Zurriel stood at a road leading into the woods.

"What——? What just happened?!" Lukas said, dazedly, as he held his racing heart.

He looked around; the town was back to normal. The people walked about the streets as if nothing had happened. All was right in the town once more, as if Lukas' unique experience had only been a dream.

"Here we are," Zurriel spoke up, waking Lukas from his confusion. "Follow this path. It will take you straight to the monastery."

Lukas looked at the weird man in amazement.

"What did you do?"

"Never mind that," he said dismissively. "You have to find the Sword. Now, off you go."

Lukas went cold.

"H-how did you know that?!" he said, suddenly alarmed.

"I know many things, young Lukas." He said with a smirk. "This is but the first chapter of your life. Now go! Perhaps what unfurls along your path will bring us together again." Zurriel turned and began to walk away. "Who knows? But, either way...it all begins with you finding that Sword."

Lukas didn't know what to say. He felt a sudden unease. *Who was this man? How did he know what he knew?*

"And with that, I bid you farewell."

"Who are you!?" Lukas demanded as he whipped around.

But, it was too late.

Zurriel had disappeared into the crowd.

VII

The Heart of Hearts

Lukas ran up the small stone driveway that led to the monastery. The path was long, and Lukas had no idea that the place where he was raised was so far secluded from the town. Eventually, he came to a clearing and realized that he was at the entrance to the isolated cathedral.

What time is it? The thought raced through his mind, echoing endlessly. *He's probably gone by now! It's probably way past noon already!*

As he eyed the ruined temple he could see the damage that was done a few nights prior. The large steeple of the cathedral lay upon the ground, worn and crumbling; the walls of the abbey had been blown to bits.

Did those two men do this *much damage?*

Here and there, monks and nuns alike were working on cleaning the area and mending the grounds.

Lukas looked around. The Inquisitor, and his blue-haired knight, were nowhere to be seen.

"I *knew* it!" Lukas cursed himself. "I wasn't fast enough."

As he got closer, he stopped at a piece of the ceiling that was dismembered from the rest. It was the mural of the man in armor, with the age-old paint slowly crumbling away. The artwork was covered in blues and golds, depicting the man holding a shining sword. He was lost in it for a moment. Now that it was right in front of him, he could see just how intricate it was. He reached out his hand to feel the smooth stone. It was cold against his palm.

"Admiring the artwork, are we?" A voice startled him.

Lukas turned around to see Eldric limping toward him.

"You!" he gasped, "You're still here?!"

"I am." The old mage laughed, "And *you're* late."

"Late? T-then why did you stay?"

"Because," Eldric started as he blew out a ring of smoke, then smirked, "I knew you would come."

Lukas bowed his head for a moment and looked at his trembling hands. He felt a welling relief overflow his heart; a lift of heaviness fled from his shoulders.

"Master Inquisitor..." he said as he wiped his eyes. "T-thank you."

Eldric laughed, his hearty old voice bellowing across the ruins.

"It's nothing, young Lukas." He put his free hand on the orphan's shoulder. "You see, I knew you would come. You're a lot like me...and I know me."

Lukas turned back to the artwork.

"The art draws your eye, huh?" The Inquisitor blew out another ring of smoke.

"I've just...never seen this one...up close. That's all."

"It is a fancy piece, isn't it? It is actually a piece depicting the legend of the Heart of Hearts."

"Heart of Hearts?" Lukas turned to the old man. "What does that mean?"

"You were raised here, yet you don't know? By One, child!" he exclaimed. "Have the monks failed you?"

Lukas gazed into the painting. He could see the figure pointing the bright sword skyward.

"Master Inquisitor—?" Lukas began.

Eldric broke into his sentence.

"Please," he said, "call me Eldric. I'm...not one for the titles."

"E-Eldric. What does that mean? 'Heart of Hearts,' that is?"

Eldric turned his eyes to the art that lay before them.

"It is an old tale. One thousand years old, actually."

A light breeze crept beneath the surrounding forest. Faint specks of midday light soaked the ancient depiction, bringing out the fullness of its colors.

"You see the giant tree below the figure with the shining sword?" Eldric pointed out.

Lukas nodded.

"It is the fabled 'Cosmic Tree,' *Yggdrasil*, the source of all life. Now, the tree itself has many names: 'The Freedom of Life,' 'The Heart of One,' 'The Breath of All.'" He scratched his head, contemplating his words. "Supposedly, it is the source of the supreme god, One, the creator of the mortals and Aeons."

"Aeons?" Lukas had heard the word before spoken in prayers by the monks.

"Yes, Aeons. They are...well...divine beings, created by One. They each hold a certain dominion over a part of reality, and, in some ways, they are fragments of One himself, yet...even that is not truly correct. They are mysterious beings, and they've even been known to interact with mortals on rare occasions."

Eldric blew a ring of smoke. "We will get to that part soon enough."

"You see, there is much speculation around the myth. No one knows where the Sword Durandal came from, or how the Philosopher King came to wield it. According to legend, the Philosopher King was a man of the lost lineage—but that is only spoken among esoteric fools. Those scholars believe he was one of the *Starborn*, but that is all mere guesses at this point. The general consensus is that he was a man of pure heart and mind, and was thusly given the Sword by One. 'Heart of Hearts' was a title given to him. What it means, however, is unknown to me as well.

Eldric ran his finger down to the next picture. Lukas beheld a drawing of a man dressed in white holding hands with a woman dressed in black.

"He soon met Lunae, the Aeon of Wisdom. Long story short, they fell in love. He sat with her as she explained to him all of the mysteries of the universe, and his knowledge grew. Despite this knowledge, however, he saw the evil in the world around him and wanted the answer to stopping it. So, he begged Lunae to give him her eyes, but she refused. Filled with anger, soon the evil of mortals overwhelmed him. He took the Sword Durandal, then entered the holy realm of Empyria one last time."

Eldric pointed to the final piece on the wall. It was a drawing of the man pointing the Sword at the woman in black.

"Once there, he offered Lunae a deal. More a threat, really. She finally gave in, and in exchange for one of her eyes, he would give her his Heart of Hearts. The Aeon Lunae loved him deeply, you see, and she knew that it was the only way of preserving his heart from the darkness. So, begrudgingly, she agreed. The eye gave him sight, but without a heart, he was driven into a dark madness..."

Eldric removed his hand from the stone and looked into the blue sky.

"What happened to the guy?" Lukas asked, his eyes stuck on the depiction of the man in armor.

"After that, there are no other mentions of him in any history book. It's as if he simply...disappeared, or..." the Inquisitor shrugged, "never existed to begin with."

Lukas looked at Eldric, bewildered.

"What does any of this have to do with me?" he asked.

The Inquisitor looked at him and smiled.

"I have no clue whatsoever."

Eldric's answer caused Lukas to contort his face.

The wizard blew out another ring of smoke.

"Why you can hold that Sword is a complete mystery to me. Oh, and *believe* me, we tested the myth. My knight tried to lift the blade and it wouldn't even budge, and I guarantee you, her strength is far beyond yours. Why the Sword allowed you to draw it is beyond me. But, you will be meeting with his Holiness, Archbishop Marven Ferrenvaal, when we return to Mhyrmr. Perhaps he will know."

Lukas opened his mouth to speak.

"Master Inquisitor," a female voice broke in from behind them.

The two turned to see Snow. She looked at Lukas and smiled.

"It seems our young Lukas has made a nice recovery."

Eldric put his pipe back in his pocket after cleaning it out.

"Well, I assume we should be going then." He gave Lukas a nod. "You ought to go get the Sword and say goodbyes. Oh, and pack lightly. You'll find that everything you need with be furnished for you at Mhyrmr." He pointed to a black automobile parked by the woods. "I'll give you fifteen minutes."

Eldric patted Lukas on the back reassuringly, then followed Snow.

Lukas walked into what was left of the crumbling Zerlina cathedral.

All around him, destruction desecrated the reverence and beauty he once saw in this holy building. The walls had fallen in; the glass from the colorful windows was scattered across the floor.

He looked forward. Just as the wizard had said, the Sword Durandal lay in the exact spot where he had dropped it. Lukas stood over the Sword. He gazed curiously at it's sterling white blade, it's elegantly ornate hilt covered with gems.

It had...changed? No longer did it appear rusted and chipped. *What happened to it?*

Would it let him hold it again? Surely he wasn't dreaming? Seeing the Sword laying on the ground, and not in the stone, was proof of that, right? Lukas took a deep breath. In this blade lay a future he had never predicted, far from his old life, far from the days of being an orphan at the Zerlina monastery. He thought back to the days before, of playing with Nox in the fields. It had only been *two* days ago, yet it seemed as if many years had passed instead.

He bent down to pick up the holy blade. Breathing in to prepare himself, he grabbed the hilt, and, to his surprise, lifted it from the floor with ease. Durandal was weightless in his hands. Lukas swung the blade a couple times.

It was true. He now knew...

He was the Heart of Hearts.

Whatever that means...

"L-Lukas..." a voice stuttered.

Lukas looked up.

"Brother Claus?!" he gasped.

"You're leaving, aren't you?" the monk asked.

Lukas could detect a lowness in the monk's voice. In a way, he could tell that Brother Claus was probably just as broken in this situation as he was.

"Yeah, I am."

Lukas could feel the awkwardness in the air as he looked into the man's droopy eyes.

"B-Brother Claus," Lukas finally spoke up. "I know I wasn't your favorite, and I know that you even wanted Nox to stay away from me." Lukas put his fist to his heart. "But I want to assure you that I will do *everything* in my power to find her."

Brother Claus smiled, his eyes soft and morose.

"Thank you, young man."

Lukas bowed in respect.

The monk bowed in return, his hands clasped around prayer beads.

"May the light of One guide your heart...Lukas."

"Thank you, Brother Claus."

Lukas turned from the monk to see Eldric limping toward him, using his cane to balance himself.

"I would tell you to pack your things," he scratched his head as he looked at the rubble of the monastery around him, "but, I assume that wouldn't be possible in this...situation?"

"It's fine." Lukas looked at the Sword Durandal in his hand. "I have all I need right here."

Eldric began limping toward the black automobile behind him. Snow was standing at the car door, preparing to assist the Master Inquisitor to his seat.

Eldric waved his hand for Lukas to follow.

"Come along, then. Let's not dillydally."

Lukas gave Brother Claus one last bow in respect, then ran toward his ride.

VIII

The Devil's Blood

Lukas met Snow and Eldric at the car. He had no sheathe for his sword, so he wrapped it in a cloth that he had found among the destruction. The Sword surprisingly wasn't heavy, and Lukas found he could carry it quite effortlessly.

"We await your orders, Master Inquisitor. We disembark upon your cue," Snow said with a salute.

"Let us not dally on here any longer." the wizard said as he motioned his hand. "Come, young Lukas. Take your seat."

Lukas did as commanded and sat across from the old man and his knight. As he sat, Lukas sank into the soft leather seat, and he instantly took note of how surprisingly comfortable it was.

The ride was silent, but not awkward. Lukas was preoccupied by the sights outside of his window. He'd never ridden in an automobile before, much less through all of Zerlina. He was consumed by the sights of the tall buildings and the smells of the foods and smoke that wafted in through the open window. For a moment, he had almost completely forgotten about the other two passengers.

"Sightseeing, are we?" Eldric spoke up.

Lukas snapped out of his trance and nodded in agreement.

"You really haven't ever been off of the monastery's grounds, have you?" Snow asked.

"No," Lukas replied, "but I always dreamed about it. I always wondered what was out there. Me and Nox both did..." Lukas tailed off.

Eldric and Snow saw the change in expression that cast over the orphan's face, the shade of silent darkness that was now present. The two knew how he felt, or at least tried to know.

"Worry not, young man." Eldric reached for his tobacco pipe. "I will help you."

Lukas looked up at the Inquisitor and smiled. Eldric knew this grin was just politeness, but, for now, politeness would have to do.

"Lukas, was it?" Snow said with a smile. "I'm Snow, by the way. I don't believe I ever mentioned my name."

"Yeah, it's Lukas." He smiled with a nod. "Nice to meet you, Snow."

The knight pointed ahead. "If you look forward, you can see the aerodock!"

Lukas stuck his head out the window. A cool breeze brushed his face, a fair day in the fair weather of southern Aestriana. Ahead, he could see the large metal building. Steam softly misted off the ground in puffy plumes of white, then dissipated into the atmosphere as the airships flew by.

Lukas put his head back inside of the vehicle.

"That's an aerodock?!" he exclaimed with outright amazement.

"If you think that's something, it's going to be fun showing you the airship," she giggled in a strangely feminine way.

Lukas looked at her for a moment. She was so different than when he had last seen her. Her light, azure eyes were softer, not like the soul-stabbing glare he had seen once before, not like the eyes of the Snow that had jumped to his rescue two days ago.

Lukas looked at the Inquisitor.

She's a lot like him, I guess.

"Ah! The Airship *Orca is* a beauty!" Eldric began, trailing off into a tangent.

The breeze from the window died down as the car slowly came to a stop.

"It appears we're at our destination!" Eldric put his pipe away.

The driver opened the door and Lukas stepped out first, then Snow, who assisted Eldric.

"The Zerlina Aerodock, Master Inquisitor!" the driver stood at salute.

"Most gracious," Eldric said as he handed the man a tip.

The facility was humongous; mammoth stone towers protruded into the sky, cut off by the clouds of smoke that were expelled by the vessels flying above. Lukas stood in amazement; the building was so different from the old stones of the monastery that, truly, it stunned him.

"Wouldn't you like to look inside?" Snow said, waving her hand in front of his face.

Lukas nodded and they began climbing the stairs.

Once inside, he was instantly overtaken by the sights and smells. Snow, on the other hand, did what she was trained to do, her keen eyes searching for anything even remotely sinister. She had two people to protect this time. Lukas looked over his shoulder to see her quick, azure, eyes darting back and forth, detecting at speeds his human eyes could not.

"Are you the Master Inquisitor? *The* Eldric of the Black Flame?!"

Eldric turned to see a little Abdian girl walking up to him.

"Why, yes," he chuckled. "And who might you be?"

"My name is Enlil! It's such an honor to meet you! I think you're so cool!" she said with a starry gaze as if she were the luckiest girl in the world.

"Well, now," the old man blushed, "I'm not *that* big of a deal."

"But you are!" the girl said in excitement. "You're *the* Master of the Inquisition!" she held out her hand. "Can I," she stuttered, "can I shake your hand?"

Eldric held out his old, leathery hand.

"Of course," he laughed.

As their hands met, Eldric looked into the young girl's pale, green eyes. For a moment, they seemed to swirl into a kaleidoscope of green hues. The more he gazed into them, the more they seemed to...soothe his mind with their shifting waves.

She released his hand.

"You have safe travels!" Enlil waved as she began to walk off. "Thank you, Mister Eldric!"

As she passed Snow, the knight grabbed the girl's arm in a single, quick motion. Lukas could see the strength in her grip; it seemed almost *inhuman.*

"You're hurting me!" Enlil cried out, her face contorting in agony.

"Why don't you give the Inquisitor his pipe back?" Eldric smiled.

"Okay, okay!" she cringed as she pulled Eldric's tobacco pipe from her pocket. "Here!"

Snow took the ivory pipe without a word and let the girl go. Enlil ran off into the sea of people—vanishing just as quickly as she had come.

"A pickpocket!" Eldric chuckled. "I would have never guessed. And what an impressive steal!"

Snow handed the pipe back to Eldric, who put it into his pocket.

Lukas looked bewilderingly at Snow.

"How did you see that?" he asked.

"She's a half-Elf, Elven blood makes her a bit more...acute...than us." Eldric limped onward. "Let us continue."

They walked through the crowded alleyways of the aerodock. Lukas took in the sights of his surroundings. Amazed, he saw everything from the building's architecture to the salesmen and all of their strange wares.

The group came to the dock where the *Orca* was stationed. Eldric stopped and pointed at the large, metallic vessel.

"She's beautiful, isn't she?"

Lukas had never seen an airship up close. He had seen them fly in the sky but never had they been right in front of him. He saw the gears and sails and lights, and his eyes sparkled at the sheen that the midday sun cast upon its metallic hull.

"Master Inquisitor!" the captain called out as he walked down the loading ramp. "The crewmen are all at attention. We await your orders!"

Eldric motioned his hand forward. "Let us go ahead."

"As you wish." The captain walked busily up the ramp.

"Snow." The Inquisitor added. "Show our young guest to his room."

"Yes, sir."

Lukas turned and looked back at the aerodock behind him. So quickly had a future, unknown, swept him up. He watched the ramp slowly lift.

He felt so far from home, and he knew he would only grow farther.

Snow marched down the halls of the *Orca's* living quarters. The ship's crew stopped and stood to the side, saluting as she passed by.

"They really respect you, don't they?" Lukas asked observingly.

"I'm not one to misuse their respect. But, though I have earned it, I must maintain it."

"I see why they respect you." He paused. "Back at the clinic, I noticed you had bandages wrapped around your stomach. Are your injuries bad? If you need to stop and sit down we can—"

The knight smiled.

"I indeed was injured. I was stabbed, but I am okay. It will take more than that to kill one with *my* blood."

She stopped and opened a door. Lukas looked inside the room. It was well furnished with a bed, a desk, a bathroom, and a window.

"Here you are."

"Thank you, Snow. You've been so helpful."

"No problem, Lukas."

Right then, a voice came over the loudspeaker.

ALL HANDS ON DECK, WE'RE CLEARED FOR TAKE OFF!

Snow pointed to the window. "Look outside, you'll see what it's like to take off."

"Can I go up to the deck?"

"No. You can when we're afloat, but you'd need a safety line during takeoff, given the power of the wind when we lift. Without a line, you'd be blown off."

Lukas gulped.

Snow smiled.

"But I picked a room with a big window. Go on, look."

Lukas walked anxiously over to the window and watched. Steam burst from the side thrusters, creating a thundering noise as a giant, glowing ring began to form around the hull, making a zinging noise as it awakened on the bottom of the ship, causing the vessel to rise.

Before he knew it, he was above the clouds. Lukas watched with eyes full of amazement.

"How did we do that?!"

"I'm not an engineer, but the glowing stuff in that ring is called 'aether.' It's created from a special ore that, when melted, holds a high electrical charge. The liquid powers the magnetic thrusters, which keeps us airborne."

She could see the sparkles in his eyes as he watched the sky outside of his window.

"Well," Snow began to walk out the open door, "get some rest. We will be at Mhyrmr before you know it."

She exited and closed the door. Lukas stared outside until dark.

The night air was thin and cold in the skies above the province of Aestriana. Lukas had opened his window so that he could see the ground below; however, on a moonless night such as this one, the ground below was but a dark mass save for the dots of lights from houses.

Lukas inhaled the chilly air, then fell back onto his bed.

He surveyed the room that was his quarters. The walls seemed to show some attempt of decoration, as they were boarded with red cedar. Rugs covered the floor, and swords hung on holders along the wall. Lukas raised up again, and this time, moved a chair to the window and sat in it.

The absence of the moon only complimented the brightness of the stars above, enhancing their glow. Lukas had always liked the stars; their enigmatic glow perplexed his young eyes.

I'll go up on the deck.

It seemed a favorable idea, so he got up, put the chair back, and left his room.

The halls of the *Orca* were nicely lit. Lukas locked his door behind him then made his way down the hall, doing his best to stay out of the way as he meandered to the stairwell and up the stairs. The airship was noisy, and steam from the engine hissed so loudly it could be even heard on the highest floor.

On deck, crewmen carried on about their duties, none of them giving Lukas any attention.

The orphan wandered to an uncrowded rail and looked skyward. The stars above were everything he'd hoped they'd be. Never before had he seen their crystalline glints seem so pristine. He closed his eyes, took a deep breath, then exhaled and watched them once more.

"Stargazing?" Eldric said in a jesting tone as he approached the rail beside Lukas.

"Something like that."

"They're marvelous, I know."

"Mesmerizing, even."

"They say the stars are the eyes of One looking down upon us. That, however, is just an old superstition. An ancient one that so happens to still exist...it is a nice thought though, I assume. To believe that he is always watching." Eldric chuckled, "Sounds comforting."

"I've always found them comforting." Lukas smiled. "They remind me of Nox. The monks and nuns used to say that she fell from the sky."

Lukas smiled

"So, for me, looking at the stars sorta makes me feel...a bit closer to her."

"You and your friend—Nox, I mean—you are quite close, aren't you?"

"Yeah," Lukas said in a wistful tone, "she's my best friend."

"I see. Well, a good friend is a most valuable thing."

"I agree."

The two quieted, watching the black night.

"Eldric," Lukas said. "That man at the temple, the one who took Nox, said that you have the blood of the Devil. Are you—"

The old man burst into laughter.

"No, young man. I am not the son of the Devil."

"Then what did he mean?"

"It's a disease; the 'Devil's Blood' is a disease. A rare one, in fact."

"You mean—?" Lukas' eyes widened. "Are you, like, dying?"

Eldric chuckled once more.

"It is not a disease of the flesh, but one of the spirit. It began around three thousand years ago, back when the race of angels still ruled the world. Legend has it that, back then, a person was created from pure darkness—someone that never should have been made. This person was the first to experience the disease, and...well, I guess I am of their lineage."

The old man smiled.

"Unlucky, wouldn't you say?"

Lukas looked at him in disbelief. To be able to look at life the way he did, to be able to reject the world in such a way, to harbor such raw optimism, Lukas wished he could do so, as well.

"The Devil's Blood warps the afflicted's magic. Mine just so happens to manifest in the form of those black flames." He smiled. "I wouldn't touch them, though. They'll eat your soul, and..."

The Master Inquisitor looked upward and smiled. Lukas looked into his white eyes and noticed not a single star reflected off of them.

"Eventually, they will eat mine, as well."

Suddenly, the old man chuckled heartily.

"Don't worry yourself with my old man troubles, lad! You're meeting the Archbishop tomorrow!"

"What's he like?"

Eldric stroked his beard.

"He's serious...a bit of a sourpuss, actually. But, a good man, nonetheless."

The air whistled between them as they stared into the night.

"Young Lukas," Eldric said finally. "Come, you need rest."

IX

Meeting the Archbishop

The morning sun arrived suddenly; Lukas awoke to a single strand of light, which pierced his window and unfortunately cast over his face.

He rose and dressed himself, combing his hands through his long, platinum-blond hair, then opened the curtains of the window. Outside, the sun bathed the clouds in scarlet light, illuminating them in rose-like hues. He marveled at the scene for a moment, then walked out into the hall.

The halls were busy with shipmen coming and going, attending to their duties.

ALL HANDS ON DECK! a voice over the loudspeaker commanded. *WE WILL BE LANDING MOMENTARILY!*

The voice startled Lukas, but his surprise was soon replaced with excitement and curiosity.

Landing?!

It was difficult to imagine at first. Everything seemed to be happening so fast that it almost made his head spin. Anxiously, yet filled with anticipation, the orphan made his way past the rushing sailors and up to the top deck. Upon opening the door to the top floor, Lukas was greeted by a rush of cold morning air. He looked around, only to see that there was nothing but clouds. Upward, the sky was a bright, whitewashed blue. He made his way to the rails and looked out. Before him, atop the highest peak of the rocky mountain, was the ancient temple—the Church of Mhyrmr.

Even from a distance, Lukas determined that this was the

largest structure he had ever seen. Its old, stone walls and high spires made it just as imposing as it was majestic.

"I was just as thrilled upon my first time flying, as well." Snow said as she walked up beside him at the rail.

"It's beautiful," Lukas said, starstruck.

"It is, isn't it? It is the home of the Inquisition, established one thousand years ago."

"I'll meet the Archbishop now, won't I?"

"You will. Do not worry. He is a good man."

"Have you ever met him?"

"Here and there, but he and Eldric are childhood friends."

As the ship descended into the port, Lukas could see the stonework of the temple more clearly. He awed at the intricacies that were put into them. Within the solid walls were etchings of trees and angels, adding to the temple's enigma.

"Follow me." Snow motioned with her hand as she spoke.

As they walked though the ship, the crew stopped to salute the knight as she led the orphan down the halls.

"Where are we going?" Lukas finally spoke up.

"To meet the Archbishop. We have to rendezvous with Master Inquisitor Eldric first."

Lukas could suddenly feel a lump in his throat. He had never really thought of meeting such a prestigious person before, but now that he was, the idea daunted him.

Eldric waited for them at the end of the hallway, smoking tobacco from his pipe.

"The big day?" he chuckled, "Follow me."

The airship hangar was busy with mages going in and out on church missions; Lukas noticed the other soldiers and Inquisitors salute the old man as he passed them by.

"He's a really important guy, isn't he?"

Snow smiled softly at the orphan's lack of manners.

"He is. He's second down from the Archbishop."

Lukas felt his face burn red.

"H-he's second in line?!"

"Yes. He's the leader of the Inquisitorial Force, the 'Master

Inquisitor.'"

The orphan watched the old, worn man. He was so...unassuming. All of these people revered and exalted him, yet, from what Lukas could see, Eldric never treated any of them as inferiors. He remembered how the old wizard defended him in his dire need back at the ruined cathedral; he remembered the sheer, unbridled force this careless man possessed. And, he could see why they respected him, and Lukas realized that *he* respected him, as well.

Lukas surveyed the bright decorations of Mhyrmr as they passed through the labyrinthine halls of the giant temple. He saw depictions of heroes and stained-glass windows that illuminated pictures of angels.

Eldric led the three to the sanctuary, a gargantuan room lit by the ethereal colors, illuminated by the sun. This was to be his new home, for all he knew. He found it somewhat comforting. He had lived in a temple his entire life, so moving to a new one wasn't all that bad.

Archbishop Marven rummaged through the papers on his desk as he mumbled to himself, when a knock came to the door.

"Who is it?"

"Eldric."

"Ah!" he stood, remembering the meeting he was to have with the orphan. "Come in!"

Snow opened the door in Eldric's stead. Marven scurried around in an attempt to clear spots for his guests among his heavily cluttered office.

"Your Holiness," Eldric said as he seated himself, "I want you to meet Lukas."

Lukas bowed.

"So," Marven said as he observed the Sword, "It's true. You hold Durandal. There's no mistaking that sword." He cleared off a small table. "Here," he commanded, "place the blade on the table."

Lukas did as he was told.

Archbishop Marven reached down and gripped the hilt of the

sword. The three watched as the Archbishop struggled, trying to lift the blade to no avail.

"I see..." he whispered to himself, then turned to the boy. "It seems this era has brought the Heart of Hearts upon the continent of Lythia."

Lukas spoke up. "I came here because Eldric—the Master Inquisitor, I mean—said you'd help me find my friend."

"Ah, yes." Marven began, "Eldric has told me of your situation, and I believe it is within my power to help you. But. In return, you will stay here and become a Inquisitor. A mage, like us."

Lukas stopped for a moment. "An Inquisitor? But, why?"

The Archbishop held up two fingers. "For one, tutoring you will allow me to keep my eye on you until I decide just what it means for you to be wielding that blade. And two," he took a sip from his glass, "we will teach you for your own good."

Lukas stared back. He knew it was true. He looked back at the few days before his arrival to Mhyrmr; he remembered, placing himself in the very shoes he wore when he stood in front of Iago...in front of those phantom blades.

Scared, kid?

The Elf's words reverberated through his mind.

"Your Holiness," he began, "I know that I may not know much about the world, and that I was raised secluded from it for all of my life. But, I stood in front of that Elf, Iago, and I felt a terrible fear. I wasn't sure at first, but now I know." Lukas clenched his fist. He felt as if waves had filled his heart, crashing against it's confinement forcefully to escape the space within.

"I know that one of the reasons that Nox was taken was because *I* was scared—because *I* was terrified and powerless."

Marven placed the glass on his desk.

"Then you agree with me?"

The orphan and the Archbishop met eyes. Those eyes, Lukas thought, were much different from the strange white and black eyes of the Inquisitor. Marven's eyes were a deep brown—a hard color to match a hard man.

"Yes, Your Holiness, I do. You're saying that, even if I were to find Nox, I'm in no place to be any use in aiding her. Not as I am now."

"You're a clever boy, it seems." Marven smiled. "Snow, show him where you will be training him, then take him to his room, and," he slightly laughed, "pick a nice one for him."

"Yes, Your Holiness." She turned to Lukas. "Right this way."

Lukas followed the knight out of the room. Eldric turned to follow them.

"Eldric." Marven spoke before the Inquisitor stood. "I wanted to ask you something."

"Yes?"

"His friend, Nox, is she the one with the red eye?"

"Indeed. I confirmed with several witnesses. One even reported a rumor that the girl 'fell from the sky.'"

"A red eye is a bad omen at the least. Do you believe...?" he trailed off.

Eldric blew a puff of smoke from his newly-lit pipe. "I can't say for sure. There are far too many mysteries in the world for such certainties."

Marven tapped his fingers upon his desk.

"Red eyes, the Heart of Hearts...it's all...so sudden."

Eldric sat, silent.

"I know what you're thinking, Eldric. And *I* think it's crazy."

Eldric smirked. "And what do you think I think?"

"That boy..." the Archbishop said. "You think that he might be one of the *Starborn,* don't you?"

"I'm..." the Master Inquisitor paused, "not truly sure."

"But the *Starborn* never existed—"

"Never is *never* a possibility." Eldric smiled. "You know that, Marven."

Marven laughed. "I only wish I could have your composure, my friend."

The Inquisitor nodded. "All I am saying is that it will play out eventually. Whatever happens will happen."

"That is all, Eldric." He turned to the mound of paperwork and sighed, "I must get back to my papers now."

Nox sat, trapped within a large birdcage. All around her was darkness, save for the light from a massive stained-glass window, which ascended the length of the wall.

"A temple?"

"No," a voice caught her unexpectedly from within the void. "It is the library of V'rezen Myur."

Nox looked in the direction of the voice. On the opposite side of the bars stood the large, blue Darkling from before.

"Who are you?!" she yelled. "What do you want from me?"

"I am Agnon." The large Abdian said as he walked into the cold steel bars of the cage. Black clouds formed on his skin, allowing him to pass through the bars as if they weren't there. "And it is not what *I want*, but the wishes of my Master."

"Master?" she whispered. "Look! I don't know who you think I am! I'm just an orphan! My name is Nox, and I've *always* been Nox!"

Agnon stood in front of her. She could see how gargantuan he was as she looked up into his pale, green eyes.

"Silence," his deep voice growled. "You may not know who— or rather *what*—you are, but that is not the point. My Master wishes you unharmed, but only until your usefulness expires."

Expires? A chill ran up her spine.

"Now stay silent." Agnon waved his hand, and a black cloud appeared.

He stepped into it and was gone.

Nox sat for a moment, then turned her eyes to the large window. The ancient glass stretched high unto the ceiling. The art seemed to be of a large, intricate tree. She ran her eyes up the length of the artwork to see the image of a black, crescent moon at its height.

She stared at it curiously.

Dark as obsidian, its wide crescent arch dominated the top of the window, it's ebony glass blocking any light that tried to enter through it.

A black moon?

She stared at it, and, for some reason, she felt as if she knew what it meant.

X

The Prince and the Orphan

The next day, Lukas awoke early, as instructed by Snow, and made his way to the training yard.

The area was spacious and almost empty save for some practice dummies that lined the surrounding walls. As he had expected, Snow was waiting for him, dressed in a casual shirt and jogging pants. He found it strange to see her in normal clothes. Her figure was tall and lithe, and Lukas couldn't help but think that she was actually rather...beautiful.

"You ready?" she smiled as she picked up one of the wooden swords from the rack.

Lukas drew the Sword Durandal. "Ready."

"So, tell me, is that sword light or heavy?"

Lukas raised the Sword, "It's light as a feather!"

"Good!" she said as she tossed Lukas one of the practice swords. "Use this instead!"

Lukas quickly caught it and was almost toppled over by the surprising heaviness.

"Hey!" he yelped.

"Oh, c'mon!" Snow smirked. "It's only thirty-five pounds."

"Only?!"

The knight winked. "Yes. Only. We have to get some muscle going on that scrawny body of yours." She looked at her practice sword and twirled it a bit. "We'll have to cut those long, luscious locks, too."

"But...I like my hair long!"

Snow turned and pointed her wooden sword at Lukas. "I don't."

He looked into her azure eyes and shivered.

She turned. "Now, let's work on basics."

Eldric emptied his pipe into the ashtray on Marven's desk.

"I hear today is our young Lukas' first day of training!" the Inquisitor said excitedly. "By the way, who will be his magic tutor?"

Marven picked up some papers and rummaged through them. "One of your best Inquisitors, of course. I chose Blake. Blake the Snowbird."

Eldric gave a hearty chuckle. "That will be interesting! Um...but, you know, Blake isn't necessarily the...uh...nicest of people."

"I am aware. She is one of the best, though."

"She definitely is. And, now that you mention it, that girl does need to get out of her comfort zone a bit."

"My friend," Marven laughed, "I'm glad you see my point."

Lukas nearly jumped from his skin as the boisterous blast of a trumpet resounded and ricocheted off of the courtyard walls.

"Turn around," Snow commanded.

Lukas did as he was told. Before him, all of the knights in the courtyard had knelt to one knee. Six men stood at the opposite end of the space, most in bright silver armor, their white clothing marked with insignia of a red raven.

"Who are they?"

"Him," Snow said as she pointed to the two men in the middle. Both were dressed extravagantly, however, Lukas only found his eyes drawn to one of them—a man with a brilliant red uniform, decorated with medals.

"You may want to kneel..." Snow whispered, still standing herself.

"Young man!" One of the armor-clad soldiers pointed in his direction.

Suddenly, Lukas felt his pulse speed up.

"Me?"

"Too late..." Snow smiled.

"Have you no etiquette?! Kneel!"

"No." The decorated man held up his hand.

Lukas' began to sweat as the man in red walked past the reverent knights. As the man approached, Lukas could see just how tall he was. His shoulders were broad, only to match his muscular frame. The young orphan felt the weight of the man's firm grip on his shoulder. Their eyes met. This man, his eyes were not grisly like the rest of his body. Instead, they were a soft, light brown. Lukas didn't know why, but in that look, he felt a strange assurance.

"A man who is not afraid to stand before royalty," the rest of his face relaxed into a smile, "is my kind of man."

"I a-am?"

The other decorated soldier approached them, smoke seeping from his mouth as he exhaled from his cigarette. Lukas could see that this man was much different. He was slimmer, with short, sandy-colored hair.

"What's your name, kid?" the soldier asked, flicking ash onto the ground

"L-Lukas," he nodded, "Lukas of Zerlina—sir."

"Zerlina?" the large man said curiously. "Then you must be the one I've heard so much about."

"Y-you have?"

"Of course!" he smiled, "News travels fast, young man. Let me introduce myself." The large man took his hand off of Lukas' shoulder and smiled a friendly smile. "My name is Alexander Clement zel Reethkilt, Crown Prince of Aestriana and commander of the Red Ravens." He pointed to the other soldier. "And this is Captain Havell Maro."

"Prince?!" Lukas' jaw dropped. He'd thought meeting an Inquisitor was impressive, but never had he imagined he'd meet a prince.

"Of course," the man replied, "But please, call me Clement."

"Hey, Clem," Havell said, "he's the Heart of Hearts, isn't he?"

"I assume so," Clement replied. He turned to Lukas, "Is this true?"

"T-that's what they say?" Lukas stuttered, suddenly anxious after learning the man's status.

"Well!" Havell exclaimed as he drew his longsword. "Let's go a round, Luke!"

"W-what do you mean?" Lukas asked, wide-eyed.

"He wants to spar," Snow cut in as she approached them.

"Snow," the prince bowed, "how fare you today?"

"I fare well, Commander. And what brings you to the top of our lonesome mountain?"

He smiled. "I come to bring a word from my father to the Archbishop. It is a rather quiet issue, unfortunately."

"I understand." Snow turned to Captain Maro and handed him her wooden sword, "Put the real sword away. Can't go hurting him too bad."

Hurting me...too bad?!

Lukas gulped.

"Master Inquisitor!" a young woman exclaimed as she stormed into Eldric's office. "What is the meaning of this?!"

Eldric looked up from the papers on his desk, his eyes slightly enlarged by the lenses of his reading glasses.

"What is the ruckus for, Blake?" he said, startled.

"You assigned me to some random," she shook her head, "orphan boy?!"

The Master Inquisitor suddenly burst into laughter.

"Is *that* what this is about?"

"I-it's" Blake pursed her lips, "it's not funny! You know I don't work well with people! And he has literally no experience! Do you *want* him to die!?"

Eldric picked up his beer mug filled with water and took a sip. "He has Durandal. He'll be fine! Snow herself is in the training yard with him as we speak. Besides, *you're* going to be the one to teach him how to use a Word of Heart."

He mumbled to himself. "I wonder what his will be..."

"Are you even listening?" Blake put her hands on her waist.

"Oh, I assure you that I am, however, the order supersedes mine. It was Marven who assigned you to the Heart of Hearts, not myself."

Blake bit her tongue and groaned. "Archbishop Ferrenvaal?"

"Indeed. If you have an issue, unfortunately, you'll have to take it up with him."

Blake sighed, her shoulders relaxing. "I see. So there's no way around this, is there?"

Eldric chuckled. "Not one that I foresee." He took another sip. "You know, Blake. This might be a good exercise for you. Lukas is a quite likable young man. And who knows? You may even accidentally make a friend."

Blake gritted her teeth.

The old man reclined in his chair and swirled the water in the glass mug. "Just try to look at the beer mug as...half-full, you see?"

She took in a deep breath and exhaled as she walked toward the door. "I guess..."

"Quite good." The old Inquisitor smiled. "Oh, and Blake. One last thing..."

She held the door and looked back.

Eldric laughed as he took another sip. "Try not to be so sour when you meet him. All will be well."

Blake turned her head, rolled her eyes, and walked out.

Havell Maro stood directly in front of Lukas, his wooden sword held loosely in his right hand and a lit cigarette in his left.

"Now, it's not every day that someone gets to say he sparred the Heart of Hearts, now is it?"

"They say that's what I am," Lukas shrugged, "but, don't think too highly of me."

"Don't worry, young man. You're definitely humble, but you won't make it high on the list just because you hold a shiny-special sword."

Lukas smiled and readied his stance. "Good to know."

The training yard had mostly cleared. All around the Lukas and the captain, soldiers and knights had stopped what they were doing and gathered around to watch the fighting.

"You got a lotta eyes on you, kid." Havell pointed his sword towards his opponent. "Better make a good impression."

Go!

Lukas broke into a sprint.

"First mistake!" the captain laughed.

Lukas' swung his blade horizontally at head level. Havell Maro ducked his head just in time and swung upward. The motion took merely a second, but Lukas felt as if he watched the upward arc of the captain's parry for an eternity.

He's so quick!

The wooden sword cracked as the blade collided with Lukas' chin, causing the skinny orphan to rise from the ground. A plume of dust surrounded Lukas as he fell on his back, yelling in pain as he held his face.

"Listen, kiddo." Havell Maro blew out smoke from his cigarette. "Never. And I mean *never* attack first in a sword fight. It's better to be the one who parries than the one who is being parried."

"Got it..." Lukas said through a sore jaw as he stood once more.

"That's one," the captain said. "You get three."

Lukas wiped his eyes and took his stance once more.

Okay. So, if I don't attack first, I'll be on the defensive. But. If he doesn't attack either, we'll just be standing here looking at each other. He sighed. *Here goes nothing!*

Lukas sprung forward once again, his blade rising for a vertical attack.

Prince Reethkilt, Snow, and those in the courtyard watched intently, but Lukas was unaware. To him, all that existed in this moment was Captain Maro and how he was going to defeat him.

Lukas' blade descended quickly. He felt the surprise of cutting air as his opponent spun to the right.

"Not quick enough!"

Feet planted firm, Lukas ignored the taunt and focused on blocking. The force from the wood clashed, pushing his stance off balance.

Lukas yelped as he suddenly felt a pain in his side.

"That's two," the captain laughed. "But you're getting better, for sure."

Snow and Clement watched from the sidelines.

"You know," Snow smiled, "he reminds me of you when you were his age."

"Yes." The prince smiled softly. "I see it as well."

"By the way, what is *our* score by now?"

"Our score?" Clement turned to see Snow wearing a mocking smile. "Two hundred and fifty to two hundred and fifty-one, I believe."

"Ah, I remember now. So, is the great Commander of the Red Ravens finally ready to admit defeat?"

He laughed. "I think you know better than that, Snow."

"It's exactly *that*." Snow turned back to the fight, "I see it in *him*, too."

Lukas stood, though much slower this time.

"Your footwork needs improvement," Havell Maro said as he blew out smoke, "but, you're doin' fair enough, I guess."

Lukas readied his stance for the third time.

I got a block in...let's aim for a strike!

Lukas burst forward, his blade ready.

Don't strike first. Simply close distance.

"Stalling won't work, either!" Captain Maro laughed as his blade fell in a straight line for Lukas' head.

The orphan slid his feet sideways to evade the blade as it sliced beside him.

"I won't be so dumb a third time!" Lukas roared as his blade came around his head for a counter.

"That's good to hear!" Havell laughed as he threw a counter of his own. The two blades made cracking booms as they collided with each other in a great rally.

I'm doing it! I'm keeping up!

Clash after clash, the sounds of the wooden blades crashing into each other filled the courtyard.

"Where was this two points ago?!" Captain Maro smirked as he flicked his cigarette onto the floor and held his blade with both hands.

"I don't know!" Lukas yelled back, distracted.

The captain raised his blade high before bringing it down. Lukas could see the sheer force in the swing as it descended.

"It's been fun!"

Now!

"Perfect!" Lukas yelled. His blade rose in an uppercut arc as he pivoted his stance to accommodate his sword hand's movement. The blade rushed toward Havell Maro's face. "Here's strike one —!"

Lukas blinked.

Suddenly, he felt a weightlessness...a certain free-fall. He opened his eyes to see the space in front of him empty.

What was I doing? Where am I?

His mind felt fuzzy.

"Forget something?"

Lukas felt a heavy weight come crashing down on his shoulder. He opened his eyes once more.

He was on the ground.

"A bit much, Havell." A shadow stood over Lukas. "Young man, are you okay?"

Lukas looked up to see Clement standing over him with an outstretched hand.

"Yeah," Lukas groaned as he lifted his battered body, "I'm alright."

"You did pretty good for a sheltered orphan!" Captain Maro lit another cigarette.

Lukas laughed as he stretched his sore muscles. "Thanks, Captain!"

"Call me Havell." He blew out smoke. "You've earned that, at least."

"You did better than most," Snow said as she approached. "Not many people even get that close against Maro, much less make him use that little technique of his." She turned to the smoking captain. "Maybe he's getting soft."

Clement and Lukas faced each other; Lukas became unaware of the bickering captain in the background; he disregarded the commotion around him as soldiers passed him by.

He focused only on the tall commander in front of him. The prince placed his hand on Lukas' shoulder once more.

"Young man," he began. "In the path ahead of you, you will most certainly face true peril. Ahead, you will encounter people much stronger than my playful captain—people who want with everything in them to end your life. So I wish to impart two words of advice."

Lukas watched the prince's eyes soften. He felt the man's grip, firm on his shoulder.

"Lukas of Zerlina. No matter the odds, always fight, and—" He looked off. Lukas followed his gaze. Before them, the sterling Sword Durandal lay against a sword rack. Lukas watched it in the red light of the evening. For a moment, it seemed as if the sun itself were trapped within the silver blade.

Clement released his grip.

"And," the prince continued, "when you swing that sword—no matter why you swing that sword—swing it with complete resolve. For a blade of skill will slay an army, but a blade of resolve will win a war."

"I—" Lukas thought of what he had told the Archbishop—that he had only failed in protecting Nox because he had been afraid. He looked into the eyes of the Commander of the Red Ravens, perplexed. This man—his eyes had been so soft, yet so strong in the mere minutes Lukas had met him.

"I will."

Clement smiled. "Good man."

"I am not getting soft, *Snow.*" Havell griped in the background.

"Then why don't *we* have a sparring session right now, too?"

Lukas saw the captain physically repulse.

"That's what I thought," she said as she walked toward Lukas and turned to Clement. "Is our lesson over for the day?"

The prince laughed. "It is indeed. And perhaps upon my next visit, *we* can spar. Like old times."

Snow nodded. "I would have it no other way."

"Besides, I need to catch up, right?"

"It *is* two-fifty-one to two-fifty."

Clement bowed. "Then it will be done." He turned to the captain, and then to the other Red Raven soldiers. "Let us go. We have spent far too much time here, and I must speak with the Archbishop."

"Yeah, yeah..." Havell said through a puff of his cigarette.

Lukas watched Prince Reethkilt walk away. He didn't know why, but, for some reason, the prince's words made him feel strong.

XI

The Black Moon

Agnon sat in dark silence, amid the forlorn tomes of V'Rezen Myur, whispering to himself.

"I hear you have been successful, Agnon." A disembodied voice filled the spacious library.

Agnon opened his eyes and bowed his head.

"Master. You have returned."

The air in the room began to thin as a tall, cloaked figure approached.

"I take it you have found her, Agnon?"

"I have, Master."

The hooded figure raised his hand, motioning for the Darkling to rise, then continued to walk by.

"Then let us go see her."

Nox watched herself as a child encircled by faceless children.

"Look out! She's a witch! She'll cast a spell on you and turn you into a lizard!"

"No I won't! I'm not a witch!" She could hear herself crying, echoing off into some distant somewhere.

"She's a devil! She'll drink your blood at night!"

"No, I'm not! I'm not!"

"Then why's your eye red? Nobody else's eyes are that color!"

Nox tried to stand, but she could feel a heavy weight on her chest as the children pushed her back onto the ground.

"I'm not..." She could hear herself whimper. "I'm not. I'm not.

I'm not."

Suddenly, she looked up to see a boy standing in front of her.
"I told you I'm not a witch! I already said it!"
"I don't think you're a witch!"
"You don't?"
"No! And even if you were, I wouldn't care. I mean, how many people could say they're friends *with a witch?"*
"But..." Nox could hear herself echo. "My eye is red? You don't think it's scary?"
"Lemme see!" The boy put his hands on his knees as he leaned over to get a closer look.
"See!" Nox said as she opened her eyes really wide. "It's red! Blood red! Doesn't that scare you?"
"Nope." The boy smiled. "Red is my favorite color! And, I think it's kinda pretty!"

You remember this, don't you? It was at this moment, wasn't it?

Nox could hear a strange voice as she watched the scene play out in front of her.

That was the moment? That was the moment you felt it, right?
"Y-you think my eye is pretty?"
The boy held out his hands.
"Yeah! Let's be friends!"
Nox watched herself take his hands and lift off of the ground. She watched herself dust off her yellow dress.
"O-okay! I'm Nox! What's your name?"

It was this moment that you knew, wasn't it? This very moment?
The boy smiled.
"Oh, I'm..."

When you knew you were going to give it to him.
Nox mouthed the words along with the boy.
"I'm Lukas."

Nox awoke.
"Lukas?" she mumbled to herself. "But, that voice?"
She turned her eyes to the gargantuan window, focusing upon

the ebony moon placed at the top.

"It looks familiar, doesn't it?" a voice said from the door of the birdcage.

Nox's head whipped around to see the imposing figure of Agnon alongside another, tall man, hidden in a dark shroud.

"Who are *you*?" she could hear the quivering in her own voice. She didn't know why, but something about this man was different, even from the brooding mass that was the Darkling beside him; this man—though she had only just seen him—incited an acute fear, far more than that of the grim Agnon.

"Of course you would know what the Black Moon means." The Master said, disregarding her. "Of course you would recognize your own depiction. Isn't that right, *Lunae*?"

"L-Lunae?" Nox's heart began to race. As far as she was concerned, a knife to the chest wouldn't have hurt worse than hearing what she had just heard.

Whoever this man was, he thought she was an Aeon.

"A bit confused?" the Master laughed, amused at her trembling body. "You mean to tell me that you never contemplated your origins? Falling from the sky? Your left eye being crimson? You never thought it was strange?"

"I already told you people! I'm Nox, and I've always been Nox! I'm not Lunae, or anyone else. I'm just Nox!"

The hooded man tilted his head.

"Are you? Why then can I hear the frantic beating of your heart? If you were Nox, you would know it, right? But if you were Lunae...you'd know that too, wouldn't you?" he laughed. "So tell me, which are you? Can you say either with *certainty?*"

Nox gripped her chest. She knew what he was saying was true. She didn't know *how* she knew—but he was right—the beating in her chest was proof enough.

"What do you want with—?" Nox started.

"Our talk is over," the Master interjected.

The final words of the cloaked man reverberated throughout the darkness of the vacant library, as well as in her mind, as she sat in the middle of the large birdcage, listening hopelessly as the footsteps of her captors walked down the stairs and through the doorway.

Her heart pounded; her breath was heavy.

Nox looked back at the glass moon.

XII

The Word of Heart

The snaps and cracks of wooden blades filled the courtyard with zipping noises that bounced off the ancient stone walls.

Lukas struggled to lift one of the weights off of the ground; Snow, however, stood beside him, gracefully lifting one that was easily three times the size of his.

"How is that so easy for you?!" Lukas exclaimed through heavy breaths.

Snow smiled and flipped her short, azure hair. "It's all in the blood."

"Are Elves, like, super strong or something?!"

Snow switched the weight to her other arm.

"No," she said casually, "it's in my *other* blood. I'm a half-Elf."

Her other blood?

Lukas watched the knight for a moment. There was so little he knew about her, yet, in the air around her, he felt rather...at ease. He had watched her face down a mage in Zerlina with merely a sword in hand; he remembered her inhuman speed in detecting the pickpocket. Truly, she was an admirable person. So quickly had he come to respect her. And, he realized that he respected her greatly.

"Is he mine yet?" Lukas and Snow turned to see a young woman with silver hair, tapping her foot impatiently.

"If you must, Blake," Snow smiled.

Blake disregarded the knight's words.

"You must be Lukas?"

"Yeah!" Lukas waved, "Nice to meet—"

"Follow me." Blake cut into his greeting and began to walk away. "Magic study. Now."

Lukas looked at Snow, who only shrugged, then he followed.

Archbishop Marven sat amid a pile of papers as Clement stood on the other side of his desk.

"Prince Reethkilt?" he said as he poured himself a glass of wine. "What brings you here so unannounced?"

Clement bowed his head. "I apologize if I have appeared rude, your Holiness, but I was sent here upon the request of my father, Ahmaal zel Reethkilt. He was quite forward and urgent with his order, so he never made the traditional arrangements."

Marven furrowed his brow as he took a sip of his wine.

"Very well." He motioned downward with his free hand. "Take a seat. Would you like a drink?"

"I dare no." The prince smiled politely as he sat. "Those with the blood of the Aeon Vhryt are not meant for drink."

"Ah, that's right!" Marven chuckled. "The Aeon of Wind." He filled his cup once more. "Anyway, what importance brings you here so quickly?"

"Something happened two weeks ago," Clement began. "An occurrence at the capital. I will start from the beginning, if you will allow?"

"Well," Marven sipped his glass once more, "that *would* be best."

"Verily so." The prince cleared his throat. "Recently, my father told me that the Voice of the Wind has been speaking to him in a rather stranger tone than usual, and he has been a bit...on edge. According to him, a figure appeared in his chamber two weeks ago, referring to itself merely as '*The End of the World.*'"

Marven narrowed his eyes.

"End...of the World, you say?"

"Yes," Clement nodded, "that is correct. My father claimed he called loudly for the guards—fellow Red Ravens, that is—yet, they did not come. When the guards *were* found, it appeared as if they had gone completely mad. According to the reports I read, they were found crawling on the ground and speaking incoherently." A grim visage cast over the prince's face. "They were dead by noon."

"By the One!" Marven exclaimed as he set his glass on a stack of papers. "Why did he not inform me until now?"

"I do not know. My father's will is his own, I assume. Yet, he did not even mention the figure to me until he had heard of the incident at Zerlina and the drawing of the Sword Durandal."

Marven exhaled and began to scratch his head. "So, what does he wish to do?"

"He wishes to call the nations to conference. A gathering of Aestriana, Mirea, and Abdiah. I believe he wishes to tell them what I have just told you."

The Archbishop nodded his head. "I will make it happen. And, if it is well with you, I will have Master Inquisitor Eldric give his report of Zerlina as well?"

Clement stood and bowed his head. "I believe that must be done, as well."

Marven bowed back. "Good."

Clement raised his head and turned to walk out of the room. "Prince!"

"Yes, Your Holiness?"

"Tell your father that I am glad he is well."

The prince smiled. "I shall. He will be grateful to hear it."

Blake made no attempt to speak as she led Lukas down the ancient halls of Mhyrmr. Many times did *he* consider speaking, but the sheer tension that surrounded her caused him to reconsider each time.

This girl—she was...definitely different. The air around her was cold. It wasn't like the warmth of Nox, or even Snow.

Lukas found himself shivering.

What am I getting into?

They continued down the dim corridor until Blake reached a door and stopped.

"You," she said as she opened the door and pointed into the

pitch black room. "In. Now."

Silently (cautiously, rather), Lukas entered.

"W-where are we?" he finally mustered the courage to ask.

"This is where I'm going to tutor you. It's quiet here."

Lukas looked around in the pitch blackness. "But, I can't see a thing?"

Blake didn't acknowledge the orphan's comment.

With the snap of her fingers, the globes on the walls and ceiling were suddenly filled with a bright, blue, flame.

Lukas watched the room illuminate. He could see just how big the space actually was, with the globes hanging over tables that were piled with dusty books.

"This place looks like it hasn't been touched in ages," he said without realizing it.

"Sit." She pointed at a chair. "I'm not going to be repeating myself over and over, so listen up."

A sudden nervousness washed over Lukas, so he felt it was probably best to silently do what he was told. He walked over to the chair and sat. The simple, wooden chair wasn't necessarily comfortable, and the creaking it made as he sat wasn't necessarily reassuring, either, but Lukas also knew that he would rather fall onto the floor than incur Blake's wrath.

"I'll start from the beginning. So listen up!" she sighed. "In our blood lies a unique element that we called 'zellinium.' We don't know why it's there, or for what reason, given that it appears to have no real evolutionary value. Ancients referred to this chemical as 'Presence,' and there are many different speculations on how this element got there, but none are conclusive. It is the most basic form of spiritual energy, and, it's your very breath of life. That said, it lies...well, dormant most of the time. Thusly, Magic is the art of manipulating and materializing this energy into the external world."

Lukas was reminded of Zerlina—of how Iago was able to create his blades from thin air.

She continued. "Magic comes from the heart, the spiritual wellspring of our being."

"I remember," Lukas spoke up, "that when I saw Eldric and Iago use magic, they yelled words before they used it. Like a spell?"

"Shhhh!" Blake raised her finger. Lukas looked into her white-blue eyes. Their very color filled him with a wintry chill.

Everything about this girl, he thought, *is frigid.*

"I'm getting there." She cleared her throat. "Every person's heart is different, therefore, every mage's magic manifests differently. The words they spoke before they used their magic is called a 'Word of Heart.' Those words are more a...prayer than a spell. By vocalizing the heart's true name into the air, one's spiritual Presence is awakened. Think of it like this: In everyone, the true powers of the heart lie sleeping. But. The heart is constantly sleep talking, calling out it's name, waiting for someone to say those words back in return."

"Sleep talking..." Lukas said under his breath.

"Catch your breath, just so you don't feel suffocated." Blake said as she stepped into the middle of the room and took a deep breath. Suddenly, a light breeze swept through the area, slowly flipping the pages of the open books upon the tables, and a thin blue aura engulfed the mage.

"Nix Celshior."

Lukas watched a veil of frost lace around her body like a dainty dress. The temperature in the room suddenly plummeted; the once fair breeze became a biting cold.

"T-that's incredible!" Lukas exclaimed as flurries of snow began to form in the air. "So those words are what activate your power?"

She shrugged apathetically. "You must listen, hearing your heart's cry, then you must join it in its song. Hearing your heart's voice and calling its name are the true weapons of the Inquisition."

Lukas watched Blake, now even more intimidated than he was before. She was so young; he knew she couldn't be much older than himself, yet, she had this amazing grasp of her powers.

"So, every mage's Word of Heart is different, then?"

"Are you even listening?" she groaned, "I said it comes from the heart. No two people possess the same heart, so no two mages wield the same magic. I've already gone over that!"

Honestly, the concept daunted Lukas. Seeing it happen was hard enough to comprehend, but, invoking it within *himself*...well...that seemed even *more* far-fetched.

"How do I do it?"

"The key is in your breath. Breathe deep and focus inwardly. The heart is never silent; it speaks even when *we* are silent."

"Never silent, huh?" Lukas said under his breath.

"What was that?" Blake said as she crossed her arms.

"I was—" Lukas gulped, "J-just repeating what you said!"

"Whatever," the ice mage sighed as she walked toward the door. "We'll have our next lesson here at the same time tomorrow, so don't be late. Until then, leave me alone."

Lukas exhaled a nervous breath as she walked out.

XIII

The First Mission

Three months went by for Lukas, the silence of the passing days more excruciating than the last. Each day, he woke up at the first light of dawn to meet Snow in the courtyard for combat training. Next, he would make his way down the dim hallways of Mhyrmr to practice magic with the unapproachable Blake.

His time with Snow had been fruitful, and the sword practice had quickly become his favorite thing about his new home. Quite quickly had he come to enjoy his time with the blue-haired knight. Despite the severity of her training methods, Lukas had found that she had a rather warm and caring personality.

The time with the cold mage, however, had been the most difficult, to say the least. In three months, he had been unable to hear his heart's call. Each time, he was reprimanded with some slight curse or openly blunt remark about how his concentration was off, or something like that. Regardless of her superficial corrections, Lukas was positive that Blake had given up on him by his second try. Archbishop Marven, however, still insisted that she spend regular time with him until he had made progress, but the lack of said progress was the most grueling aspect.

In the three months he had spent with the seemingly unavailable tutor, he had learned nothing of her. To him, she merely remained a mystery. She spoke nothing of herself, and he dared not ask anything of her.

Lukas lay in his bed, pondering his new life.

The morning had just begun, and the beams of red light had

only started to peek through his ancient window. Snow had told him that there would be no combat training today, which was a strange thing for her to say given her ascetic regimen.

Is today special or something?

The change in schedule made him a bit...uneasy.

Blake strode down the hall, muttering angrily to herself.

"I can't believe he assigned me to..." she shook her head, *"babysit!"*

Light filled the sanctuary, shining upon the ancient artwork heroes and angels. The walk to the Archbishop's office was always the most scenic, or at least she thought so, and, despite her disdain, she found the route to be enjoyable. As she walked, she considered what awaited her in his office.

And, she loathed the idea already.

He's basically sending that boy to his death, she thought. *But it's not* my *hands that will be bloodied, at least.*

She knew what awaited her, or rather what awaited *them.*

And she didn't like it one bit.

Lukas showered and dressed for his day—a day which he believed would be free of tasks. In other words, a day he felt would be boring. He stared at himself in the mirror for a moment. Honestly, he didn't think he would like his hair if it were cut short, but as he stared at it, he had to admit it didn't look as bad as he had thought. His platinum-blond hair appeared a rather strange color, and he couldn't decide if it looked more white or if it looked more golden.

"Sir Lukas!" The knock on the door caused the orphan to jump.

"Yeah?" he said as he looked through the peep hole to see a fellow knight standing stern on the other end.

"Archbishop Ferrenvaal wishes to see you. Please, prepare and follow me."

Lukas did as he was told. He really had no choice in the matter, as he didn't know how to get to the Archbishop's office. And, secondly, a summons from the Archbishop couldn't be ignored, so it wasn't like he could refuse, even if he wanted to.

As they walked from the orphan's room to Marven's office, Lukas couldn't shake a sudden anxiety.

So that's why there wasn't any training today! he thought. *Because the Archbishop had something for me to do...but what? Why would he be so secretive? I mean, couldn't he have just given me a heads up?*

The cryptic nature of the summons frankly invoked a fearful, unsettling knot in his stomach. They walked silently down dim hallways, through the courtyard, into the sanctuary, and up the stairs. Soon, Lukas stood at the large wooden door to Marven's office.

Soon, but a bit sooner than he was prepared for.

"Here we are, young man," the soldier said.

Lukas nodded and watched the soldier disappear down the stairs. He turned to the door, took a deep breath, then entered.

As soon as Lukas entered the office, he noticed that Blake was also present. The elderly man sat at his wooden desk, surrounded by an ocean of papers and loose files. Lukas scanned the massive mess and wondered to himself if this man ever got anything done.

"Lukas," Marven said as he beckoned with his hand, "so good of you to join us." He pointed to the chair beside the one that Blake was sitting in. "Sit. We have much to talk about."

Lukas looked at Blake and nodded as he took his seat. She, however, merely looked away.

Lukas sighed.

This is going to go well...

Archbishop Marven cleared his throat. "I have been hearing great things from Snow in regards to your physical training, and, although Blake has made it clear that your magic training isn't going...well...the best, I have decided that some time on the field would be the most beneficial thing for you right now."

Lukas heard Blake groan.

"Do we have to do this, Your Holiness?" she pointed at the orphan, "I really don't want to carry back a cadaver."

"Now, now, Blake." Marven said as he picked up his wine

glass. "Even though his magical skills are not necessarily existent, he can still serve you as a knight." He took a sip and then turned to Lukas. "Besides, there is a *special* reason for Lukas to attend this venture."

Blake turned to Lukas. Although he didn't return the look, he could feel her freezing gaze chilling his body.

"What sort of 'special reason,' Y-Your Holiness?" Lukas asked.

Marven nodded at the orphan.

"You see, when you arrived, I promised to help you find your friend, yes?"

A sudden sense of surprise cast over Lukas. Though he didn't realize it, he had figured that the Archbishop had forgotten, or even *lied,* just to keep him there. The agonizing anxiety in Lukas suddenly lessened at the old man's words. Maybe—just maybe—he didn't forget.

"I remember, Your Holiness." Lukas could barely hide the excitement behind his voice.

"I will be sending you and Blake to northern Aestriana, to the mountain town of Ildar. The town is humble and out of the way, but has one unique attraction."

"The Oracle," Blake said under her breath.

"Yes," Marven continued. "The Oracle of Ildar. I believe that her magic might be able to aid you in the finding of your friend."

"So what's the *actual* mission?" Blake sighed.

"Well..." Marven set his wineglass on the table and picked up the bottle to pour another glass. "We've received word that the Nightshade Court has taken up a headquarters there. According to our intelligence, they've seized the city."

Blake cleared her throat and pointed her thumb in Lukas' direction. The Archbishop could see the lost expression on Lukas' face.

"The Nightshade Court is a criminal organization of vampires. They specialize in the creation and distribution of a highly potent drug called 'Blood Dust.'"

Lukas suddenly felt uneasy. Training was one thing and actual combat was another—but vampires were a factor entirely to themselves.

"Sounds fun," Blake said dispassionately.

"The man you're after is the vampire lord known as 'Damasko the Bloodletter.' He's an extremely wanted man, and a master of the Sanguine Call." Marven turned to Lukas. "'The Sanguine Call' is what we call vampire magic."

"And you're only sending two of us?" Lukas failed his attempt at hiding the quiver in his voice.

"Well, I'll be sending just the two of you from Mhyrmr. You'll be rendezvousing with Captain Havell Maro of the Red Ravens. They will be your ground force, and your allies." He glared at Blake. "So play nice, little Snowbird."

Blake stood. "Is that all? I'm guessing that we leave now?"

"It is. And yes, you will be departing immediately. I have arranged for you the usage of the Airskiff Cavalier. You'll be packing light, as well."

Blake left the room silently. Lukas sat for a second and looked at Archbishop Marven. Marven smiled and shrugged.

"Well, Lukas. Best of luck in dealing with her."

Lukas sighed, then followed his partner.

Blake and Lukas separated as they each went to their respective rooms to prepare for the journey ahead. Blake moped down the dim-lit corridors in no real hurry.

How could he do this to me? What's gotten into Archbishop Ferrenvaal? He's sending this boy to his death. And even worse, *I have to put up with it?!*

The very thought bubbled in her stomach in a boiling rage.

"Flustered, are we?" came a female voice from behind.

Blake turned to see Snow.

"I don't understand, Snow. Why would the Archbishop send someone so combat-ignorant onto the field? He's only been training for three months—and he's completely useless when it comes to magic! He isn't able to even call upon his Word of Heart."

Snow smiled and put her hand on the mage's shoulder. "He

may be a bit naive, that is true. But." Blake turned to face the half-Elf. "Don't worry. He's a resilient young man. I'm sure he will do just fine.

"Whatever."

Blake brushed the knight's hand off of her shoulder, and walked off without another word.

Lukas gazed at his reflection in the mirror once again. For a moment, he didn't recognize himself. Between his short hair and newly grown muscle, he had almost utterly transformed from when he was the scrawny orphan from the remote Zerlina monastery.

"Hey!" Lukas heard Blake banging on the door. "Can't you hear me?! We have to leave. *Now.*"

Lukas jumped and frantically grabbed his travel bag.

"What are you doing?!" The voice said as the pounding increased in force.

"Sorry! I was packing!"

"Well hurry up. We were supposed to leave, like, *five minutes* ago!"

Lukas hastily put on his shoes and ran to the door, opened it, and was face-to-face with an irate Blake.

"Are we *finally* ready, princess?"

"Princess?" Lukas could hear the crack in his voice. "I'm a guy!"

"Yeah? Well you definitely prep like a princess. What? Did you have to do your makeup?"

"Hey!" Lukas retorted.

"Come on." She turned and walked away. "We have to get to the hangar."

The airship hangar was just as Lukas remembered it to be. He followed Blake past the countless airships to a small dock with a small aircraft, less than a fourth the size of the ones they had previously passed.

"It's tiny," Lukas said as he scratched his head.

"It's an airskiff." Blake replied dryly. "It's not supposed to be big." She pointed to the passenger seat. "Just get in."

Lukas did as he was told and entered the cockpit, followed by the taciturn Inquisitor, who sat at the yoke. Lukas made comments about the design, but his voice was unintelligible as the ice mage started the machine.

She pointed to three tiny gauges, filled with bright teal liquid. Lukas watched the indicators as the liquid all became evenly leveled.

Blake reached to her left side and picked up a small radio receiver.

"Aether gauge at equilibrium."

Lukas could barely hear a static-veiled voice from the other end, and then the door began to open.

"You can fly this thing?!" Lukas' voice cracked slightly.

"Don't talk. You'll bite your tongue off."

"Bite my—?"

Suddenly, the small airskiff shot forward with blinding speed. Lukas held his breath as a heavy weight pressed upon his chest. For a moment, he felt as if he were being flattened under the pressure.

"Calm down," Blake said flatly as she shifted gears.

Lukas fell forward as the aircraft halted and was caught by his harness.

Blake sighed. "First gear is a bit rough, but you'll get used to it."

Lukas was caught aback. He tried to speak, but he could feel his heart beating against his sternum.

His partner looked forward, disregarding him.

"Just shut up until we get there."

There was a moment of painful silence.

"Blake." Lukas said as he sat upright in his chair. Never before had he tried to address the mage directly, but he couldn't help but discern her complete distrust in him.

"What?"

"I know—" Lukas stopped and thought. "I know you think I

won't be of much use, but I wanted to let you know that I'm going to try my best to be a useful knight to you during this mission."

Blake let out a groan.

"Just stay out of my way, okay."

XIV

The Oracle of Ildar

The flight to Ildar had been an extensive journey, filled with an even more extensive silence. Lukas watched below as the small craft traversed over the tops of the Drezen Mountains. The greens of the evergreens below danced amid the mountain breezes, shaking off their snowy caps, the flakes falling like glitter upon the crystalline floor.

This scenery, however beautiful it may have been, did little to pierce the grueling quiet which pervaded within the cockpit.

They had traveled for a whole day, yet Blake had said little more than was necessary. Lukas, on the other hand, had attempted to formulate something—*anything*—to talk about.

He found it futile.

"So," he finally said. "When I learn my Word of Heart, h-how will I know how to use it? Like, do I have to practice a lot?"

Nothing. Merely the hum of the engine and the winds outside.

"Well, it's a part of you," Blake finally said, the irritation in her voice obvious. "You'll most likely know how to use it instinctively." She paused. "I mean, that doesn't mean you can't get creative or whatever."

Lukas was silent then; he had long decided that his partner had no desire to talk.

So...I'll just know how to use it, huh?

Snow poured heavily, a thick powder that covered the dark

town of Ildar in its chilling embrace. The biting wind swiftly flowed through the thick fir and small houses only to be halted by the thick walls of the castle of Ildar, the Baronwatch. The ancient stones had worn with time and weather, which seemed to spite its stalwart walls. The fortress seemed uniquely (and blatantly) out of place compared to the rustic setting which surrounded it, a monolith of an age long gone.

Amid the silent snow, the melodies of melancholy strings filled the air, thrown about by the winds. Damasko the Bloodletter stood, perched upon the walls of the forlorn fortress, the bow of his violin gracefully slicing upon the strings. The frigid winds whipped around him, scattering his long, black hair with its passing.

"What a rich melody, my lord." A woman's voice entered the air.

Damasko opened his eyes to see another vampire, a tall, curvy woman in a pink dress.

"Magenta," he said, "what is it?"

"The Red Ravens are camped just at the base of the mountains. I assume they plan to attack."

"They will be fools to try it."

"And," Magenta's voice was smooth, "I have heard the Church is sending an Inquisitor to aid them."

"I see...why don't you send them your little puppet-plaything? The old doctor, Nils? They'll never expect that one."

"He does need something to do." Magenta laughed. "It will be done, my lord."

The winds whistled and zipped around the vampire lord as Magenta made her exit.

"An Inquisitor, in this frozen land?" he laughed as he put his violin under his chin once more. "I wonder if it is *her*."

Softly, he placed his bow upon the strings and made them weep.

"Oh, dear Snowbird, I shall play for you a *lasting* dirge!"

The Oracle stepped out into the encroaching morning. From her temple at the top of her mountain, she looked down at the dark and desolate town of Ildar, consumed by a black mist—the peculiar feature, the one that she observed for two weeks now. The sun broke the horizon, a blazing beacon which lit the clouds in songs of pink and red, chasing the night with its presence.

"Is it still the same?" A voice approached her. "The same as yesterday?"

The Oracle lowered her pipe and blew out smoke. She observed from her mountain spire. Though the morning sun had now risen fully, its light did not pierce the dark veil that engulfed Ildar.

It is the same, Vilkar, she said wordlessly, her voice resounding in his mind. *The light dares not enter the mist.*

Vilkar stood beside her, his tall, lanky, figure towering over the short and withered old woman.

He pointed to the forest below them. Vaguely, in the shadows of the thick fir, a camp could be discerned.

"And yet the soldiers fight it? They wish to fight vampires at night?" he snorted. "A fool's quest."

Perhaps not. The Oracle puffed her pipe. Her solid black eyes bore a faint hint of red as she stared off toward the fiery horizon.

One comes...one comes who is different from all the others.

"Different how?"

It is too soon to say. She paused and looked down at the camp below. At the foot of the hill, she could make out the darkened figures of soldiers as they moved about in the impending dawn. She turned. *We will go see them.*

"Go..." Vilkar stopped, "to see them?"

Yes.

Captain Havell Maro leaned against a crate as he smoked his morning cigarette and watched the sky. He was looking for the aircraft sent by the Church. Earlier in the day, he had his scouts use the Aether Scry to determine the exact positioning of the Inquisitor's aircraft. He had determined that aid would be with them within the hour. He also knew that the reverse was just as true. Whoever was piloting the Church aircraft would be using the same technology.

At least I get to have my smoke in peace. He thought as he exhaled a large, white cloud.

The minutes passed; Captain Maro kept his eyes on the sky, though, every so often, he'd scan his soldiers to make sure all was well. Eventually, his idle gazing turned into daydreaming, and he found himself drifting to the ancient temple that loomed ominously over their meager camp. Even from the bottom of the mountainous terrain, he could make out the decrepit stone of a structure desperate to escape the flow of time.

The Oracle...

The thought was curious to him. Does that ancient woman really live in such frigid solitude? There were many legends surrounding the witch-like woman. Some said that she had existed for thousands of years. Others claimed that she could truly see things that mortals—even the mages of Mhyrmr—could not. And, some resolutely disbelieved her existence entirely.

"Cap'n Maro!" a soldier's call broke his trance. "The Church's craft is headed our way!"

Havell flicked his cigarette into the snow, then stood.

"Lead the way."

The Airskiff Cavalier descended softly onto the mountain floor. Outside, soldiers stood at attention, awaiting the arrival of an Inquisitor. The cockpit opened, and Blake and Lukas rose from their seats and climbed down to the ground. As Lukas' feet sank into the knee-high snow, he watched Blake move nonchalantly past the saluting soldiers. As he caught up to her, he noticed how lightly she was dressed. He, himself, was dressed head to toe in thick fur, worn over his silver breastplate. Blake, however, merely wore a casual dress, pure white, with sky blue frills.

"Aren't you going to freeze to death?!" Lukas trembled from the cold.

Blake looked in his direction; a slight streak of anger contorted her face.

"I'm an ice mage. You really think I *get* cold?"

Right...right...

Lukas dropped the subject.

"Oh thank the Aeons that old man Ferrenvaal still has some sense!" A gritty voice came from the back of the camp.

"Hello Captain Maro," Blake sighed as the soldier approached.

"You're as chipper as ever," Captain Maro laughed. He turned to Lukas. Lukas could see a sudden hint of excitement cast over the captain's face. "Luke! What's up?!"

"How's it going Havell!" Lukas raised his voice.

Blake's cold eyes shot at Lukas. "Did you just call a *captain* by his first name?!"

"Bah!" Havell laughed. "Me and Luke go way back!" He took hold of the young man's shoulder. "Looks like Snow did you a solid! You've definitely filled out! You might be able to take me next time we spar!"

"Whatever." Blake scoffed. "So tell me what—"

"Captain!" A soldier called as soon as Blake began to speak.

"What's up?!" Captain Maro called back in a stern tone. "Can't ya see that an Inquisitor is speaking?"

"Yes, sir!" the soldier replied with a bow. "But, sir! A woman arrived just now—says she's the Oracle!"

"Ora—" the captain stopped mid-sentence, "Where is she?!"

Here, Captain Maro.

A woman's voice thundered throughout their minds.

All stopped and turned to the old woman walking toward them. She was accompanied also by a lanky man, much younger than herself.

Silence ensued as everyone in the camp watched the ancient woman anxiously.

Why do you stop? her voice said. *Am I such a spectacle to you?*

"How is she—?"

"Projection magic," Captain Maro interrupted Lukas' sentence. "In other words, it's psychic power. It's what I used on you when we sparred. Remember how I made you forget what you were doing?"

The Oracle stared at Lukas. Lukas could see into her solid

black eyes. As they stared back at him, they seemed less like eyes and more like pitch dark pits.

And you have much to learn, Heart of Hearts.

"H-how do you know that?" Lukas' eyes widened.

She pointed at the Sword Durandal in it's leather sheath on Lukas' back.

You carry the First of Three, no? You carry the Sword Durandal, yes?

Lukas looked at the blade on his back.

Then you are *Heart of Hearts.* The old woman slowly walked closer. As she approached, Lukas caught the stark scent of tobacco on her breath.

Questions filled his mind, a plethora of inquiries wrapped in his awkward silence. This woman knew much—but, did this woman know *too much?*

You seek what you have lost, no? You seek her. You seek Lunae.

Lukas stopped. A dreadful shock stunned him.

L-Lunae?!

"The girl I'm looking for is named Nox!" Lukas blurted out, his voice a bit louder than he had intended. "Lunae is an Aeon! Nox is a girl—she's my best friend!"

The Oracle blew out smoke mixed with warm breath.

But the eye is red, no? The sky from whence she came, no?

Lukas froze, the mystic's voice resounding through his mind.

"How did you know that?

Your friend, the old woman ignored Lukas' question, *you never stopped to wonder* what *she was? Why she was so different?*

Lukas' mind was loud with confusion. Why? Why was he listening to this preposterous woman—and why—*why* did he believe her?

Lunae?! he thought. *But how? Why?*

Lukas suddenly felt a strange heat in his heart; a certain ember filled his body.

Heart of Hearts, the woman's voice said, *you know what is right. But you do not know what lies ahead. Your path is perilous and wrought with grief. In order to survive, you must not be what you are.* Her voice carried through his mind like a faint breeze, a soft whistling of wind through a silent forest.

In your greatest peril—you must only be yourself, for if your spirit is anything else, you will not survive.

"What do you mean? Lukas asked.

But she had already disappeared back into the woods.

XV

The Eternal Night

The sun rose steadily into the noon as a figure in scrappy clothing limped desperately to the Red Ravens' camp. Sunlight struggled to peer through the thick and snow-capped fir trees, reaching the bottom in some places to alight the pure white blanket which smothered the ground. The rays that eyed the man stumbling below revealed his bloodied skin, dotted with bruises and the pink of newly-formed scabs. Ahead of him, he could barely visualize the smoke of the camp through the dense canopies. In the vagueness of the shade, soldiers ran toward him. Blood stung his eyes as he squinted. On their coats, a red insignia —the sign of hope.

He felt his heart skip as his knees buckled beneath him. The snow was cold on his exposed skin, and he prayed that death wouldn't take him.

Vilkar aided the Oracle through the voluminous mountain snow. The journey uphill to the temple always revealed itself to be taxing for the tall and thin assistant, but never once did he see any evidence that his limping mistress fatigued as well. Although he had spent his entire life at her beckon, he had realized many times that he knew almost nothing about her. She was an enigma, a living relic lost to the ages. But, how much time? He did not know; he could not infer, even after she had raised him, just how long she had truly lived.

"What was so special about that boy?" he asked, breaking the lengthy silence of their trek.

He wields the Heart of Hearts. Her voice was a whisper in his mind, a faint breeze in his ears. *He wields the Sword Durandal, the First of Three.*

There was a slight pause filled with the faint patter of falling snow.

He reminds me of him. *He reminds me of Lucyn.*

"Lucyn?"

The first Heart of Hearts. They are very much alike—but that was long ago.

"I see."

They walked on for a while longer.

Just like him, the Oracle thought to only herself, *tell me, boy, do the stars flow in your veins, too?*

The man who passed out in the snow awoke to the faces of Lukas, Blake, and Captain Maro looking down upon him. Like a lucid dream, their faces were akin to a mercy he'd felt impossible, given his odds.

"You're awake, friend." The captain's words were soft. He nodded to the soldiers to raise the man up. "You got a name?"

The man looked around. Surrounding him, a giant tent shielded them from the cutting winds outside.

"Nils," he said. "I am Nils."

"You're a lucky man, Nils." Captain Maro said, his voice muffled behind his hand as he lit a cigarette. "You just so happened to pass out on a patrol route."

Nils examined the decorated captain, his eyes drawn instantly to the insignia of a crimson raven, woven onto his uniform.

"Red Ravens?"

"Yep." Havell blew out smoke. "You wanna tell me what you were doing out there? You look like you've been mauled by a snow leopard."

Blake held her thumb to her chin for a moment, silent.

"You came from Ildar, didn't you?" she said finally.

"You think he's—" Lukas said under his breath.

"I did." Nils hung his head. Lukas could see the indigo bruises along his shaking arm.

What happened...to this man?

"Interesting," she said dryly.

"So." Captain Maro blew out more smoke. "How about you tell us how you got out of there."

"And while you're at it, tell us just what the Nightshade Court is doing down there." Blake added.

"They came one night—the Court—about two weeks ago. We were completely helpless; our town guard was swept away in the blink of an eye. After that, they chained us in the town prison and began taking our blood to make their 'Blood Dust.'" Nils looked at his arms. "They take our blood until we pass out, leave us alone for a few hours, then return for more. It..." he paused. Lukas could see the fine tremors coursing up the man's arms, "I thought it would never end..."

"And just how did *you* escape such conditions?" Blake said with one eyebrow raised.

"I died," Nils coughed. "Or, they thought I had died, at least. They threw me into the cave—with all of the other bodies. I woke up and just started running. I saw the smoke from this camp, and I...just ran..." Nils lowered his head, "I just ran..."

Blake put her finger to her chin ruminatively.

"So it was just a sheer fluke that you're alive, huh?" Captain Maro shook his head with a slight laugh.

Lukas clenched his fist.

This man has been through hell.

"Inquisitor!" Nils exclaimed suddenly. "I can take you to the cave. *Please.* Let me take you to the cave!"

Blake narrowed her eyes. "So soon?"

"Yes." He nodded. "I'm the town physician. I can't abandon the ones I swore to heal! Please. You can reach the city through the cave. It's perfect!"

Blake narrowed her eyes as she judged the battered old man. Was he telling the truth? She was almost positive that he wasn't, but...if they went in the daytime, with a large number, then there was probably no harm. *And,* an opportunity like this was honestly what they'd been waiting for.

"Okay," Blake said finally. "But Captain Maro and a squad of Red Ravens come too."

"Of course!" the captain answered.

Blake turned to Nils. "It's not that I don't trust you, doctor. I just don't trust you."

"You don't trust him?" Lukas spoke up.

Blake turned to Lukas. He could see that familiar frostiness in her stark blue eyes. "I don't trust anyone."

Right...right...

"Rest up, Nils. Tomorrow morning, you take us to your little cave."

Darkness filled the vast chapel of Baronwatch save for several islands of light provided by hanging chandeliers, ablaze with blue flames. Below the dim beacons, Damasko the Bloodletter sat upon a worn throne before three kneeling figures.

"It has been done?" The vampire lord's voice echoed throughout the chamber.

"It has, my lord." The woman in the middle smiled as she bowed her head. "The one who escaped—whether he knows it or not—he will bring us the Inquisitor."

A Cheshire grin crossed the lord's face.

"You have done well, Magenta. Never before have I had the blood of an Inquisitor, and to think my first sip will be from *her!*"

"So funny and simple the living are." The woman laughed as she pointed to her head. "You put one little thought in their minds and they dance like puppets."

"Go now, Magenta." Damasko pointed to the exit. "Go and reap my prize."

"As you wish, my lord." She smiled as she rose and walked away.

Damasko turned to one of the men still before him.

"Vermilion," he summoned.

Of the two men bowing before him, the short, fat, one raised his head.

"Yes, Master," his soft voice hissed.

"What of production?"

"The slaves work well." He smiled. "The constant supply of Beastfolk is working to our favor. They themselves are immune to vampirism, yes." He paused. "But their blood makes the finest Blood Dust known to Lythia."

"Wonderful," Damasko laughed as he reached into the pocket of his coat and pulled out a cigar case. "Remember, Vermilion, we wish to keep our client happy."

"Of course." Vermilion said.

"You may leave."

Without a word, the fat vampire rose and slithered off.

Damasko turned to the third, a gargantuan man, just as broad as he was tall.

"Sanguine." Damasko lit his cigar and exhaled a thick, red cloud.

"Yes." Sanguine's voice thundered throughout the room.

"Is the Emulator running as planned?"

"Yes, my lord. The Stone seems to power it flawlessly."

"Good," Damasko laughed.

The vampire lord rose from his seat.

"With the stone in place, we shall continue our Eternal Night."

Night passed slowly for Nils, his dreams clouded with flashing images and disembodied voices. Guards were posted outside of his tent, but his high-pitched wails could be heard all throughout the camp. As soon as dawn broke the horizon, they woke him and began their journey to the cave.

Everyone but Blake wore heavy coats and masks to keep themselves from the wind's spearing sting. Blake, however, wore merely a small white dress. As he watched her move effortlessly through the knee-high snow, Lukas couldn't help but ponder her eccentric mannerisms. She repulsed others without prejudice, and she seemed to have no qualms about rejecting friendships. She was, he thought, in every sense, a lone wolf.

Nils led the excursion through shadowy fir, which were covered in white pillows and brushed merely by the vague screeching of the forest winds. Lukas admitted to himself that he'd never seen such a place that was just as beautiful as it was forlorn. Ahead, down the slope, a dark miasma swallowed the small, unfortunate, town of Ildar.

"We turn here." Nils raised his voice above the winds. "The cave is below this hill."

The followers looked at each other, then nodded.

The hills steepened as they descended the frozen mountain. They guided their feet carefully along the little walking space they had. All but Blake, that is, who seemed to have no qualms with her movement around the slick terrain. The trek seemed endless to Lukas when Nils abruptly stopped and pointed to a small chasm in the ground.

"Tiny, huh?" Captain Maro griped.

Nils looked at Lukas and Havell. "You'll probably have to give your weapons to me. I'll hand them to you once you're through the hole."

The three followers stopped and looked at each other. As their eyes met, Lukas could discern that the other two felt the same as he did.

Distrusting.

"Me, Lukas, and half of the squad will follow you," Blake said, "We keep our weapons. *And.* Havell stays outside with the other half."

"She's right," the captain said. "I wouldn't want to make mutiny *too* easy, now would I?"

"And my sword is magical," Lukas added. "Only I can lift it."

The doctor looked at them blankly for a moment, then nodded.

Captain Maro watched Blake and Lukas follow the man into the deep crevasse and disappear into the darkness.

The forestation covered the mountain absolutely, causing the vast shadows to conceal the denizens which dwelt within their depths. A multitude of deranged villagers shifted from their positions, their eyes locked onto the figures of Captain Maro and the Red Ravens, who stood unaware. They peered through the shades at the vulnerable men before them.

Controlled by strings unseen, they leapt forward.

Blake, Lukas, and the rest of their squad followed the perturbed doctor through the darkened cavern. Their steps lit only by the dim light of an aetherlamp, nothing was visible outside of it's small glow.

"We turn here." Nils said as they came to a trickling stream.

"For a man who has only traversed this cave once, you know an awful lot about your whereabouts," Blake said incredulously.

Suddenly, a melodic whistling echoed down the corridor. Nils suddenly stood upright and looked around frantically.

"Where am I?" He yelled in terror. "How did I get here?" He turned to his two companions. "Who are you people?"

"Nils?!" Lukas said with a streak of terror.

"The living are such quirky little playthings!" a woman's voice laughed from within the darkness. "You put one little thought in their minds and they just *obsess*!"

Lukas and Blake shielded their eyes as a bright blast of light filled the room. In the now visible cave, a woman in a tight pink dress sat lazily upon a shelf of rock. The three looked around to see the corners of the room cluttered with vampire soldiers.

"Let me introduce myself," the woman said as she levitated slowly from the overhang and landed on her feet. "My name is Magenta the Seductress."

"M-Magenta?!" Nils screeched as he dropped to the ground.

"Little Nils," she laughed, "you've been *such* a help, my lovely!"

Quickly, Lukas drew the Sword Durandal and stood in front of Blake. He looked around the room. Fanged smiles had them completely surrounded. Even if they were to fight, he thought, there's very little possibility that they would win in a head-on collision like this—regardless of their numbers.

"You sure sound confident," Blake smirked as she stepped

forward, covered in a light blue aura.

Suddenly, Lukas could feel his breath being sucked from his lungs.

"Slow down," Magenta sang as she snapped her fingers, "magic is a no-no here! You wouldn't want your lovely captain and his men to get ripped apart, now would you?"

"What?!" Blake exclaimed, her aura dissipating.

The Inquisitor and her Knight halted in horror as three vampires carried out the limp body of Captain Maro into the light.

Blake gritted her teeth as Magenta revealed a fanged smirk.

"Good girl!" Magenta smiled. She pointed at Lukas. "Put that pointy thing away. You won't need it where you're going." She snapped her fingers once more. "Take the men and put them in the factory. Take the Inquisitor and bring her to Lord Damasko. He'll be absolutely *thrilled* to have her company."

"Blake! What are you doing?!" Lukas roared as he waved the Sword Durandal at the encroaching hoard. "Take me, not her!"

Magenta laughed and snapped her fingers. "How valiant! But, you're not the one he wants. No...he wants the *Snowbird*."

Lukas felt a sudden pain on the back of his skull, a sudden heaviness took him as he turned around to see Nils holding a large rock.

"Nils?!" Lukas whimpered as he hit the ground.

Nils faced the knight, tears streaming down his face, then collapsed.

Lukas could feel himself drifting; his last image was the pain in Nils' face.

XVI

Lyrlark

Lukas stood in an endlessly vast darkness.

"You're conscious!" a soft voice echoed throughout the void.

Lukas spun around to see a young woman with deep violet hair and deep violet eyes.

"Who are you?!" an unnerved Lukas demanded.

The girl simply smiled.

"I have many names, used by both men and gods alike. To your kind, I am the Oracle. But, my dear Heart of Hearts, you may call me by my true name: Lyrlark, Aeon of Dreams, Revelations, and Prophetic Vision."

"Aeon?!"

Lyrlark touched her fingertips together and smiled.

"We look surprised?"

"I would say I'm a little more confused than anything," Lukas sighed. "Where am I, anyway?"

The Aeon put her finger to her chin. "We're inside your mind. You took quite a blow to the head." Lukas watched her eyes. They seemed to sparkle with unique flair. "But, don't worry. You're still very much alive. You might have a nice headache when you wake up, though."

"What do you want from me?" Lukas raised his brow.

"You seek my big sister, yes?" she smiled. "You seek Lunae— the one you call '*Nox*.'"

"So, Nox really is..." he trailed off.

"An Aeon, yes. Though, I do not think even *she* is aware of who she truly is."

Lukas lowered his head and clenched his fists. "Tell me. Is she okay?"

Lyrlark frowned and looked upward longingly. "I do not know. I cannot hear her heart over the screaming songs of the world."

"The world is...screaming?"

Lyrlark smiled. Lukas couldn't help but draw his gaze to the lush purple of her eyes. The more he looked, it seemed as if they sparkled with faint freckles of lights. He wondered, thinking about Nox's eye, if all Aeons had these strange optic qualities about themselves.

"Everything sings a song, Lukas of Zerlina; everything has its own voice. As Heart of Hearts, you above all should know that."

"'Heart of Hearts.'" Lukas said. "What does that mean?"

"The Heart of Hearts is the hearer of all things. It is the Heart above all others. And, it is the wielder of the First of Three."

"You're talking about Durandal, aren't you?"

Lyrlark simply nodded. "Yes. The blade you call 'Durandal' is but one of three pieces—one of three Starswords."

"So I need to find the other two?"

The Aeon craned her neck as if peering into the blackness around them.

"No," she said casually. "That would be impossible. The three Blades were once united into one; that is true. But, now, they are scattered—lost among the stars. Who is to say where they exist— or if they exist?" Lyrlark's eyes met Lukas'. "You do not need the others. You only need Durandal. The Heart of Hearts and the First of Three are kin just as the heart and the soul are kin. You must learn to hear the voice of the Sword just as you must learn to hear the songs of all things. Call its name, and it will come to you."

Lukas pondered. In the brief experience with the Aeon, she had only been victorious in producing more questions than answers.

Durandal...has a voice?

"Lukas of Zerlina." Her voice cut into his meditation. "You must begin by listening to the cries of the First of Three. Hear its cry, and the rest will follow."

Their eyes met. The violet phantasmagoria of her shifting irises seemed so soft, so warm.

"That is all, my dear Lukas." She smiled. "I will tell you one thing before I leave. That is, you may experience a bit of dizziness when you wake up. I don't know why this is, but it seems to be a side effect of my dream-walking."

"What—!?"

"Until later!" a giant smile crossed her lips as she snapped her fingers.

Suddenly, everything went black.

Lukas awoke and tried to move, only to find that restraints prohibited his body from doing so. Bright white lights in the ceiling blinded his view, and he blinked a few times before anything became visible.

"And now the other is awake as well," a raspy voice hissed. Lukas turned his head to see a short, fat, vampire standing beside a captured Havell Maro. "Anyways, my dear Captain, why don't you tell me why you and the Red Ravens are in the mountains above Ildar?"

Captain Maro smirked. "Why are you asking stupid questions, you fangfilth? You really think I'm going to give you classified information?"

"No matter." The round fiend cracked a fanged smile. He reached into his pocket and produced a tiny, red stone. "Tell me, Captain, do you know why they call me Vermilion the Bat? You see, it's really quite simple," he said as he crunched the stone in his mouth and swallowed it.

Lukas watched in horror as Vermilion's hand began to morph into a large, black talon.

Havell...no!

"You see, the Blood Dust we get from the veins of your inferior species allows us to tap into our true potential, our 'Sanguine Call.' We each have different powers, just like your kind. You've already seen the aptitude of Magenta's thought control. But, you see," Vermilion put his claw on Havell's bare chest, "some of us

119

are a bit less...subtle."

Havell tensed and grunted as he felt the claw glide across his chest, it's razor tips creating shallow scrapes along the captain's skin.

"Oh how easy it would be," Vermillion chuckled, "to tear you to ribbons."

"Havell!" Lukas roared. "Leave him alone!"

Vermilion turned to the knight.

"Ah, yes," he hissed, "the Inquisitor's gallant knight. Tell me, do you feel your own failure? The very one you were supposed to protect—no—the *only* one you were supposed to protect, has now become my Liege's prize."

"Where is she?!" Lukas squirmed frantically to no avail. "Where is Blake?!"

"'Blake the Snowbird?' I'm sure you know nothing about her —or how grave her sins are..." He smiled. "How *vast* her sins extend."

"Sins?" Lukas paused. "I don't know what you're talking about! Blake is a good person!"

"You're very naive for a knight," the vampire laughed. "But that information will do you no good at this point. *She* is with Lord Damasko, and *you* are here. Indefinitely."

"You bastard..." Lukas trailed off.

"That is all." Vermilion waved as he turned to leave the room. "Collection time will happen soon. Until then, adieu."

Lukas looked over at Havell Maro. The captain returned the glance with a smile. Lukas knew that it was meant to keep his spirits up, but he couldn't help but notice that the captain...was crying.

Damasko looked at the large stained-glass window above the altar, its bright blue and golden tiles formed into the image of a heavenly woman with bright, gilded hair.

"This chapel is truly ancient," he began. "One could speculate that it dates back to the time when angels still walked among us, before their race was eliminated, three thousand years ago."

Damasko paused. "This window is quite eloquent, wouldn't you say, Snowbird? It depicts Myrsa, who was worshiped by her people as the Angel of Deliverance. Ironic, considering how cruel and oppressive the angels were."

Under the faint blue flames of Baronwatch Chapel, Blake stood upright, her hands and feet bound by shackles and chained to a post.

"I'd rather you not struggle, dear." Damasko grinned as he chomped on his cigar. "You'll only do yourself more harm that way."

"Where're my comrades?!" She writhed. "Where is my knight and the captain?"

"Oh? Have you such empathy now? That's quite a surprise, Snowbird. Do not worry, they are in my laboratory right now, aiding me in creating the finest Blood Dust known to Lythia. The other Red Ravens may have joined them by now, as well."

Lukas...Blake thought, though, she could not tell why. She thought of him—she thought of how annoying she found him, how stupidly naive he was—but she also thought of just how little he deserved the fate he had received.

"You..." Blake trailed off into whimpering.

"Have we found sudden humanity? Aren't you the feared Snowbird? Aren't you the genius mage, famed far and wide by her chilling demeanor?" Damasko lifted her chin with his fingers. "Such infamy, and yet accompanied by such...beauty."

"You cold-hearted bastard!" she raved, "How dare you do that to them! How dare you do that to the people of Ildar! How dare you—"

Suddenly, a sharp pain flared against her cheek as Damasko's hand crossed her face.

"You say I'm cold-hearted?" he laughed. "How hypocritical coming from such frigid lips." Damasko grabbed Blake by her hair, puffed his cigar, then blew red smoke into her face. "You think I don't know anything about you, Snowbird? You think I don't know how much blood is on your hands? Would you say more than one thousand people? Two thousand, maybe? I mean, to kill your own home like that—to snuff out such bright flames in the mere blink of an eye..." he released her, then turned to walk down the aisle. "You see, my dear," the lord's words echoed throughout the vast chamber, "I may be cold-hearted, but *you...you* are frozen solid."

XVII

Frozen Solid

"You have such a lively smile, sweetie!" The florist told a seven-year-old Blake with a pat on her head. "It's hard to believe that vile Dominik is the father of such a kind child." She reached behind the counter and pulled out a starkly red flower. "Red Nightshade? What would bring you to ask for such a strange flower?"

Blake's face shone brilliantly. "It's Mama's birthday!"

"Oh! Aren't you just the sweetest!"

Outside, the sun was still young upon the horizon. The almost-noontime sky reflected a faint blue veil, unblemished by clouds. Blake scurried through the market square. She passed the butcher's shop, the produce stand, and the jeweler (whom she wished she could buy from). But, the whispers were all the same —she could hear them even as she hurried by.

"I can't believe his daughter is so sweet."

Of course, Blake didn't blame them; honestly, she couldn't. Her father *was* a bad man.

The sheen of the morning sun had already broken the horizon, enveloping the town of Malka in it's pristine light. Blake stopped for a moment, turning her eyes to the sun...

Today was a new day...

A new day, her heart aflutter.

Blake turned her eyes from the sun and rushed down the historic district, her wondering eyes admiring the ancient stones as he zipped past them. She ran until she came to a small house painted in white with a bright red door.

"Mama!" Blake called out giddily as she opened the door.

"Quiet down!" a gruff voice exploded from the other room.

Blake felt herself shiver as a tall, fat man entered the room.

"What have I told you about yelling?" His voice was like jagged stone.

"I'm sorry, Papa!" Blake bowed her head.

A silence filled the room for a moment.

"Where's Mama, Papa?"

"She's not here," he said without hiding his irritation.

"W-where did she go?"

"She left," the fat Dominik said as he entered the room. "She's not coming back. Go to your room."

Blake's arms fell to her side; the red nightshade made no noise as it fell to the floor.

Mama was gone.

And little Blake was left behind...

Why would you leave, mama?
    Why would you leave me?
        Why would you leave me with him?

Three days passed, the violent pangs in Blake's stomach increasing with the end of each one. She couldn't sleep; she couldn't eat; and, to add to her misery, she couldn't breath.

Long had an odor invaded the house—a putrid, desecrating smell. So much so that the smell made her continually retch.

Her father, however, seemed to be unaffected by the stench. Why? Perhaps there was no smell within his room.

That was worth investigating, she thought.

So, decidedly, she left her room and snuck down the hallway. Her father had long sentenced her to her room, and she had worn socks to limit the sounds that her footsteps made. Softly and slowly, she reached her father's room. The door was open, so she silently slipped in.

Inside, the lights were rather dim, limiting her vision. In the vague lowlight, she could make out strange red stones on the night stand; but, she had come on a mission—she had come to find the smell.

Stealthily, she worked her way around the room, sniffing to see where the ghastly odor was most present.

She came to the closet, and promptly opened it.

Suddenly, eldritch horror engulfed her.

"MAMA?!" Blake shrieked as wracking nausea overtook her body. In the closet floor, amid the bloodstains, lay the half-eaten remains of her mother.

Blake felt her knees buckle as she hit the ground and her stomach gave way.

I threw up all over the floor, Blake remembered.

"Why are you out of your room?!" her father growled.

Blake hid her face in the ground, trying to muffle the sound of her cries on the wooden floors without avail.

"What happened to Mama, Papa?!" an acute crack spurred in her wails. "What did you do?"

A forceful hand grabbed her by the neck and lifted her off the ground.

"The same thing that will happen to you." In the faint closet light, Blake could see the fanged smile of her father. "I really hoped to leave you out of this, but it doesn't matter either way."

Blake gasped for air, her voice halted under her father's massive grip.

"Papa?" Blake mouthed.

"Shut up," Dominik growled as he clutched his hands around her throat harder. "I'll eat you!" he laughed. "Just like I ate your mother!"

That's when I heard it. Blake thought, her stomach curdling as she recalled the event. *It was a vague whisper in my heart, something I'd never heard before, but...it was the only thing that felt as frigid as my hatred.*

Blake writhed, desperately trying to pull his vice grip from her throat.

Those two words...

My salvation...

And my burden.

'*Nix Celshior.*'

Suddenly, frost spouted from her eyes, glazing her body. Blake fell to the ground as her father released her. Ghastly screeches filled the room as Dominik flailed and clawed at his skin, desperately trying to scrape the frost off of his arms. Blake watched as the ice crept up his arms despite his vain attempts to rid himself of the bereaving cold. Spots filled her vision as she saw her father freeze completely solid.

She threw up once again, then all went black.

Blake awakened the next morning to pure silence. The events of before still fresh in her mind, she looked around. Before her, her father stood frozen, imprisoned in ice. She almost slipped as she tried to walk, the icy ground like a thick film.

And when I went outside. I found that it was not only my father...

All around her, the entirety of the city of Malka—her beloved hometown—had frozen still. Blake walked around aimlessly looking at the endless sheets of ice. She stopped and looked upward. Above, the morning sun had broken the horizon, it's light shining upon the solid ice, pure and prisine, glinting around her like a world of diamonds. A luster, beautifully eerie, sparkled around a shattered girl.

As she walked down the market district, she could see the frozen corpses of the townsfolk, frozen solid, sculptures caught in whatever actions they were doing at the time.

Blake could feel the tears freezing as they streamed down her face, dropping onto the frozen ground like small drops of glass.

"It appears someone survived?" a raspy voice chuckled. "You truly are lucky, my dear. Living in this for a whole two days? How'd you ever do it?"

Before her, a middle aged man rested upon a cedar cane, a tall, blue-haired girl, in silver armor behind him.

"I've been asleep...for two days?"

"A horrid thing has happened to you, hasn't it? But, do not worry, young one," the man said. "My name is Eldric." He pointed to the blue-haired girl. "This is my knight, Snow. We are from the Church of Mhyrmr, but do not fear. I am not here to do you harm."

Suddenly, Blake let out a ghastly shriek as she hit the ground and wept frozen tears.

"W-what did I do?!"

Above them, the skies of Aestriana reached a noontime pinnacle. The bright light of the sun reflected off of the glass-like ice, a blinding mirror that draped the deadness of the town in elegant sparkles.

"You had what is called an 'Awakening.' Usually when someone calls upon their Word of Heart for the first time, it is more powerful than usual. But, this is to be expected, given that the zellinium in your bloodstream is the most potent the first time. Tell me, did you hear anything strange, like a song in your chest...a faint breeze? And did you repeat its words?"

Eldric furrowed his brow as he watched the small girl look at the ground aimlessly.

He extended his hand to me. I remember so vividly.

"What is your name, young one?"

Blake trembled as she raised her hand toward his. The man wobbled slightly, the knight coming to his aid. Eldric took her hand, frost creeping up his arm. Upon contact, bright, black flames covered his skin, causing the ice to disperse into blue shards.

I remember that I screamed. Those flames...seemed so demonic...

"Do not worry," the Inquisitor laughed. "My flames will not burn you, child. I am here to help, I promise. Now, let's start with your name."

I can still see that smile, Blake could still see the moment perfectly. *How it seemed to defy everything around me. I told him my name; I told him everything. I had only known him for a moment, but he was all I had left. The world around me—my world—was dead and cold.*
That world around me froze on that day...

She could feel the warmth of her tears as they ran down her face. Chained to a post inside of the Baronwatch Chapel, she turned her eyes to Myrsa.
And so did I...

"Are you considering your deed?" The sound of Damasko's voice echoed throughout the Baronwatch Chapel, breaking Blake's remembrance.

"How did you know about me?" Blake said through gritted teeth.

Damasko smiled a fanged smile. "Echoes travel far in the night, my dear. How could I *not* know? You killed your father, Dominik. But much greater, you killed his shadow. He was my friend, my ally."

"He was a *monster!*" she growled.

"There are always two sides to the coin, my dear. To you, a monster. To me, a friend." Blake suddenly felt the vampire run his fingers through her short, white, hair. "And just as you took his life, I take yours. Such are the laws of vengeance."

"I hate you!" Blake screeched as she pulled her head away, the sounds of her outburst ricocheting off of the ancient stone.

"You can hate me all you want," Damasko said as he began to walk down the aisle, "but you shall still pay for your sins in blood."

Blake watched him disappear into the darkness of the chapel. She looked at the stained-glass window, the image of Myrsa, her white wings spread wide. And, for the first time, she feared for her life.

XVIII

The Princess of Thieves

The black mist over the town of Ildar denied the sun entry within its walls. Though the plants and trees were all but dead from the darkness, a solitary figure thrived as she moved through the black. Enlil made her way through the dim-lit halls of the castle Baronwatch, using its advantageousness to swiftly sneak past the vampiric guards. She breathed slowly, her pale green eyes swirling with psychic energy. She had to admit, Projection magic was not known to the layman—whether man, beast, Elf, or vampire—but each of them held the *potential* to do so. Anything with a brain could use Projection, she was taught; anything with the capacity for cognition could acquire such power, though the ability itself must be sculpted through arduous contemplation and meditative practices.

She merely considered herself lucky to hold such power at the meager age of thirteen.

Lucky as she may be, she still knew the detrimental effects of using the ability for too long. With this in mind, the young burglar assessed her situation in increments, strategically using her instincts as well, as to not rely fully upon her psychic prowess.

She came to a corner and stopped. Falling back into the darkness, Enlil closed her eyes and steadied her breath.

All became dark; she exhaled, and her mind's eye opened. In her vision, she could see faint pink clouds moving back and forth.

Two guys ahead, two guys below...the Stone is below them, she thought as she peered into the void. *They sure did a good job of hiding it.*

The Stone. She had so quickly taken the job to retrieve it—partially because she imagined all of the *other* things that she could steal upon meandering through the large complex. But mainly she was curious about this Stone. According to her superiors, the treasure being held here—the supposed source of all of the thick mist which blanketed the town of Ildar—was this one Stone.

But is it shiny? Or does it glow?

She mused upon this conundrum absentmindedly.

Enlil sifted through the passageways soundlessly, slight energy rushing through her body, allowing her eyes to see through the blackness. She slipped past the guards and descended the stairs until she came to a large door. From behind the corner, she could see two faint, pink clouds guarding it.

She smiled for a moment—they couldn't have made it easier. On that thought, however, she realized that they probably had not considered that their base of operations would be penetrated.

Oh well.

With lightning fast speed, Enlil sprang from the corner, a wave of psychic energy preceding her. The blast hit the soldiers as soon as they became alert, and, for a moment, they looked at each other obliviously.

"Forget where you are?" Enlil smiled as she leapt into the air, slamming her boot into the first guard's head. His skull collided with the metal door, the recoil of which dropped him instantly. Gaining sentience, the second guard reached for his blade. Moving incredibly fast, the small Darkling grabbed his wrist and twisted. A wave of energy rode up his arm like a circuit. The guard shivered for a moment, then fell, unconscious.

Enlil exhaled and began to search their pockets.

Oooo! Prettyyy! She grinned as she pulled out a silver pocket-watch.

But this was but a trinket compared to the treasure in which she sought.

She approached the metal door, and, holding her fingers to the keyhole, she took a deep breath and twisted her wrist. She smiled as the lock clacked and the door opened.

The room was vast and dank, with mold obviously growing upon the ancient stone walls where the water of melted snow had reached its way into the deepness of this underground hollow. Despite the decrepit state of the basement, her target was quite visible from its red glow. Before her was a mammoth machine, with the Stone in its center. Large, convoluted tubes extended into the ceiling. She knew what this was, though she didn't think even the people of Ildar knew. It was easy...or maybe a bit more complicated, but all she knew was that somehow—some way— this Stone was responsible for the black mist that pervaded over the town.

But even more so, this stone was worth quite a fortune—and *that* was all *she* cared about.

Enlil moved through the dim light of the silent room, slowly approaching the infernal rock.

"You are not wise, thief," a deep voice growled from behind her. Enlil spun around to see a gargantuan vampire behind her. "How did you get in here?"

"Well, your security here is terrible, so..." The tiny thief smiled. "It was pretty easy. I basically just walked in here."

The faint glow of the strange Stone illuminated the bulky vampire, revealing his fanged grin.

"What is your name, young one?"

Enlil laughed, "What sorta wierdo question is that?"

She watched the hulking shadow walk closer in the dim glow. "One should at least know the name of the life he takes, no?"

"How sweet." The small Abdian smiled, "I'm Enlil."

"I am Sanguine the Silencer."

"Fun, fun," Enlil giggled. "That's a cute name."

The two were silent as they stared each other down. Only the faint hum of the machine filled the space between them. Enlil closed her eyes and took a deep breath, letting the psychic energy flow from her mind into her body. She opened her eyes, swirling with bright green glow, and charged forward.

As she approached, their eyes met.

Enlil felt a strangeness in her body as her gaze met his. Her body slowed and became seemingly...heavier. For a moment, she told her arms to move; she tried to move her legs.

But, to no avail. Instead, her eyes were stuck on his. Her body, she realized, had frozen.

Sanguine's spoke grimly.

"I am no fool. I saw your eyes, Darkling. But psychic or not, you will not escape my halting gaze."

Enlil looked deeper into the vampire's dark eyes.

Dang it!

The Oracle stood upon the balcony of her temple, gazing down at the black dome of mist that swallowed the forlorn town of Ildar. Beside her stood her aid, Vilkar, and around them was but quiet snow.

It is ready. Her thoughts projected into her assistant's mind.

"What do you mean, Mistress?"

All of the pieces are in play. She smiled. Vilkar looked at her face, which contained a specific youthful spirit despite its ancient appearance. *Tell me, Heart of Hearts, what will you do?*

Damasko's throne sat squarely in the center of the Baronwatch Chapel, the captured Blake chained to a post to his left and the mosaic window of the Angel of Deliverance behind him.

"You're hurting me, you big blob! Don't you know how to treat a lady!?" Enlil shrieked as Sanguine threw her on the ground before Lord Damasko.

"A thief," Sanguine's deep voice reverberated through the vast amphitheater, "and a psychic one as well. She is bound in necronite, accordingly."

"Thief, you say?" Damasko chuckled as he rose from his seat and approached the little girl. "No, Sanguine, she is no thief—or at least no *ordinary* one. Sanguine," he snapped his fingers, "Take off her shirt."

"Pervert!" Enlil screeched as the large Sanguine ripped her shirt from her body.

"Her abdomen..." Blake whispered as she watched helplessly.

"Yes." Damasko narrowed his eyes. "Just as I thought."

Even in the dim blue lights that were suspended above, Blake could still see it. Upon the girl's stomach was a large tattoo—a marking of a black rose.

The vampire lord laughed. "Sanguine, you've snagged not a thief, but an *assassin*. Tell me, girl...are you here to kill me?"

Enlil smiled and stuck out her tongue.

"If I were here to kill you, you'd already be dead!"

This girl, Blake thought as she watched in silence, *who is she?*

"Such a sharp tongue," Damasko laughed. "So, then you are here for the Stone?"

"Bingo! And I almost got it too..." The assassin furrowed her brow and pouted.

"No, no, no..." Damasko laughed, "I can't have you do that. You see, the Stone in the Emulator is very important to me. Unlike you." He nodded to Sanguine, who nodded in return.

"What are you doing to her?!" Blake yelled as the large vampire dragged the small Darkling away into the darkness.

Damasko watched until she was gone, then turned again to the window depicting Myrsa.

"The Angel of Deliverance," he said with a smirk. "Tell me, Inquisitor, do you believe in One?"

"You bastard!" Blake shook her chains.

"The god of all things, born from the Cosmic Tree, Yggdrasil."

"Shut up!"

"Angel of Deliverance," he laughed to himself, then turned to Blake and smiled. "Hear this, for there is *no* deliverance from the night."

Shivers crept up her spine.

In his eyes, she saw delusion.

XIX

The Iron Door

Lukas woke to the same grim reality—the same reality that he had hoped so many times was a dream.

But, it never was.

Still, he lay on a stretcher, his body strapped down. It only been a mere day and a half in this hellish state, but the time had seemed to all run together into a slight delirium, so it felt as if it had been weeks, if not months. He looked around the room to see the same blaring lights casting down upon his squinting eyes. Lukas realized that Nils was right, but he couldn't decide which he hated worse: having his blood taken every few hours until he fainted, or the haunting wails of the other prisoners.

But the time he had spent here was not all for naught, that much he was sure of.

"Havell," he finally whispered.

"Yeah," the weary other replied.

"I think I can get us out of here." Lukas turned his head to face the captain. "I have an idea."

He didn't return the glance, but Lukas saw it...

The captain smiled.

"This should be interesting, Heart of Hearts. Let's hear it."

To Enlil, the hellish sounds of torment that filled the dungeon fell on deaf ears. It was not that she was apathetic, but rather that her lifestyle had rendered her immune to the sounds of human suffering. After all, she had heard many of the same noises from those that found themselves at the end of her blade. Some might have assumed that thirteen was a rather young age to slay a man, but she'd become accustomed, and never really considered her age a factor in her line of work.

The large vampire, Sanguine, led her down the forlorn halls of the Ildar jailhouse, her hands bound by the magic-canceling chains. She simply observed her whereabouts as she walked. In the cells, the citizens of Ildar were bound to stretchers; in other cells—*many* other cells—were beastfolk, bound to their beds in the same chains as herself.

Beastfolk?

It was true, but weren't they awfully far from the Folke Lands? *One...two...three...five...eight...twelve...*

There were too many to count. Walking, being pushed down the hallway, Enlil determined that there were actually *more* beastfolk than there were Ildarians.

What is going on here?

She felt Sanguine push her as her pace slowed. They continued down the corridor, the bright white lights blaring down upon her face, causing her to squint. Eventually, they came to a small, isolated, cell containing a single stretcher with which she assumed was prepared just for her extraction.

"Now lay down," the vampire growled.

Enlil looked at the stretcher, then the IV, then at Sanguine, his dark eyes seemingly glowing even in the bright light.

Great...now what?

Lukas and Havell quickly hushed as the sounds of footsteps became increasingly louder. It wasn't time for another harvest, was it? It shouldn't be. No, it *couldn't* be. If the vampires extracted from Lukas once again, it would destroy his plans. Time was crucial, and Lukas knew that he was already almost out of it. He held his breath and watched the door. The soft tapping of boots became louder still, when, suddenly, they stopped. Time felt as if it abruptly halted. What was but a moment felt like an hour until the sounds of steps faded into the distance.

The knight's sigh was audible.

"So," Havell whispered, 'what's this plan of yours?"

"Do you remember Nils?" Lukas began. "You know, the guy that got us into this mess?"

"How could I forget 'em?" Havell's whispers were scratchy.

"I don't think that was really *him* that led us here. I think there's more to it than that. Y'know, more than meets the eye."

Havell contorted his face curiously.

"Just what are you getting at, Luke? It was obviously a trap."

"It was. That part is true. But, I've been thinking about what happened. Hear me out. You stayed outside of the cave, which is where you were ambushed while waiting outside. But Nils, Blake, and myself all entered. Nils seemed to know exactly where he was going, but then we heard that Magenta woman, and he suddenly didn't know where he was. That leads me to believe that he was —"

"Hypnotized," Havell finished the other's sentence.

"Exactly. Whatever that Magenta woman did, she was using it to manipulate his mind."

"Okay..." Havell said in slight confusion, "How does this help *us*?"

"Well," Lukas smiled, "I think you can do the same thing. Think about it—back when we sparred in the training yard at Mhyrmr, you used Projection to make me forget where I was for a little bit..."

"That's my Scatterflash Technique," Havell coughed. "It only works for two seconds, and I can only make someone forget where they are."

"That may be true," Lukas said, "but, it's a foundation. You've gotta hear me out, Havell. It's at least worth a shot. If you could use your Projection to trick a soldier into releasing our straps, we could at least have a slim chance at rescuing Blake and the others."

Havell lay quiet for a moment.

"You're crazy, Luke," he said. "I think that's why I like you so much."

The Iron Door was at the very end of the alleyway, far from the other prisoners. Anyone could tell that this door was no ordinary door—its gargantuan size and complex locks ruled out that possibility. The prison was brightly lit, filled with blinding white lights in each cell and adorning each corridor. But the Iron Door was different; the lights became fewer as they approached its peculiar form, fading in number until they finally ceased to be, and thusly, this particular remained shrouded in a cloak of shadows.

From his office within the prison, Vermilion had placed boards over the window that faced the direction of the Iron Door. He did not fear it, but it made him rather anxious. As a matter of fact, it wasn't the door itself that made him uncomfortable, no, it was what was beyond its metallic barriers that brought him unease.

And so, he did himself the favor of simply not looking at it. After all, he decided, there was no use in worrying about something that would never happen—and, despite himself—he had no say in the matter.

It was not of his volition, but rather the powers that lorded over him. It served Lord Damasko, so it equally served him in turn. As for his Lord, Damasko was being commissioned heavily by a mysterious client—one that he was unaware of and had long come to the conclusion that he did not *desire* to know personally.

However, whoever was supplying his Liege with blood was a matter of knowledge that he felt was of no use to him.

"You worry too much," Magenta's smooth voice seeped into his mind, breaking his concentration. "He's not going to escape."

"I am aware."

"The man behind the Iron Door, you fear him, don't you?" she laughed. "It's a shame that you're afraid of a doomed man. I didn't know you were so weak."

"Silence, hag," Vermilion hissed. "That 'doomed man' is no ordinary man." Vermilion paused and looked in the door's direction once again. He stared at the boarded window in his office and shivered. "That man is the very flames of revolution."

Time passed slowly; Lukas could feel his stomach churn anxiously. Would his plan work? Was Havell truly able to successfully attempt mind control? He knew that if it failed, and the vampiric soldier did indeed detect that the captain was trying to hypnotize him, then their chances of survival would be slim.

Havell was silent.

Both of them knew that it was almost time for another harvest; both of them knew that their lives were hanging merely by a thread.

Moments passed and, eventually, they heard the footsteps of the guards approaching. Lukas gulped as the sounds grew closer and closer. The door opened, and in walked the soldier, his metal chains clanking as he moved.

Havell closed his eyes as his captor approached him.

Alright. Breathe. Go to that place in your mind. This is no different than battle. Just go farther. He felt a sort of falling sensation as he slowed his breath. Suddenly, all went black. His pulse slowed.

NOW!

Havell opened his eyes, swirling with psychic energy.

"Release me!" he commanded as the soldier met his gaze. Immediately, the vampire reached down and released the straps.

Like a flash, Havell sprung upward and pulled the guards blade from its sheath. In one fell swoop, the sword arced, and the vampire's head rolled around on the ground.

Havell turned to Lukas with a smile.

"I did it!"

"Nice!"

Havell began to release Lukas' restraints. "Now what?"

The knight pointed to the corpse.

"Put those clothes on."

XX

The Road to Dawn

A disguised Havell Maro led Lukas down the halls of the dungeon. Thin binds were wrapped around Lukas' wrists. The captain had done so, making sure they were tight enough to appear effective, yet light enough to unravel should things escalate. Despite this act, the two of them found themselves baffled at just how little traffic there was among the corridors of the jailhouse. Surely, there would be more guards standing watch, wouldn't there? It seemed as though they would heavily patrol the very production of their so coveted Blood Dust concoction.

But no. Instead, the halls were filled less by patrolling soldiers and more by the eerie cacophony of human agony.

They stopped. Lukas inhaled sharply.

Even the air stank of blood.

Though he knew that the air wasn't pleasurable—rather bloody *and* musty—it still caused his stomach to churn. He had to admit, he wasn't in the best of shape. He turned to Havell, who was leaning against the wall with one arm.

"You alright?" he said as he propped his back beside the captain.

Havell merely nodded with a grunt in reply.

"Just a little winded—" he said as he collapsed against the wall.

Lukas quickly pulled his bindings apart and sprang forward and caught his falling comrade.

Now what?!

Thoughts raced in his mind as he looked around, the

unconscious captain in his arms. He was admittedly lucky, given that the halls were empty. But for how long? That remained, now more than ever, to be a pervading question within his mind. All it would take was a soldier to round the corner and discover them. That was all it would take for the two renegades to be quickly—and easily—silenced.

Lukas looked at the door to the closest prison cell.

I guess I have no choice...

"Lord Vermilion!" A breathless soldier barged into the warden's room, "The captain and the knight—" he gasped, "they're not in their cell!"

For a moment, Vermilion merely gawked at the soldier, the words slowly seeping into his brain.

"*WHAT?!*" he erupted as he slammed his hands on the desk so hard that it made small cracks form in the wood. "What do you mean 'not in their cell?!'"

"W-well, sir. They aren't in the cell we placed them in, and—"

"There's no way!" The fat vampire sprung from his desk and rushed out into the hallway, shoving the messenger as he shot past him.

Vermilion strode down the alleys, eying each cell until he came to the one that had previously held the two escapees.

"*HOW?!*" he fumed as he scanned the room.

The cell was barren, save for the stretchers with cut bindings and the beheaded corpse of a soldier. One of them, then, must be in disguise. Vermilion felt his blood heat as anger engulfed him. What had they done? How had they escaped? Where were they? What if Lord Damasko found out? What if they released other prisoners? What if—what if they opened the *Iron Door*?!

He knew he had to find them, and he had to find them *quickly!*

He rushed back down the corridors and into his office to set off the alarm.

I can't let this happen. I won't. *When I find those two I'll skin them alive!*

Lukas jolted as the sirens rang throughout the hallways.

NO! His mind swirled as he slowly came into a state of awareness.

It wasn't time for another harvest, was it? It couldn't be, Lukas was sure. There was *no way*.

But, it seems he had merely miscalculated. Hours and hours inside what seemed like a timeless space seemed to undo him.

*What now? What now?! h*e thought as he looked at the barely conscious Captain Maro at his side.

"Hey!" a voice suddenly barked over the blaring noise. "You gonna help me or what?"

Lukas turned to the prisoner bound to the examination table in the center of the room. Before him, a small girl, a Darkling, stared back at him with bright, pale green eyes.

"You—?" she squinted, "I've seen you somewhere, right?"

Lukas stopped. She was right...or at least it seemed so.

"I'm Enlil!" she yelled, "Blah, blah, blah—now release me, Mister Boy-I-Think-I-Know!"

Havell groaned and cleared his throat as he held up the set of keys that came with his uniform. Lukas stared at him blankly for a moment.

"Worth a try, at least," the captain said.

Lukas nodded and hurried to the mysterious prisoner, releasing her binds and helping her to stand.

"Ugh," she groaned as she wobbled for a moment, then stretched, her arms reaching skyward. "Wobbly-wobbly!"

"That tattoo," Havell's voice was raspy as he too stood and stretched. "Aren't you a little young to be a Black Rose?"

Lukas turned and stared at Captain Maro blankly.

The captain merely sighed as he scratched the beard that had grown during his captivity.

"Assassins Guild."

"Yup!" She smiled with sudden effervescence. "Name's Enlil!"

"That's it!" Lukas snapped his fingers, "You were the girl I saw back in Zerlina—the one that tried to steal Eldric's pipe!"

"Yeah!" she said with brightening eyes. "You're that kid that had that shiny sword!"

"Right!" He smiled. "I'm Lukas!"

"Lukas..." Enlil whispered, "Cool!"

"I'm Captain Havell Maro," the other said with a gruff in his voice. "It's nice to make friends and all, but now what do we do?"

For a moment, the three looked at each other. Contemplation replaced excitement as the sounds of the alarms echoed down the hallways.

"We're stuck," the captain finally spoke up as the sounds of footsteps rushed by the doorway, "We can't take them all at once!"

"But," Lukas said as he pointed to the doorway, "if we had numbers...?"

"Hm..." Havell scratched his beard, then looked at Enlil. "I didn't think of that."

"Luke has a point, Cap'n," the little assassin said as she smiled. "You guys just waltzed right into my room, so why can't we just do that with *everybody* else?"

Havell shrugged, then nodded.

"Well...it's worth a shot!"

"It's a good idea...I guess," Havell Maro said as he sheathed the vampiric sword, and stretched his neck. "But *how* are we going to do it? Those fangfilth are flooding the halls."

"Pfft!" Enlil laughed, "Easy-breezy!"

The captain and the knight glanced at each other, and then at the little girl. She closed her eyes and slowed her breathing.

"No way..." Havell mumbled as he watched Enlil's eyes open to reveal a bright, swirling green.

Projection? Lukas suddenly remembered meeting her at the aerodock. *So* that's *what she did back then.*

"Perfect!" Lukas smiled.

Without another word, Enlil stepped toward the door, her movements flowing as if a veil caught in a light breeze. She gripped the door handle and turned to the two behind her.

"Okay, I'm going to open it. There are two guards outside this door, so you'll have like..." she trailed off, "three-ish seconds to

The Heart of Hearts

take 'em down once I hit them with a Shockwave."

Lukas gulped as he looked at the captain. The captain, however, looked back at him and nodded.

"GO!" she exclaimed as the door flew open.

The two guards on patrol spun around too late as Enlil's psychic blast collided with them. They stood for a moment, glancing around in an abrupt confusion.

Instantly, Captain Maro burst from the open doorway, swinging his blade. The lights above reflected off the sterling blade twice, and the heads of the guards rolled upon the floor.

"Fun, fun!" Enlil snickered. "You're not too bad, Cap'n!"

"We have to hurry," Lukas said as he unsheathed the blades on the corpses' belts and handed one to the Darkling, "Split up," he pointed to the other doorways further down the hallway, "We have to release as many prisoners as we can—and as *quickly* as we can!"

Without another word or acknowledgment of the other two, Lukas opened the closest cell door and entered. Once inside, shivers ran up his spine. Before him, beaten and bruised upon a stretcher, lay Nils.

"Lukas?" His voice was small. Lukas felt as if he could detect a hint of fear. "Have you...have you come for revenge? I promise that I'll accept it if you have."

Lukas gripped his blade as he approached.

"Please." Nils' voice cracked as he closed his eyes. "Do it."

He exhaled. Suddenly, there was a ripping sound, and the weights of the binds loosened.

Nils opened his eyes to see a smiling Lukas.

"There's no need for that!" The knight said as he helped the doctor to his feet.

"But—" Nils exclaimed as his knees buckled, leaning upon Lukas for support. "I'm the reason! I'm the reason you're in here at all!"

Lukas stopped and helped the man to his feet.

"That's true, Nils. But. If you didn't lead me here, you'd still be on that stretcher, no?"

Nils watched the young man's face. For some reason, he still felt guilty. For some reason, the boy's smile pierced his chest. *How? h*e thought. How could, after all the hell he had caused this boy....how could he still smile? Nils looked at Lukas' arms, spotted in bruises and pricks. For a moment, his mind calmed, and tears rushed to his eyes.

"Lukas..." His voice gurgled as he wept. "Thank you."

"Of course!" Lukas nodded and took the man's hand. "I know it wasn't your doing. Hear me out, Nils: This time, we will put an end to this—for me, for you, and for *all* of Ildar!"

The knight held up a clenched fist and nodded.

"I promise you, Nils, you *will* see the sun again!"

"Lukas," he paused to calm his breathing, "you're right. We will...we will..."

Lukas smiled, then turned away.

Lukas quickly found that Nils had, through whatever had happened to him, not yet recovered from his condition. Carrying him upon his back, the knight exited the cell to find Enlil, Captain Maro, and several beastfolk and villagers waiting outside.

Before the beastfolk lay several vampiric corpses, their necks visibly warped and broken. Lukas stared at the strange men before him, noticing that there were several dots and scratches upon them from where the vampires tried to bite them in retaliation.

Lukas stared at them confusedly; one of them took notice and smiled.

"We are beastfolk," he said as he wiped the blood from his arms, "vampire bites do not work on us, and they cannot cut our talons with their swords."

Lukas observed their strange figures. They seemed so alike to his own, yet their shoulders were covered in brown feathers and their fingernails were long and razor sharp. He stared into their yellowish, hawk-like eyes.

"We need to move!" Havell cut into Lukas' mind. "They know where we are."

"They're headed here! Lots of 'em!" Enlil called back to the group, her pale green eyes swirling with strange energy.

The beastfolk simply looked at each other, nodded, then walked in the direction of the approaching guards.

"Y-you're going the wrong way?" Lukas said, more of a question than a statement.

They turned. As Lukas looked into their eyes, he shivered. Those eyes—he'd never seen the like before. Not even the vampires had those eyes. The bird-mens' eyes were filled with a bright rage.

"No," one said, "we are not."

Lukas, Enlil, Havell Maro, and Nils hurried down the halls, Nil's upon Lukas' back. Behind them, the sounds of battle filled the hallway, mainly the shrieks and wails of vampires overshadowed by the screeching of birds.

"They were serious!" Lukas said through panting breaths.

The knight turned just in time to prevent himself from slamming into Havell Maro, who had abruptly stopped.

"Damn it!" Havell said as he spit on the floor.

Before him, a large vampire stood, a giant longsword held by both hands.

"Luke," the captain said. "You know how I told you to never strike first?"

Lukas nodded.

"Well...I lied."

In a flash, the captain bolted from his position, blade drawn and ready. The vampire raised the giant blade high, bringing it down with crushing force. But Havell was ready, and quickly spun to the left, his blade glinting in the light as it sped toward its victim's throat. This one, however, was not a fool. The blade came down just as it's target's hands pushed Havell away.

Quick. But just not quick enough.

A great scream could be heard throughout the halls. Lukas, Enlil, and Nils watched in horror as the vampire's forearm lay dismembered upon the floor.

Havell swung again, only to slice thin air as he watched the large vampire escape down the corridor and around the corner.

"Damn it again!" he sighed.

"But you got him!" Lukas said, smiling.

"Even that won't kill a vampire," Havell groaned. "Gotta sever the neck."

"Nice and all," Enlil cut in, "but we're gonna be surrounded soon, guys."

"Damn it *again*!" the captain repeated, "Now where to?"

Lukas turned around. He hadn't noticed it before now, but once it caught his eye, it was as blatant at a red dot on white paper.

"Let's try this one..." Lukas pointed.

Enlil and Havell looked where the knight's finger directed.

Right behind them, was the large, Iron Door.

"We can at least hide behind it, I guess?" Enlil shrugged. "Best thing we can do at this point, probably."

"But all of those locks?" Nils coughed.

Enlil didn't reply. Instead, she merely approached the locks.

"Don't tell me you're about to try and *pick* all of them?!" Havell complained. "There's at least ten, and we *don't* have time —"

"Shush!" the little assassin shot back. "Give me a few seconds."

She closed her eyes, and took a deep breath. Lukas watched the curious little Darkling as she held two fingers to the keyhole of the lock. She paused, then turned her wrist as if she held the key in her hand. The others jumped back in amazement as the lock fell to the ground, unlocked by whatever she had done.

She turned and smiled.

"There's one!"

Within no time at all, the small girl had finished the process. Havell and Lukas pushed the heavy door open, and the four of them slipped behind it.

It was dark inside, strangely. Lukas definitely found that peculiar. The rest of the prison had been acutely lit, so much so that his eyes took a longer moment to adjust to this alien blackness. Lukas suddenly realized something. This room was actually rather small.

"Boy."

A deep voice called from within the dark. The four escapees jumped, their attention directed to the back of the room. Lukas noticed the dark, hulking figure of a man, chained to his knees against the back wall.

"You are the one that is unlike any other," the voice thundered.

Lukas looked deeper into the darkness. Suddenly, a pair of bright, iridescent, orange eyes lit the void.

"You are the Heart of Hearts."

XXI

The Phoenix King

Vermilion sat at his desk, his head in his hands. Before him, the armless soldier stood, his injuries from the bout with Captain Maro already healed completely.

"You're *sure?!"* the fat warden thundered.

"Positive, my lord! I fled after sustaining injury, and when I returned...the door still shut, but..." he paused nervously. "It was unlocked. How they unlocked it is unclear to me—"

"You imbecile!" the vampire lord screamed as he flipped his desk. "Do you have *any* clue what will happen if that man runs free?"

"Well, I—"

"Well, I" Vermilion mocked. "You fool!" he exhaled as he rubbed the sides of his head with his fingers. "Well, there's nothing that can be done about it *now.*" He turned to the armless soldier. "Gather everyone, and I mean *everyone,* and get ready at the door. If he is released, he will fall before he has a chance to strike."

Without a word, the soldier bowed, then, frightfully, ran out of the office.

"Well..." Vermilion said as he reached into his desk and produced one of the red stones of Blood Dust. "I'll end him where he stands."

He crushed the stone in his mouth, then walked out the door. As he exited, he felt his body change. Sinews and muscles became denser, larger. Short hairs grew upon his skin. He hunched over as wings sprouted from his back and razor sharp talons replaced his hands.

He was a ferocious beast; he was ready for war.

As ready as he could ever be.

"You," the chained man said, "you are the Heart of Hearts."

Lukas stared into the prisoner's bright orange eyes.

"How do you know that?" Lukas' asked, alarmed.

The man said nothing. Instead, his figure remained still, a silent monolith, shrouded in shadow.

"The birds told me," he finally spoke.

"The birds?" Havell cut in.

"The birds, yes. They see, they hear, and they tell."

Enlil leaned forward, her eyes swirling. "You're a bird-man, right?

Havell cleared his throat. "Just tell us who you are, and save us this trouble."

The man was silent again.

"I," his voice was thick and imposing, "am Edmund Vargrave Hallow-Talon."

"What the hell?!" Havell suddenly exclaimed, startling the others. *"You're* the Phoenix King? You're the ruler of the Folke Lands?!"

"At one time, yes..." he replied.

"Well!" Lukas said, "Let's get you out of here and you can go back to your kingdom!"

The bird king's brilliant eyes moved slowly toward Lukas.

"The birds say you are the Heart of Hearts, but you do not wield the Sword Durandal. Why?"

Lukas stopped. The king was right. The knight had been so caught up in his situation that he'd forgotten all about the mystic sword. But, he realized the one problem...

He didn't know *where* Durandal was.

The cave!

He realized that it must still be within the depths of the crevasse —lost.

"You don't have it, do you?"

There was a pause, the question hanging heavily in the air.

"I thought as much..." Hallow-Talon sighed. "What a fool."

"L-listen to me." Lukas clenched his fist, frozen under the large man's accusation. "I may not have Durandal. I'll even admit that I *lost* Durandal. And I don't know who you are, or how you know I'm the Heart of Hearts, but I couldn't care less about that stuff right now." He straightened his back and walked toward the shadowy hunk. "Hallow-Talon, hear me out! I don't care if I don't have a magic sword or holy heart! None of that matters to me, because regardless, I am who I am! I have a friend who is in dire trouble here, and I need to help her—sword or no sword! Heart or no heart! Because, in the end—well—she's in danger and I...I refuse to stand around!"

Hallow-Talon's eyes pierced Lukas'. Lukas could feel his heart pounding. The man was chained, but still, his presence was massive.

Lukas felt sweat drip down his face.

Suddenly, Hallow-Talon exploded into rolling laughter. Lukas jumped back at the beastfolk's sudden outburst.

"What is your name, Heart of Heart?"

"L-Lukas?" Lukas said as a question, unintentionally.

"I like you, Lukas. You seek to help your friend? I, too, have a friend in need." He paused. "Listen to me, Heart of Hearts. I am looking for someone who is very important to my kingdom. He is an Elf named Lyon, and he is the only Elf I trust. My country is under attack by the Elven kingdom, Mirea, and we will indeed lose our homes if I do not find him."

"So," Lukas smiled brightly, "You'll help us then, right?!"

The king nodded. "Release me, Lukas, and I will show them the very wrath of hell itself.

Vermilion approached the front lines, the hallway packed full of soldiers, blades ready. He watched the door.

Why? The thought spiraled through his mind. But why, indeed? He fancied himself one of the strongest vampires alive. Of course he was! He was one of the Red Three, the highest officers in the service of Damasko the Bloodletter.

Exactly!

"Exactly!" he cried aloud. "What is there to fear!?"

Suddenly, there was deafening noise.

The Iron Door burst from its hinges under the pressure of a large explosion, a fireball filling the room with brilliant red blazes. Soldiers fell to the floor as the flesh on their faces melted, burning through the ligaments and muscle tissue.

TELL ME, VERMILION...

Vermilion froze.

DO YOU REMEMBER MY VOICE?

"No! No!" the fat vampire's voice cracked as he watched the outline of a figure appear within the flames. "Not *him!*"

"I," Halow-Talon's voice exploded as he came into view, *"am Edmund Vargrave Hallow-Talon, High Chieftain and Phoenix King of the Folke Lands."*

The bat-like vampire gulped as he viewed the released prisoner. Hallow-Talon was tall, towering over him. The red feathers upon his shoulders were blazing, bright red tongues of flame reaching high into the air. Even as he approached, the heat caused the bat to sweat.

What are you doing?! His inner voice screamed. *KILL HIM!*

"Y-you!" Vermilion exclaimed, raising his bat-like talons, "I-I'll kill you."

With one swift motion, Vermilion rushed forward, his flesh-cleaving claws slashing quickly.

Slowly, Hallow-Talon raised his palm.

"You will..." the Phoenix said as a ball of red flame formed within his hands.

Vermilion closed in quickly, talons extended.

Hallow-Talon stood still, giving no ground.

"...do no such thing."

At the Phoenix King's command, a blast of bright red flame erupted from his palm, completely consuming the vampire.

Lukas, Enlil, Havell, and Nils walked from the doorway as they watched Vermilion fall to the ground, his flesh singed and red.

Lukas looked out into the hallway. Before him, countless vampires lay mangled and fried upon the ground.

"Thank you, Heart of Hearts." Hallow-Talon's voice echoed along what was now an eerily silent prison.

Lukas looked at the large man. Even from a distance, he had a mammoth figure.

Their eyes met.

Hallow-Talon was smiling.

XXII

The Mad Dash

Smack!

Vermilion's painful shrieks resounded through the hallways of the prison, audible for every released prisoner to relish in.

"WHAT DO YOU WANT FROM ME?!" the vampire bellowed as he looked at Havell and the others, tears dripping down his singed face.

"Listen here," Havell said as he slapped the vampire's charred abdomen once more, "I haven't had a smoke in a *long* time, so I'm not really in the *best* of moods." Another smack on the belly. "If I had no other engagements, I'd make you pay for the nice little scars you gave me on my stomach, but I need to know things, and you *will* answer me."

Smack!

"Okay! Okay!" Vermilion begged as he writhed and wept.

"Good." Havell cleared his throat. "First, *what* is causing the black mist around Ildar?"

"It's caused by the Emulator!"

"Not specific enough!" Havell exclaimed as he raised his smacking hand.

"E-emulator! I-it's a machine! In the cellar of Baronwatch! Please, stop!"

"We're not done yet!" The captain wiggled his fingers. "How do we stop it?"

"Ooh! Ooh!" Enlil spoke up. "We need the glowing stone that powers it!"

"Yes! Yes!" Vermilion gasped. "The Antithicite! I don't know what it's made of, but it was given to us by someone. Damasko won't tell us the rest!"

"Yay! I got one!" Enlil giggled. She turned to Havell and pointed at Vermilion. "Can I?!"

Havell smiled maliciously, "Be my guest."

Enlil jumped into the air to gain height, then swung her hand down swiftly onto the vampire's burned body.

SMACK!

Vermilion yelped and whimpered. Enlil giddily returned to Lukas and Nils and smiled.

"He let me do it!" She beamed.

"You bastards!" the vampire said. "Damasko will kill all of you!"

"Yeah, yeah..." Havell coughed. "Tell me one more thing. Why are so many of your prisoners Beastfolk? The Folke Lands are *way* too far from here for such a large migration."

"We were sold here," Hallow-Talon spoke up, "we were prisoners in Mirean mines, and Prime Minister Zilheim thought kindly enough about us to send us here."

"Yes! Yes!" Vermilion said. "Please! Let me go!"

"I got one right, too, it seems," Hallow-Talon said with a sadistic glint in his flaming eyes. "May I?"

Havell moved his hands in a welcoming motion.

Hallow-Talon raised his hand high. Lukas watched the dark skinned bird-man's arm. He could see each giant muscle move as it rained down onto Vermilion's midsection.

SMACK!!

"Why are you asking things you already know?!"

Havell laughed.

"It's fun to watch you squirm."

"You vermin!" Vermilion thundered. "You may have bested me, but Damasko will skin you alive!"

"Vermilion!" Lukas finally spoke up. "Where is Blake?"

"B-Bl—you mean the Inquisitor?!" he raised a singed brow.

"Of course he means her!" Havell raised his hand again.

"S-she's with Damasko! I-in the Baronwatch Chapel! Please! NO MORE!"

Lukas and Havell met eyes. Lukas smiled.

"Be my guest, Havell."

The captain turned to his prey with a big grin.

SMACK!!!

Blue flames decorated the chandeliers hanging above Damasko's throne. Beside the large chair, a captive Blake remained chained to a column. In the ethereal light of the azure fire, the depiction a Myrsa was illuminated. The Inquisitor tried her hardest not to look at the antiquated mosaic, for it simply caused her to shiver. She couldn't really put a finger on the cause of her distaste for the window. Perhaps it was because she knew that, though the artwork was meant to emulate that of an angel of deliverance, the angelic race had enslaved man long ago. But, she knew that angels didn't exist anymore, so that couldn't be it. She finally gave up, resorting to believe that it was merely the lighting that caused her discomfort.

Deliverance... she thought. *Pathetic.*

"Tell me, dear Inquisitor," Damasko's voice echoed throughout the sanctum, "have you finally accepted your fate?"

Blake slowly raised her head, watching her captor approach her.

"We are silent?" he laughed, "Where has all of our rebellion gone? Our *spunk*? Our *spirit*?"

Damasko smiled, his eyes running the length of her body.

"So lithe. And your skin, pale as a wedding dress," he said as he lowered his mouth to her neck, gnawing softly on her flesh, "and so...*tender.*"

Blake jerked on her chains, swinging her head side to side to repulse him.

"You sicken me!" Her tone was rigid and sharp.

"Is that so?" Damasko smirked as he grabbed her chin and pulled her face toward his.

Blake yelped as she felt her body stretch past the extent of her restraints.

"Listen to me, my poor prey." She felt his warm, wet breath on her face as he spoke, "You are mine now. None will come to save you, for you are now lost." He smiled as he gritted his teeth and brought them an inch away from her lips. "You have no hope, and soon—very, *very* soon—I will drink your blood from your lips."

Blake squirmed and mumbled as he brought his lips closer to hers.

"*My lord!*" a smooth female voice said as the doors to the chapel opened. "Vermilion has fallen! We've lost the prison facility!"

"*WHAT?!*" Damasko erupted and he spun around, jerking his hand from Blake's face.

He turned to see Magenta striding up the aisle.

"Indeed, my Lord. The fat fool seemed to be unable to hold his own, and our subjects seem to have escaped. The Beastfolk and Red Ravens are headed this way." She smiled and bowed. "What shall I do?"

Damasko stood silent for a moment, his fists vibrating. He exhaled, then turned and looked upward to the large window.

"Bathe the ground in red."

Magenta smiled and licked her lips.

"Absolutely."

Nils had stayed behind, though the more Lukas considered his choice, the more sense it made. Nils was a good man; however, Nils was not a warrior.

"Luke." Captain Maro's weathered voice caught the knight's attention. "You're going after Blake? For real?"

Lukas nodded. "I can't just abandon her, Havell. You know that."

"Without Durandal?" The other coughed. "Are you crazy?"

The captain was right, Lukas thought. It *was* crazy. He knew that going into a battle without the mythic blade would be a major disadvantage for him, but he had no time to look for it.

You must learn to hear the voice of the Sword...

The Oracle's words flashed through his memory.

Lukas smiled.

"You're right, Captain," he said. "But, I have an idea of where to find it."

Ahead, torches burned in the darkness, only illuminated dots in the dense black fog. Almost nothing was visible save the dark silhouettes of the surrounding buildings. Lukas had only been exposed for a short time, but he instantly saw why this imposing veil was so oppressive.

"They're waiting," Hallow-talon's voice rumbled. He squinted his eyes. "And Sanguine is among them."

"This is where we split," Havell said as he turned to Enlil. "You wanted that stone so badly, right kid? Well, I think I'll let you take it."

"Such a kind old man!" the small Darkling beamed as she darted off.

"Watch it!" the captain shot back.

"I'll go with her," Lukas said as he began to follow, "Damasko is in that castle! And if he's there, Blake is too!"

"Wait, Lukas—!" Havell stopped.

Lukas had disappeared into the mist.

Enlil moved seamlessly through the night, gliding from cover to cover. So much so that Lukas felt, at certain points, that he had lost her.

She truly was a strange little girl, Lukas had to admit. Though, despite her oddness, he couldn't help but feel she exuded a feeling of intense sincerity. She certainly wore her heart upon her sleeve, that much was sure. And, Lukas felt rather at ease around her. However, his eyes strained to trace her flitting in the darkness. All around him, houses were but angular black blocks in the deepening mist, empty phantoms, devoid of all signs of life. Lukas looked ahead. Enlil had stopped. A gargantuan wall towered over them.

Lukas realized instantly what it was.

It was the wall of Castle Baronwatch.

"How do we—"

Suddenly, Enlil cupped her hand over Lukas' mouth and pointed upwards.

You can't see it, but there's a guy up there. He's on the stairs, but those stairs are where we need to go. Enlil's voice rattled in Lukas' mind. She pointed to her forehead. *I can make him forget his stuff for a few seconds, but you gotta steal his sword before he remembers. That way, he won't go alerting his buddies, okay?*

Lukas' eyes were wide with fear. *In all honesty,* he thought, *how wild is this kid?*

Okay! Great! Before Lukas could prepare himself, she abruptly began to slither up the stairs.

Lukas followed, the wind growing sharper as he ascended. He could feel his blood pumping in his neck, his heart rising to his throat. They perched themselves just below the soldiers, and Enlil pointed.

Now! Go get 'em!

Lukas bolted from the darkness, quickly rising the stairway. Startled, the vampire fumbled for the sword at his side. Suddenly, the soldier stopped for a moment and held his head.

Now! he thought as he drew the enemy's sword from its sheath. He raised it high, and, in a split second, the vampire's head rolled down the steps.

Lukas panted, his heart racing. For a second, he looked at the river of blood as it spouted from the vampire's head, then he retched.

"You have a weak stomach, Luke!" Enlil said almost as a cheer when she passed by him. "But the second time won't be as bad!"

Lukas wiped his mouth and looked at the small girl. She walked ahead to a small door and placed her fingers to the lock. She twisted her wrist, and simultaneously the lock clicked and the door opened.

He wanted to ask how she did it, but the thought was fleeting in his mind.

The inside of Baronwatch was cold and gloomy, but at least not dark. The hallways were lit by light blue etherlamps. Also, the two of them were quick to notice that, besides the initial guard, the insides of the castle were rather deserted. It appeared as ancient on the interior as it was on the exterior. The air was thin and damp— and, most of all, the cold stones did nothing to protect its inhabitants from the frigid snows outside.

Lukas found himself shivering, his teeth chattering as his jaw quivered.

Enlil turned to him and smiled.

"Sorry to ditch ya so early on," she said, "But I've gotta find the shiny stone."

Before Lukas could answer, the small Darkling was already departing.

"Good luck finding whoever!"

Lukas sighed as he watched the little girl turn a corner and disappear.

Oh well...

Now, he had a problem: He didn't know where the chapel was.

I mean, it can't be too hard, right? he thought. *If I can just find a way outside, I can see where it's at!*

But now, that proposed another problem—that being *where* he was in the castle and *where* the outside was.

No! He shook his head. *Blake is in trouble! It doesn't matter where anything is. I just have to* go!

He began to walk in the opposite direction from where Enlil had gone, his steps quickly developing into a stride, then a run, then, a sprint.

His mind raced as he barreled down the dim, labyrinthine hallways. He ran with no interruption—no signs of any soldiers or remaining villagers. No life at all roamed the corridors save for the faint sounds of mice heard vaguely over the sounds of his footsteps. The boots he wore now—the boots he had taken from a dead soldier back in the prison—were heavier than what he was accustomed to. They were less boots, and more greaves, really; the shins were covered in a light, black metal, and the toes were covered in a thick steel. Running was a bit unorthodox, but it did not matter.

All that mattered now, all that consumed Lukas' mind, was finding the Inquisitor before it was too late.

*Too late...*he thought.

What could that mean? Was it *already* too late? For all he knew, she may no longer be in the castle.

NO!

She was there. He was *sure* of it.

The paths wound until he came to a large, glass door, which led to the castle's frosty exterior.

"Found it!" he exclaimed.

Suddenly, his smile faded. He could hear noises from the outside—the sounds of armor clinging and clacking as a soldier moved. Lukas went static, his breath halting. He thought to run, but it was too late. A silhouette had already emerged behind the glass. Lukas watched as the doorknob turned and the door opened.

GO! GO! GO! His mind blazed.

"Well, well." The vampire licked his lips.

Lukas watched him raise a large mace.

"Looks like I'll have some dinner after all!"

"I can't let that happen!" Lukas shot back as he brandished the sword he used to kill the last soldier with.

"Cheeky!" the other grunted, bringing the giant mace downward.

But not fast enough. The lithe Lukas easily strafed to the left, his short sword swiftly arcing toward his opponent's head.

"You little monkey!" the vampire said, swinging the mace sideways.

Remember, Snow's words flashed in Lukas' mind, *there are people in this world who are incredibly strong.*

Lukas ducked as the huge club swished over his head. With another loud grunt, the weight of the weapon caused the vampire to sway.

But.

Lukas burst from his position, his sword slicing cleanly apart the vampire's exposed neck.

If you're fast enough, you can always use their blunders against them.

Lukas exhaled as his enemy's head rolled at his feet. Unlike outside, he could smell the blood of his opponent drip from its corpse. The smell of putrid iron caused Lukas to look away.

It's easier the second time?

The thief's words slipped through his mind as he heaved his empty stomach.

"Yeah, right..." Lukas grumbled.

He had no time to feel sick. Gathering his composure, he walked past the corpse and out into the night air.

He noticed it immediately.

Below him was a building with a giant stained-glass window.

The chapel...

XXIII

Golden Sun Rises

Lukas peered off of the balcony, viewing the large mosaic window below.

This was it. He knew Blake was down there. And he knew that he was running out of time. If the vampires had rallied at the front gates, it surely meant that Damasko was aware of their escape, which in turn meant that the chances of the vampire lord disposing of her were steadily inclining.

What if she's already dead...?

Lukas shook his head violently.

NO! he told himself. *She's alive! She* must *be alive.*

Regardless of her situation, he still faced the problem of how to reach her. Certainly he couldn't scour the maze-like castle in search of the right door. Not only did he not have the time to do so, but he didn't have the energy to fight the waves of soldiers that might still inhabit its halls.

He looked around, begrudgingly.

Standstill—

The thought was barely finished when it occurred to him. On the railings of the balcony, he noticed a thick wire. Lukas leaned over the side and followed it with his eyes. The wire was long, a binding of multiple, smaller, wires, extending downward with small flags along it. As his eyes ran down the metal rope, his heart leapt.

This rope ran downward to the chapel, ending at the top of the large stained-glass window.

Inside the chapel, Damasko stood upright, arms held behind his back, gazing upward at the mosaic of Myrsa.

"They are at our gates now," he began, "and at their very demise."

Blake stood silently, her arms chained to the post behind her.

"You are still silent?" he said as he approached her. "Is that because you have finally lost hope?"

For a moment, he stared at her. Blake turned her face from his gaze, but she could still feel his eyes piercing her.

"How beautiful is your despair," Damasko said softly as he raised her head. "The smell of fear is intoxicating, no."

Blake gritted her teeth. Why speak? This was the end, after all. She knew it would come, though she didn't think it would be so grisly.

Damasko lowered his mouth. Blake shivered as she could feel his breath on her neck.

"And now," he whispered in her ear softly, "I shall partake."

For a moment, Blake's life slowed. As she felt his teeth gnaw her flesh, not yet piercing the skin, she thought of her mother.

Why? Why didn't you run? Why did you leave me? Why did you have to die? Why did anyone have to die?

She thought of the captain, and of Lukas. In her mind, she could see his smiling face—something she knew she'd taken for granted.

But that was over now, and she closed her eyes.

Oh, great god, One, she prayed desperately, *I don't want to die!*

Suddenly, a great force collided with the window of Myrsa, causing both within to jolt violently.

Blake looked among the shattered glass, her eyes widening.

"Blake!" Lukas' voice hit her ears like the power of a symphony.

"L-lukas!?" Her voice trilled more than she'd expected.

Lukas ran toward her, not noticing that the vampire walked toward the window.

"You're okay!" he exclaimed, "You—"

Blake noticed his expression darken.

"Lukas?"

Lukas balled his fists; he could feel his fingernails dig into his palm. Even in the dim light, he could see it.

"He hit you..." the knight trailed off.

The room fell silent, all but the howl of the wind through the shattered window, blowing gusts of snow between the two parties.

"Are you the one they call Damasko the Bloodletter?" Lukas said as he turned to face the vampire.

"Lukas, what are you doing?" Blake felt her blood run cold at his tone.

"I am." Damasko replied blankly. "And who the hell might you be?"

"I've seen what you've done to these people," Lukas growled, ignoring the other's question. "How could you do such a thing? You've put these people through hell for what?! For your drug? Your own personal gain?

"Yes," Damasko laughed. "Look, boy! Look at the world around you. The eagle eats the fish; the cat eats the mouse; the wolf eats the rabbit...the strong devours the weak. It is only *natural* for the weak to be sacrificed in the powerful's favor.

"Natural?!" Lukas felt his blood run cold. This was no ordinary opponent. This wasn't Havell or even Snow in the training yard; this wasn't a small vampire or even an armor clad one.

No.

This was a highly dangerous fiend.

Lukas felt his knees grow weak.

NO! He caught himself.

This was no time to run. He knew this feeling; he knew this fear well. What he felt right now was the same thing he felt as he stood between Nox and Iago.

And he knew *this time* he wasn't going to run.

"LUKAS!" Blake's sudden shriek caught his ears. "Run! Please! Leave me!"

Lukas kept his eyes on the vampire before him.

"I can't do that, Blake."

"What...?" her voice was a mere whimper. "What do you think you're doing?"

And what indeed? All this time, he'd not even considered *what* he was doing. But, now that the question surfaced, there was no need to consider.

Despite his anguish...

Despite his fear...

He knew what he was doing...

"Blake." Lukas turned and smiled. "I'm getting in your way."

"In my...way...?"

It couldn't be...

But was.

That smile. That *same* smile. She knew that he was afraid, there was no hiding that. But, in that moment, he reminded her of Eldric.

"How sweet," the vampire laughed as he turned from the broken window. I shall eat you as well."

"Listen to me, Damasko." Lukas straightened himself. "I'm going to cut you down. Right now!"

"Are you trying to intimidate me, boy? Are you trying to scare me with threats?" the other jeered. "I smell your fear, and you have no weapon to do said 'cutting'?"

Alright, Lukas thought. *One shot.*

Without a word, Lukas extended his arm to his side, opened his hand, and closed his eyes.

Durandal's voice? he thought, trying his best to block out the sound of his frantic heart. *Well, listen to me, I don't know where you are, but if you can hear me, Sword, I command you...*

Blake watched as faint white flames began to engulf Lukas' arm.

White flame? she thought. *This isn't a Word of Heart. What is this?*

"*COME!*" Lukas exclaimed as a brilliant blast of white light exploded from his open palm, causing the room to flinch.

Lukas blinked as his eyes adjusted. He looked at his hand.

In his hand, he held the Sword Durandal.

"I see..." Damasko sneered. "So you've some magic, as well. Unusual for a knight, I must say."

From behind him, still bound to a post, Blake looked at Lukas, her eyes studying him intensely. In that moment, she saw someone entirely apart from the ditzy, daydreaming orphan she'd been teaching for the past months. In his stead, another young man seemed to be. She watched his hands.

He's shaking. That idiot.

"Tell me this, boy," Damasko's voice hissed over the snowy winds as he stared at the shattered window, "why do you fight for her? You know not what she's done; you don't know the extent of her crimes—how many lives are bloodied on her hands! She should die for merely being born. And yet," he paused, "you would still brandish your blade in the face of peril—all for a simple witch?"

Lukas breathed inward. For some reason, memories of Nox filled his mind, flashes from childhood at the monastery.

Why are you playing with her?! Didn't you hear? She's a witch!

"You're right," he began, steadying his breath. "I don't know what she's done, nor do I care about any accusations that come from *your* lips."

Her eye is red because her mom was a witch that hides in the woods.

"But, I've been by her side for a while now, and yeah, she may be a bit rough around the edges or even a bit coarse."

She's weird! Her eye is red! She'll put a curse on you if you be her friend!

"But I know that, deep down, she's a good person! So, you can say she's evil all you want, but..."

She's not a witch! She's Nox, and she's my friend!

Lukas pointed the tip of the Sword Durandal forward.

"No one deserves to die for just being born!"

Snow slowly melted as it hit the cold, stony floors of the chapel. The wind whistled as it whipped about outside.

"What a fool!" Damasko suddenly burst. "With such *fiery* blood!"

Without warning, Lukas bolted forward, blade ready.

He's off guard! His mind raced. *If I can close in quick enough, I can strike—*

Suddenly, Lukas felt a sharp pain shoot through his shoulder, causing him to drop and shriek in agony.

"You're a quick little monkey," Damasko snickered. "But I'm no fool."

Lukas watched in horror as a long, razor-sharp, spear retracted back into the vampire's finger.

"You may be a magic wielder, but you're nothing to my prowess."

Lukas writhed upon the ground, a bloody hand held to his shoulder.

"You see," the vampire said as he reached into his pocket and pulled out a silver cigar case, "you might have been able to fool that slob, Vermilion, but—" he put the cigar in his mouth. Damasko snapped his fingers, producing a bright, blue flame, "—I am not as easy."

He's right, Lukas thought. He had not fully realized until now, but he had never truly fought anyone with any sort of magical ability, and now that he was locked in combat, he had scarce room for error.

This, he realized, was a duel to the death.

"I can see your trembling, boy," Damasko laughed through a plume of dark red smoke. His eyes shifted to black; his body began to contort, sinews shifting alongside convulsing muscles. Lukas and Blake looked onward, eyes widened as the fiend's body mutated behind the thick, crimson clouds.

Before Lukas reached a full stand, three blood-red spikes shot from behind the fog. Without thinking, Lukas reacted, his body strafing to the right. His feet slid as he frantically tried to find his center of gravity.

Suddenly, a beast shot from within the haze, a great spear exploding from its fingertip.

Drop! Lukas commanded his weary body. He could feel himself growing more and more lightheaded as his wound remained open. His body grew heavier and heavier. He readied the Sword Durandal for a parry as the spike closed in with astounding momentum. The sound of the impact rang throughout the chapel, the force of the clash of spike and steel knocked Lukas upon his back, winded.

"Tell me, boy, do you still have such resolve?! Do you still wish to save these *wretched* fools?" Damasko said as his monstrous form loomed above the knight, pinning him down with bulky arms. Horror filled Lukas' eyes. The once slim and suave vampire had become something entirely abominable. It stood tall and hulking, its skin a vague gray. Lukas looked into his solid black eyes. His breath was warm, saliva dripping from small, needle-like teeth. Spit dripped onto Lukas' face as the beast let out a gurgling chuckle.

"I'm going to eat you alive!"

"Lukas!" Blake gasped as Damasko sank his needled jaws into Lukas' shoulder.

The knight wailed as the teeth slowly split his skin. For a moment, Lukas could feel a suctioning pull.

Then, the beast stood still.

Abruptly, Damasko pulled back and retched, vomiting profusely upon the icy ground.

"What?!" he said through gagging breaths. "Are you?!"

The beast leaned back and screeched, brilliant white flames exploding from his mouth.

Of course...

Blake didn't know why she hadn't considered it before.

Pristine flames enveloped Damasko, slowly melting away the hulking muscles to reveal the thin figure of what he was before.

"Lukas!" Blake shouted over the screaming, "He can't drink your blood! You're—!"

"Heart of Hearts..." Lukas finished her sentence, slowly rising to a stand.

The two looked at their enemy as he lay sprawled upon the

ground.

Lukas smiled wearily and turned to Blake.

"I won!"

Snow filled the darkness, made visible only by the multitude of dim torchlight, which illuminated the gates of Baronwatch. From a distance, Nils trekked hastily through the bitter cold to catch up to the rebel army. Unarmed, he knew the dangers of his mission, yet, as a medic, felt internally compelled to complete it. He watched the faint lights of the castle grow ever more visible as he approached, and he prayed to One for protection.

Ahead, Hallow-talon and Captain Maro stood face to face with the vampiric guardians amassed to prevent their entry into the castle. The gargantuan figure of Sanguine stood amid the front lines, his shadowy presence intensified by the mist.

The parties stood in silence, only the air of impending bloodshed between them.

Captain Maro waited and watched Hallow-talon. There would be a signal, he knew. As the vampires waited for their arrival, the two leaders of the militia of prisoners agreed upon a strategy. Both Havell and the Phoenix were aware of the beastfolk's immunity to the vampire-morphing disease, so they had agreed that Hallow-talon's legion of birdmen would lead the charge. This was fine for the captain, who wanted nothing more than to storm the ancient fortress.

Because he knew he needed to do one thing: get rid of the mist.

But more importantly, he *needed* to retrieve the stone that powered it.

"Kill them." Sanguine's voice boomed.

Silently, Hallow-talon pointed forward, and his men responded.

Many times had Havell been on the battlefield with soldiers—men, women, even dogs. But never had he seen such power. Within an instant, great hawk wings sent cracking gusts as large birds ascended into the air, razor-sharp talons ripping through vampire flesh. Haunting wails filled the air as limbs dismembered and guts spilled upon the ground.

With a quick signal, the remaining Red Ravens followed their captain's commands, blades drawn, slicing through the few that dared give them mind. Distracted by the onslaught, the army of vampires remained oblivious as the captain slipped through the gates.

Enlil swept down the barren halls of the fort, her third sight navigating her passage to the cellar where she had discovered the Glowing Stone. As she descended the stairs, she could see the faint blue clouds that indicated that the psychic sight had detected humans within the entrance to the castle; below her, she saw pink mist.

Vampires.

Her mind was calm; her answer seemed clear.

Just down the stairway, Captain Havell Maro could hear the approaching calls of what sounded like a young girl. His mind instantly knew who it was, and his eyes quickly confirmed his hypothesis.

"Hey! Cap'n!" Enlil exclaimed as she ran past them. "First one to the stone's a rotten egg!"

"Hey—" the captain began, but seeing the young Darkling scurry down the hall, he knew he had little time.

He gave the signal, and his men followed in pursuit.

Blood of both beast and vampire flooded the grounds of the courtyards just within the gates. The once advantaged hawks had now been halted as arrows rained down upon them from the tops of the walls.

"Tell me, Phoenix," Sanguine said as he approached the beast king, "Where are your mighty flames?"

Hallow-talon observed the vampire's ripped clothing, deep cuts speedily healing, his large body muscular and defined.

"Are your flames asleep?" he laughed, "Or is there just too much *moisture* in the air?"

He was right, the king thought. There was. The wetness of the snow and howling winds were too cold and wet for him to summon his raging blaze.

"What does it matter," Hallow-talon smiled. "I can still beat you to death."

Great orange wings burst from his back. The giant Phoenix leapt forward, flying straight for his enemy. He reared his fist.

Sanguine merely stood, unaffected by the other's advance.

Their eyes met.

Without warning, Hallow-talon's body hit the ground limply. He tried to move, but his body simply wouldn't. He tried to move his arm. Open his hand. Twitch his finger.

No use.

"You see," the vampire said as he bore his heel on the bird-man's face, "anyone I make eye contact with becomes limp for ten minutes. That means one thing for you, *bird*."

Sanguine took time to aim, then with a burst of unreal force, kicked the limp bird in the gut. Hallow-talon retched as the vampire's foot dug into his abdomen, sending him crashing into a far wall."

"It means that, for at least ten minutes, I will make you wish you were still in prison."

"The key..." Blake shook her chains. "It's on his left belt loop!"

Lukas quickly hobbled over to the fallen Damasko and wriggled the key from the loop. He returned to Blake and searched her chains until he found the lock.

She felt a wave of relaxation flow through her veins as the thick links fell from her hands.

"Got—" Lukas suddenly felt empty, he could feel himself begin to wobble, and all went black.

Blake jerked, the weight of his body causing her to fall as he caught him.

Shit! She felt her pulse quicken like a fire through her body. *He's dying!*

The doors to the chapel swung open swiftly, causing Blake's head to jerk. A lone, blocky silhouette, strode up the aisle.

"Inquisitor! Inquisitor!" the voice echoed throughout the

chamber.

That voice...

"Is that Lukas?! Did he make it?!" Nils shouted as he came into view.

Blake suddenly went on edge.

"What do *you* want?"

Nils dropped to his knees.

"Inquisitor." His voice shook, "I know I have done you and your party great wrongs, and I know that I must pay for them, so please, on my honor as a doctor. No. On my honor as a *man!* Let me treat him!" He set a first aid kit and other bags upon the cold stone floor. "Let me save that young man's life!"

Blake stopped and looked at Lukas, his face now pale and his body covered in blood.

"Nils." She smiled. "Please. Please save this young man's life."

Blake softly placed Lukas' head upon the ground and stood. Suddenly, the snow began to grow heavier.

"I have something I need to do."

A vast sheet of ice followed at Blake's heels as she strode down the hallways, suffocating the walls and etherlamps as she passed them by. Mist swirled off of the frigid crystal as it raced behind her pace, matching the maelstrom of her mind.

He was right... she thought as tears froze as they left her eyes, hitting the stone floor like drops of glass.

Memories were spotty in her mind, each image a fleeting specter beckoning for her to fall prey to its vicious designs. She could see her father, the town—everyone she knew, standing still, frozen in time and chilled to death.

But she kept her eyes ahead, walking hastily toward the open courtyard. Screams echoed from the outside—wails of men giving their final breaths—but she couldn't hear them.

She couldn't hear over her own cold breathing.

A breath, frigid as winter.

Outside, her presence brought upon snow. All around her, soldiers stopped as they watched ice engulf the walls of the castle entirely.

"You!" her voice was sharp, cutting the air and filling the silence with deathly shivers.

At the opposite wall, the hulking figure of Sanguine was but a grim shadow looming over the worn body of the Phoenix.

"How did you escape?" his dark voice boomed over the whistling winds.

"Damasko has been dealt with," her voice growled, "and I need someone to take my anger out on." Blake scanned the courtyard, the faces of vampires were filled with a stunned uncertainty. "I think you and your army will do just fine."

Time seemed to stop, those in the bloody field stood still, anticipation pumping through their hearts. Snow bombarded the ground, filling it higher and higher with the passing moments.

"You're cocky, Snowbird," the other laughed as he slowly approached, his eyes desperately searching for hers. Sanguine knew her prowess in the snow was magnanimous, but he was aware that she would be useless without the use of her body.

All he needed was a little eye contact.

Blake took a deep breath, frost glazing her skin like a dress. Thoughts filled her mind as she watched the multitude of vampires approach her, each waving their blades hungrily.

He was absolutely *right...*

The temperature in the air dropped; the wind became blistering. Each hawk lay upon the snow, their feathers doing little to aid them in this blizzard. Hallow-talon, through his bloodied eyes, watched intently. What was she doing? Why would she warrant her own death like this?!

But Blake merely raised her foot.

"Now!" At Sanguine's order, the army charged, full speed.

Blake snapped.

"I deserve to live!"

Nix Celshior! She exclaimed as she stomped her foot upon the snowy floor.

Suddenly, frost exploded from her foot, covering the snow in solid ice. The hawks lay wide-eyed, lost and dumbfounded. In an instant, the courtyard was silent, all but the patter of the snow.

Hallow-talon dropped his jaw.

This was it. *This* was the power of an Inquisitor. Before him and his hawk militia, he saw Sanguine and the army of vampires.

They were frozen...

Frozen solid.

It was definitely a challenge, Havell thought as he and his small unit bolted down the hallway, trying their best to keep up with the small thief ahead of them. Through twists and turns she took them, constantly making the captain wonder if she even knew where she was going.

He got his answer.

Descending several flights of dimly lit stairs, the chase produced a room with a large, iron door.

"It's inside." The small thief nodded.

"Well..." the captain twisted his wrist as if turning a key, "go on..."

Enlil took a deep breath, held her fingers to the lock, and turned her wrist.

A great creaking noise echoed through the chamber as the door flew open.

"You brought me guests, Captain..." a woman's voice giggled.

Before them stood the tall Magenta, her body covered by a short, light-pink dress.

"Well, well," Havell began as he smiled, "I would kick your ass alone, but I knew some others who would like to join me."

The seductress bit her lip and ran her hand through her long, jet-black hair.

"Sounds kinky, Captain."

"You won't think that once your head is rolling on the ground!"

"Oh?" Magenta said as she snapped her fingers. "You want to *play*?"

Suddenly, Havell felt a warmth in his chest, as if all of the enmity of the world began to melt from his shoulders.

"Captain?" Her voice was smooth and sweet.

"Yes?" he looked at her. Magenta was so beautiful—her long black hair, her starkly pale skin, her voluptuous curves—just beautiful.

"Come to me, Captain."

He grew near her—he *wanted* to be near her, to hold her, to be with her. Captain Maro held his eyes upon hers—her beautiful black eyes. He walked toward her. Suddenly, a black flash sent the idol flying into the wall.

"You're a real dummy, Cap'n!"

"Enlil?!"

It was her! He looked around to see the other Red Ravens slowly gaining their sanity back, as well.

"You little *worm*!" Magenta shrieked as she exploded from the wall, psychic energy engulfing her and her dagger high in the air. The lithe fiend descended upon the small child, a blast of energy exploding from Magenta and colliding with Enlil. But the thief stood, unscathed. The seductress closed in quickly, jabbing her blade forward.

Enlil moved with a flash, and, in an instant, Magenta lay upon the ground, her arm contorted in an unnatural way—snapped backwards.

The soldiers all looked at each other, baffled.

"What did you just do?!" Havell finally exclaimed.

"Oh!" she smiled, "Just something my big brother taught me!"

"Your—" he began before cutting himself short, "whatever."

Simultaneously, they turned their eyes to the stone.

"Look, I need this thing." he began.

"Nope!"

"Okay. Look," the captain groaned. "Whatever. You can have it! Just take it! If you blow up, then whatever!" he shivered, "I just need a smoke."

"Sounds like a personal problem to me," the little Darkling sang as she approached the giant, rumbling machine.

"Maybe you'll die if you touch it," Captain Maro cursed under his breath.

"It's Antithicite," she retorted as she scooped it in her hands.

"It's okay to touch it, as long as it doesn't come in contact with zellinium."

"Is that so?" Havell said blankly as he motioned to his men. "So you can't use magic while you hold it?"

"Yeah—!" Enlil said before the hilts of two swords clanged against her head.

Enlil fell to the ground, unconscious.

Nils applied salves and wrapped bandages around Lukas' unconscious body.

Please, son...

Thousands of thoughts filled his mind, but he couldn't help but wonder one thing: Why was Lukas' body not falling victim to vampirism? He had taken serious bites to the shoulder, but yet his body showed no signs of change.

"Lukas..." he said to himself, "what *are* you, boy?"

He hurriedly tried his best to do what he could, applying pressure to the small wounds created by the needle-like marks made by Damasko's teeth. Upon a quick scan, he determined that no bones had been broken, but the wounds to his shoulder had been about an inch deep, so he needed now to focus on stopping the bleeding.

Nils looked at Lukas' face. For some reason, his visage seemed lighter. The doctor scanned the chapel. It seemed he could see better than before.

No...it can't be...

Nils turned his gaze to the large, broken window. Outside, the sun was rising.

XXIV

Leaving Ildar

The message came in the dead of the night, wrapped in mysterious material and with seemingly no sender. The messenger had delivered it sometime soon, and it was now that the soldiers had begun to carry it to whom it was addressed. In big, bold letters at the top, it read "ELDRIC."

Who was sending this to the Master of the Inquisition was a mystery, but the soldiers had opened the letter to check for poisons or other devious means of assault and had found nothing of suspicion, so the letter was sent through, and, due to its mysterious nature, was sent to the Master Inquisitor directly, to be placed upon his desk for inspection.

The courier carried the letter from the mailroom, through the corridors that led to the courtyard, then through the sanctuary, and up until the great wizard's office. He carried on up the stairs, and, despite the midnight hour, the Inquisitor still sat diligently at his desk, writing furiously.

"Master Inquisitor!" the courier said with a salute, "A letter, sir. I think it may be in your interests."

The old man looked up curiously. The soldier could see the bags under the elder's eyes. *He must be putting in many nights of work,* he thought.

"Let me see," Eldric said as he took the letter.

The soldier watched as the old man's calloused fingers unraveled the mysterious linen.

Eldric carefully took the piece of parchment from the parcel. He looked over it for a moment, then his face contorted as if in epiphany.

"You are dismissed." Eldric waved his hands, his eyes locked upon whatever was written on the sheet. "And, thank you. You've done well."

The soldier saluted and left. Eldric leaned back in his chair, stretching his clubbed foot.

He gazed over the paper multiple times, reading it repetitively. He was sure it was the same words he had read...the same words of the same places, over and over.

It was the name of the prison in which Valter Rivyra was held captive.

On the paper, four words were written in large letters. The paper simply read...

"AVELLE'S BROOK. TWO DAYS."

Lukas found himself surrounded by darkness. He blinked a couple times, then wiped his eyes and stood. As he rose, he immediately noticed that he felt no soreness whatsoever. He had a vague memory of the past few days—of his imprisonment and his fight with Damasko—and he knew that he sustained some injuries, so why didn't he feel any pain?

Unless...!

Frantically, he patted down his body.

"Oh, come now!" a young woman's voice echoed throughout the nothingness. "You aren't dead!"

Lukas jerked as the body of Lyrlark materialized before him.

"Parhaps a bit reckless, but not enough to wind up dead." She smiled, her glittery eyes squinting. "I will say, what you did was rather heroic!"

"So, it's only you..."

"Indeed," she said as she approached him. "You've done a lot in the past few days, and you learned something important, didn't you?"

"Uh..." Lukas began, "I did?"

"By Empyria, boy!" Lyrlark exclaimed, furrowing her brow. "You really can be quite a ditz, you know that! I'll give you a hint: What you learned is like the sound of the wind sweeping across a field of barley—it's but a soft hum, yet wild and free. You know?"

Lukas held his hand to his heart.

"You're right," he said softly. "The voice of Durandal. It's there now. It's soft and faint, but I hear it."

"Well," the Aeon said and smirked, "it seems you're truly growing accustomed to *his* heart."

Lukas stopped and raised his eyes to meet the goddess'.

"You remind me of him," she continued. "Lucyn, I mean. You remind me of him a great deal—more than you know, actually."

"Lucyn..." he said, "you mean...?"

"The first to be called 'Heart of Hearts,' yes. He was the one you call a 'Philosopher King,' or whatever. But his real name was *Lucyn*. I can't believe it has truly been one thousand years. I thought that surely I'd never see a mortal like him ever again." Lyrlark giggled softly, her laughter echoing along the void, "I see now why my sister is so drawn to you. You have a certain..." she held her finger to her chin, "charm. Yes?"

"Lyrlark." Lukas' voice became suddenly grim. "What is the Heart of Hearts? Is it even really mine, or do I have another? How did I get Lucyn's heart? I have so many questions, and every turn I take—every path I follow—I find more mystery and less answers. Who am I? What do those men want with Nox? *Where* is Nox?" She could hear a sudden trill in his voice. "Please tell me."

"My dear Lukas," she began, "I don't know the answer to any of your questions. I'm sorry, but I truly don't. I may be an Aeon, but even we Aeons are not omniscient. I am truly sorry to have to part ways with you under such circumstances—" she stopped. "I am sorry."

Lukas closed his eyes, and silence filled the space between them. A soft hand took his. He opened his eyes to meet the Aeon's gaze. He stared deep into her galactic eyes, watching them as their stars swirled and shifted.

"Lukas of Zerlina. Please be careful. One who seeks answers must always be prepared to find truth, but we don't get to decide what the consequences of that truth might be."

Lukas held her hand in his, and for the moment, he felt as empty as his surroundings.

"Avelle's Brook, huh?" Archbishop Marven said as he scratched his balding head.

"Yes, it is indeed interesting," Eldric replied as he blew rings of smoke from his pipe. "And the nature of the letter is just as curious."

"Why would they notify us?"

"Exactly the mystery to me as well." Eldric laid a piece of paper on the desk. "However, it seems that this is the exact reason. I'm sure of it."

Marven picked up and scanned the paper. Suddenly, his face became pale.

"Valter Rivyra?"

"Yes. Also known as 'Legion.'" Eldric took his pipe from his mouth. "I believe that they will try and free him."

"But..." Marven said slowly as he placed the paper on his desk, "No one has ever breached the prison at Avelle's Brook."

Eldric sighed.

"I believe the Abdian—the one that I met at Zerlina—can."

"What should we do?"

"Meet them there. I'll be going with Snow and soldiers. Contact the Red Ravens." Eldric puffed his pipe, "I'm going to welcome them."

Lukas groaned as he awoke to soreness in his shoulder. Opening his eyes, he realized he was in an unfamiliar place. The room was unmistakably a cabin, with the walls consisting of gargantuan logs. The roof seemed to be made of tin. The light of a lamp filled the room, and Lukas looked out of the large window beside his bed.

It was still dark. Outside, he could see the sky become blue on the linings of the horizon—the vague premonitions of the coming dawn.

"You have healed rather quickly," a hoarse voice said from the doorway, "faster that I've ever seen anyone heal, in fact."

Lukas turned to see Nils enter the room; in his hands was a tray filled with toast, some sausages, and scrambled eggs.

"Your bleeding had stopped mostly when I had found you, and if any bones had been fractured, they have healed by now. It's..." he furrowed his brow, looking for the right words, "miraculous, really. Mainly, you're just going to be sore for a few more weeks, but you'll be just fine."

Lukas took the tray as it was handed to him. As he looked at the food, he suddenly realized how hungry he was.

"Nils..."

"It's the least I can do. You beat *him*, after all. I don't know how you did it, but you defeated Damasko the Bloodletter."

Lukas stopped. The doctor was right. Suddenly, images of the battle filled his mind, of crashing through the stained-glass window, summoning Durandal, the giant beast...he recalled all of it, even if a bit hazy.

"He gave you a rather big bite, too," Nils continued. "You show no signs of Sanguine Vampiris—becoming a vampire, I mean. It's like your body has an immunity to it. I've...I've never seen that before."

"Immune?" Lukas held his hand to his heart.

The Heart of Hearts?

"I digress," the doctor said as he waved his hand, "right now, you should rest a bit more and eat. Most of the vampires died when the sun rose yesterday. Captain Maro has Damasko and the others in custody. He's holding them in the prison until he can take them to the Skyprison at Avelle's Brook. The Inquisitor you were with has been aloof. She isn't really in the best of moods, but—"

He stopped. He could tell that Lukas had somewhat tuned out, his attention drawn instead to the window. Lukas peered through the cold glass. Outside, the light of the dawning sun had doused the clouds, turning them to rose-hued plumes upon the horizon.

The two watched as the rays of the triumphant orb broke the gloom of the dark. The sun was rising, chasing away the shadows of night. Lukas turned to the doctor who had, only a day earlier, saved his life.

"Hey, Nils..."

Their eyes met; Nils could see the deep greenish colors of the young man's hazel eyes.

Lukas smiled and nudged his head, directing the doctor's attention to the rising sun.

"What did I tell ya?"

Nils stopped. He inhaled deeply. He remembered.

"You did..." Lukas heard an audible crack in the doctor's voice as he watched him turn away. "You did tell me."

He turned his face toward the orphan.

"You were right." Nils smiled as his eyes seemed to wander out the window. "Isn't the sun...so beautiful."

In the bright light from the window, Lukas could see that Nils was crying.

Captain Havell Maro made his way down the prison halls, met by a fellow Red Raven.

"Captain, a word?"

The captain exhaled smoke from his cigarette and nodded.

"Damasko the Bloodletter," the soldier began, "He *was* a vampire, right?"

"Aeons, boy!" Havell shook his head. "Why do you think we were here?! Of course he's a vampire."

"W-well," the soldier startled, "if he *was* a vampire...let's just say that he's *not* a vampire anymore."

The captain stopped.

"What?"

Damasko's cell was dark and chillingly damp. The distant sound of water dripping onto a small puddle echoed from somewhere in the room—the most unlivable cell, picked just for him. He sat in silence, the memories of the prior days flashing through his mind like lightning. In the distance he heard a door open, followed by footsteps. The steps became clearer and clearer until he could see a light coming down the hall.

"Damasko the Bloodletter," a voice said through a cough. Damasko squinted his eyes at the light. A Red Raven stood, cigarette in his mouth.

"What do you want, Red Raven?"

"Not so tough now, are we?" Captain Maro said through a puff of his smoke.

Damasko spit upon the ground.

"Why don't you tell me about your little operation here?" Havell said, his face hardening. "Starting with the 'client' that Vermilion mentioned."

"That fat bastard..." Damasko mumbled, "My client? I can't tell you that. My client does not act alone, you see. And angering the *other* would not be...to my best interest."

"Other?"

"He is 'The End.' He's a man of great and terrible power. He's unlike us. He's stronger than any of you mortal fools." Damasko leaned forward and spat at them. "He'll kill you all. He'll destroy everything you know and love. I can't *wait* to see you suffer, you dog!" he laughed.

"Well," Havell turned around and waved to the others, "I'm sure you'll have plenty of fun in Avelle's Brook."

The captain tuned out the wails of his prisoner as he walked away.

"He's *not* a vampire..." he muttered to himself in confusion.

It was strange for sure, but Havell thought he knew what had happened. Of course. That *had* to be what happened. He saw the marks on Lukas' body. Damasko had bitten him—he had tried to drink his blood. And, according to the doctor, Lukas seemed to show zero signs of Vampiris.

To Havell, there was only one solution...

Lukas' blood had cleansed Damasko of vampirism.

The halls once filled with wails of torture were now silent as the grave. Either way, Captain Maro was oblivious to it, instead focusing on the little presence shadowing him.

"For an assassin, you're not doing a very good job," he coughed as he inhaled smoke. "You're not getting the Stone, so you might as well give up."

From within the shadows, the figure of Enlil emerged.

"That's not fair!" she pouted. "I even saved your life and stuff!"

"And *that* is why we haven't arrested you like we should have." Havell smiled. "I figured giving you your freedom would be enough payment. Besides, I don't have the Stone anymore."

"You *what?!*" Enlil yelled louder than she intended.

"I gave it to the Inquisitor." Captain Maro took another drag of his cigarette. "It's obviously magic...and the Church is better at studying magic-y things."

Enlil groaned as she disappeared back into the shadows.

"I don't like you, Cap'n!"

Havell chuckled.

"It's probably better that way."

Lukas, against Nils' better judgment, had put on his winter coat and left the humble clinic. Before leaving, he took time to thank the doctor for all he had done, and he also left a word of farewell, as well as a word of encouragement to assure the man that any damage he had done to Lukas and his companions was forgiven. The physician, though he tried to hide it, cried a bit more before wishing Lukas well on his journey. And so, Lukas ventured out into the morning, knowing what he must do.

He knew he had to find Blake.

Asking Nils about where she might be produced no fruits. The doctor merely shrugged, honestly apologizing for not knowing the answer to what he had been asked. Lukas, however, had somewhat expected that. It didn't matter, because he knew where she would be.

The heavy snows from before had calmed with the dissipation of the dark mist, and were now replaced by a soft flurry, carried by a light breeze. As Lukas walked past the boundaries of Ildar, he took in his surroundings. What was once a dark shadow was now illuminated to reveal deep, green, fir trees topped with silver snow.

He looked ahead as he walked onward. The ground, though covered by snow, gave way to small mountain streams, clear as glass, with colorful rocks at the bottom.

If he remembered correctly, the Airskiff Cavalier was parked somewhere north of the town, and, after a few moments of trekking, he found it.

And, as he approached, he saw Blake.

"Hey!" he called out as he rushed toward her, "What are you doing out here all alone like this?"

Blake stirred momentarily.

"I didn't really care for the...revelry," she muttered.

"Well, everyone was wondering about where you went. Nils told me all about what you did. It was amazing! You saved their lives. Surely they would like to thank y—"

"Why?!" Blake's sudden outburst caused Lukas to jump.

"Wh-why what?"

"Why are you so stupid?!" Blake erupted. "Why did you do *anything* for me?! All I ever did was push you away!"

"Well," Lukas said softly, hoping to diffuse the other's anger. "You're my friend. Why would I not help—"

Lukas suddenly felt a harsh sting as Blake's palm crossed his cheek.

"You put your life in unnecessary danger!" she yelled. "Are you really so dense?! *You* are the Heart of Hearts; *I* am just some Inquisitor." She shook her head violently. "I don't get you! Can't you see that I never wanted to teach you?! Can't you tell that I just want to be left alone?! Why, then?! After all I've done, why didn't you just let me die?! Why didn't y—?!"

"Oh, shut up!" The sudden, unusual, force in Lukas' voice caused Blake to freeze.

Lukas exhaled.

"Just because you *think* no one cares, doesn't mean it's true! And how are *you* so dense that you can't see a friend when they're right under your nose. Get this through your thick skull, Blake! I came for you out of my own volition because I care about you and value you as a friend." Lukas grit his teeth. "There's *no way* that I would just abandon y—"

Blake raised her hand once more. Lukas flinched, closing his eyes, preparing the best he could for her slap.

Suddenly, he felt pressure around his chest. Lukas opened his eyes to find Blake embracing him tightly. Her arms wrapped around him felt unnatural, as if she'd never done it before. Her body was cold. Lukas held still as she starkly trembled.

"Lukas," she whimpered with a shaky voice. "Thank you."

For a moment, he remained still, slightly in shock. Never before had he ever even seen the stoic Inquisitor smile, much less weep. But, he knew she had to be human somewhere, deep down.

He held her there as the wind blew the thin flurries through the trees, and he couldn't help but smile.

"This is a one time thing, okay? If anyone asks," she gasped, "I don't cry."

"Right, right," Lukas laughed.

They released each other.

"So, we're friends now, right?"

"Don't push it," Blake smiled as she wiped her eyes.

She looked at the Airskiff, then back in the direction of Ildar.

"Go get Durandal," she said with a wave of her hands. "Or do that little...thing you did?"

He remembered what had happened in his battle with Damasko. So, standing there with Blake, Lukas held out his hand. Blake smiled as small white flames surrounded Lukas' arm.

"Come."

At his call, a white light exploded from his hand, and with it, he held the Sword Durandal.

"That's awesome," Blake said. "If you're doing what I think you're doing, then you'll just need to focus a bit more to hear your Word of Heart." She held her chin. "Though, I've never heard of white flames...that is strange indeed."

Blake trailed off into thought, and both were silent. The sounds of the mountain forest surrounded them, the sounds of snowbirds singing mixed with the whooshing of the winds through the trees.

Blake took a deep breath, then motioned for them to climb

aboard.

Hallow-Talon and the remaining birdmen soared through the air, now miles away from Ildar. The southern winds blew warmer breezes, a more welcoming weather to the king and his men. Flying in a V-formation, none stopped to ask where they were headed or what they would do now that they were free.

It was all too obvious and none *needed* to ask.

They were on the hunt to find *him*.

They were on the lookout for Lyon.

XXV

Day One

Nox sat silently inside the large metal birdcage, her eyes fixated upon the large, stained-glass window. It was truly an enigma. She couldn't think of how or why, but the depiction of the tree upon the glass felt...familiar. Even more so, the black moon at the top made her feel unnerved.

Nox turned around and sat, leaning against the bars. The library was deathly silent, all but the intermittent rustle of Iago turning the pages of the book he seemed so lost in. Despite that, he remained silent as well.

Nox had long decided that he wasn't assigned to watch her or anything, but rather he sat there because it was the place underneath the sunroof where light was brightest. He perplexed her, truly. She couldn't really tell why, but he was different from the other two. Even though his personality appeared combative, she couldn't help but be unafraid of him.

Perhaps he just wasn't as intimidating as the others.

"What are you doing?"

Iago flipped a page, his eyes still peering into the book.

"What? You never seen a book before?" he said derisively.

"I know what a book is," Nox shot back.

"Well, there you go."

Nox sighed.

Really? she griped in her mind.

"Well, what's it about?"

"You're a captive," he groaned, "be quiet or I'll hurt you."

"You won't hurt me."

Iago closed his book and stood.

"Won't I?" the Elf snapped his fingers. Suddenly, several phantom blades surrounded her. "Are you sure you want to test that?"

Nox stepped forward to the bars of the cage. She stared into his eyes, all but ancient metal between her and Elf.

"I don't fear you, Iago."

Iago met her gaze. He looked into her multicolored eyes.

"I don't know why," she said, "but I don't believe you're as evil as those other men."

The Elf remained silent.

Iago clenched his jaw. Who was this stupid girl to say? She knew nothing about him. She knew nothing about what he had done—about the prince and the revolution—she knew *nothing*.

"Don't pretend you know me, Lunae," he growled. "Don't be so naive."

He walked to his chair, picked up his book, then stormed off, disappearing into the darkness.

Nox watched him leave. She sighed and returned to gazing at the window. She thought for a moment about what she had just witnessed. Before he stormed off, she saw his eyes.

They weren't eyes of anger.

No.

In Iago's eyes, for if just a split second, she saw *pain*.

Lukas slept soundly as the Airskiff *Cavalier* swiftly cut through the morning air. Blake sat quietly as she manned the small vessel, her pale blue eyes focused ahead. She heard the long yawning of her companion as he stretched his arms and legs, straightening his body.

"How far along are we?" Lukas said as he lay back in his reclined seat.

"Just starting. You've only slept about thirty minutes."

Lukas rubbed his eyes as he raised his seat. The sky was a sheer blue, with no clouds to prohibit the graceful rays of the high noon sun. Lukas winced once more at the soreness of his shoulder.

"Don't try to over-exert yourself," Blake said with a soft voice. "You can sleep more, if you wish. We'll be flying for a while." Her eyes became wide as she looked at the meters, "Nevermind. Looks like we're going to be making a stop."

Lukas stared curiously at the Inquisitor, more surprised by her tone than the present malfunction. Ever since their argument at Ildar, she had changed. Her once antisocial personality had been replaced by a milder, more accommodating one. The more Lukas considered it, the more honored he felt. Eventually, he finally decided: *This* was the *real* Blake.

"The engine is running hot," she sighed without hiding her frustration. "I can keep it cool with my magic, but I can't sustain it long enough to get us all the way to Mhyrmr. We're going to have to land."

Lukas sighed as well.

"I hate that I'll have to find a mechanic," Blake said under her breath.

"Where can we stop?" Lukas asked, looking out his window at the endless treetops directly below him.

Blake pointed. "There, outside my window." Lukas looked over Blake's seat to see a large white tower ascending into the sky, surrounded by a nicely-sized city.

Lukas fixated his eyes upon the tower.

"Avelle's Brook," Blake started, "home of the most securely locked-down prison in the entirety of Lythia. Why they put it in the middle of a city," she shrugged, "your guess is as good as mine."

Lukas watched the city grow closer and closer as the now fuming Airskiff Cavalier descended into the aerodock. Smoke wafted from the small vessel, filling the cockpit with the smell of burning oil until, finally, Blake was able to land in an unreserved spot.

"By the Aeons," Blake growled as she stepped out of the driver's seat and down the stepladder.

"Um...what now?" Lukas said at the sight at the smoking

Airskiff.

"I guess we find an inn," she stretched, turning around and walking away.

Lukas followed.

As they turned, the steward of the Aerodock approached them. He was a skinny man in pink, holding a clipboard.

"Here," Blake handed him a small card before he began to speak.

"Ah!" he nodded, "I will send the bill to the Church." He handed the card back to Blake, then walked away.

Blake nodded, motioning for Lukas to follow.

Avelle's Brook was a lively city, Lukas thought, as he and Blake passed through the exit of the aerodock. The streets were exceedingly crowded—much more so than Zerlina, Lukas thought. Strange smells of the strange foods being sold filled the marketplace. He gazed upward. Even from the outer ring of town, he could see the prison ominously towering over the free citizens.

"The tower is huge," Lukas commented.

"It is," Blake said. "It's the largest, most secure prison in all of Aestriana—or Lythia, for that matter."

Lukas found himself staring at it. It's pearl-white exterior appeared smooth and almost shiny, with small windows that appeared as mere specks upon it's massive figure. So marvelous was its design that he found it hard to believe that it was a mere prison.

"It's run by the Church, which makes it a neutral zone. This is mainly to keep the most dangerous criminals from the world outside. The warden is a notorious torturer. So much so that they simply call him 'The Butcher.' Rough." She motioned for him to follow once again. "Now we need to get to the Inn."

"How do you know where it is?"

Blake smiled. "Because my uncle owns it. He's my mother's brother. He's really the only family I have left."

"Really?" Lukas exclaimed in slight laughter, "No wonder you knew where the aerodock was!"

"You're catching on." She turned and began to walk away.

"Let's find that inn."

The two walked down the crowded sidewalks of the city to the inn, which was placed by the aerodock as to attract the weary traveling merchant or trader. The building, like the city itself, was in no way modest, its large stone exterior ascending several stories high.

Lukas counted the stories; there were five.

"Ugh," Blake groaned, "I can finally shower..."

"Yeah, you stink." Lukas jeeringly concurred.

"Gee, thanks," Blake replied flatly.

Lukas smiled at his companion, who smiled back.

The inside of the inn was lavish, as well. Lukas silently followed Blake to the receptionist's desk. A girl sat there, her hair a mousy brown, held back in a ponytail. It hung to her baggy green shirt, which didn't appear to fit her slim build in the slightest.

"Blake?!" the girl at the desk happily exclaimed, standing and walking around to the Inquisitor with open hands.

"Cilli." Blake smiled awkwardly.

"It's been so long since I've seen you! How are things at the church? Are they taking good care of you? You aren't in too much danger are you? Are they working you too hard—?"

"Cilli." Blake cut into the girl's frantic questioning, "I'm fine. Promise."

Cilli turned her attention to Lukas. "Who's this? A boyfriend?!"

Blake's cheeks suddenly turned blood red. "N-no!" she snapped back. "He's the knight that was assigned to me," Blake said. "He's here to protect me."

"How romantic," Cilli said slyly, eyes darting at Blake.

"Good to see you too," the Inquisitor sighed, exasperated. "Where's Ralf?"

"At the bar, where do you think?" Cilli laughed. "He's *your* uncle. I shouldn't be telling you this; you should be telling me!"

Blake sighed once more.

"You guys looking for lodging?"

"Yeah," Blake said, rolling her eyes. "Our Airskiff broke down."

"Ugh," Cilli mirrored the other's attitude, "the worst!" She reached over the desk. "Rooming together or separate?"

"Separate," Blake and Lukas replied in unison.

"I'm only joking," she laughed as she handed them each a key.

Lukas followed Blake away from the lavish lobby and to the staircase.

"This place is incredible!" Lukas said as he marveled at the high ceilings and glowing chandeliers that adorned them.

"Yeah," she replied as she looked at the room numbers above the door. "My uncle's a drunk, but he's a rich drunk. He's owned this ever since I can remember. He was never around when I was growing up, and I only really met him last year, but my mother used to tell me he started from nothing."

"Wow! Are you going to see your mother while you're in town?"

"No. I can't."

"Why not?"

"She's dead."

Suddenly, Lukas felt awful for asking. "I'm sorry I pried," he said in an equally low voice.

"It's okay. It's in the past now." She pointed to a door and handed Lukas his key. "Here's your room. Now go take a bath." She mocked, "you stink."

Lukas laughed as he took the key and entered his room. She was probably right, he thought. He probably did stink. And to be honest, a shower sounded really nice right about now.

The warm water felt so good on Blake's aching body. She stayed in the shower for quite some time, but eventually she shut off the water and got out. After dressing, she looked out the window at the bustling city below. Her eyes wandered. Behind the tower, the sun shone, causing it's shadow to cast over the city right below her window. The monolith was ominous, she thought. To think that all of Lythia's worst criminals were held in bondage in that pearly spire. She looked at the streets once more—all of those people, they were so oblivious to the danger right above them.

She sighed.

Knowing that she needed to call Eldric, she sat her bag down and reached for the phone on the nightstand.

Eldric sat in his cabin in the Airship *Orca*, fiddling through papers, when the phone on his nightstand began to ring.

"Yes?" he said as he picked it up.

"Master Inquisitor," Blake said, relieved to hear his voice. "This is Inquisitor Snowbird."

"Blake? Are you still in Ildar? What happened to Damasko?"

"No, we're not. And Damasko was taken down. There were many things that happened. Damasko was using captives to manufacture Blood Dust. But that's not all. He was using a mysterious Stone to power a machine which blocked the sun from the city. We fought; we won, and I retrieved the stone from Captain Maro for testing, but maybe you should send an investigator to Ildar, just in case."

"I see. I'll send someone right away." Eldric said curiously. "Where are you now?"

"Well, our Airskiff began to have trouble. We ended up in Avelle's Brook."

"By the Aeons!" the Master Inquisitor paused, "I wonder why you ended up there..."

He trailed off.

"What's that?"

"Stay there," he replied. "You *need* to be there."

"I do?"

"Yes. Is Lukas with you?"

"He is. We've found lodgings for the night. I—"

"Something is going to happen in two days," Eldric cut in, his voice hardening. "Meet me in the aerodock early tomorrow morning. I'll brief you on the updates when I get there. Stay put, and keep Lukas close."

Blake sighed as the phone clicked, indicating that the old man had hung up. He was always this way. But why would he want them to be at Avelle's Brook? And two days?

The young Inquisitor took a deep breath when suddenly a knock came at her door.

"Yes?" she said in a raised voice as she opened the door to see Ralf standing and smiling at her.

She recognized him instantly. Ralf wasn't easy to forget. He was a very large man, more in his gut than the rest of his body, but Blake had only assumed that was caused by the excessive drinking —which, of course, was evident in the redness of his face and wrinkles under his eyes. But, despite all of this, she still found kindness in those eyes. Honestly, she had truly only known the man for a small amount of time, but he'd always been kind. *She* was the one pushing him away. On the way from Ildar, Blake had done a great deal of thinking.

No more, she decided. *No more pushing.*

"Blake!" the hefty man said as he embraced her, lifting her off of the ground. "It's been too long!"

"Hey, Uncle Ralf," Blake said with what air she had from the man's snug grip.

"What brings ya here? Is there some trouble the Church is sending you after?" he asked as he placed her down.

"No, actually. Our Airskiff broke down. We'll be here until it's fixed, probably."

"Wonderful!" the large man exclaimed, "So you'll join us for dinner?"

Blake smiled warmly at the thought. She had not been in company before, and she decided that now would be the time to start.

"I would love to." Blake nodded, showing a bit more excitement than she expected.

"Great! You'll be in for a treat! Y'see there's this strange storyteller in town. He's been doing shows for a couple days now, and I hear great reviews!" he put his hand on her head and ruffled her short, white hair with a smile. "You can bring your boyfriend, too."

Blake felt her face turn hot again. "He's not my boyfriend."

"Sure, sure," Ralf teased. "That's fine."

Blake looked at him blankly for a moment.

"Need a fresh change of clothes? I'll be right back!"

Blake smiled as her uncle walked away, then closed the door. For the first time in her life, she was home.

It still was nice, Lukas thought, to finally take a bath, the feeling of the warm water shooting on his aching muscles. He sat in the shower for a time, letting his body relax before getting up and turning off the water. He took one of the large towels from the stack next to the sink and began to dry himself. He ruffled his blond hair (which had now grown out a bit), then patted his back with the towel. He exhaled, feeling revitalized by the steam, then walked out of the bathroom and began to dress himself. He had packed one more pair of clothes, a piece of advice given to him by Snow before their departure to Ildar—a piece of advice he was now glad that he had heeded.

He took his clean shirt from the bag. It was one Sister Helga had bought him for his birthday, and was one of his favorites. He held it up and inspected it for stains and spots. Its yellow triangles decorated the collar, and the rest was a deep blue. Upon deciding that it was acceptably presentable, he put it on. Next, he took his pants from the bag. They were soft material, slightly tight, but he liked their black and white stripes around the waist band. Lastly, he threw on his black jacket, which just so happened to be his favorite article of clothing. He shook his hair, attempting to help it dry quickly.

Lukas looked over to the window. Even from the other end of the lavish hotel room, he could see the gargantuan tower ascend into the heavens. He thought of Blake's words regarding it, that it was the most secure prison on the entirety of the continent of Lythia. Still, the sight of it gave him a chill. Lukas shook, then turned to leave his room. He wouldn't go far, he thought. He may not be as lucky this time if he were to get lost. He wouldn't have the mysterious magic of the even more mysterious Zurriel to guide him this go around, so he decided he best stay close to the inn. He would just check the lobby, he thought. That way, he wouldn't get lost.

With that decided, he left the room.

Lukas walked down the long hallway, examining the pictures on the wall. There were paintings of landscapes from far and wide. For a moment, he stopped and gazed at one—its large purple mountains in the distance, far away from the hills covered in white flowers. He took in the sights for a moment, then turned and moved on.

He descended the stairs down to the first floor and walked into the lobby. Cilli was still at the receptionist's desk.

"Hey! It's you!" Cilli called from across the room, waving her hand above the desk.

"Hey!" Lukas replied as he approached her, smiling.

"You're taking good care of her, aren't you?" She squinted her eyes and smiled. "You better be!"

Lukas laughed and scratched his head. "Of course. That's my job. I would be a pretty lousy knight if I let her get hurt."

"Good!" she said. "By the way, we're taking Blake out to dinner tonight, and we would love for you to come too. There's a traveling storyteller in town today, and we want to see his show."

"Did someone say 'storyteller?'" a deep voice spoke loudly from behind Lukas.

Lukas turned to see Zurriel standing before him.

"Zurriel?" Lukas asked after taking a moment to recognize him. "What are *you* doing here?"

"Ah!" the tall man exclaimed, throwing his hands in the air theatrically. "But I should be asking you?"

Lukas couldn't help but smile at the strange man's zeal. "I've come with a friend. Our Airskiff broke down."

"You're the one we were just talking about!" Cilli added.

"Oh, is that true?" Zurriel put his hand to his heart and bowed. "I'm truly honored, young woman."

"Yeah." She smiled. "We're coming to your show tonight!"

The odd storyteller's face lit up. "You will, will you?" He turned to Lukas, "And will you as well, young Lukas?"

The directness of the question caught Lukas off guard.

"O-of course."

"Why, wonderful! I would love to have you at my show." He threw his hands in the air again as he began to walk away. And now, adieu—until tonight!"

Cilli turned to Lukas. "He was a strange one."

"You're telling me."

The guards dragged Damasko up the stairs of the prison tower, his feet banging against each stair of their ascent. The man who was once a vampire was silent. The soldiers came to the top of the stairs, then turned down a hallway to a door. The door opened to reveal a small room, the walls slathered in blood. The ex-vampire scanned the room to see stretchers and chains.

"Well, well," a gruff voice said, "Damasko the Bloodletter. My, how the mighty fall."

Damasko raised his beaten face to see a tall, muscular man. He saw the scars that covered the man's face, determining his identity instantly.

The Butcher.

"Why the long face, Bloodletter?" The warden cracked a smile as he leaned down to the prisoner's eye level. "You didn't want to pay me a visit?"

"Not for a moment," Damasko said as he spit in the warden's face.

"Put him in the chair," the Butcher commanded his soldiers.

The soldiers lifted the tall Damasko and placed him in a chair beside a lever. The chair appeared to be solid metal, with thick clasps to keep it's victims from moving. Their captive made no effort to resist, simply limp as they placed him and locked him in.

"Now," the torturer said as he picked a long link of the metal chains from the floor, "let's have a nice little talk."

"You can beat it with your talk," the captive Damasko said, gritting his teeth.

"Beaten by a teenager?" the Butcher gave a hearty bellow of a laugh, "I thought you'd been smarter than that."

"You don't scare me, Warden."

"What a shame," the warden sighed as he pulled a lever on the wall.

Suddenly, Damasko felt a burning sensation spread through his body. Outside, the soldiers standing guard only heard the haunting wails of one who now inhabited hell.

"You see, Bloodletter." The Butcher lowered his head to speak into Damasko's ear. "You're in my playground now."

Smoke fumed from Damasko's burned flesh.

"Just you wait," the Bloodletter said through clenched teeth, "*he* will kill you all. *Every last one of you.* He's going to purge this dreadful world."

"Tell me who this 'he' is," the Butcher demanded, sending another surge through the metal chains.

Damasko shrieked and ground his teeth, the heat beginning to tear through muscle. "I don't know his name. They call him 'The End.' That's all I know, I swear," he pleaded, "I don't even know his face!"

The torturer paused for a moment and laughed.

"I'm disappointed, Bloodletter," he laughed as he pulled the lever again. "You know better than to lie to me. Let's try this again."

Wails of eldritch agony filled the room. Outside, the soldiers were impassive to the torment happening behind the door. Hours seemed to pass by, the once gritting screams now reduced to breathless gasps, vaguely heard from the outside.

For a moment, silence, then, the Butcher walked out of the room and motioned his hand dismissively as he began to walk away.

"Put him in Sector Zero," he instructed. "Bring him back in a couple hours. We'll see if he knows more by then."

Inside, Damasko sat in delirium, his mind warped from the hours of pain. The soldiers unchained him, unconcerned with his scars and harsh burns, then dragged him away.

Lukas sat at the foot of his bed, staring out the window at the ever creeping dusk, Lyrlark's final words echoing through his mind

Consequences of the truth?

For some reason, it felt more to him like an omen than advice. Even in the end, the mysterious Aeon did more *adding* to his list of questions than she did *answering* them. Even in the midst of his confusion and everything that had happened, he couldn't help but think of Nox. He had no clue where she was, or even if she was still alive. But, despite his fears, he couldn't help but feel a strange warmth when he thought of her. It was not butterflies or any tingling, nervous sensation, but rather as if he felt his heart beating outside of his chest, as if it were a distant rhythm. He pondered this for a moment, for even though his mind's constant anxiety and his stomach's rolling, he couldn't help but feel that, wherever Nox was, she was alive.

Lukas shook his fears, rose from the bed and walked toward the window. He placed his hand upon the cold glass, feeling through it the outside chill.

What should I do?

She was out there, somewhere, in the clutches of those mysterious men. Yet here he was, about to go to a show.

What a terrible friend I am.

The thought cut through his mind like a razor.

"Even the Aeons can't help me..." he said to himself as he pressed his forehead to the glass. "That sure is reassuring..."

Then, the thought hit him. He remembered.

"Zurriel!" he exclaimed in sudden epiphany. Strange man had aided him in Zerlina with his mysterious magic. Perhaps he could do so again? Lukas was sure the peculiar Storyteller could help him. He laughed at his sudden idea, and his spirits lifted.

Blake slipped into a summer dress, white with a large blue lotus flower painted on the front. It was cute, she had to admit, and with her yellow cardigan, she felt beautiful as swayed in front of the mirror, trying to see her front-side as well as her backside. She combed her short, white hair. However, as merry as she was *supposed* to be, she couldn't shake a tensity from her shoulders.

"Eldric..." she said as she daydreamed blankly into the mirror.

What could be so pressing that the Master Inquisitor himself would be in such a hurry to address? Why would he be so sudden on the phone? It was unlike him, she thought. Master Eldric was usually so nonchalant. She shook her head. Whatever it was, she decided, they'd be ready.

"Hey!" a muffled voice shouted from the door. Blake calmly walked to it and opened it. There stood Cilli, dressed in a pink, flowery dress.

"We're both wearing flowers!" she exclaimed with a hug. "You ready to go?"

"Y-yeah." Blake said awkwardly.

Cilli smiled and took Blake by the hand, surprising the Inquisitor, and pulled her down the hall.

The lobby was fairly empty as dusk had quickly turned to night. Blake descended the stairs with Cilli to see Ralf and Lukas waiting at the bottom and Ralf impatiently pacing back and forth.

"You women ready yet?" he said in a mix of jeer and irritation.

"As we'll ever be!" Cilli replied, dismissing his sour attitude.

Ralf smiled and began to walk toward the door.

"You're coming too, right Lukas?"

"Yeah! I'm excited to see it!"

Cilli smiled cleverly at Blake; Blake rolled her eyes.

"Lukas knows the guy, too! How crazy is that?" Cilli said in a bombastic voice.

"He does?" Blake turned her head to Lukas curiously.

"Yeah!" Lukas laughed. "I met him in Zerlina. I got lost in the city and he helped me find my way."

"He's really weird, but likable," Cilli added.

"Are you coming?" Ralf asked impatiently from a distance, "We need to get our seats."

Cilli turned to Blake. "Someone's cranky," she laughed. "But don't worry. We have reservations."

The venue was packed. Lukas and his party began to filter in with what felt like was the entire city. He looked around the giant amphitheater, the size of which astounded him. Two stories tall, the room was filled with tables for the audience to sit and eat while they enjoyed the show.

"We're right up front!" Cilli smiled as she took Blake's hand to guide her through the crowd.

And Lukas found that she was right. The four of them were seated just at the foot of the stage.

"All this, just for him?" Lukas added as they took their seats.

"Nah," Ralf laughed, "He's just the opening act." The large man waved to a waiter. "I'll take an ale!"

It was not much longer until a lanky man took the stage.

"Please take your seats, everyone. Today, we have a very unique guest. A man who knows no home, yet knows each well— a gatherer of stories and legends far and wide—the one known as Zurriel!"

As the audience roared, Zurriel took the stage, his coat of silver fur glistening under the stage lights. Lukas observed him. He had only met the man twice, yet he felt as if he had known him all along. Something about this man made him feel familiar, but the knight could never pinpoint just what it was.

The room quieted, and the lights were silenced, as well.

"My beautiful audience!" Zurriel exclaimed as he held out his hands. "Today, I shall recite a poem lost to time!"

Lukas could feel excitement bubbling in his heart. Since he left the monastery, he had experienced many things. He had learned combat, felt the rush of peril, and ever mastered small measures of magic.

But never had he experienced this...

Never had he been to a *show!*

Zurriel raised a finger and cleared his throat.

"Tonight, I will tell you the story of *Vespira the Blessed One!*"

The audience shuffled, then silence filled the room. All eyes locked upon the enigma before them. Zurriel stood, as if a lucid dream—

A sage.

A wise man.

An esoteric fool.

He began.
The Cosmic Tree, Yggdrasil, has always been...
Alas it willed, and it bore fruit.
The fruit grew strong,
And from it, a being was born!

Even this being himself
Did not know for sure
If he came from the tree...

But. It made sense.

He is known by many names,
Spoken by many peoples
Across the worlds so vast:

Prime mover...
Precursor...
Enchanter...
Starbreather...

He was born,
The Great God...
One.

Lukas looked around the room. Even in the darkness, he could see an entranced crowd, and, he must admit, he too was drawn to the story. He had heard many tales as he grew up in the Zerlina Monastery. He knew some stories more than others, but he had also concluded that his knowledge was not comprehensive.

Yet, still...he couldn't help shake a familiarity in Zurriel's telling. A strange pull. Was it the man's voice? The story itself?

He didn't know, so he shrugged the feeling off and listened to the storyteller continue.

For some reason,
One decided to create
By calling upon the roots
Of the tree.

First, came the Angels!
They lived in peace momentarily...
But, soon,
They cried out...

'Give us dominions
Over the universe!
Give us the powers
Of the Aeons,
So that we will be mighty!'

And so the Starbreather
Felt compassion
For his creation
And enchanted
Their blood.

"This!" Zurriel broke character. "This is how the Angels became blessed with the powers of old!"

He cleared his throat.

Next, the Starbreather
Called upon the tree
And created beasts:
Creatures of land, air
And sea.

They, too lived peacefully,
But soon cried out:

'Give us beauty
As the Angels,
That we will not
Be grotesque!'

One felt compassion again
And granted them
The forms of men...

"These!" he said. "These are the Beastfolk!"

A third time
The Prime Mover
Called upon the
Cosmic tree, and
Formed the Darklings.

And once again...
There was peace, until
They, too, cried out:

'Unlock our minds!
Give to us the secrets
Of life itself!'

Begrudgingly, One
Had compassion once more.
He touched their brains,
And their third eyes opened wide!

"Projection!" he exclaimed.

And, at last,

The Creator decided
To make one last time...

These
Were the humans.

They were frail and weak,
And they, too, demanded power...

This, however,
Deeply saddened One.

In agony, he cried out:

'My creations only want power!!"

Disgusted, the Starbreather
Sat alone in his garden
And was immensely grieved...

Zurriel stopped. The crowd stopped as well. Lukas looked at his table, and then back at the stage. Zurriel had shifted his eyes from the crowd.

Lukas suddenly felt a chill; he noticed that the sage staring directly at *him*.

"But," he continued. "That is merely where *our* story begins."

In a crooked world,
Only a young girl,
A sickly human,
Dared enter the garden...

Her name,
Was Vespira.

Joyfully,

She wept at
One's feet and cried:

'Thank you for giving me life!'

The Starbreather was moved
At the sight of the
Young girl's humility
And took her hand.

And thus he spoke to her:
'I will give you the greatest gift of all...'

'I will breathe the stars into your veins!'

Lukas paused for a moment, his mind harkening back to Zerlina. It was a vague memory at this point, but he faintly remembered the word spoken to him by Eldric...the word *"Starborn."*

"And thus," Zurriel began, "Vespira became the first to wield the legendary *Starblood.* Is the story true? Is there really such a thing in the world? Do, perhaps, they walk among us? That, my good people, is for *you* to decide." Zurriel bowed his head. "Thank you!"

Suddenly, the audience went into ecstatic uproar, clapping and cheering as Zurriel bowed and bowed again. He walked off of the stage, the people cheering and waving as the host took the stage again.

"My good people," the host exclaimed, "Are you prepared for our next event?"

The people roared once more.

"Then take your seats!"

Lukas sat, thinking as he held his chest.

Starborn, huh?

"My good man," a familiar voice snapped him out of his daydream. Lukas looked up to see Zurriel standing by him. "May

I take a seat?"

"Of course!" Lukas said as he moved over to make room.

Zurriel sat and turned to Lukas. "How did you like the performance?" he laughed.

"It was awesome!" Lukas lit up. "How did you know it so well?"

Zurriel smiled. "I'm a storyteller. I devote my life to histories and myths and legends. They interest me." He tilted his head curiously. "What brings you so far from Zerlina?"

"I'm looking for a friend!" Lukas was glad the storyteller asked. "I was wondering if you could help me find her!"

"A friend?" he laughed. "I commend your nobility." He sighed sadly. "But I will be unable to accompany you. You see, I will be leaving tonight. I have three more shows to attend over the next three days. The life of a storyteller is a hard one." He patted Lukas on the back, "But, may I have the honor of eating with you?"

Lukas' face lit up once again. To have the life of the party eat with him was a great honor.

"Absolutely," Cilli answered for Lukas, shoving the bread in his direction.

Lukas ate that night, and, for the first time since his departure from Zerlina, he felt happy.

The night air was chilly as the Airship *Orca* descended upon the aerodock in Avelle's Brook. Eldric stood in the cockpit, watching as the captain landed.

"It's a grim sight for such a lavish town, eh, Eldric?" the captain commented.

"Indeed it is," Eldric replied, "but the Butcher keeps the city safe, I assume."

"We will be landing in about ten minutes," the captain mentioned as Eldric walked out to find Snow on guard at the door.

"Master Inquisitor," she said as she followed him. "I await your orders."

"Good." Eldric looked out the window. Below, the town was lit with blue and yellow etherlamps. He couldn't help but notice just how peaceful it seemed. "This city is about to get much louder."

XXVI

Day Two

Damasko's skin stung where the clasps had been placed, the scars of blackened flesh exuding a rancid smell. He sat on the ground, groaning as he writhed. The room was dark and the air stale. There were no windows or vents. There was only a faintly dim light bulb to illuminate the confinement of the cell.

How did he get here, he thought faintly as he lingered upon the fringe of lunacy. He raised his singed arms and stared at his hands. *That wretched boy with the sword*, he thought. It was that kid that was his undoing, that was for sure, but now what...?

His thoughts trailed off as a black cloud filled the room. In it, he could make out the vague shadow of a tall, muscular man.

"Damasko..." the voice called.

He knew that voice better than any other he was aware of, and he knew what it meant.

"Agnon," he whimpered as he clenched his teeth from the pain.

"Why have you betrayed me, Damasko?"

"Betrayed?" Damasko said, wide-eyed. He could feel his heart begin to race. Here he was, trapped with this large, violent man. "How have I—"

His words ceased quickly as the dark sorcerer grabbed him by the throat and lifted him from the ground.

"You have failed your client," the grim man whispered in his low, growling voice. "And by failing the client, you have thus failed my Master."

"I..." the slim prisoner choked out the word.'

211

"It is too late." Agnon began as he held the damaged Damasko in the air. "You have deprived yourself of your usefulness."

"Wait—"

Suddenly, Agnon slammed Damasko's head repeatedly against the stone wall, creating sickening crunching sounds. Damasko seized for a moment, then went limp. The taciturn Darkling dropped the prisoner to the ground, then whispered under his breath and waved his hands in the air. The air became thin, and the black cloud appeared once more. The silent man stepped into it and was gone.

The morning sun softly broke the horizon, rendering the Prison Tower an unholy obelisk amid the shadowy town below. Eldric sat in his cabin, watching eagerly as the Airship *Orca* landed within the aerodock of Avelle's Brook.

Outside, Blake waited with equal anticipation as the fumes from the giant vessel filled the hangar. Gears clanked and spun as the metallic door descended from the hull. All around, travelers and merchants had stopped to watch the old Master Inquisitor limp down the ramp, followed by Snow, and surrounded by soldiers.

"Master Inquisitor," Blake bowed as she approached.

"Civilian clothes, I see." Eldric laughed as he dropped some tobacco into his pipe, "Backpack included?"

"No," Blake said, looking down at her floral dress. "I don't want to joke. Why are you here so quickly? What is happening?"

"No, no." Eldric waved his hand dismissively. "First things first. Where is this Stone you mentioned?"

Blake sighed, reached for her backpack and handed it to a soldier.

"Such a mystery." Eldric smiled with a nod to the carrier. "Tell me about it."

"Well," Blake began, "I don't really—uh—know anything about it. It was being used to power a giant machine that could somehow control the weather." She paused. "And, according to Captain Maro, it has the ability to negate magic, sort of like

Necronite, but..."

"Exciting." Eldric narrowed his eyes as he stroked his wispy beard. "So strange..."

"Now." Blake shook her head impatiently, "Why are you here so quickly? What is happening?"

Eldric took a puff of his pipe and silently limped past her.

"Blake," he said, "Where are you staying? Where is Lukas?"

"An inn," she replied, raising an eyebrow, "and...he's there. Why? What's happen—"

"They are coming." Eldric cut her off.

Blake stopped. There was no need to continue.

She knew who *they* were.

Lukas awoke late that morning, not really to his surprise. He rose from his bed, washed in the washroom, then put on his clothes.

The night before danced in his mind. The story of the *Starborn*, and the mysterious Storyteller himself still caused him to smile. His smile, however, vanished as he began to think of the old Storyteller's disagreement to help him find Nox. But, he knew, as Blake had told him on their way to the show, Eldric would be arriving today. He knew *that* could possibly mean getting one step closer to finding her. Blake had informed him to rest up and stay at the hotel until she returned.

After getting dressed, Lukas exited his room, slight anxiety filling his mind at the thought of the Master Inquisitor's arrival. He made certain he had his room key on his person, then began to walk down the hall. Once more, he admired the paintings and flowers that decorated the corridor. The flowers enticed him, their vibrant blossoms alive in bright yellows and refreshing reds. Lukas observed them for a moment, then continued his short walk to the end of the hall and down the stairs.

He reached the lobby to find Cilli sitting at the desk, inspecting her fingernails out of boredom, which were painted a light blue. Lukas looked around the lobby, simply because he had not done so before. The wide, open room had many decorative flowers along its walls as well. A painting of distant mountains veiled in indigo was the centerpiece upon the wall, placed so that any who entered the doors could see it hanging majestically. But it was the flowers that caught his eye. They were strange and alien looking. Still true that they looked like red and yellow flowers, but Lukas couldn't place his finger on what was so off about their appearance. He walked closer, inspecting their otherworldly texture.

"They're fake, you know," Cilli said from behind him, spooking him.

"Fake?"

"Yeah, you know, not real?"

Lukas smiled, slightly laughing at his naivety. He'd never seen, nor even considered that someone would make a fake flower.

"You really were missing a lot, being trapped in that monastery and all," Cilli giggled.

"I guess so..." Lukas blushed, "I realize that more and more every day. How did you know about the monastery?"

"Blake told me. Girls talk, don't you know?"

Lukas smiled again, honestly happier that Blake had a friend than anything else.

"It's okay though." She smiled back. "You'll learn one day."

"Lukas!" Lukas recognized Eldric's voice as the front doors opened, revealing himself, along with Blake and Snow.

"Eldric!" Lukas walked quickly to the old Inquisitor to greet him.

"Well met!" The careless Eldric waved his hand.

"Who's the old guy?" Cilli said flatly.

Blake suddenly turned red with embarrassment at the blatant disrespect.

"He's the Master of the Inquisition," she snapped, "second to only the Archbishop."

Cilli suddenly matched Blake's embarrassment and bowed frantically.

"My apologies, Your Holiness!"

Eldric laughed, amused by the secretary's sudden humility. "No harm done. Now," he said, "I need a room."

Blake looked at Cilli expectantly. The receptionist looked back. "Right this way, sir!"

Cilli turned. The others followed, and soon the secretary caught on to the fact that the Master Inquisitor had a limping pace, and so she slowed to accommodate the honored man's speed. As they approached the stairs, Snow held the old man's free hand, helping him stabilize himself during the upward climb. They slowly ascended, then, once reaching the second floor, Cilli guided them to the end of the long hallway.

"This is one of the suites," she said. "I'm sure it will be good enough for your stay, your Holiness."

"Thank you, young lady." He smiled. "And call me Eldric. The whole 'Holiness' business was never right with me."

Cilli stared at him a moment, speechless. The familiar attitude of someone of such high status was unheard of in her mind.

"Y-yes," she said, "Eldric. Enjoy your stay."

"Thank you, young lady," he chuckled, "And your name?"

Cilli looked at him for a moment, dazed.

"Cilli!"

"It's good to make your acquaintance, Cilli."

Cilli thanked him and scurried away.

The suite was quaint and homey, with gray sofas surrounding a coffee table made of dark wood. The kitchen was placed beside the door to the balcony, in which one could see the fabulous market district of the town. The four entered, Eldric first, then they each sat upon the furniture in the living room area. Once they were all seated, Blake and Lukas turned their eyes expectantly to the Master Inquisitor.

"Now," the old man began, "Blake, I assume you've been quite curious as to my cryptic nature as of yesterday." He sat up and leaned on his cedar cane, "Allow me to tell you the situation in full."

Blake and Lukas nodded, fully captivated by the unusual grimness in the normally carefree Inquisitor's tone.

"I received a letter. One that I believe indicates the ones who attacked the monastery in Zerlina will also attack Avelle's Brook."

"But why?" Blake said, shocked.

"My intelligence was given to me by an anonymous letter, addressed to me, that I believe was sent by the assailants." He leaned back. "I believe they're after a man by the name of 'Valter Rivyra.' He is a man of great danger. In fact, he was the Master Inquisitor before I was, imprisoned after an assassination attempt on Archbishop Marven's life. Also, he has the name 'Legion,' because his Word of Heart allows him to mask himself and recreate his likeness."

"What does that have to do with Avelle's Brook?" Blake asked sincerely.

"Valter Rivyra," Eldric paused, "is currently held under apex security in the prison here in Avelle's Brook."

Blake was silent for a moment. Lukas watched her face. There was no fear in her eyes; only the same, cold blue.

"What do we need to do?" she finally said.

"We've received some backup from the King of Aestriana. Prince Reethkilt and the Red Ravens will be arriving immediately." He yawned. "For now, stay here. We can use the inn as a home base."

Blake nodded as she stood. Lukas followed her lead.

"I will bring the prince here," Eldric said as he limped past them. "Consider my words while I am gone."

The old man limped to the door, followed by the silent Snow, opened it, then left.

Blake turned to Lukas.

"What do you think?"

Lukas looked her in the eyes. She'd never seen his eyes that way. They were lit, like the bright vigils of a torch. She knew already what he would say.

"This time," he said, "I'm not going to run."

Prince Alexander Clement zel Reethkilt walked down the landing ramp of the Airship *Wyndrake*. It had been some time since he had visited Avelle's Brook, and, now that he looked around, he decided that not much had changed.

Soldiers filed out of the ship, passing by him and out into the aerodock.

"Prince!" Eldric said as he slowly approached.

"Master Inquisitor," Clement replied, stepping forward to meet the old man. "Snow."

"Hello, Commander." Snow smiled with a nod.

"So." He turned back to Eldric. "What is this about an attack on the city?"

"I do not know if it is the city they are after," the old sage replied, but *who* is in the city."

Prince Reethkilt raised an eyebrow.

"I believe they're after a man—former Master Inquisitor Valter Rivyra."

"I see..." the commander replied. "Then we need to..." He trailed off.

Eldric took a puff of his pipe and blew out a plume of smoke.

"We need to see the Butcher."

Valter Rivyra sat in his cell and stared blankly at the windowless, concrete walls. The vague light of the lightbulb hung by single worn cable flickered above his head. He hated that lightbulb. Its faint light hurt his eyes. He wondered, as he did every second, how he got into this. He knew, however, how he got into it; he knew very well how he'd ended up here. It was no secret to him. Attempted murder was a harsh crime—but attempting to assassinate the *Archbishop* was unforgivable. But Marven had it coming. He shouldn't have become the Archbishop, Valter thought. No, Valter should've ascended to that power. But Marven was a crowd favorite, so he usurped it from poor Valter.

I was only taking what was rightfully *mine!*

The air suddenly thinned as a black cloud formed in the room, blocking out the lights. The imprisoned mage coughed as he inhaled the thick smoke, then looked up to see a large, dark man before him.

"Valter Rivyra," the grim man said as he overshadowed the short Valter, "I have come to bring you atonement." The large Agnon reached out his hand. "If you take my offer, you will win your freedom. If not, you will continue to rot in this place until your death."

"Well," the prisoner said with a crooked smile, "who are you? Where will you take old Valter?"

Agnon was silent, then moved his hand. At his command, the black cloud filled the room.

"My Master can give you the head of Ferrenvaal," Agnon said finally.

Valter laughed as he stood up. "Then, by all means, lead the way!"

Agnon reached into his black cloak and pulled out a piece of parchment, laying it on the bench in which Valter once sat. He turned at once to the cloud.

"Come," he commanded as he disappeared into the black mist.

Uneasily, Valter stared at the cloud for a moment, then decided that it was better than the prison. He entered it, the cloud dissipated, and they were gone.

The entrance to the Prison Tower was heavily guarded, yet served no issue for the passage of such esteemed men as Eldric and Prince Reethkilt. Upon their arrival, the guards saluted and bowed, welcoming the two men to their domain. Upon entering, the Butcher was waiting to greet them with welcoming eyes.

"Master Inquisitor! Young prince!" he said as he bowed, "I have been expecting you two."

"As we have you," Eldric laughed.

"I'm sure you've come to investigate?"

"Indeed we have."

The warden paused for a moment. "I assume you wish to go to the cell housing Legion?"

"We do." Eldric said, "I want to replace him, as to throw off our...guests."

Clement smiled slightly at the cunning of the old Inquisitor.

"Nothing gets by you, does it, Eldric?" the Butcher laughed, "I see you're just as witty as ever."

Eldric laughed. "I try."

The Butcher nodded to two of the guards.

"Let us go give our man in question a little visit, shall we?"

Eldric nudged Clement at the Butcher's jolliness, then he, Snow, and the prince followed.

The prison was large as they walked the stairs, which seemingly ascended to the heavens.

"I apologize for the upward trek," the Butcher said to Eldric, hearing his heavy breaths. "The Prison Tower extends high into the sky. It was built hundreds of years ago, and is much taller than Mhyrmr. It's actually the tallest in Aestriana, and, maybe, all of Lythia."

"No problem," Eldric said in slightly heavier breaths. "I may be old, but I can do this."

Their climb up the large monolith was short lived for Clement, yet a bit longer for the old Eldric.

"We keep Valter on the eighth floor, in the back," the Butcher said almost jeeringly, "It's a quaint little home. No windows, just concrete walls and floors. Oh, and a lavish single lightbulb dangling from a chord at the top." He laughed, "Just short enough so that he can't hang himself."

The hall was dark, with soldiers standing every few feet, blades drawn and spears ready. The door to Valter's cell was a thick, windowless, steel door with several locks and bolts. the Butcher motioned forward to the soldiers around him. They nodded, then walked to the door, working their way with the locks and bolts, the sounds of such echoed down the hallway. The guards drew their swords as the door swung open.

Then, a chilling wave washed over them.

The room was empty.

"What?!" the Butcher exclaimed in outright rage. Eldric's eyes widened. Clement stared at the empty cell in amazement.

"But how?!" Clement's voice carried down the hallway.

"It's them," Eldric said calmly, "It's the same that happened to Iago. Doors were locked, yet he simply disappeared." The Inquisitor walked into the cell.

"Gone," the prince said as he looked up at the dim light bulb swaying back and forth, "but, from the swaying of the light, he hasn't been gone long."

"You're right, Commander," Snow said as she held up the piece of parchment that was laying on the bench.

"And it seems he—or someone else—left us with a few words," Eldric said as his knight handed him the paper.

His eyes widened in sudden alarm.

It read simply: *ZERO*.

XXVII

Zer0

Blake sat on her bed, twiddling her thumbs frantically as she thought about the Master Inquisitor's brief words. She looked up from her hands and turned her sight to the creeping dusk outside of her window. The nearly set sun cast a yellow veil along the horizon, chased away by the dark blue waves of night. What could that silly old man mean by "consider" his words. What was there to consider? She didn't care for consideration; she wanted action.

Down the hall, Lukas paced back and forth along the lavish green rug, scraping his feet as he walked anxiously, Eldric's words repeating in his head. What did Eldric know that Lukas didn't? If it really were the men that attacked Zerlina, then this could be his *only* chance at perhaps finding out where Nox was. The ideas swirled in his head. But, the thought came to him as he looked out the window at the now pervasive night, even if he were to come in contact with Iago or the large man that took her, what would he do? He couldn't summon his Word of Heart. He knew his defeat of Damasko was sheer luck; he was more than aware of that. Lukas pressed his head against the glass, discouraged.

Suddenly, a boisterous blast sounded from outside. Lukas jumped for a moment, surprised, then looked out the window. He could see it, though the smoke was faintly lit by the street lights; a building had just exploded.

Lukas sped to the door and opened it only to find Blake outside of her room. For a moment, they looked at each other, then she nodded and they bolted down the hall.

Two dark, hooded figures slipped unnoticed through the crowded streets, which were filled with the distracted citizens of Avelle's Brook. Beneath his hood, Iago walked quietly behind the Master as they moved down the back alleys to a cramped area.

"Agnon," the Master commanded into the air. Suddenly, the small area filled with a black mist. The mysterious Agnon appeared alongside another man. "You have succeeded, I assume," the Master laughed, his face darkened by his heavy hood.

"Valter stands among us," Agnon said as he took a knee, bowing before his leader.

"Valter," the Master said in a commanding voice. For a moment, Iago felt the power in the man's tone, seeming to almost shake his soul.

Who was this man? Iago had wondered since he had been released. This man with such power that his mere words could pierce the very essence of his being.

"Who are you? Why did you free me?" Valter began to question.

"Silence!" the hooded man yelled. Valter stood, terrified by the man's presence. The Master paused, then spoke. "You have a part to play in this story."

He turned away.

"Now," the Master said as he began to walk forward, motioning the others to follow, "we will begin."

The three men followed the Master as he stepped onto the streets of the filled market district and stopped.

Iago watched as the man extended his hands in the direction of a large building. People passed by, keeping the men close together. Iago felt as if the air were being sucked from his lungs as his Master closed his eyes and began to whisper, his hood ruffling underneath the lightened pressure. The people around him took alarm to the suffocating air, turning to face the wizard, staring at him in expectant horror.

"Perish, Avelle's Brook!" he exclaimed as an emerald blast exploded from his hands.

The sound of the explosion rang throughout the city, even through the thick stone of the Tower in which Eldric resided. The Master Inquisitor turned quickly to the Prince, who turned to the Butcher. The warden returned a quizzical glance when a soldier came running down the hall toward them.

"Warden!" he exclaimed in a panting frenzy. "There's been an attack on the market district!"

Suddenly, another deafening blast shook the ground.

"Such power," Eldric said, startled.

Without a word, the silent prince shot down the hall. The Butcher turned to follow. Snow turned to Eldric. "Master Inquisitor," she said in her unbreakable composure, "I have to get you out of here if the blasts are getting closer to the Tower."

Eldric nodded, then took her hand.

Blake and Lukas hurried through the streets as quickly as they could, making their way toward the ever-moving explosions. Lukas led the way, his sheer determination to confront the mysterious assailants overpowering his creeping fears. He would be ready this time; he *had* to be ready!

Blake kept up with the speedy knight to the best of her ability, trying with all her might not to lose him in the maelstrom of fleeing citizens. Who were these attackers? She'd not had as many run-ins with them as Lukas. The thoughts and questions coursed through her mind, racing with her panting breaths. Where was Eldric? She looked around her at the soldiers trying desperately to make sense of the flood of people frantically evacuating. She looked forward, then she felt her heart drop.

She'd lost sight of Lukas.

Iago sat upon a toppled wall as he waited for the soldiers to come find him and spring into action. He sighed as the soldiers around him drew their blades.

"We really gonna do this?" he groaned as he called out his Word of Heart. Suddenly, phantom swords materialized at the throats of the soldiers. He could see the fear in their eyes as they all turned to run away, horrified at how easily he could have blotted them out.

"Lame," he said to himself as he stood and began to walk across the rubble and toward the Tower.

"Iago!" a voice yelled from behind him. Iago turned to see a panting Lukas.

"Well, well," the Elven mage laughed, "isn't this a coincidence?"

"Where is Nox!" Lukas yelled furiously. "Tell me!"

"You don't think it's really *that* easy, do you?" Iago scoffed, "Besides, I want a *show* first!"

Suddenly, ten translucent blades formed around the Elf, dancing in the wind.

Lukas stood straight in front of Iago, and the longer he stared into the other's eyes, the more the reality of danger became apparent. Lukas felt his legs grow weak.

But, this time was different; this time *must* be different. Lukas knew he'd grown since the attack on Zerlina; this time, there was no running.

"Still a scaredy-cat, it seems," the tall Iago taunted with a smile, "but I won't let you live this time."

Lukas could see the sincerity in Iago's eyes.

"I won't die!" Lukas yelled back. "Tell me where Nox is!"

"I already said it's not that easy, kid?" Iago laughed as he pointed his finger at the Knight. "Get real!"

The ten blades shot from their orbit, one by one, spiraling forward. Lukas held out the Sword Durandal in front of him. In that moment, a split second that seemed an eternity.

There was no one to save him this time; Blake or Snow weren't here to bail him out.

The Heart is never silent.

Lukas closed his eyes and took a sharp breath.

Iago watched in horror. Truly, he wasn't seeing what he thought he was seeing?

What was this? As the orphan held out the mysterious blade,

white flames engulfed his body.

Lukas felt a spark run through his being, a certain lighting ran through his veins.

All went silent but a single, vehement voice.

My heart's name...

Thunder roared through his chest, like the heat of the sun itself.

LUCYN REJIIS!

Instantly, a bright blast of white light shot from his body and ascended into the sky like a pillar. Iago held his eyes from the blinding light as a forceful gale collided with his body, almost toppling him.

The wind died down, and Iago rubbed his eyes and blinked rapidly, trying desperately to refocus. He looked back at his opponent.

"The sword..." he trailed off for a moment, then exclaimed, "turned green?!"

Lukas felt his clothes ruffling under his white aura. Truly, he'd seen, and even felt, the power of magic as an onlooker, but now, as he stood, he felt it; he felt the power coursing through him. In this moment, he felt the power of the Heart of Hearts. Lukas pointed the Sword Durandal forward.

It was true. The once silver blade had turned an emerald green.

Blake hopelessly forced herself from the torrent of the fleeing townspeople, convinced she'd never find Lukas at this point. Moving upstream through the panic was tiring enough, and not knowing where her partner was or what even was happening, didn't do anything to relieve the situation. *Where is he?* The thought came quickly, mixed with her rushing fear.

Where?

At that moment, a bright white light shot into the sky. She could see it in the distance, and she knew; she knew that whatever that light was, Lukas wasn't far behind.

Iago and Lukas stood, deadlocked, staring into the other's eyes.

"So," Iago said as a gray aura surrounded him, "You've got a special sword now? Big deal!" his face turned intense, *"I've got a thousand!"*

Lukas beheld the Elf's power as hundreds of phantom swords filled the air around them, creating a dome of razor-sharp edges, all pointed at the orphan. Lukas could feel his breath leaving his lungs; the lightness of the air felt as if he were in a vacuum. But, what now? He had summoned his Word of Heart, but how would he use it, especially against the thousand swords pointed directly at him.

But his opponent would give him no time to think.

At Iago's beckon, the blades descended, spiraling toward the knight.

I'll just know, *right?*

In a wild abandon, Lukas swung the green blade, and, to his surprise, a bright shockwave of light spit from Durandal's edge, slicing through the air, speeding toward the Elf.

"Idiot!" Iago said as he pointed his finger fiercely at the quickly approaching slice.

The bright gray blades obeyed and speedily clustered together in front of their owner. Lukas' shockwave slammed into them, and shattered both itself and the phantasms.

"You really don't learn, do you!?" Iago laughed as he pointed to the ground.

In rapid succession, the translucent blades howled as they rained downward toward their target.

*Was this it? t*he orphan thought.

Is this the end?

*No! h*e shrieked. *I REFUSE!*

Suddenly, Lukas felt as if his heart burst within his chest. With an acute gasp, the orphan dropped to his knees as an immense energy exploded from his body.

Iago staggered as the blast slammed into him like a stone wall. He opened his eyes and froze. Before him his army of blades misted downward in bright gray shards, dispersing in small pops as they hit the ground.

"You..." He coughed blood, falling to his knees, "My swords?

You destroyed——? You destroyed them all?!"

Lukas himself couldn't believe what had actually happened. His aura was gone, and Durandal returned to silver. He approached Iago, pointing the blade at the Elf's throat.

Iago looked up at him with remorseful eyes.

"Heart of Hearts," the Elf sighed, "I have no reason left to live. Just kill me already."

"No." Lukas sheathed the sword Durandal.

Iago let out a grieving groan. "Why not?! Why must you mock me further?"

"Shut up!" Lukas fumed. "I won't kill you!"

"Why?"

"Because." Lukas turned and looked at his beaten opponent. "I heard your heart. It was just for a split second, and..." Lukas paused. "You're not a bad man, Iago."

Iago looked into the other's eyes. They were pure, full of light. They were so unlike his own. For a moment, he envied them, but he also knew that they were not the eyes of a killer.

"You two really are the same..."

Lukas looked at him quizzically. "What?"

"You really are a virtuous fool, Heart of Hearts."

"Lukas!" Blake exclaimed as approached frantically. "I found you! What happened?" She looked to see Iago.

Lukas smiled. "It's a long story."

Suddenly, translucent blades appeared at their throats.

"Iago!" Lukas said in panicked surprise.

"Never look away from an opponent, Heart of Hearts," he laughed. "That's rule number one!"

Lukas felt the cold air from the sword at his throat.

Suddenly, a black cloud filled the air, and the large, dark Agnon stepped out of it.

"Iago," he began, "it seems you've won."

"I guess so."

"You've done well, Iago," another voice laughed.

"Master," Agnon said.

Lukas turned to see whom the large Darkling was addressing.

Suddenly, a frigid shiver coursed up his spine. Lukas knew the man who stood before him was the orchestrator of all of this madness.

The man who stood before him was Zurriel.

XXVIII

Leaving Avelle's Brook

"Z-z..." Lukas' words came as a mumbling whimper as he looked at the storyteller in horror. "Zurriel...?"

"Finally," Zurriel's wolf-like eyes seemed to peer into the young man's soul, "we meet in honesty, Heart of Hearts."

"But, you're..." Lukas felt his legs grow weak. "You're a Storyteller!"

"Oh, you liked my little disguise?" the Master laughed. "I've played it for so long now that I've grown rather adept at acting it out."

"You!" Blake screamed as she stood, also frozen by the once friendly man.

"Ah, and you," Zurriel's cloak blew in the breeze, "Snowbird, right?"

"Are you going to kill us?" Blake snapped back as she rushed to Lukas' side.

Lukas shook his head and pointed Sword Durandal at Zurriel. "Where is Nox!?" he cried vehemently.

"Not so fast, Lukas," the man said he held his hands out theatrically. "We've just only made introductions!"

Lukas could feel the cold air of Iago's blade as his neck.

This was it, he thought. Caught, like a mouse in a trap.

"What did you do to her?!" Lukas raged.

"Nothing yet, but her usefulness will expire quite soon." Zurriel turned around and waved his hands. "Yours, however, expired some time ago."

Blake clenched her jaw, knowing that nothing could be done with the spirit sword at her neck.

"Agnon!" the Master said as he walked away.

"Yes, Master." the large Abdian held up his hand.

A black aura suddenly encircled him, his black robe flowing as if in a breeze.

Nuun Graviikka.

Suddenly, a black cloud enveloped Lukas and Blake, their screams filling the air, then, in a split second, they went silent. The cloud dispersed, and the two were gone.

Zurriel walked on; his men followed.

"Goodbye, Heart of Hearts..."

Snow carried Eldric on her back as they rushed toward the location where the pillar of light had been, the other two at her heels. The lithe half-Elf had no trouble carrying the light old man, and they had both determined this to be the best way to reach their destination, especially for the limping Inquisitor. Prince Reethkilt carried himself immediately behind the knight, his broadsword drawn. The older Butcher struggled somewhat to keep up, but the pumping of adrenaline through his body kept him from realizing his body's limits.

"What do you think it was?" Snow yelled back to Eldric through panting breaths.

"Only one thing," Eldric replied, "It happened once before in Zerlina."

"You don't think?" the prince breathlessly asked the Inquisitor.

"Of course I do."

"I agree," the Warden spoke. "Light like that can only can only mean one thing..."

Eldric turned his head forward. "The awakening of the Heart of Hearts."

The alleyways were empty mainly with most people evacuated. Snow simply led the pack out of her acute senses, quickly determining the routes as they sprinted down the alleyways then into a destroyed clearing. In front of them stood Valter and three other men.

"Valter Rivyra!" the Butcher exclaimed as they approached.

"The old Butcher," Valter laughed as he saw the Warden approach. "It seems we're on even terms now."

Zurriel stepped forward.

"So," he laughed as he held his arms open, "This must be the famed Warden of the Sky Prison Tower, and" he paused, "the Master Inquisitor? You actually came!"

"What have you done with the Heart of Hearts?" Eldric thundered irately.

"Oh." Zurriel cocked his head and smiled. "Lukas and his little Inquisitor friend won't be coming back from where Agnon sent them."

Sudden despair cast over the Master Inquisitor's face.

"You bastard!" the Warden erupted as he drew his blade.

"Now, now, Warden," Zurriel taunted. "Is there really the need to jump straight into violence? We've only just met." He smiled a cavalier smirk. "I'm sure we can be civil and get to know each other first!"

"I want no conversation with criminals!" the Butcher said as he rushed toward Zurriel, his blade brandished high.

"As you wish," Zurriel sighed as the Warden rapidly approached him.

With a great battle cry, the Butcher thrust his blade directly into Zurriel's abdomen.

A moment passed, and the Butcher came to his senses. Surely, he thought, he had struck his opponent. Surely! He looked forward. He *had* struck him. Actually, he had pierced him through! The Butcher froze. From his blade, ripples resonated from where he'd thrust, as if he had disrupted water.

Zurriel burst into a manic laugh.

"Tell me, Butcher." He grabbed the Warden by the throat and lifted him. The Butcher watched in fear as the place he'd penetrated returned to normal. Untouched. "What is the one thing that binds all mortal men?"

"What are you?" the Butcher gasped under the fierce grip of the wolfish sorcerer.

"The question is rather rhetorical," Zurriel laughed. "You see, all things cling desperately to life, yet realize not that their ambitions are naught. Your thoughts, dreams, loves...they must all come to an end. Such is the way of the world."

The Butcher grabbed Zurriel's hand, desperately trying to free himself. He pulled, but Zurriel's grip was absolute.

Eldric, Snow, and Prince Reethkilt watched in horror as the smoke cleared. Surprise took them, and their stomachs turned. Zurriel still held his grip on the struggling Butcher, hanging him above the ground.

"You see, Warden," Zurriel's demeanor had quickly turned grim, his once taunting face now had become dark visage, stricken with doom. "The one thing that binds all mortal men is the *fear of death itself.*"

He held his other hand over the Warden's red face and called into the air. A green aura surrounded him; his cloak swayed under a fierce gale.

The onlookers grabbed their throats at the extreme thinness of the air. Eldric turned to Snow, who met his gaze. Many times before, they had felt the thinning of the air as an Inquisitor called upon a Word of Heart, but never to this degree.

Nyhilo Zurriel.

They watched as green flames flickered at the tips of his fingers. The Butcher suddenly began to shriek and writhe, and, as soon as Zurriel dropped him to the ground, he began to claw at his now ghost-white face. He pressed his fingernails upon his face so hard that they could see red blood begin to seep from the cuts. The Butcher slammed his head against the ground over and over, until, after a moment, he squirmed, then lay motionless.

"What...?" Eldric's words trailed off as he stood in eldritch awe.

"Now," Zurriel said as he turned his attention from the dead the Butcher onto the three standing to oppose him, "I'm so glad you could make it, Master Inquisitor."

"And for what reason have you made it so blatant that you wish for me to come here?" Eldric's once impassive attitude was replaced by a fiery fierceness.

"It's really quite simple," Zurriel said as he turned around and faced the distant Sky Prison Tower. "Behold."

The ground began to shake as the mage raised his hand. The green flames danced on his fingertips; Snow and the prince both jumped to keep the crippled Master Inquisitor from toppling over under the rumbling force radiating from Zurriel.

A blast sounded from the direction of the Tower. Eldric, Snow, and Clement turned their eyes toward the Tower.

"By the Aeons...!" Eldric exclaimed as he watched, stricken with fear.

Giant cracks formed in the heavenward spire.

"O, mankind!" Zurriel yelled into the air. "The End is nigh."

The crevices in the Tower crawled the length of its ascension as the earthquake shook the foundations.

"Eldric!" Snow cried as she quickly lifted the Inquisitor from his stand. "Commander! Run!"

Prince Reethkilt reacted wordlessly, speedily turning to follow the half-Elf, matching her sprint.

Eldric turned to see Zurriel and his subordinates grow farther and farther away. He watched in astonishment as the Tower began to fall to the ground.

"Snow!" he screamed at the top of his lungs as he watched the monolith come down. "The Tower!"

Without a moment of thought, Snow turned and grabbed Clement, throwing him through the doorway of a shop and jumping in after him. The cracking of the Tower was boisterous and overpowering. Snow grabbed the commander once again and lifted him, the man's eyes full of surprise at her raw strength. Carrying both men, she rushed to the back of the store and down into the storage cellar.

"Get down!" she yelled as she dropped Prince Reethkilt and placed Eldric on the ground.

A blast sounded, followed by sounds of ripping and tearing.

Then, everything was silent.

Eldric slowly limped up the stairs, aided by Snow as Clement walked ahead.

"I forget your strength, Snow," the commander began as he made his way to the top. "The blue hair does not lie."

Snow smiled and combed her hair.

"So easy to forget, is it?

Clement reached the top of the stairs first, the door broken and hanging hopelessly from only one hinge.

"How did you know this store had a cellar, Snow?"

Snow smiled slightly. "I guessed."

"Master Inquisitor," the prince began as he opened the loose cellar door, "who was that man?"

"Your guess is as good as mine," Eldric groaned, "but he's the one who sent me that letter; that I'm certain of."

Eldric reached the top of the stairs after wobbling a bit, his old body aching. The shop that they had hidden in was mostly decimated, with only half of the frame still intact, the force of the gargantuan Tower's collapse shattering the wooden beams like glass.

Snow and Clement, ever-watchful of Eldric's condition, walked out into the night air, now turning dawn as the sun began to light the horizon

"By Empyria..." The words escaped Eldric's mouth unknowingly. The prince and Snow looked around.

"My men!" Clement erupted. All around, the bodies of unfortunate townspeople and soldiers littered the streets.

"It really happened," Eldric said as he looked in the direction of where the Tower once stood. "It's really gone..."

"Commander!" a voice echoed down the desecrated street, followed by the sounds of marching. Clement Reethkilt turned to face captain Maro, covered in dirt and sweat.

"Havell!" he replied. "You're alive?"

"Thank One! *You're* alive!"

"Are there other survivors?" the commander asked quickly.

"Yeah! We began to round up the civilians as soon as the first blast sounded."

"Good man," Clement sighed.

"We've already begun to evacuate the citizens. The survivors will be taken to the nearest settlements. We've sent word to your father in Crown City, too."

"Good." the worn Clement relaxed his shoulders. "We'll have to add this to the list of things to mention at the Conference." He turned to Eldric and Snow. "Shall we finish this together?"

Eldric smiled.

"We shall." The old man nodded to Havell. "Take us to the aeroedock, please. I must make my way to Mhyrmr. The Archbishop must hear about this."

Clement shifted his eyes from Eldric over to Snow. He knew she must have been as ragged as he—if not more. He quickly nodded in agreement.

"Let's go."

Snow aided the limping Inquisitor as they were led first by Captain Maro and immediately followed by Prince Reethkilt.

"Master Inquisitor," Clement spoke up after several long moments of walking in silence. "What do you think happened to the Heart of Hearts and Snowbird? Do you think they're—?"

"I do not know," Eldric said quickly, knowing instantly what the tall commander was insinuating.

Clement looked into the morning sky and sighed.

The city lay in shambles, and the aerodock wasn't much better. However, out of all of the destruction, the aerodock received the least amount of it. The port was positioned on the outer rim of the city, so it was some distance from the Sky Prison Tower. The boulders of cement strewn from the walls of the random shops clogged the once marvelous streets; several bodies lay underneath them.

Snow guided Eldric around the debris. They walked for a small amount of time before they reached the tall, arched opening to the aerodock.

Inside, Eldric saw the surviving citizens of Avelle's Brook huddled together as he approached.

"Inquisitor!" Cilli exclaimed as she and Ralf rushed toward the worn mage. She looked over the party and gasped as her eyes widened and she covered her mouth. "Where's Blake and Lukas."

"They made it out, right?" Ralf added, matching her fear.

Eldric sighed as he hung his head. He looked up at the two, "I'm not sure where they are. They were sent elsewhere, and I will do my best to find them."

"What do you mean?!" Cilli became suddenly indignant. "What do you mean they're not here? What did they do, vanish into thin air?!"

Snow looked at Eldric. For the first time, she saw grief. Never before had she seen it; he was always so calm and nonchalant. Never before had something unnerved him so visibly.

"We admit we lost your companions," Commander Clement spoke up, bowing before the irate Cilli. "We must admit we are only human. We will do all we can to rectify our failure." He knelt and bowed his head before the girl. "As your prince, and future king, I have failed you." Clement turned to the other citizens, who were huddled together. "I will ask that you find it to forgive us— even if only superficially."

Everyone stood speechless, their eyes curiously fixated upon the kneeling prince. Suddenly, Ralf hung his head and placed his hand on Cilli's shoulder.

"F-forgive?!" Cilli exploded. "You lost my Blake! My precious Blake!"

Yet, Clement remained bowed.

"I know you can hear me!" she raged as she took hold of him and shook him violently.

Onlookers watched the crazed girl as she threw the prince upon the ground.

"Unhand him!" Several surviving Red Ravens rushed to the prince's aid. But Clement merely held up his hand to halt them.

"Why?! Why didn't you save her?!" Cilli's voice shook and gurgled underneath her tears.

The prince straightened himself and bowed his head once more.

"Hear me, young lady," he began. "I cannot control the past, nor can I undo it, or undo any action that was false on my part."

The prince took the girl's hand gently; the woman, trembling, fell into his arms.

"But I swear to you, to *all* of you, I *will* set things right."

Cilli looked into Clement's eyes. They were so soft and kind.

Snow looked at Havell. They returned smiles.

Even Cilli knew, as she stared into his eyes, that he meant those words.

The *Orca* sat in the hangar, its gigantic sleek figure unharmed. Eldric, Snow, and the Prince approached as the landing ramp opened, beckoning the Inquisitor and his Knight.

"I believe this is where our paths shall diverge." Clement said.

"You have my thanks." Eldric smiled as he bowed to the tall soldier.

"I will return to my father and report my experiences here."

"And I shall do the same for Archbishop Ferrenvaal."

The commander turned to Snow and bowed.

"Snow," he said as he rose and put his hand to his heart, "you have my thanks. If it were not for you, I probably wouldn't be able to thank you now."

Snow bowed in return. "I take your gratitude with pleasure, Commander."

He turned back to Eldric.

"I shall take my leave. Safe travels, Master Inquisitor."

Eldric waved as the commander left the hangar.

"He's a good man." Snow smiled.

"And he'll be a great king," Eldric replied.

With everyone boarded, the *Orca* rumbled as it took to the air. Steam filled the aerodock as the large metallic vessel disembarked.

Inside, Eldric sat on his bed, his eyes mystified by the sight of the mysterious Stone that Blake had obtained from Ildar. Whatever Damasko was doing there, he thought, he wasn't acting alone. More so, the Inquisitor determined, he was positive it had something to do with the mysterious man that he'd just met hours before. Eldric looked over at the ship's phone, picked it up, and called Marven.

"Eldric?!" the words sounded frantic on the other line.

"Marven?" Eldric replied.

"Oh thank the One," Eldric could hear the deep sigh of the Archbishop on the other end. "I've received news of the destruction there in Avelle's Brook, and—well I thought I'd lost you for sure!"

"No," the Inquisitor chuckled. "You know it would take more than that to bury me. I am quite disappointed in you."

He could hear the Archbishop return his laugh.

"So," Marven said, "tell me what happened."

"Right." Eldric paused for a second, grasping for the right words, "You see, while in Ildar, Blake seemed to stumble upon a mysterious Stone. I have it here on my desk. I'll be sending it to the labs. Other than that, we made contact with the one I believe is the ringleader of the...operation."

"I see," Marven said, drifting into deep though., "And what of Valter?"

"He escaped as well. As long as they have that Abdian in their midst, they can pretty well go anywhere except Mhyrmr. The Darkling is powerful, but not enough to break our barriers."

"So he's among us now?" Marven's voice turned grim.

"Indeed he is," Eldric sighed.

"I see. Well, this is but another thing to add to the list of discussions to be had at the Conference."

"But of course."

"That's happening in a week, you know. I'll need full reports for the presentation, but" Marven waved his hands, "just rest for now."

Eldric nodded as they ended the call.

He reclined upon his bed, and soon was fast asleep.

XXIX

In the Northern Sea

The rays of the desert sun were brutal, bearing down upon Lukas and Blake as they walked aimlessly.

"Where are we, Blake?" Lukas' voice was frantic.

"A desert?" Blake replied as she held her cardigan over her head to shield her from the scalding light.

They seemed to have been walking endlessly, the sun sapping their energy as they progressed through the deep sands. There were no trees; there was no water; there was not even stone. There was only the sun above them, and the hopeless trek in front of them.

"How did we get here?" Blake cried as she fell to her knees.

"That guy," Lukas said as he stopped walking, "the Abdian. I think he can use that black cloud to go anywhere he wants."

"So he..." Blake trailed off, "sent us *here*?"

She looked at Lukas; he nodded in reply.

"How far can we go?" She took sand in her hands and watched it sift through her fingers.

"I don't know," Lukas said through a clenched jaw, "but we'll make them pay."

The sudden intensity in his voice caught her off guard. She'd heard this in his voice only once before; it was the same tone she heard when he stood against Damasko.

They began walking once more.

Thoughts swirled in Blake's mind. What were they doing? They'd been traveling ever since their arrival, and she had no clue where they were. It was dawn in Avelle's Brook, but here the sun had been high in the sky for quite some time. Where were they going? She felt the waves of hopelessness wash over her worn body. She could feel the heat rising to her head. She hadn't eaten and was extremely thirsty.

Before them, the ground began to rise. Quickly, Lukas summoned the Sword Durandal as he and Blake watched a lump appear.

"No way!" Blake suddenly yelped.

A scorpion the side of a man rose from the heated sands, its tail drawn and ready to strike.

Nix Celshior! Blake called into the air almost instantly, her fighting instinct taking over. The blue aura surrounded her, and the air lightened.

But, nothing happened.

"The heat!" she said as the large arachnid's tail rose to strike.

Blake closed her eyes; the fear mixing with her exhaustion caused her to fall upon the ground.

Lucyn Rejiis!

Blake felt as if she were being choked for a moment. Then, there was a loud bang.

Blake opened her eyes, shocked. In Lukas' hands, he held a green Durandal. She turned her eyes to the large bug before them. Whatever he had done, he had severed the bug cleanly in half, straight down the middle. The arachnid hissed and then fell over, dead.

"How did you?!" She turned to Lukas. "What did you do?! Was that your..." she trailed off, "Word of Heart?"

Lukas turned to her and smiled, then dropped onto the warm sand, completely drained. She could feel the sands calling her name, as well.

Was this it? Was this the end? She felt the sandy heat on her back as she fell. She knew she couldn't sleep. No...not after a monster just appeared...she couldn't...shouldn't...

Was this what she thought it was?

Was it really it?

Yes, she knew.

This was death.

And all was dark.

V'rezen Myur was deathly and painfully quiet, which Nox had become accustomed to as she sat in the isolation of her large birdcage. Every now and again, Iago would come and silently read under the sunroof or, once a day, bring her dinner, which was a conglomeration of fruit and gruel. She didn't necessarily find it pleasing to taste, but she didn't complain. She couldn't complain. The Elf would, for the most part, remain speechless in his delivery, however, every other occasion, she could hear him mutter under his breath or tell her to "eat up" while she could. She could sense a change in him. Ever since their confrontation, she found she didn't fear him at all. She wasn't really sure what had changed, but she no longer saw him as the taunting villain he was when he attacked Zerlina. Something about him, she thought, was...gloomy.

After considering this for some time, she found that she was indeed unafraid of him.

What she felt for him was pity.

The mysterious Master, she thought, hadn't spoken to her since his initial revelation that she was the Aeon, Lunae. He perplexed her; his words were mysterious, yet, they somehow seemed less foreign the more she pondered them. She had always known she was different; something had always been there. Deep in her heart she felt it. Brother Claus never spoke of it, and acted weird every time she brought it up. She fell from the sky, he said, yet, he never questioned it. The monks and nuns kept it secret for some reason or another...and then, her eye...her crimson eye. In those days, the children would humiliate her.

Thought took her for a moment. She thought of Lukas. Where was he? Had he come after her? Surely he did; if she knew him at all, she knew he *would* come for her.

The sounds of footsteps echoed throughout the chamber, and the shadowy outlines of four figures approached.

"Lunae." The voice of the Master sent tremors up her spine.

"Who are you?!" Nox yelled as she gripped the bars of the cage and shook.

"My name," the tall man said as he stepped into the light, the dim sunroof illuminating his gaunt face, "is Zurriel."

"What do you want with me?!"

"It's really quite easy," Zurriel said as he turned to Agnon. "Release her and open the portal."

Agnon called upon his Word of Heart as Iago opened the door to the cage and took hold of Nox. The black cloud filled the area, blocking out all light. The thinness of the air caused Nox to take in deeper breaths as she held her eyes shut in fear. Suddenly, she felt a frigid wind across her face, seemingly reaching to her bones.

"We're here, Lunae," Zurriel laughed. "We've reached the end of our journey together. With the Heart of Hearts disposed of, you shall be also."

"Heart of Hearts..." For some reason, she felt she knew who the wicked man was referring to. "Disposed of...?"

Zurriel laughed deeply.

"Yes, yes. Your precious friend is dead. Long gone."

Nox was speechless; quiet tears spilled from her eyes. No, she thought. It wasn't true; it *couldn't* be true. She refused. She refused to believe it, but yet, she knew it *could* be true.

"Welcome to the Northern Sea," Zurriel said as he held out his hands theatrically. "Look at where you are now."

Nox looked around the cliff in which they stood, a stark drop into the dark, watery abyss just off its fringe.

"In the middle of the sea," he said. "Where you shall rest for eternity!"

Nox swung her hands frantically as Zurriel took her by the throat, her flailing arms passing through him like a phantom. The small girl gasped for air, but the man's unwavering grip held her as she felt her head begin to pulsate, her blood desperately trying to circulate.

"And now," he began as he held his hand over her face, "you have something *I* want."

Nox felt a slight pull.

Nyhilo Zurriel.

Suddenly, green flames sparked from his fingertips. Nox felt their heat as she desperately searched for air. She felt her red eye begin to tug from her face, the pain of which forced her to breathlessly scream. The flames shot into her eye socket, plucking her eye from her head.

Zurriel threw her to the ground thoughtlessly.

Nox slammed onto the stone, shrieking as she held her bleeding face.

Zurriel held the eye up to the moon. "It's finally mine. The Eye of Lunae."

He turned to Agnon and nodded dismissively.

The large Abdian followed his Master's command, lifting the hysterical Nox and casting her over the edge and into the sea.

Iago walked to the edge and watched her drop, then sink.

I don't know why...but I don't think you're as evil as those other men...

You're not a bad man, Iago...

Their words lingered in that moment, both Nox's and Lukas'.

His mind wandered momentarily, the thought of her eyes in the dim light. Only once before had he seen eyes as determined as those; only once before had he seen eyes like hers.

And for a split second, he could hear the voice of another...

Her.

Immediate, unconscious emotion filled Iago's veins.

"Amalia!" he screamed as he hurled himself over the edge of the cliff and into the cold waters of the Northern Sea.

Agnon and Valter stopped and looked at Zurriel, who merely gave an accomplished grin.

"Let us go," Zurriel said as he turned away, the Eye held carefully in his hand. "It seems we have killed two birds with this stone."

Agnon nodded, then called upon his Word of Heart.

The cloud formed, and they were gone.

The cold water stunned Iago's body, and the salt stung his eyes as he swam, panicking, toward the sinking Aeon.

The waters swirled beneath him, their dark veils an all-consuming reaper to those foolish enough to enter them.

Where are you?! The thought drove his body forward as he swam deeper and deeper into the blackness.

His eyes were almost useless in the depths, but he tried his best focus.

Then, he saw it. He wasn't sure at first, but the closer he came, the more astonished he became. Right below him, he could see a faint, red light.

He knew what it was...

It was Nox.

He reached the light, and there she was suspended like an ornament, a bright crimson light pouring from the empty eye socket.

But he knew he had no time to ponder. The ocean was cold, and he needed breath. Quickly, placing his arm around her, he began the swim speedily toward the surface. He felt his lungs plead heavily for air, begging for it in an instinctual fury.

Iago heaved as his slender face escaped the water.

"No, no, no," he begged breathlessly as he held the unconscious Nox in his arms, "don't die, you can't. *You can't.*"

He looked at the cliff face before him, its tall stone daunting him. But there was no time to think. Nox needed help, and she needed it *now*.

He looked to the distant shore.

Could he make it? No! He *would* make it.

With desperation mixed with the sheer will to live, he pushed his freezing body through the tumultuous waves, careful to keep Nox above the sea, coughing as the water jumped into his mouth. The rocky walls extended high above the ocean, but he could see in the faint distance the light colors of a rocky shore. Challenging as the distance may be, he determined he had no time for doubt. He began to swim.

The waters were frigid, and the Elf could no longer feel his limbs. He felt no tingles, but merely the dead weight of his arms as he held Nox and paddled onward. He knew that he was in peril; he knew that they were *both* in peril.

But that didn't matter now. All that mattered now was getting to the shore.

As he approached the rocky beach, he dropped the girl as best he could, laying her on her back.

"I won't lose you!" he screamed as he pressed his numb hands upon her chest.

"*Not like I lost them!*"

He pushed and pushed, their bodies turning darker from the cold.

"*Not like I lost her!*"

He pressed between her ribs, checking constantly to see if she was breathing. She coughed, and her breathing lightly returned, her pulse faint.

She won't last long. Not like this.

Iago panicked in a rush of emotions, his thoughts passing at an immense speed.

Was this the end? Was it all going to come to an end like *this*? What an idiot, he was. Why did he jump? Why didn't he just let her die?

But, he knew; he knew he *couldn't* let her die.

He turned to the dark sea, then he saw it. It was distant, but there was no mistaking it. He saw the light from a ship on the waters.

That's it!

Faintly, Iago summoned his Word of Heart. Countless bright gray blades shot, one by one, into the air. This would work, he thought; this *had* to work.

He finally fell backwards, his benumbed body unfeeling as it slammed against the rocky ground. He could barely feel the small pebbles as he hit the floor. He didn't know if the ship had seen him. He didn't know if this was the end. He thought of his father. He wondered how the old man was doing. Then he thought of *her*, her eyes like bright flames. He could almost see her face in his ever faltering mind. Would he die here? Was this it? What a lousy life, he thought. What a *stupid* existence. To be imprisoned for some stupid politics. He smiled faintly. After all of the death he had been through—after all the pain—maybe, just maybe, he deserved it. His mind drifted as he slowly lost consciousness...

What a fool you are, Iago, he thought. *What a fool...*

The SS *Beartooth* cruised quietly along the Northern Sea, a ride of luxury and pride. On board, giant men sat upon gargantuan seats of oak. On the bow, a large man stood, watching into the fog of the ghostlike sea. He stared around, his long, blue hair and full beard battered by the freezing gales. The fog was seemingly pervasive above, however, given how it lingered above one could see quite clearly below at the unforgiving and icy tides of the ocean. He was a watchman, and he quite honestly found the job boring. He watched, though, as was his duty. Staring into the dark beyond, he saw a reflecting light ahead. Perhaps a trick of his mind? He watched further. More and more, he saw flickering explosions of gray shards, bursting in the clouds with only their mere sparkles to distinguish them.

An attack? No. He looked closer, his eyes catching sight of two small figures beneath the moonlight.

He knew now.

It was no attack.

It was a cry for help!

The giant watchman sprung from his post and ran down the deck of the massive ship, causing the other large men to look at him worriedly. An attack, they thought? No. It was something else.

"My Jarl! My Jarl!" the blue-haired man yelled as he entered the ship's cabin. Inside, a regal Giant sat at the head of a long table. The man wore the fur of bears, with a crown of antlers sitting atop his head.

"What is the meaning of this commotion, Leifgar?" he said calmly as he ate a cooked goat leg.

"Jarl Agmundr! I see a cry for help! Two people on a deserted beach!"

The Jarl suddenly straightened his back. "Steer forward!" he demanded as he pointed to the others at his table. "By my honor, I will not desert those in need!"

The men at the table sprang from their seats, the oaken chairs hitting the ground with a thud. They rushed through the ornate doors onto the deck, yelling their Master's command. The others, heeding the demands of the Jarl, rushed to their stations. The captain spit his orders with surety. Jarl Agmundr stepped out of his quarters and stared upward.

Above him the moon was crescent, and he wondered what that meant.

The SS *Beartooth* anchored adjacent to the island, utterly dwarfing it by its sheer size. The Thane rowed a smaller boat to the shore, struggling to balance as it swayed under his size. He bent down, carefully picking up the unconscious bodies of Nox and Iago in each hand and stepped back on the deck of his own ship.

"Their bodies are cold!" he yelled as he returned to the *Beartooth*.

"Are they dead?" one questioned in reply.

"I do not believe so!" he said, "I feel their beating hearts. Very softly, but still there."

"Caedmon!" the Jarl commanded. "Take them to the engine room and warm them by the engine."

"Yes, my Jarl!" the Thane nodded as he hurried into the ship.

"A young man and woman?" one of the crewmen commented. "How did they get all the way out here?"

Agmundr sat in his stone chair, positioned in the center of the lavish wooden vessel as it disembarked and left the forlorn island behind.

"Perhaps we shall find out soon enough," Agmundr replied. He raised his hand to the captain. "We return now to Hawkhaven!" The Jarl's deep voice resonated like thundering clouds.

The Giants' long blue hair swayed in the numbing wind as the ship sped through the sea, steam billowing from the pipes as the vessel carried onward. Soon enough, they were on the sea, free as the birds.

The other crewmen rushed around the busy engine room as Caedmon bellowed out commands.

"We need to take their wet clothes off!" he yelled. "Do we have clothes for Smalls?"

The other men scratched their heads as they looked all around the ship, then returned empty-handed.

"We have no clothes for Smalls!" they cried.

"Then wrap them in blankets and place them by the heater!" Caedmon directed. "We need to take their chills away!"

Speedily, the other Giants took the death-like Nox and placed her by the warmth of the engine.

"My Thane!" one called over to Caedmon.

"What is it, brother?" he replied.

"This Small, the girl..." he trailed off for a moment as if to double-check, "She's missing an eye!"

"By Lyhaal!" the Thane exclaimed. "Get the Witch Doctor down here!"

The Giant wrapped Nox in the cloth and placed her by the heat of the engine, then ran up the stairs and was gone.

"My Thane!" another exclaimed, holding a naked Iago. "On his back! Look!"

Caedmon's eyes widened. On Iago's back, the tattoo of a white bird was distorted by the scars of major burns.

"What the—?"

"You called, Thane?!" The voice of the old Witch Doctor cut him off. He turned to see the withered old man, his graying blue beard now a strange turquoise color.

"Indeed, Jargar!" Caedmon motioned his hands to hurry the old Druid to Nox's unconscious body. "She's missing an eye!"

"By Lyhall!" Jargar said in surprise, reaching in his satchel for medicine. "Quickly, rub this on the eye socket!"

Caedmon motioned his hand. The other Giants hurried to

follow their superior's command. They retrieved the leaves and began to rub them against her eyes.

"Gently, you fools!" Jargar scorned. He turned to Caedmon. "It's best she was unconscious. The oil of a Ghardrel Leaf is quite painful to the skin."

"Will it work?" the thunderous voice turned the heads of everyone in the room.

"My Jarl!" they all shouted in bewilderment at the kingly Giant's presence.

"Will they live, Jargar?" Agmundr asked candidly.

"I believe we found them in opportune time," the healer replied with a bow.

"Good," the Jarl sighed. "It would shame me if a young woman, even if she is a Small, were to die on my ship."

"Of course, my Jarl," Caedmon bowed as well, which in turn convinced the others, along with the engine room staff to do so also.

Agmundr walked over to the wrapped Nox and Iago.

"We had no clothes for them, my Lord," Caedmon said as he stood, "this will have to do for now."

The Jarl looked at the motionless Nox, her pale face slowly being transformed by a slight hue of redness.

"Her face is returning color," the Jarl said with a smile. He turned to Caedmon and his men. "You've proven yourself quite well, my men. There will be much feasting in my halls back at Hawkhaven, and we will sing songs of their rescues—rescued by the warriors of Caedmon."

He placed his hand on Caedmon's shoulder as he walked by and up the stairs.

Caedmon thanked the Aeons, then sat and watched the now sleeping Iago and Nox. It was true; the color was returning in their faces. They slept now, and he knew they needed it.

XXX

The Assembly of Nations

The winds of autumn brought snow to the top of the mountains. Stalwart as ever, the gargantuan temple of the Church of Mhyrmr stood, not bothered by the light flurry.

From a distance, Prince Reethkilt sat in the command deck with his father, both of them watching the approaching cathedral as the airship *Wyndrake* carried forward.

"It really is a beautiful sight when covered in snow." King Ahmaal zel Reethkilt said through hoarse coughs.

"I agree, uncle," a voice laughed. "It stands so tall, yet looks so peaceful in the snow."

"I think so, as well, Marko."

Clement turned to see his cousin walking toward them. Marko was a tall, slender man, with obvious laugh lines upon his face.

"So good of you to join us, cousin!" Clement laughed as he placed a hand upon his cousin's shoulder. "This will be your first time at Mhyrmr, no?"

"That it will, Clement. And, I'll finally get to meet that girl you speak so highly of. Snow, was it?" Marko snickered. "Maybe I can share with her all of the details about how you *really* feel about her? No?"

"Marko Jharres!" the prince retorted awkwardly, "Y-you will do nothing of the sort!"

"I can see it now! The Crown Prince of Aestriana falls for a mere knight! A fairy tale in the grandest sense!"

Marko turned to his cousin and laughed.

"I only jest," he yawned. "You should learn to relax your shoulders, cousin."

Clement looked into his cousin's dull eyes. The man passed him and took a seat beside the king. He sat, shuffled for a moment, then pulled out a deck of tarot cards. He flipped through them for a moment, then began to shuffle the deck.

Ah, Marko. Clement smiled. *Like a dear brother.*

It was true, or, it *felt* true. They were cousins. Marko's mother was his father's younger sister. Regardless, once she had passed away, the young Marko Jharres came to live with the king. In those many years, the prince had grown less to think about his cousin as a cousin, and their bond became more like that of brothers.

"It seems my two boys are in high spirits today." King Reethkilt smiled.

The king looked through the large windshield of the deck and coughed.

"Let us hope that is a good omen..."

"You don't feel anxious, do you, Snow?" Eldric said as he stood upon a balcony and watched three large airships come closer and closer to the lonesome temple.

"I am never anxious, Master Inquisitor," the knight replied flatly.

Eldric puffed his pipe and pointed to a massive, golden airship in the distance.

"Not even in the presence of *him*?"

Snow looked outward for a moment, then returned her eyes to the Inquisitor with a quizzical glance.

"That's the airship *Golden Gavel.* Largest in the world and personal taxi of the Mirean Prime Minister, Eizen Zilheim."

Snow was sullen for a moment. She touched her pointed ears, then her hair.

"Do not worry, Snow. I will not let him dishonor you."
She smiled.

"You need not protect my honor, Eldric. I am not ashamed of

only being half Elf." Snow placed her hand upon the old man's shoulder. "A certain someone once taught me that being different isn't so bad. And, I believe he is right."

"He must have been very wise," Eldric chuckled.

"He is." Snow smiled. "When he wants to be."

The airship *Efreet* cruised effortlessly through the wispy clouds surrounding the temple of Mhyrmr. High Priestess Marise Myi Kefnir stood upon the bow, watching as the church upon the mountain grew ever nearer.

Beside her, a man in solid white robes stood beside her, the tattoo of a white lotus barely visible through the blank fabric.

"Such a forlorn location, Your Holiness," the robed priest said.

"A place of wretched magics," she replied.

"Worry not, My Lady," the man began, "for the Aeon of Death, Obsidian, gives punishment to all accordingly."

She smiled.

"Not even the god of death can wash away their blemishes. As a White Lotus, you should know that."

The Priestess waved her hand for him to leave. The man bowed, then left her side.

Kefnir looked at the encroaching temple.

"How disgusting," she said, "those who would warp their spirits for a little power."

Archbishop Marven paced up and down the length of the conference room, his eyes set upon the ground.

"Nervous?" A voice penetrated his thoughts.

Marven looked up to see Eldric limping toward him.

"Now *this* is a rare sight. And I thought that 'Archbishop' had gone to your head all these years..."

The Archbishop chuckled. "You haven't changed a bit, my friend. Perhaps some maturity would do you some good?"

"Would it now?"

"Maybe not." Marven shrugged, his eyes drifting along the stained-glass windows that lined the spacious hall. "Whether you know it or not, I'm glad that you've remained yourself through all of these years."

"Is that sincerity I'm detecting?"

"Perhaps."

Eldric pulled a chair and sat, leaning on his cedar cane. In the lights that peered through the golden glass, Marven could see his white pupils.

"They always thought it was strange, your eyes," the Archbishop said.

"And they were right," the Inquisitor replied. "I'd have run from me too. I cannot blame them. I cannot control what others will think of me, but their thoughts do nothing to determine my worth."

Marven merely smiled.

It's like you've never changed...

"You're nervous, aren't you, Marven?"

"You read me like a book."

"A book with *large print.*" Eldric reached for his tobacco pipe. "I can't blame you. I've never remembered a time when the three Great Nations have come together to convene."

Marven took a deep breath. "I don't know how they will act once all together."

"Do you remember when we were children, and those boys from down the street took my cane?"

"Yes." The Archbishop said sharply. "I wove a ward and trapped them in a pig pin."

"They never messed with me ever again." Eldric laughed. "As a matter of fact, no one ever did. They feared you, Marven. You had a temper and you were boisterous and defiant. They feared you, but *I* respected you. I knew why you did what you did, regardless of your methods. Because I knew that you did it to protect the weak. And you knew that the purpose of the strong is not to abuse the weak, but to defend them."

Marven chuckled. "You're right, my friend. You're quite right."

The two turned their gaze to the large window at the end of the court. Golden light spilled through its glass, bathing the room in a bronze color. Eldric blew out a ring of smoke.

"You're strong, Marven. *That* has never changed.

XXXI

The Conference of Nations

The airship *Golden Gavel* descended into the Mhyrmr aerodock, met with the complete silence of the onlookers. Inside the vessel, Prime Minister Eizen Zilheim waited impatiently behind the landing ramp, tapping his foot and eying his pocket watch.

Foolish trifles, he thought as the ramp began to descend.

Outside, everyone stood in grim silence, but Zilheim paid them no mind as he walked down the ramp and through the crowd. Each and everyone in his way scurried off to let him through, for none would dare to busy the Elf with their unwelcome presence.

Zilheim kept his eyes forward, his back straightened, and walked with his hands behind his back.

"Vondell," he snapped.

A decorated Elven soldier rushed to his side.

"Look at them, Vondell," the Prime Minister said as he motioned his hand to the crowds.

"I see them, Your Honor."

"Tell me," he began. "Why again must I lower myself to a meeting with such beasts?"

"It is a conference, My Lord." Ellier Vondell replied as he bowed his head. "Of international importance, at that."

"Conference," Zilheim almost spat the words. "Do they not know of the war in Mirea? We're trying to subdue beasts! I have no time for the squabbles of inferior races."

"Yes, My—"

"Don't speak," Zilheim waved his hand dismissively. "Let us get this over with."

Time had passed. Archbishop Marven Ferrenvaal sat at the head of a large table. He had watched anxiously as the leaders from the three nations had filed in. He looked around the room. To his left sat King Reethkilt, Clement, and Marko Jharres. To his right, Eldric had taken his side, and Snow stood behind them, her ever-watchful eyes scanning the room for danger. Before him, on opposite sides, the High Priestess of Abdiah sat across from Zilheim, Prime Minister of Mirea.

Marven stood.

"We have gathered here today to speak on the topic of several terrorist attacks which occurred on Aestrian soil. I have the witnesses of the royal family, as well as the Master Inquisitor." He turned to King Reethkilt and nodded.

The old king did not stand.

"One month ago," King Reethkilt began, "I was visited in the night by a figure, a man who called himself 'The End of the World.'"

"Master Inquisitor Eldric and I can concur..." The Prince began.

Zilheim sat in boredom as the meeting continued on and on. He looked around the room; he looked at High Priestess Kefnir and whispered to Vondell.

What a fool. She denies magic for a god? *Weak.*

"And thus," King Reethkilt concluded, "I wish to ask the nations of Lythia and Abdiah to aid me in the destruction of these criminals—"

"Absolutely not!" Zilheim burst into raging laughter. "So you admit you are a weaker race? That you cannot defend your existence without the help of the Elves?!"

"It is not that, Your Honor," Eldric spoke up. "The king is merely asking for cooperation, not deference."

"Cooperation?! *Us,* help *you?"*

"Did you not come to us for the arrest of Iago of the Thousand

Swords?" Marven began, "Was that not—"

"Cooperation is not the same as bottom-feeding. I merely gave you Iago because he was not worth my time."

"Truly the races can come together?" Kefnir began, coming to the others' aid, "I see the removal of this threat to be vital to the spirits of the world."

"Come together?!" Zilheim spat and pointed at Snow, "And what would you have? More *halflings?!*"

"That is enough, Prime Minister!" Clement yelled as he stood.

Zilheim clenched his fist. What do they know? He wondered why he even came. They cared nothing about Mirea! They only wanted to help themselves. They *will* pay for their folly.

"Do you wish to stake your blade in her defense, *Prince*?"

Clement put his hand to his heart.

"I would stake my very blood with it!"

Snow sighed as she clenched her fist.

"No! If he has a quarrel with me, then it should be *my* sword that crosses his face! It should be easy for someone as superior as you to defeat someone like me, right?" She touched her blue hair. "Or do you *fear* my blood?"

"Silence, *knight!*" Zilheim growled. "Know your place in a room of kings."

Marven gulped.

"Please! Please! Let us focus on the task at hand!"

"I will do no such thing," Zilheim said as he began to walk away. "I don't know why I even agreed to meet you fools."

The leaders all looked at each other. Everyone became silent as the sound of the Prime Minister slamming the door behind him resounded throughout the room.

Marko looked around. He could see the dumbfounded faces, the results of the chaos that had just ensued.

This.

This made Marko smile.

"We're leaving, Vondell," Zilheim raged as he stormed down

the hallway, motioning for his soldiers to follow.

"So, it was a fool's errand after all?"

"As I predicted," Zilheim scoffed. "Nothing but ants building a nest before the fall of rain."

"The nest will not shield them, Your Honor."

"Yes, and I shall be the rain," he laughed. "*I*. The thunder *and* the lightning."

"So, you weren't going to comply at all? Sounds like a wasted trip?" a voice whispered in his ears.

The Prime Minister turned to see a figure walking beside him. The hallway was empty, all but the Elven soldiers who marched around him. He knew who the figure was.

"Wasted?" Zilheim laughed. "It was not wasted, for it blustered my hate for them."

"Oh? So you will use the power of hate?"

"Yes, Zurriel. Hate is a wonderful fuel."

XXXII

The Need for Theatrics

Dusk approached an unsettled world as the conference abruptly came to a close and all made their journeys back to their respective kingdoms.

Within each royal vessel, all dwelt with anxiety.

All but one.

Marko Jharres sat in his cabin, staring at the figure across from him, sitting at the far side of the room.

"Why didn't you kill them?" Marko began. "You could have saved yourself a great deal of trouble if you just offed everyone right then and there. Then there would be no Church, no Kingdom, and, most of all, no Heart of Hearts," he paused. "And, no Lunae either."

"You truly are perceptive, Marko," Zurriel laughed. "But, you lack one virtue."

"Oh? And what might *that* be?"

"Yes. You forget the need for *theatrics*! I am a storyteller. So why not, while the time is given, tell the grandest story of all?"

"How grand can it be? Your Heart of Hearts is dead, so who will take the protagonist's stage?"

"Dead? Who can say for sure if he is dead? Perhaps he is dead, but, perhaps I still hear his beating heart."

"So, are we just not going to mention the eye, or what?"

"Ah!" The wizard touched his red eye, "Ah! Yes, the *Aeonic Object*. With it, I may read the hearts of men."

"So you can also see what *I want*?

259

"Oh. No," the wizard laughed. "I knew *that* from when we first met. You want something I can give, don't you?"

Marko smiled as he walked over to his cabin window. Outside, he watched the red light of the setting sun soak the white clouds in bright red hues.

"Me?" he chuckled. "I just want to watch the world burn..."

XXXIII

Hawkhaven Blues

Nox stood in a vast wasteland where her sight was vague, and
the objects in front of her danced like water upon paint.
Regardless of the state of the area, however, it was obvious where
she was; it was all too blatant what was before her...

Nox stood at the cusp of a massive graveyard.

Gone! Nox! The World!

The sudden wail caused the girl to jump. She looked at her feet.
Before her, a naked child held desperately to a gravestone.

"Lukas?!" Nox's shriek echoed throughout the void.

To her horror, the child took form. It *was* Lukas, but not as she
remembered him. He was frail and withered, his face gaunt and his
eyes watery.

It's all gone, Nox!

"What's gone? What are you talking about? Why are you here?
W-where are we?!"

It's the time of loss, the age of death...

"I don't know what you're talking about?!"

The phantom of Lukas fell to the ground. Nox looked at the
name upon the gravestone. It was scratched away, almost as if
worn from time. She eyed the stone further, deciphering the image
of a feather carved below the inscription.

"What are you trying to say?"

It is the time...

For brother to slay brother...

Country to kill country...

And then...and
then it shall be true...

Nox shook her head in frustration.

"What will be true?"

The child peered upward, Nox following his gaze. Above them, she could see a crescent moon, black as night, cast upon a brilliant blue sky.

He gave a ghostly howl.

The End.

Nox awakened, slowly opening her eye to the warm air. The surroundings startled her, their differences stark from the cold library of her captors beforehand. The smells of burning cedar filled the air, the aroma of the forest wafting in the room.

She stared upward as she lay upon her back, gazing at the extremely high ceilings, composed of large, long, wooden planks. She placed her hand upon her empty eye socket, now covered by a bandage, as if to fully realize that it had indeed been taken.

Nox rose from her soft bedding of straw and hide, her body aching, and looked around the room. All around her, giant versions of furniture were placed decoratively. She gazed curiously, even wondering for a moment if she had shrunk to a smaller size. The fireplace was humongous as the bright flames crackled and cackled. She held her head; the pain was dull, then, she realized that she was wearing a different change of clothes, her old, worn, dress had now been replaced by a soft white gown.

"You're finally up." A high-pitched voice startled the young Nox.

She turned her head to see a Giant, blue-haired woman sitting on a wooden chair at a table full of food.

"Where am I?" Nox blurted out unknowingly.

The large woman laughed gaily.

"My, my! Aren't we lively all of the sudden!"

Nox could feel herself blush. For some reason, she felt strangely...at home here. Whoever this woman was, Nox felt somehow that she meant no harm.

"You're here," the woman replied. "In Hawkhaven."

Nox stared at the woman quizzically, holding her head from pain.

"Why is everything so big?"

"Well," the woman smiled kindly, "you're in Hawkhaven, the land of the Giants, so, everything is taller than you, Miss Small."

"Miss Small?" Nox laughed softly. "Well, how did I get here?"

"For that, you need to thank that Elf boy. He's in another room." She took her large knife and cut off a piece of meat, placed it on a wooden plate, and put it by Nox on her bed, "But now you need to eat."

"Elf boy?" Nox asked rhetorically. Suddenly, she felt a small shock of realization. "Iago?"

For a moment, she couldn't believe it, yet, she knew it was true.

"Eat, and be merry! You've been asleep for three days. You must be starved."

"Three days?!" Nox exclaimed in a sudden burst of surprise.

The blue-haired woman laughed casually.

"You were almost taken by the chills. If it wasn't for that boy, you both would both be in the afterlife by now."

Iago, Nox thought, would he really have saved her? The thought was a strange one, yet also one that seemed oddly plausible.

Nox took the piece of meat in her hands. Suddenly, she felt the weight of her hunger. She admitted, it had probably been way longer since she had eaten, and it was an even longer time since she had a good meal. She bit into the piece, and she quickly found herself scarfing it down quickly.

"Someone was quite hungry, weren't they," the old woman smiled, "But please, rest for now, your body needs it." The old woman placed some small clothes on Nox's giant bed. "We had a bit of trouble finding clothes for Smalls, but I have those for you to change into when you are ready."

"Thank you," Nox said as she smiled.

"My name is Trina, by the way," the old woman smiled as she walked out the giant door. "It's good to meet you."

When Trina had left the room, Nox lay back on the warm bed. Was it really Iago that saved her? Could that be true? To be honest, Nox vaguely remembered anything from three days ago. She remembered the dark library, then the cliff. But, after that, she only remembered the sharp pain as Zurriel took her eye before everything went black.

"'Elf,' huh," she said as she stared up at the tall ceiling.

It had to be him. She laughed slightly.

Things had turned out so...bizarely.

Iago awakened from a dreamless slumber. His eyes opened slowly and, for a moment, he stared aimlessly at the ceiling. The wooden beams of the roof seemed to extend exceedingly high.

"Giants?" he said as if alone in the room.

"You're correct," a deep voice startled him.

Iago quickly rose, spiting his worn, sore body. He turned to see a gargantuan man in extravagant robes. The Elf quickly examined the man, noticing the scar across his eye and the crown of elk antlers that he donned upon his head.

"You're a long way from Mirea, Elf. How did you end up in the Northern Sea?"

"I don't even know who you are," Iago snapped back. "Do you always quiz everyone you meet?"

"Sharp tongues wont help you here, Elf," the regal Giant snapped back. "I am the king of this castle; I am Jarl Agmundr the Bear." He paused. "Tell me, Elf. How did you end up in the Northern Sea?"

"None of your business," Iago replied, shooting a sharp glance at the large king.

"I see," Agmundr said with a hearty laugh, then, in an instant, his face turned dark. "You saved that young lady. Who are you?"

Iago stared at the ceiling, hopelessly averting himself from the Jarl's eyes.

"I'm no one."

"That's not true." The Jarl said as he stood. "We both know that. Who are you?"

Iago looked at the man's height. It was true, he was somewhat intimidated by the Jarl's tallness.

"You heard me the first time," the Elf said, this time more assertively. "I'm no one."

Agmundr laughed.

"We both know that is not true." He sat once more, reaching for a large beer mug. "So, I'll ask one more time. Who are you?"

Iago gulped, nervous. He felt his hands become clammy with sweat. Could he tell this man who he was? Could he really admit his identity?

"I saw it," the Giant's words cut into Iago's mind.

"You..." Iago's eyes widened in fear as his words trailed off.

"On your back, you bear the symbol of the White Dove. I know who you are; you're—"

"*Stop!*" Iago exclaimed in a sudden outburst of aggression. "I can't bear to hear that name again."

Agmundr stepped back, taken off guard by the Elf's sudden explosion.

"I know! I know! I know you know who I am!" Iago clenched his fist. "Just shut up! This ghost follows me everywhere, I don't need it spelled out for me." He breathed deeply. "Please. Spare me that dreadful name."

"Ghosts of sin will follow a man to his grave, but," the Jarl took a drink from his mug, "you obviously saved that girl, regardless of the circumstances. For that, I will not dishonor your name."

Iago laid back down, dwarfed by the giant bed on which he lay.

There was a moment of silence.

"Thank you..." Iago finally mumbled.

Agmundr smiled.

"You know," the large Jarl said as he calmly stood and walked toward the equally large door, "I am hosting a feast tonight to honor Caedmon, my Thane. He is the man whose quick thinking saved you and that young woman from the chills. I would like for you two to join us. There will be lots of food. I'm sure you're hungry after a three day slumber?"

Three days?! The thought was a sharp flash throughout Iago's mind. Well, he decided, he *was* hungry.

"Sure," Iago said as he rolled over, his back facing the Giant. "Thank you again...or whatever..."

The Jarl laughed heartily, then walked out of the room.

Agmundr walked laxly down the hallway, seeing the paintings that decorated it. All along the corridor were portraits of the previous Jarls of the hold of Hawkhaven—his father. His father's father. And so on.

The Jarl took great pride in his family.

He walked past several of the rooms along his palace, rooms of servants or warriors. To him, all of the men and women under his name were treated to the paramount of his ability. Not one of them would ever go hungry or without rest. That he made sure of, by his honor. He approached the door to exit the hallway when suddenly it swung open with massive speed, surprising the Giant king as a soldier rushed in and stood before him, gasping for breath.

"By Lyhaal, man!" Agmundr exclaimed, placing one comforting hand gripped on the man's shoulder. "What is the rush about?!"

"My Jarl!" the soldier said breathlessly, "There's been another attack!"

Agmundr's eyes widened in fear.

"Is it...?"

"It was another Dragon attack!" the soldier said, finally catching his breath. "We're certain of it!"

"By the Aeons!" Agmundr exclaimed.

"We saw it last flying over the Hjargen Mountains to the North."

"So it has left us again," the Jarl said, almost as if to himself. "I will send another detachment to the villages on the outskirts. Go get some food and drink, young man. You've fought bravely."

The soldier nodded, then hurried out the door from where he had come.

Agmundr stood for a moment, impassive. Out of a window, he

could see all of the land that he owned; he could see his whole kingdom. He stared woodenly, his reflection visible as if a phantom trapped within the glass. He could see his pale blue eye, his massive blue beard which was graying with time; he saw the scar that pained his face in its deep reddened color. That scar. He brushed down its length with his worn, roughened fingers.

That scar cost him his eye!

He was stagnant as he looked at that faint reflection, his gaze looming back onto his kingdom. Agmundr took in a deep breath, then sighed deeply as he bowed his head.

"Why did you do it, Beogar?" he said under his breath.

"My Jarl!" a soft voice came from behind him.

Agmundr turned to see Sunniva, the head chef, her hands at her side.

"Is it ready?"

"Indeed, my Jarl," she said gleefully, "We will be able to celebrate, as planned. You told me you wished to choose which of the cattle to be slain?"

Agmundr's face lit up, and he motioned for her to lead on.

An old, scrawny man, shrouded in a worn gray cloak scurried about in the darkness, gathering things here and there amid the cold dampness of the cavern. Only a faint torch lit his way as he strode down the chasms, his cloak wet from the puddles upon the cave's floor. Above him, faint light peered into the craggy grotto only to be lost within its recesses. The small man rushed down a familiar path, illuminated only dimly by his the fainting embers of the torch he carried.

"Beogar!" he called out. "Can you hear me, Beogar?"

There was nothing but silence as the cloaked old man heard the last of his words echo into the darkness of the cavern. He could even hear water dripping somewhere below.

"Beogar!" he called once more, his hoarse voice spilling out into the blackness.

Suddenly, he heard the echoing sound of boots coming from deeper within the darkness.

"Beogar?" he said, this time louder. "Is it you, Beogar?"

"What do you want, you tiny old man?" the coarse voice reverberated like thunder, shaking the walls of the cave.

"I have news for you, Beogar." The small old man replied.

A large, muscular Giant walked into the low light of the cave. The old man felt chills every time he saw the behemoth who towered over him acutely. The scarce light cast a shadow over the man's eyes underneath his large brow. A red tattoo placed on his face was fashioned into the likeness of a skull.

"Athor, you'd better have something useful to say," Beogar said as he clenched his large fists."

"Of course, Beogar," Athor replied, "Would I do anything to do you wrong?"

The Giant was silent. Athor looked up at his gloomy face.

"Agmundr exiled you, and I took you in," the old man said in his raspy voice. "I care for you as if you were my son!"

Beogar sat upon the wet ground, his heavy mail jingling as it hit the stone floor.

"Agmundr was jealous of you, you know? The previous Jarl, well," the old mystic paused, "he loved you. He wished for you to be Jarl—not that wretched fool, Agmundr." Athor placed his old wispy hand on the giant Beogar's fist in an attempt at consolation, "But now, I have more news for you..." he squinted his eyes and smiled wolfishly.

Beogar turned his head to the small old man. Athor didn't even come to the height of his elbow. The old man was right, however. The mystic *had* be there for him in his exiled state. As far as he knew, the old man helped him simply because he gave him some company. Company that even he, reluctantly, desired as well.

"What is this news you have for me, mystic?"

Athor waved his hands dramatically and bowed. Beogar watched as the old man's hood completely shadowed his face.

"There will be a feast soon," he laughed. "The ravens have told me so. One of the men, a Thane, has done an honorable act." he threw his hands up vehemently. "And you know how much that Agmundr is an *idiot* for honor and glory, pride, and respect..." He let out a disgusted groan. "Regardless of that, Beogar, I'm sure that the great and glorious Jarl would *love* to see his baby brother in such a time of celebration, no?"

Beogar sat silently for a moment. Athor could hear the deep breaths from the gigantic man as he considered the mage's words quietly. After a short moment in dark quietness, the Giant smiled and let out a deep laugh.

He stood.

"I believe you're quite right, Athor," the faint light cast over his face to reveal his wintry blue eyes, "I think I will go see my big brother..."

XXXIV

The Dinner for Caedmon

Nox sat on the edge of a giant chair. She wore a clean pair of clothes and now sported an eye-patch to cover the hole where her red eye once dwelt. She felt as if she sat upon a large swing, her feet dangling off. She looked around the room, humming a tune in which she improvised as she went along. The ceiling above her was exceedingly high, so much so that she doubted even the Giants could reach it.

"You're healing well, I see!" Trina's high-pitched voice echoed throughout the wooden room.

Nox turned to the old woman, who seemed to tower over her.

"I am!" She smiled. "And thanks for the eye-patch!" Nox made a hook with her finger. "I'm a pirate now!"

"You're optimistic, it seems," Trina laughed. "It's good to see that you have such high spirits for someone who has been through so much!"

"It was hard." Nox smiled. "That's true..." she paused. "But I'm safe now, and that's all that matters."

"We're having a feast tonight!" Trina spoke excitedly. "The Jarl, Agmundr, wishes for you to attend. The Elf boy, too."

"A feast?"

"Yes! It's to honor Caedmon, the Thane and the one who saved you and the Elf boy from the chills. His Majesty wishes to give you and your friend the seats of honor by his throne, as well!"

Nox felt a giddy sensation in her chest. She'd never been outside of the monastery for most of her life—but, now...*now*, she found herself being invited to a feast with Giants? It was like something out of one of the fairy tales that Brother Claus used to lull her to sleep with.

No. This, she thought, was much better!

"I would love to come!" Nox's words sounded a bit more excited than she had intended.

Trina laughed loudly, amused by the little girl's sudden enthusiasm.

"Well then," she said, placing some clothes beside Nox on the large chair, "I've brought you some nicer clothes! The chefs are preparing the fattest lambs for the feast! It's quite an honor to dine in the Jarl's hall, you know."

Nox's eye was simply sparkling at the thought of this. To be in the presence of the Jarl! She didn't know what a Jarl was, but he sure sounded fancy. Maybe he was like a king of some sort? The thought of a Giant king filled her mind with a gleeful curiosity.

"I'll leave while you dress." Trina said as she walked out of the room.

Nox stepped down onto the stepping stool that Trina had placed for her at the foot of the chair. Once on the ground, she held out the clothes that the large old woman had brought her. She unfolded the long, emerald green tunic and marveled at it for a second. The lengthy shirt was woven in the softest cotton she'd ever felt. It was so soft to the touch that she felt as if she were holding a cloud. She eyed the frills at the hem. It was the most beautiful shirt she'd ever seen. After removing her old clothes and donning the shirt, she looked down at the pants, and, picking them up, she looked curiously at the long tassels and buckles that seemed to lace around the knees. She put it on as well, then climbed another stepping stool to the bed and sat there, watching the fire.

Thoughts swirled in her head. Her life had taken another drastic turn from when she had been living in the monastery. For a moment, she thought of Brother Claus. He must be worried sick. She could only imagine how angry he'd be. Or not? Because, after all, all of this really wasn't her fault, she guessed.

But what of Lukas? Her stomach writhed for a moment, causing her to wince. She remembered what that man—the one called Zurriel—said when he took her eye.

"Disposed of?" Nox could barely stand to hear the words roll off of her own tongue.

No. She knew it wasn't true. She didn't know how she knew this, but she did. It was a familiar warmth in her chest; it was a small warmth, but it was there.

He's got to be alive, she thought. *He would never leave me like that.*

"He must be looking for me," she said with a small whisper as she reclined backward onto the bed, "I *know* he is..."

"You're ready?" Nox jumped at Trina's somewhat cracking voice.

She quickly sat up and nodded.

"Well." The large Giant motioned with her hands. "Right this way!"

Nox quickly forgot her worries at the chance to walk around the palace. If you call a Jarl's place a palace, that is. She stepped off of the bed and onto the stool quickly, then jumped to the floor.

"I'm ready!" Nox exclaimed as she followed the large woman out of the room.

Iago reclined on the large bed and stared aimlessly at the ceiling. He'd been through a lot up until this point, and it was the first time that he actually had rested since he'd started this crazy adventure. He rolled over and watched the fire. It was only a small ember now, but the size of it still heated the room.

"Young man!" a voice thundered from the door.

Iago looked to see a Giant man standing in the doorway, covered in fur and worn armor.

"What do you want?" Iago asked, slightly intimidated by the man's large form.

"I have brought you clothing for the feast tonight!"

The big man threw a small sack at the Elf, who quickly caught it.

"Dress, and be ready!" the large warrior laughed deeply. "We will honor the Thane tonight!"

"Right..." Iago trailed off impassively.

As soon as the man had exited the room, the Elf undid the ties on the satchel, and grabbed the clothes within it.

Inside, there was a leather shirt and leather pants. He held them to himself to see if they would indeed fit him. Even though he was Elven and tall, the clothes seemed to fit well enough.

He had to admit, he was rather nervous. Meeting a Jarl—a king of Giants—was mildly nerve-racking. He entertained the anxiety for only a mere moment before deciding that his current situation was better than any of the others since his escape from the prison. Besides, he thought, what had he to fear? He was Iago of the Thousand Swords, one of the most feared and infamous men in the world since the death of that stupid prince. Ha! This was nothing! His anxiety slowly simmered down.

"Are you prepared, Elf boy?" the warrior's loud voice shook the room.

"Yeah, yeah," Iago said harshly, slightly stunned by the Giant's sudden entrance, "I'm ready."

The Giant man laughed as he held his round belly.

"Follow, young Elf," he said as he turned around. "Tonight you shall feast as never before!"

Agmundr walked gallantly down the hallway, stroking his full blue beard. Giant servants rushed past him, all moving out of his way as they passed, speaking excuses. He made his way down the hectic hallway and into the kitchen.

"Looks yummy!" the large Jarl exclaimed with a blast of laughter. "When shall it be done?"

"Quiet down, you old goat!" a large, round woman yelled back at him, shaking a ladle in his face. "It'll be done when I say it's done! That's when!"

"Oh, old Ferma," Agmundr laughed harder. "You cook so well! I can hardly be patient!"

"Well, you want me to cook the best for your Thane, don't

you?!" she said as she tapped the ladle on his shoulder with a noticeable amount of force. "The best takes time, you impatient goat!"

Suddenly, a well-dressed man entered the room.

"My Jarl," the man said with a bow. "The table has been set. We await your arrival."

"Ah!" Agmundr faced Ferma once more. "I await your feast, dear Ferma."

She turned with the ladle in hand, and chased them out the door.

"Out, Agmundr!"

Trina led Nox down the long, tall hallway. Nox, as she walked, was left in a daze, taking in all the sights around her. She remembered a promise to Lukas that they would see the world—which saddened her that she couldn't share this moment with him. Even in a low mood, Nox was distracted greatly by the large pictures upon the walls and the men painted on them. The men depicted in the tall paintings all bore a mixture of fur and armor.

"They're the previous Jarls of Hawkhaven," Trina said, noticing the curious sparkles in the girl's eye.

"Were they all kings, too? Just like Agmundr?"

Trina smiled.

"Indeed. They were all great men of great valor." She beckoned her with her hand. "Now hurry up, young Nox."

They reached the dinner table shortly after the dazzling (or so as Nox thought) walk down the hallway. The servants scurried about; large, blue-haired, men in warlike attire lined the seats down the extent along an exceedingly long wooden table. At the head, three chairs sat. The middle chair was lavish, seated under the mounted head of a large bear. The bear was larger than any animal Nox had ever seen, but, given that she'd never really had the chance to see any *other* large animals, she still admired it just as so. On each side of the ornate throne sat two smaller chairs.

"You will sit on the left side," Trina said to a curious Nox, "the seat on the right hand bears much respect among our people, and goes to the Man of Honor."

Nox looked up at the giant woman in wonder.

"What's wrong with the left hand?"

"Nothing," Trina laughed. "But the right is better."

Trina picked up Nox and placed her on the chair, which had been placed preemptively for her, and stared down the length of the table. All the way down, men and women in assorted animal furs talked and laughed jovially with each other. As she watched them, she felt a sense of warmth in her heart, a fluttering feeling. It seemed all the bad things had come to an end, and she had turned out alright.

Suddenly, a joyous laugh burst from behind her as a large hand placed a disgruntled Iago at her side.

"Hello, young lady!" the Giant man said, "I hope you enjoy our food tonight!"

Nox smiled and thanked him.

Beside her sat Iago; Nox's mind abruptly filled with thousands of questions.

"Iago," she blurted out without thinking.

The Elf sat silently for a while, his face averted from her.

"What," he said harshly after the moment of silence.

"You saved me, didn't you?" Nox paused. "The Giant woman, Trina! She told me you did."

Iago said nothing, his face contorted as if perturbed. Time moved rather slowly, and Nox began to wonder if the Elf would ever answer at all.

"What of it?" he said finally.

Nox smiled softly.

"I just...wanted to say thank you."

Iago turned away from her.

"You're..." he sighed. "You're welcome."

Nox laughed serendipitously.

"I knew you weren't a bad person!"

The Elf groaned.

"Whatever..."

"I knew it! I knew it!" Nox laughed as Iago steamed.

Suddenly, everyone stood.

"My Jarl!" they all cried simultaneously.

Nox turned to see a large man dressed in an extravagant robe, and a crown of deer antlers woven into a circle upon his head.

"Be seated, my men!" his voice echoed within the now silent wooden hall. "Caedmon! Come to my right hand!"

A man dressed in worn armor walked toward the Jarl.

"Today, men," Agmundr said, "we honor Caedmon, who saved the Smalls!" He turned to Nox and Iago. "And we also celebrate the life that has been saved. We also honor the Smalls!"

Agmundr motioned to the servants who brought large portions of food to the table.

"LET US EAT!" he commanded in a boisterous tone.

At his word, the men and women of the table began to dig in.

Outside, the townsfolk stared fearfully at the man walking among them. Beogar trudged along the path to the palace with heavy steps. As he passed, parents held their young ones protectively from his gaze, while all of the men of the village grabbed their farming equipment, should the giant outcast try to strike them. Beogar kept his eyes forward, paying no attention to the powerless threats around him. The early moon cast beams down upon his face, illuminating the blood red tattoo of a skull that covered his ire stricken grimace. When he reached the palace courtyard, he eyed the beautiful mountain flowers that bloomed wildly over the grass.

Disgusting that his brother lived in such a place, he thought.

"Beogar!" one of the palace guards approached him, "Have you come to celebrate as well?"

"Or have you come to cause trouble," another said, sword drawn.

Beogar shifted his eyes to the blade at his chest, noticing the guard's shaking hand as the cold iron pointed at his heart.

"I've come," he said as he grabbed the sword by the blade. The guard instantly dropped it out of fear, "Just to talk to my dear older brother." Beogar smiled wolfishly as the iron blade warped under his monstrous grip.

The giant guards began to shake in fear.

"G-g-go on ahead." They bowed as Beogar passed by them, throwing the mutilated blade upon the ground.

The feast carried on into the early night as the Giants at the table laughed and sang songs of the great heroes. Nox found herself somewhat intoxicated in the excitement of the moment. She took her small slice of the gargantuan lamb that sat on the table, cooked and steaming.

"You seem to be enjoying yourself, small one," Agmundr said when he noticed Nox laughing at a joke she overheard one of the Giants tell.

"Mr. Jarl," she began, pointing at the overgrown lamb on the table. "Is everything in the Giant Lands super huge like that?"

"Of course!" Agmundr laughed. "How else would we eat if we only had small animals? We'd all starve!"

Nox giggled at the large king's enthusiasm.

"By the way, young girl," he began. "How exactly did you lose your eye?"

"Someone took it," she said flatly.

"Took it? Why would someone do that?"

"I don't know," Nox replied as she took a large bite of her food. "It was crimson red though!"

Agmundr's eyes widened.

"Red, you say?"

"Yeah." Nox shrugged. "He captured me and put me in a big bird cage! Then one day, he took me to that cliff and took my eye."

Iago, beside her, felt a sharp pain course through his heart. He had aided in the very thing that she was talking about. *He* was to blame, yet, she never mentioned a single word negatively of him. Instead, he could hear her words—words more painful than blame.

"But Iago saved me! And I'm here now."

Agmundr rolled in thunderous laughter, so loud that all of the members of the court stopped and turned to see what was so funny.

"Well, young one," he said as he pointed to his left eye. Nox had never noticed before, but a scar ran down the side of his face, which was a solid white, filmy color. "I, too, have lost an eye!"

Nox looked at him, surprised.

"What happened?"

"I got into a fight with my brother, Beogar, a long time ago." He waved his hand dismissively. "But, tonight is no night for sad memories." He raised his mug of beer and called out, "men and women of my court, let us have a drink for the Nox and Iago!"

Cheer exploded from the court as the revelry of jokes and boasting continued.

"Hello, Big Brother!" the deep, rugged, voice seemed to pierce the commotion.

Suddenly, all became quiet as the court looked at the Giant in the doorway.

"Beogar..." Agmundr said as if no one was in the room.

"What? Miss me?"

The large king stood suddenly.

"Of course I miss you!" he held his hand out in invitation. "Have you come to celebrate with us?"

"Celebrate?" Beogar scoffed. "What's there to celebrate?"

"We're honoring Caedmon, who saved the Smalls!"

"Bah!" Beogar exclaimed in a disgusted tone. "You really are a deluded fool, Agmundr!" He walked over to the table and grabbed a drumstick from another's plate. "You and your 'honor.' How vain you've become."

Agmundr sighed.

"If you have not come for my feast, then why have you come."

"Because," he said as he put the bone back down on the plate, "Athor says you have two days left."

"Athor?!" Agmundr fumed instantly. "You know that man has poisoned your mind, brother!"

"And you haven't?" Beogar snapped back, "He's a strong man. Much stronger than you." Beogar began to walk away. "You have two days until the seal is final."

"Give her back, Beogar!" Agmundr's plea echoed throughout the silent court. "Give me back my Emalyn!"

The ruffian stopped, laughing under his breath.

"No."

The king dropped to his seat. Beogar laughed louder.

"You really are a weakling..."

Just as quickly as he had come, he was out the door, and the night was ruined.

XXXV

The Soothsayer and the Black Moon

The ceiling seemed to extend for eternity. It almost appeared as an optical illusion to Nox, who held her arm out in what seemed to Trina as a vain attempt to reach the roof.

"It's a long ways up, isn't it?" the old Giant chortled, her big voice cracking as she cleared her throat.

"It's just so high!" Nox replied.

Trina placed a small plate of glossy wood in front of Nox. Nox marveled at the gorgeously cooked mixture of vegetables and meat before her.

"Eat well, child." Trina smiled. "I must go see the Jarl now. He has been summoned by the Soothsayer."

Nox's ears perked in wonderment. Trina smiled, knowing the curious twinkle in the youth's eyes.

"The Soothsayer lives behind the strange door beside the dining hall. She is a mysterious woman who has advised many Jarls before Lord Agmundr. Only the kings are allowed to be in her presence. None of us have ever seen her. According to the Jarl, she never eats or sleeps. Even he says that he knows not how long she has truly lived. She is very mysterious indeed.

"Woah!" Nox exclaimed, "Can I come?"

"No, unfortunately, the Soothsayer's fortunes are only for the king to hear. It is forbidden for anyone else to speak to her," the large old woman said. "The Jarl has ordered you to stay in this room."

"Oh..." Nox said, disappointed, "Alright then."

"Eat up," Trina said as she walked out of the room, "and get some rest."

Nox watched Trina leave, then fell backward onto her bed and turned her gaze once again to the tall ceiling.

A Soothsayer, huh? The thought resounded in her mind like a gong. *Maybe she could tell me if Lukas is alright.*

It only took a fleeting second for Nox to make up her mind.

I'm going to find that Soothsayer!

But how? The answer to that question was not as apparent as the conviction which preceded it. She looked around the room.

I can't just leave and take the hall, she thought, *and I only* think *I know where the dining hall is!*

Moments passed as Nox contemplated her escape, or what seemed as such at the time. True, she didn't want to anger the Giants, yet still, she felt a *need;* no, she knew she had to find out where Lukas was.

She climbed down from the bed and onto the floor. She stood on the stool and scanned the room.

Bingo!

She saw it, in the wall, a slight opening between the boards. Nox climbed down and scurried to the place in the wall. The medium-size hole was just wide enough for her to squeeze through.

"Perfect!" Nox exclaimed to herself.

Agmundr walked down the hallway to the dining room, Caedmon at his side.

"So you really think the Soothsayer will know what to do about the dragon attacks?"

"Indeed," the Jarl replied. "Her sight has never failed me before."

"Aye," Caedmon said as he lowered his head in thought. "We have only two days left to deal with the dragon before...well, so said your brother." Caedmon caught his tongue. "Beogar."

"No, my Thane, he is indeed still my brother." Agmundr held

his hand to his heart as he walked on. "Somewhere in there, he is indeed my brother."

They walked behind the throne and down some stairs to a large, ornate, door.

"This is where we part, my Thane." Agmundr said with a heavy hand gripping Caedmon's shoulder.

The other nodded in agreement, then walked away.

Agmundr stood before an enigmatic door. For a moment, he eyed the strange sigils etched into its oaken frame. This was always an interesting experience, he thought. It was a door without a handle or lock or key. No. For this door, he knew, could not be opened by the meager metals of man.

This door opened only to the ones it wished. The tricky part, he pondered, was not necessarily the door itself, but rather its apparent will. To whom it opened and why was merely its own machination.

"Here we go..." he said as he placed his hand upon the door.

Instantly, the runes upon the wood illuminated into a bright blue, only to fade. Agmundr waited a moment as the door slowly opened, then entered.

Nox easily slipped through the grotto in the wall. Once inside, she was astonished by the amount of freedom of movement she had.

*Now...*she thought.

She had spent so much time trying to get out of the room that she didn't know *where* to go or *how* to get there. She knew how to get to the dining room. It was a simple right down this hallway, then another right once at the end of said corridor.

"I remember there was a hallway behind the chair at the head of the table," she muttered to herself. "It was super spiffy." Epiphany came to her. "That must be the room!"

Elation filled Nox at her sudden realization. She looked down the alleyway that was the inside of the palace walls.

"But how to get there," she sighed to herself.

She sat for a minute, then came to her conclusion.

Nox began to walk down the hallway from within the walls, but, the more she traversed, the more insane her plan appeared to her.

What have you gotten yourself into? she thought to herself. *You don't want to anger the Giants, do you?*

The sheer thought of angering these colossal people sent paralyzing shivers up her spine. But—she knew—she had to figure out where Lukas was, or if he were even still alive.

"I *must!*" she said to herself, finalizing her conviction.

She began walking down the hallway, moving through the dusty cobwebs and trying to blindly navigate herself to the throne room blindly from within the walls. She could hear everything that took place from within her position—warriors laughing and servants scurrying to whatever their business may be.

She climbed over wooden blocks, her still-weak muscles flexing as hard as they could to push the weight of her small body over the obstacles.

She walked further down the hall.

For a moment, she wondered what she would do if she were caught. After deep consideration, she decided. *I'd just tell the truth, I guess,* she thought.

The trek was smooth mostly, then there was a bone-chilling hiss. Nox felt her blood turn cold as she looked upward in the direction of the hissing screams.

How else would we eat if we only had small animals? We'd all starve!

Nox remembered the Jarl's words.

"Oh, right! Everything is bigger here!" Nox said as she looked upward. Suddenly, she stopped cold in terror. Directly above her, in the wall, sat a colossal snake—and more so—it saw her as well.

In that moment, she heard only her heartbeat in her throat and the hisses of the giant serpent, its large golden eyes locked onto its prey.

Do I run? The thoughts were silent in her mind. *What do I do?!*

Before she could think, she bolted down the hallway—a vain, mad dash toward the exit. But it was too late, the slithering fiend was already on her tail, chasing her at lightning-fast speed, its body sliding smoothly upon the ground. Nox climbed swiftly over the large blocks of timber inside the walls, rushing toward a small crack in where, she hoped, the horrendous creature could not follow. At break-neck pace, she slipped through the small crevasse and onto the other side. She looked around for an exit.

Nox stopped to catch her breath, looking behind her.

The beast was nowhere to be seen.

Maybe he gave up! Nox exhaled, then turned around, finding herself face-to-face with the hellish serpent.

She shrieked as the gigantic beast tried to surround her. One by one, its fangs came down. Frantically, Nox held them in her hands, straying from their poisonous kisses.

What do I do? What do I do? Her mind was screaming. *It can't end like this!*

"NO!" she screamed as she lifted with all of her might, finally pushing the beast off in a burst of sudden adrenaline. Quickly, she looked around, picking up a large splinter.

The snake rose once more and rushed at her, hissing wildly. This time, Nox charged too, the splinter in her hands, held as a lance. The fiend struck once more, and Nox shoved her splinter forward, holding it tightly. As the serpent came down, it screamed as the wood gored its throat. Nox stood, staring at the beast.

That was all; it was dead.

She sighed in dear relief.

I've gotta get out of here.

After the perilous battle with the snake, Nox had quickly decided to abandon her plan to sneak from within the walls, and had made every effort to escape from the area. As quickly as she had found the first grotto as an entrance, she had found another grotto as her exit. Once out, she looked around. Apparently, she had moved as far down the hall to be directly at the entrance of the dining room. She looked around her. The area was unusually clear, no servants or warriors to block her way.

Alright, she thought, *what now?*

She looked at the furniture around her, then quickly scurried over and hid behind it.

The dining room was as large as she remembered it, and she quickly moved from furniture to furniture and slipped down the hallway to a mysterious, ornate door. Once there, she stopped.

Okay, she thought as he stared at the strange barrier. For a moment, she merely inspected it, looking for a door handle or any way of opening the vast chamber.

"What now?" she cursed as she sighed deeply.

Suddenly, the runes carved into the wood began to glow a violet glow.

You. A female's voice said, startling Nox. *You who once knew all now wish to know?*

"What?" Nox said in a gasp.

Without another word, the door slowly opened.

Now, Nox thought as she scratched her head, *time to find that Soothsayer!*

Agmundr sat across the table from the Soothsayer. She was a Giant woman, covered in feathers with a antler hanging from the chain around her neck.

"Oh great Jarl." Her voice sounded split, as if two were talking instead of one. "What troubles your heart?"

"I wish to know the fate of the dragon, and of Beogar, and of my Emalyn."

"I see..."

The Soothsayer placed ten cards in front of her and swayed her hands lightly over them.

Nox watched from afar. Her small frame was able to move freely since she had entered the forbidden hall, and now found herself crouched behind a pillar which was off to the side, away from the others. Nox could see everything; she watched the Soothsayer's magic intently, curiosity aflame within her.

"Let us see!" the Soothsayer's voice echoed, bouncing off of the walls. Nox watched as bright blue flaming tongues spouted from the cards, filling the room with a blue mist.

Nox felt as if the air were leaving her lungs. It almost reminded her of Iago's power when he used it back at the monastery.

"What do you see, Mystic?" Agmundr asked, his head hung humbly.

"I see a dragon; I see a mage; I see a jealous brother, lost in a poison mind..."

"What of the Dragon? What of Beogar?" he paused, "What of my Emalyn?"

"I see your brother, Beogar. He is filled with anguish and enmity. He loves you, Agmundr, but he loves Emalyn more."

Nox watched the large king; his face looked so forlorn. She saw something that she felt no one else did.

She saw that he was in pain.

"And what of the dragon?"

"The dragon shall die."

"*No!*" Agmundr thundered in an agonizing wail. He looked at the ground. "And what of Emalyn?"

"She will be lost, as well." The mysterious woman's hands moved to a card on the far right of the table, a card which burned a brilliant black flame. "I see something else, too..."

Agmundr raised his brow, perturbed.

"What is this other thing you see?" he said, almost timidly.

The Soothsayer lifted the black, flaming card.

"I've never seen this before..."

Agmundr inspected the image on the card. Suddenly, his eyes widened. Painted upon it was the image of a black moon.

"The Black Moon?" the Jarl said, alarmed by its meaning.

"Indeed," she replied, "I have never seen it burn before."

Nox was completely lost in concentration. She remembered the window back at the library.

A black moon...

She didn't know why, but she felt the card depicted her—or, who she *really* was.

"The Black Moon," the Soothsayer began, "is the symbol of the moon goddess, the goddess of Lyhaal—the Aeon, Lunae."

"Lunae?" Agmundr said, bewildered.

"It means only one thing," she replied to the king, "Lunae is here, in this court."

"By the Moths!" the Jarl exclaimed as he stood. "The girl!"

Nox knew that Agmundr was talking about her. Should she show herself? She had no idea of what to do in this situation! She pressed against the wooden column, her mind in frantic contemplation. She felt her heart race as her knuckles went white under her deathly grip.

No! She had to find out where Lukas was! Even if it meant getting in trouble with the Giants. Agmundr was aware of her supposed connection to Lunae. She knew, or at least pretty decidedly felt, that he would not hurt her now.

She waited and watched once more.

"So," Agmundr said, both of his hands now pressed against the table, "the girl is Lunae...?"

"Perhaps it is so; perhaps it is not so," the mystic replied.

"I must see her at once!" the large Jarl said as he whipped around and hurried off.

Nox felt her heart ball up within her throat. *What now?* Her mind raced. Before she could think or move, Agmundr was out of the room.

All became quiet.

"Tell me," the large diviner said finally, "why did you come?"

"Um..." Nox peeked out from behind the pillar, "me?"

"Why did you come, Lunae?"

"W-well," the small girl began, "I needed the future told, so I thought I'd come to you!"

"Then come, little goddess."

Nox abandoned her hiding space and walked hesitantly toward the Soothsayer.

"What would you like to know, Lunae?" the large mystic said as she picked Nox up and placed her upon the table, across from her seat.

"Two nights ago," she began, "I had a really weird dream. I was standing in a massive graveyard, and my friend, Lukas—he was at my feet, hugging a grave with a feather engraved on it."

Nox could feel herself begin to shake.

"Soothsayer," she said. "My friend, Lukas, I don't know where he is—or if he's even still alive! I was hoping *you* could tell me!"

"I see..." the Soothsayer said.

The mystic shuffled her deck of cards, drew four of them, then placed them face down upon the tabletop.

She lifted the first. Nox beheld a picture of two men with blades in hand.

Swords?

The next was flipped over. Upon it, a depiction of a sparrow flying across a sunset. The Soothsayer made a strange face, then flipped the third and paused.

Suddenly, a bright, white flame exploded from the card, revealing the artwork of a heart, surrounded by stars.

Nox stared at it for a moment. She didn't know why, but the image made her feel...uneasy.

The mystic cleared her throat.

"These are the cards!"

> *A game of blades will be played,*
> *where brother spills blood of brother.*
> *Against the setting sun,*
> *The bird will sing a dirge,*
> *And the stars shall scream once more.*

Silence ensued, the woman's eyes drawn intently to the cards.

"These cards...I've never seen them before..." She paused. "Lunae, there is going to be a great catastrophe, and your friend shall play a part. Whether he lives or dies, I cannot say, for the screams of the world block my vision."

She lifted the fourth card. There was a picture of a dragon.

"I do not understand...?" the mystic's words trailed off as she furrowed her brow.

"The dragon," Nox said. "You said the dragon would die, yet, Agmundr seemed so sad!?"

"Yes," she replied. "He wishes to end the powers of the sorcerer, Athor, and return his brother and his wife, Emalyn."

"But," Nox said quizzically, "what does that have to do with the dragon? If it's causing so much trouble, why would he want it to live?"

"Silly Lunae, you do not understand."

"I don't?"

"No. You see, Emalyn *is* the dragon."

Nox looked at the woman as if she had said the strangest thing in the world (which, to Nox, she had).

"He's married...to a dragon?" Nox relied, one eyebrow raised.

"You misunderstand. She was not always a dragon; once, Emalyn was a beautiful woman, loved by both Agmundr and his brother Beogar. She chose the Jarl, and Beogar became jealous and ran away. That was when the mage known as Athor used his mysterious magic to turn the queen into a dragon. You see," the mystic said, "he doesn't want the dragon to die because he hopes that, one day, she shall be set free."

Nox stared into the mystic's deep blue eyes in a mix of sadness and wonder. She had always pondered what types of mysteries and curiosities the world held beyond the stone walls of the Zerlina monastery. But, now that she saw them in person, she hardly could take in all of the emotions of fear, ecstasy, and grief.

"Young lady!" An indignant voice filled the room, sending a chill up Nox's back. She turned; it was Agmundr. "You're in grave trouble," he said as he pointed. Caedmon quickly walked toward her and picked her up.

"Do not harm her, Caedmon," the Jarl commanded.

"Wait!" Nox rebutted. "I can explain!"

Agmundr looked at Nox, then at the cards on the table.

She was having her fortune read?

His mind was filled with curiosity.

"I see," he said, "Caedmon! Take her to the throne room and give her a chair. I wish to hear this defense of hers!"

Caedmon nodded in agreement, then he walked out of the room, Nox in hand.

"What was she doing, Mystic?"

The mystic pointed to the cards on the table. Agmundr examined them for a moment, his eyes scanning the strange symbols on the cards.

He stopped at the final one.

The dragon card...?

"I see," he said, then turned and walked out of the room.

XXXVI

The Jarl's Decision

Nox sat on her knees before Agmundr, a blade at her neck.

"I gave you quarter; I fed you. Is *this* how you return my favors?" the Jarl's thundering voice filled the halls.

"Please," Nox began, her face to the ground, "I beg you! Listen!"

Agmundr raised an eyebrow. What was it about this girl? Something was off. She came to him with a missing eye, and then, the mystic drew the card of the Black Moon. Whoever—or *whatever*—this girl was, she was more than he knew, and, perhaps, more than she herself knew, as well. Regardless, she broke his command, so he must act accordingly. It was his sacred duty as the Jarl of Hawkhaven.

"I shall hear you!" he exclaimed, "But you'll have my ear only once!"

"Then, please," Nox's voice cracked. "There is someone— someone who is dear to me, and," she said looking upward at the Jarl, her eye meeting his, "he is in grave danger, and I—I have to find him! I *must* protect him!"

"You expect me to believe you?! You were in that room as well! Tell me, why was the Black Moon drawn?!" the Jarl thundered, caught by surprise at the young girl's plea. "If I am to believe you —if I am to believe *anything* you say—you must be truthful about who you *really* are." He pointed a large finger. "Lunae!"

LUNAE?! The warriors exclaimed. *The Moth Queen?!*

"Listen to me, please, Jarl Agmundr!" Nox put her face to the floor again; her tears made small puddles on the wooden planks. "Everyone says I am this and I am that, but I don't know for sure. Maybe I *am* Lunae—maybe I am this Aeon everyone says I am! But that will do nothing to change my resolve! Regardless of what everyone else calls me, I am Nox! I will *always be Nox! So, c*all me whatever name you want! Lock me in chains for all I care! No matter what you do to me, I will *never* halt my resolve! I *will* protect the ones dearest to me—even if it takes my life in the process!"

Nox raised her head, her icy blue eye drowned in tears.

"Teach me to fight, so that I can protect them!"

The Jarl stood instantly.

"You..."

Suddenly, the guard holding a gargantuan blade at her neck called out.

"Shall we dice her to bits, my Jarl?!" said one.

"Just give us your word!" cried the other.

All of the men of the court stood with their king, blades drawn.

"Little girl!" Agmundr exclaimed, then held his hands out to address his men. "Men! This little girl has shown me more honor than many of you have in a long time!" He looked down at the small girl and chuckled. "To save the ones who are dearest?"

The warriors of the court dropped their blades and watched the Jarl in awe.

Agmundr was smiling.

"Young girl," he said as he knelt and held out his hand. "Lunae or not, you have a strong heart. Hear me well, for you have shown the heart of a warrior, and I would love to have you under my wing."

He stopped.

"But I would like one thing in return."

The large king stood, towering over the petite girl before him.

"May I call you by your name? May I call you Nox?"

Nox suddenly felt tears begin to stream from her face uncontrollably. She looked around to see the smiles and tears of the warriors surrounding her. She didn't know why at the time, but soon she came to realize—for the first time in her life, she felt that she was home.

XXXVII

Training Day

Nox awoke early the next morning, her heart giddy to begin her combat training. She'd never had a real teacher before, and, given Brother Claus' constant disapproval, she'd never even held a real sword.

The excitement ate at her insides. She looked around. The light of dawn hadn't even begun to pierce the windows yet.

Great, she thought, knowing she had awakened *way* too early.

A knock at the door turned her head.

"Who's there?"

The door opened promptly and the figure of Caedmon entered her vision.

"You're already awake, little one?" he said, his voice indicating more a statement than a question.

"I am!"

"Well then," he said as he placed a hand by her bed, "come. Today is a special day!"

The training yard was filled with warriors swinging all sorts of blades and clubs. Nox observed the commotion around her with an intoxicated wonder.

"Okay," Caedmon began as he handed Nox a small, makeshift, wooden sword, crafted especially for her. "Do you know anything at all of swordsmanship?"

"No, not really," Nox replied sheepishly. "Me and Lukas used to spar when I was back at home, but since then...I haven't touched anything even resembling a sword."

Caedmon scanned the little girl before him, stroking his azure beard as if in deep concentration of what she had just said.

"Well," he said after a moment, "we will begin with basics!"

Agmundr sat across from the Soothsayer once more, his eyes moving across the table, studying the cards she had placed down.

"The serpent," the mystic said, moving her hand over a card. A bright, scarlet flame flickered at the tips of her fingers, "the serpent tells betrayal."

"Beogar..." the Jarl said solemnly under his breath.

The Soothsayer moved her hands over another card. Another red flame began to dance on her fingernails.

"The door represents closing," she paused. "It represents finality."

"So," Agmundr drooped his head, "it is true. Beogar was right. The curse is already final."

"I am so sorry, my Jarl."

"It is not your fault." She could hear a slight quiver in the king's voice. "I...I will be leaving now."

Agmundr rose from his seat and left the room, dragging his feet as he moved, then the door closed.

The mystic looked at the table. She realized that he had left before the final card was examined. Curious, she lifted it.

"I see..." her voice trailed off as she looked down at what was depicted on the card.

It was the picture of a sword.

"Well..." she said to herself, "what does *this* mean?"

"No! No!" Caedmon exclaimed, "You don't do it that way!" he held out his hand and wiggled his little finger. "The power is in the pinkie finger! You use the wrist to create leverage by applying force to the arm and little finger.

"Okay! I got it!" Nox said.

She made another vain swing with the poorly thrown together practice "sword" that the Thane had given her.

"That's a bit better, I guess," he said, stroking his beard. "But this time put your abdomen into it!" He held up his hand. "Ready? And…" He dropped his arm. "*Swing!*"

Nox followed the cue and swung with all of her might. Caedmon put his palm to his forehead.

"You're too unbalanced. Don't put *all* of your weight on one foot."

Nox contorted her face, frustrated at the many reprimands she was receiving.

"Alright! Once more!" he held his hand up again, "*swing!*"

Nox swung the wooden sword, trying her hardest to incorporate all of the Giant's many tips.

"Very good!" Caedmon's voice was ecstatic. "You did it just right!"

Nox's eye lit up at the Thane's praise.

In the distance, the sun was lowering toward the horizon, dousing the training yard in golden light.

After a time of practicing the swing, Caedmon sat upon the ground and stroked his beard.

"Now…we need to practice defense as well…but how?"

"What do you mean?" Nox asked.

"Well, if one of the Giants were to attack you, you would be squished under our power. You need a good training buddy…"

"I thought I'd find you here!" a familiar voice said.

Nox and Caedmon turned to see Iago approaching in the ever growing twilight.

"Iago!" Nox said excitedly.

"I can help with the defensive training," Iago said, a phantom blade swirling around him.

The Elf swiped the blade from the air and pointed it forward.

"You can touch them?" Nox said, her head cocked to one side. "But I thought they were spirit swords."

Iago looked suddenly irritated.

"Of course you can touch them! How else would they cut people?!"

Nox quickly felt her face become red. She hadn't thought of that, but, now that he mentioned it, it was a sort of obvious answer.

"Alright," Nox said as she readied her stance.

She could feel sweat drip down her face as she watched three more blades materialize and surround the Elf.

"Now," Iago began, "be ready! I'll send the swords at you, and you'll defend."

Nox looked at the blades that danced in her eye. Suddenly, a knot formed in her throat.

"W-what if I miss?"

Iago laughed.

"Well," he said bluntly, "if you miss, you'll get cut!"

Nox when white.

"Don't worry, you'll do fine." He pointed his finger and laughed. "I'll go one at a time."

At his command, one of the ethereal blades shot forward, the air screaming as it cut through at harrowing speed. Nox, quickly adjusting, deflected the shot with her sword, causing it to ricochet and fly off. Before she could prepare to parry the second, it sliced through the air, hurdling toward her at break-neck speed. Quickly improvising, Nox dropped her knees, feeling the wind as the translucent blade swished over her head.

"Look out!" Caedmon exclaimed as the first blade whooshed in a circle and homed in on her once more. He didn't know why he allowed this, yet he knew that the Elf was right in his unorthodox methods.

Iago was teaching her to think on her feet.

"Don't be slow!" Iago exclaimed as the two blades came whirling back, pointing directly at her. Nox stopped for a moment. Time stood still. She thought of the times she had fought Lukas; she remembered all of the times she had seen his technique. The blades closed in on her: One coming to her front, the other to pierce her back.

Think.

Caedmon watched in fear. All of the men of the training yard had stopped their sparring to observe the engrossing battle that was taking place before them.

The blades grew closer and closer; Nox could hear their

screams.

Then, the first was upon her.

Now!

With all of her might, Nox speedily sidestepped, grabbing the hilt of the phantom blade as it whirled by her. In lightning fast motion, Nox whipped about face, throwing the blade. The redirected sword sliced through the air, shrieking as it moved, crashing into the one that was to spear her back.

The blades exploded into bright, gray shards.

"You're not half bad!" Iago laughed.

"By Lyhaal..." Caedmon's words were soft.

Nox turned to see all of the Giants in the courtyard staring at her in amazed relief.

She smiled widely.

"That was fun!"

With that, the courtyard exploded with cheers and chanting.

Nox the Quick! Nox the Quick! They sang!

Nox turned to Caedmon.

"So," she said with a smile, "how'd I do?"

Caedmon laughed heartily looking at the men around him.

"I am—" he stopped. "*We* are quite impressed."

Nox stared upward at the sea of mammoth, cheering warriors. She had only ever fought Lukas, and he always won—so hearing victory cheers brought a certain heat and redness to her face.

"Incredible resourcefulness!" Caedmon praised, hands held high excitedly.

He composed himself. "That will be enough for today! I will expect you to be here at the same time tomorrow." He nodded his head. "I will tell the Jarl of your success!"

Nox bowed and thanked the Thane, then he sent her on her way. Nox watched as everyone began to separate. Even Iago was walking back to his room, which Nox quickly had deduced was the one next to hers.

"Iago!" she said as she ran up to him, waving her hands.

Iago turned, his face displaying the usual grouchiness.

"What?"

"Can I walk with you?" Nox smiled.

Iago returned her question with a look of befuddlement and slight irritation.

"I...guess?"

"Great! Your room is right next to mine, so I figured I would walk with you!"

Iago walked silently, almost as if he didn't notice her beside him, or maybe, didn't *want* to notice her beside him.

"Iago?" Nox finally broke the awkward silence. "Why did you help those men? The ones you helped capture me, I mean?"

Iago stopped for a moment as if he were contemplating something deeply.

"Because," he said as he looked away.

Shame. The thought crossed Nox's mind, then was gone as quickly as it came, a flash of lightning in the midst of a faraway storm.

"Because, they offered me freedom."

Nox stared intently at the tall Elf.

"I was jailed for killing the Prince of Mirea!" Iago looked at his open palm as he spoke, almost as if he were talking to himself.

"You helped them," Nox said softly, "even though you knew who I was?"

They walked down the hallways, through the twisting corridors of the Palace of Hawkhaven. The servants, now aware of the presence of the knee-high Smalls, walked vigilantly as to avoid bumping into the small Iago and Nox.

"I don't care who you are," Iago griped. "I never did, nor ever will."

Nox stopped as Iago walked onward.

"T-then—" Nox stuttered, raising her voice. "Why did you save me?!"

Iago turned around, the two facing each other with only a space of silence and emotional friction between them.

"Because I didn't believe you deserved to die. I didn't want to see you die. That's all. Is that so strange?"

Nox held her head.

"No..."

Iago walked on, the tension still in the air, a sense of bewilderment lingering in Nox's mind.

"Iago!" she yelled down the hall.

"*What?!*" he whipped around, eyes glaring.

"Who is Amalia?"

Iago felt a sudden chill.

She heard me?!

The thought accompanied a feeling of heat across his face.

"None of your damn business!" He raged in retort.

Nox stood, stunned by the sudden backlash. She hung her head.

"I didn't mean to open wounds," she said.

Iago held his eyes on hers. His usual fire and spite was no longer abound in his eyes. No, she knew these were different eyes. There was sadness, a certain melancholy she'd only seen once before.

"I apologize," she said.

"Whatever..."

Iago turned and walked away, leaving Nox to her thoughts.

The next day, Agmundr found himself sitting at the foot of his bed, his mind a maelstrom of numbness.

Why? he thought, *Why did you do it, Beogar?*

Time seemed to sift through the chasms of his mind. They had been so close, he and Beogar, brothers of the same womb, yet, why his brother despised him so was an enigma. He could picture their times together in his mind.

Brother!

It was as if he could hear his younger sibling's beckon. But, those days had long since passed. Agmundr hung his head.

Athor...

His mind filled with a spontaneous rage. It was *him*—that wretched wizard—who had caused so much strife in his kingdom. It was the malicious mage who tainted his brother's innocent blood.

"My Jarl!" The muffled voice of Caedmon was almost blocked out by the large wooden doors to the Jarl's quarters.

Agmundr quickly rose and answered the door.

"What is it?"

"The girl we've been training," he said, "I believe she's ready to undergo the trial!"

Agmundr stroked his long blue beard, a soft smile illuminating his saddened face.

The morning sun bathed the mountains, illuminating the billows of mist that veiled its surface. Hidden within the fog, Beogar paced impatiently within the cave.

"Athor!" he called, his deep, raspy, voice echoing throughout the chasms of the cavern.

For a moment, there was no answer.

"Beogar!" the old wizard returned. "You wish to go see him, don't you?"

"The curse is final, isnt it, you old fool?"

"It has been three days since you sent his message, so, yes, the maiden Emalyn will be a dragon forever."

Beogar laughed, his thunderous voice bellowing, bouncing off the walls around them.

"Let us go see him."

Athor looked up at the large warrior.

"Do you long for your brother, Beogar?"

"No." The Giant smiled. "I merely wish to see him struggle."

XXXVIII

Black Moon Rises

The next day came abruptly.

Nox awoke to loud laughter and ferocious knocks at her door. The day was still exceedingly young, as the mists were still cold and crisp. The young woman rose and rubbed her eye, fighting the compelling urges to sleep more.

"Nox!" the hearty voice of Caedmon resounded through her quarters. "Today is the day! Are you prepared?"

"Prepared for what?" Nox yawned.

Suddenly, the door burst open. Nox jumped, falling backward in surprise. There, at the doorstep, stood Caedmon.

"Today," he called out as if in an ecstatic monologue, "you will undergo the final test to become a warrior of Hawkhaven!"

Nox sat agape in surprise.

"A test?"

He held out his hand.

"It is time for you to undergo the Trial of Lyhaal."

"Who?"

"The great Lyhaal, founder of the Giants." He beckoned with his hand for her to hurry. "Now, let's go! The Jarl is growing impatient!"

Nox quickly scampered over to the bedside of the giant mattress, then turned to Caedmon.

"I, uh..." she said shyly, "I need to dress."

Caedmon felt his face grow hot in embarrassment.

"I-I," he stuttered frantically as he left the room, his voice muffled through the door, "I apologize, young lady!"

Nox giggled to herself, finding the giant warrior's bashfulness amusing.

A small moment passed as Nox quickly dressed herself, putting on her knee-length green dress and her long pants made of hide.

"Okay!" she called out, "You can come in now, Caedmon!"

The warrior slowly opened the door and bowed his head, placing his fist to his heart.

"I must apologize, young one, for my rudeness. I completely forgot."

"It's fine!" Nox stepped down onto the stool, stepped onto the cool wooden floors, then, quickly put on her boots. "Where to?"

Caedmon motioned out the door.

"Stay close. Where we are going is rather dangerous."

Nox looked at him, intrigued.

"...alright?"

Iago stood at the mouth of a large cave. He peered into the shadowy grotto, where he could see only vaguely the outline of a stone doorway, which was covered in what he guessed was some sort of ivy. Agmundr and three large warriors stood beside him.

"Why am I here again?" the tall Elf complained grumpily.

Agmundr placed his giant hand on the Elf's shoulder.

"You're a murderer, remember," he laughed, "and, now that we know you hold such adept magical power, I would like to keep an eye on you."

Iago groaned, "Right...right..."

He had to admit, ever since he summoned his Word of Heart in the training ground, the guards had been checking in on him more often. He knew they not only didn't trust him, but were actually rather *afraid* of him.

"My Jarl!" the men looked upward to see the forms of Caedmon and Nox in the moonlit dawn.

"A,." the Jarl said without his usual spunk, "What happens today, Nox, is a special occurrence; it is a special day." He looked into the dark cave, "Today you will undergo the Trial of Lyhaal."

Nox looked at the king blankly.

He smiled.

"Today, Nox, I am to tell you a story involving both *you,*" he said as he motioned to the others with his hand, "and we."

"Me?"

"Not you, Nox, but *you,* Lunae." Agmundr pointed to a worn flag draped at the height of the cave's opening. "What do you see on that flag?"

The young girl paused, eying the design.

"It looks like a...moth?"

"You see, there is something I have not told you," the Jarl paused, "Lunae has another name among Hawkhaven. She is the Moth Queen and the matron goddess of the Giants."

Nox narrowed her eyes.

"Moth Queen?"

"Giants have a long held belief that the souls of great warriors become lunar moths. Long ago, the Aeon, Lunae, gave an artifact to the man known as Lyhaal, who then used it to bring our race into being."

Nox contorted her face. "I...don't understand?"

"Lyhaal was a scholar and follower of Lunae, you see. He wasn't even a warrior in the slightest sense. As a matter of fact, he was a young, sickly man." Agmundr began. "It was around this time that the Aeon of war, Yeornyeim, came to Lythia disguised as a gargantuan man, a Giant—" He held his hands out to acknowledge the other warriors. "A Giant, like us. The god decreed a vast challenge. He said:'To the man who can make me bend even one knee, I will make of you a great nation. I will make your name the name of warriors and heroes.'"

"So no one was a Giant back then?" Nox asked. She stopped and looked at the others around her. She could see the pride in their faces, covered by bushy, blue beards. She looked at Agmundr. She couldn't shake it, but his face seemed so...solemn.

"No. Yeornyeim was the first to take upon the Giant's form. He was not, however, the first of *our* kind. You see," he said, "many challenged the god, and all failed. The warrior god stood undefeated. And, as soon as he was about to leave this world and return to Empyria, a man came and challenged him to a battle.

"Yeornyeim frowned as a small, weak young man approached him. He laughed: 'Warriors far and wide have come to me, and all have failed! Yet *you* believe you can make me kneel?' The god scoffed!

"But Lyhaal stood his ground. He had come prepared! For seven days prior had he spent praying that Lunae give him strength, and on the eighth, she heard his call."

Agmundr paused.

"She gave him a weapon like no other. It was a blade, black as night, that could sever any tie...it was the legendary *Nightbringer.*"

Nox watched the flag in wonderment. For some reason, this story felt...familiar.

"Their battle raged on for three days. Many from all over Hawkhaven came to watch. The giant god was fierce and strong, his blades cutting through mountains, creating the valleys, yet, Yeornyeim's might was no match for the valiant Lyhaal, Scholar of Lunae. His magic blade sliced easily through the shield of his enemy, rending the god's hand from his arm. In pain, the Yeornyeim fell to his back, and the battle was over."

Nox was utterly hypnotized by the story, her eyes locked onto the image of the lunar moth.

"The god rose and praised the victor, saying, 'You are truly worthy of my honor!'

"He granted his blessing to all of Hawkhaven, giving them forms akin to the giant god."

Nox narrowed her eyes. Something wasn't right about the Jarl. He wasn't as lively as the other times she'd seen him.

"You are about to enter the Crypt of Lyhaal." Agmundr's words perked her ears. "It is a sacred tradition founded centuries ago." The Jarl pointed into the cavern. "You are to journey into the tomb and find the furthest chamber, the 'Sanctuary of the Moth.' There, in that sanctuary, live the Moonbow Moths. Your job is to venture into the cave, catch one of the moths, and then bring it back to me."

Nox took a deep breath. There was so much information in such a short time that she felt her brain boggle.

"Alright!" she said finally, "I will undergo this test!"

"Good." The Jarl snapped his fingers. At his motion, the three other soldiers lined up and faced Nox. "As to compensate for your small size, I will allow you to take one of my men with you." He pointed to each man, naming them, "Leif. Faril. And Ragr. Choose wisely."

Nox looked at each man, each one equally covered in large breastplates mixed in with fur and hide. They all certainly looked tough, and she was sure that, whoever she picked, they would be invaluable in battle and extremely strong and quick. She eyed the long axes they carried: battle axes made of what appeared to be pure iron, engraved with depictions of dragons and wolves. She inspected each one carefully, but she'd known which one she would pick from the moment she saw him.

"I pick him!" she exclaimed gleefully, her arm held out straight, pointing.

Iago's eyes opened wide in surprise.

"M-me?" he said, bewildered.

"Yeah!" she smiled. "We're friends now, right?"

Iago looked at her as if she'd told him the strangest thing he'd ever heard. He felt his face turn hot from embarrassment. He looked at the equally astonished Giants surrounding them.

"I..." The words barely escaped his stunned face.

"Good!" Nox laughed as she took his arm and pulled him into the darkness of the cave.

The Giant king and his men watched as the stunned Elf was pulled into the crypt against his will.

Caedmon turned to Agmundr.

"You forgot to tell them about the Draugr..."

Beogar walked through the farms on the outskirts of Hawkhaven, the wizard Athor by his side.

"Fools," Beogar mumbled through gritted teeth. "All bowing to that king—that *coward*—Agmundr."

"They live like ants," Athor said as he held his hands to Beogar, "living only to toil, then fade away."

Beogar turned to the small wizard and smirked.

"Why don't you give them something...*exciting*?"

"Oh!" the mage laughed, "That *does* sound fun!"

Athor walked under a high fence and approached a large chicken.

"Hey! You!" the farmer yelled.

Beogar lifted the worker into the air.

"You got something to say?"

The farmer felt sweat drip off of his back as the large warrior held him by his throat.

"N-no" he gasped.

"Now!" Athor said as he stood at even height with the large bird. "We have some fun!" he laughed.

A dark yellow aura engulfed the wizard, causing his tattered cloak to flow as if in a breeze.

The farmers around Beogar began to shake with fear.

"He's using those curses again!" one exclaimed.

"Don't let him touch you, or you'll be turned into a frog!" wailed another.

"Fools..." Athor laughed, then grabbed the chicken by the neck. *Bel Soreska.*

The words echoed throughout the hold. At his command, the chicken began to writhe in agony as its body began to morph unnaturally. Its wings and bones shifted as muscles reconfigured.

The villagers stood, speechless and in fear. Before them, the chicken, now a large wolf, began to growl and bark at them.

"Eat!" The wizard commanded.

The giant beast howled wildly and sprung upon the fleeing farmers. Athor walked around the small ranch, turning each chicken into equally ferocious wolves. The townspeople ran, screaming, as Beogar and Athor made their way to the castle's front steps.

The distant sound of dripping resounded through the walls of the cavern.

"Me," Iago griped. "Me, of all people!"

"Hey, I'm not *that* bad," Nox laughed.

"But I helped hurt you! I took you from you from your home! I kept you in dark captivity—!"

"And then you rescued me," Nox cut in a serious tone. "I keep saying it, Iago. You say you're bad, but I know it's not true."

"You don't know that!" he exclaimed. "I could kill you right now!"

Nox abruptly stopped and whirled around to face the Elf. He stared at her quizzically for a split second as she spread her arm out wide. He looked at her in the vague moonlight that begged to enter from the centuries of erosion which created cracks above them. Her eye seemed to sparkle in the moonbeams, a frigid blue he'd not seen yet. Her face was no longer the serendipitous, care-free, smile he had seen before. This glance was biting. This look reminded him of the visage that Lukas had given him back at Avelle's Brook.

They really are alike...

"Do it, then!" Nox's words filled the cavern, echoing endlessly down the dark hole behind her.

Iago stared at her incomprehensibly.

"*What?*"

"Kill me!" she yelled. "You said you could do it, so," she continued, her eye like a stone, crushing his chest with ever-growing weight, "Do it *now!*"

Iago paused. He felt his hands become clammy with sweat. She caught his bluff; she'd won.

"No!" His voice softened. "I won't."

Suddenly, Nox's ferocious attitude melted into the old, happy girl she had been before.

Iago felt her hands take his right hand.

"See." She smiled. "I keep telling you you aren't a bad man." She looked up at him, her once chilling eye now a soft tenderness. "And I'll continue to do so until you believe me."

Iago quickly ripped his hand from her grasp and turned away. There was a silent moment of tension in the thin cavern air.

"She was my fiance..." Iago's voice cracked as he spoke.

Nox looked at him in the moonlight, his red hair cast over by a single thread of light.

"Amalia was, I mean." He said.

"What happened to her?"

"When I was arrested for the murder of the prince, she was sentenced to execution."

Nox hung her head. *How painful*, she thought.

"I'm sorry," she said.

Iago paused.

"Nox."

Nox looked at him once more.

"Thanks."

She couldn't help it, but she felt herself smile really wide. Iago looked up at her, then contorted his face.

"What's up with the goofy smile?"

"Nothing," she sang, then turned around and pointed onward. "Let's go!"

She didn't want to tell him what her ridiculous smile was about, but she knew it was because she had made a friend.

The air inside the crypt became thinner and thinner as they explored deeper, the only ventilation being the randomly placed cracks in the roof of the cavern. They traveled farther back, when, at a time in which they were unaware, they realized that they were in pitch blackness.

"Great..." Iago groaned, "I can't see anything." He held his hand to his face. "I can't even see my own hand, and I'm an *Elf*."

"I don't even know how much farther we have to go?"

"Or if we're even going in the right direction..." Iago added.

"Maybe we're lost?" Nox said nonchalantly.

Gladyus Millenio.

Suddenly, three bright gray swords materialized, dancing around Iago. Nox looked around. The blades each exuded a faint glow, vaguely illuminating the stones around them.

"Nice thinking," Nox laughed. "I didn't know they glowed!"

"Only barely," Iago said. "Just enough to let us see where we are."

"It's still better than no light!" Nox said, slightly encouragingly.

The two adventurers walked by the dim light of the translucent blades for an amount of time that they couldn't determine to be either long or short. The glow of the swords cast against the stone walls of the cavern until they slowly changed to bricks.

"These walls are definitely man-made," Iago said as he rubbed his hands across a design etched into the rough stone walls.

Nox stopped and, taking a magical blade, held it as a makeshift torch to the walls. She inspected the carvings. Within the stone were depictions of a man pointing a black blade at a giant warrior.

"These markings," she said, "they tell the story of Lyhaal. We must be close!"

Suddenly, the torches along the walls of the tomb erupted in bright red flames, illuminating the entire area. Nox and Iago stopped and stared at each other for a second before turning their eyes to the sarcophagus at the far end of the hall.

"What did you do?" Iago yelled as he summoned four more blades.

Nox stared speechlessly down the corridor. They both watched in horror as the top of the coffin began to rattle and rumble.

"What..." Nox trailed off.

"Is that thing?!" Iago finished her sentence.

The top of the coffin sprung upward, hitting the high ceilings and shattering as if it weren't made of pure stone.

Nox and Iago looked in horror at a monster as it arose from its dormancy. It's half-molded skin gave it a greenish hue; it's muscles were missing in places, showing bones. Nox immediately gagged at the rotten, putrid smell the creature exuded. True, Nox was scared. But, also true, Nox felt her adrenaline shoot through her veins.

"It's a real, *live* zombie!" she exclaimed, her fear subsiding in the heat of the moment.

"I wouldn't be too excited," Iago yelled in disgust. "It's gonna kill us if we don't kill it!"

The gargantuan ghoul stood, towering over its small enemies.

"Then," Nox said as she grabbed one of the spirit swords, "we just have to kill it first!"

The monster charged toward the two, bounding at incredible speed in large strides. Iago pointed, and his blades followed their master's command. All of the swords spiraled down the alleyway, spearing the beast in the chest. The fiend staggered, then continued its long charge. Nox stepped in and held her sword to no avail. With one giant swoop, the beast sent her flying to the walls.

"Nox—" Iago was cut short as the wight grabbed him. Iago gasped under the immense pressure of the zombie's strength.

Nox could hear her friend's screams and gasps. Her mind raced. *What do I do?! What do I do?! What do—?!*

Time seemed to stop. All she could think about was her dying friend before her, caught in the clasps of the giant abomination. She could feel it, deep within her. The more she watched the beast through a blurry eye, the more she thought of everything before. She thought of her captivity, of Lukas, of Brother Claus; she thought of just how weak she had been, and just how little power she held to defend them.

And then she felt it—

Nox felt pure rage.

LET HIM GO!

With a swift flick of her arm, a massive violet blast erupted from her fingertips, spiraling toward the terrible monstrosity.

Iago could feel himself drifting, lightheaded. He could hear Nox's scream, when suddenly, a bright flash of violet light exploded in front of him.

He felt himself falling, and all went black.

In his mind, Iago could see her. It was as if *she* were right beside him. He remembered her ruby red hair; he remembered her orange eyes. In his mind, it was as if she were still there, in his arms.

"Wake up, sleepyhead!"

He could hear her voice.

"C'mon! I know you're not dead!"

He came to reality once more.

"Amalia?"

"No! Iago, wake up!"

Iago opened his eyes to see Nox in the vague torchlight.

"Are you okay?" she asked. "You were talking. You kept calling out her name."

He felt his face turn hot.

"I...was?"

"Yeah." Nox held out her hand. "Can you stand?"

Iago ignored her hand, forcing himself to a stand, staggering slightly.

Nox smiled.

"What did you do?" the Elf said as he held his head.

Nox looked at her hands. What *did* she do? Even she was unsure. What exactly happened? What was the bright, violet flame?

The more she thought about it, the more it perplexed her.

"I..." she trailed off, "I don't know what I did. I saw you getting hurt and...it just...happened?"

Iago stared at her for a moment, bewildered.

So you really are...Lunae?

"We need to continue," she said as she pointed to the end of the corridor, "a door opened down there."

They walked in silence through the now illuminated hallway. At the end, a door *had* opened, revealing a moonlit room. Nox entered first, looking around at the spacious sanctuary. The walls were covered in crystalline rocks and filled with the sounds of bubbling springs. Filling the cavern, vibrant moths fluttered about, their bright luminescent wings reflecting off of the stones. In the middle of the open hollow, lodged into the stone, stood an ornate, solid black blade. The moon cast down upon the blade, yet it did not luster.

"This is it..." Iago said as he too beheld the beauty around him.

Nox walked through the shallow spring to the pedestal.

"All we need to do is get a moth and take it back," Iago began.

Nox slowly walked toward the sword.

"Are you listening?" Iago's voice echoed off the walls.

She felt her hairs stand on end.

Lunae...

Something was different here.

You are, aren't you...?

Nox walked toward the blade. Was it talking to her? She was certain it was.

Who's there? Nox's mind felt as if it were swirling. She moved closer to the black blade, it's lusterless edges thwarting the slant of moonbeams that cast upon it. She placed her hand upon the hilt.

Suddenly, a powerful wind exploded from the blade. Iago stumbled, catching himself before he tumbled over. Nox looked upward. Surprised, she saw a bright, glowing man standing before her.

O great Lunae, you have come to my tomb...finally...

Nox's eyes widened.

"You're..." she said breathlessly, "you're...Lyhaal...?"

You have finally returned...Lunae?

Nox was startled by his question.

"I...have?"

Do you remember my promise?

"Promise? I don't."

You've... The phantom donned a sullen face...*forgotten?*

"I'm so sorry, Lyhaal." Nox said sadly. "I know that we were probably close in a past life, but I don't remember any of that...I'm...so sorry..."

The apparition of the scholar cocked his head.

Then why? What has brought you to me?

Nox held her hand to her heart.

"I'm looking for someone, and I hear that he is in grave danger!" she stared into the specter's ethereal eyes. "And I want the strength to protect him!"

I see...

The vision placed his hand on the hilt of the black sword. When he touched it, a purple flame enveloped the blade, creeping up Nox's hand until it engulfed her as well.

I made you a promise. The ghost's voice shouted loudly, as if to shake her entire being. Nox felt herself begin to fade; she felt as if she were to deteriorate and blow away in the wind. She could see nothing but a void, a beckoning emptiness that seemed to grow increasingly appealing.

Lukas. The thought of his face flashed through her mind like a spark. *That's right! I will protect him! I will be strong!*

The ghost of Lyhaal watched in amazement as the flames around Nox began to disappear, trailing back into the blade.

This, Lunae, is the finalization of my promise...that I may now return...

Nox's eyes burst open. At the same time, the ghost exploded into bright purple fragments. Iago stood, amazed, as the winds died down.

"You—!" he couldn't believe it. In her hands, she hand pulled the black blade from its stone.

My promise...to return the Blade...and rest my soul.

"That sword!" Iago exclaimed. "That's *Nightbringer*!"

"I know!" Nox said as she turned and smiled at the astonished Iago. He'd seen this smile before; it was the same dumb, care-free smile as always.

She looked at the blade. "It's so funny how things turn out!"

Agmundr stood outside of the doorway to the palace, his eyes locked with that of Beogar at the bottom of the long stairway.

"Well, big brother..." Beogar laughed as he turned and walked back into the streets.

"Have you come back to me, Beogar?" Agmundr said as he followed him down the stairs.

Beogar stopped in the middle of the street, at the gate to the palace.

"I," he announced loudly, turning the heads of all of the fearful onlookers, "would like to see which one of us is *truly* stronger than the other, right, Athor?"

The wizard approached, riding on the back of a giant wolf. More and more wolves came to his side.

"Athor!" Agmundr yelled viciously as he marched toward the small wizard, "You've poisoned my brother's mind! This suffering is on *your* hands!"

He quickly approached the mystic, but not before Beogar stepped in the way.

"Move, Beogar!"

"No!" he said as he placed his hand on Jarl's chest, pushing him backwards.

"He is using you, Beogar!" Agmundr grabbed his brother's arm, only for it to be yanked away from his grasp.

"Athor has shown me true strength!" Beogar retorted. "He has shown me the faults of your 'honor' and 'glory!'"

"Beogar, please—"

Suddenly, Beogar's fist swung full circle, slamming into Agmundr's jaw, the force knocking him to the ground.

"You're weak, big brother. I don't understand why I *ever* looked up to you."

"My Jarl," Caedmon and the other warriors exclaimed as they rushed down the stairs to tend to their master.

"You bastard!" Caedmon yelled back as he helped his king to his feet once more.

"Athor." Beogar motioned his head.

Athor pointed, and the giant wolves followed his command. Frothing at the mouth, the beasts hurled themselves toward the unwary warriors, descending upon them like monsters. The screams, combined with the sounds of battle cries and metal blades leaving sheaths, filled the air as the wolves ran everywhere throughout the town, followed by the warriors who dared hunt them and protect the citizens.

"Caedmon," Agmundr said as he rose. "Let me deal with this; let me deal with my brother." He stood and looked at the seething

Beogar. *"Little brother. I love you."*

Beogar let out a sickened growl as his fist once again crossed Agmundr's jaw, sending him staggering to the ground. Beogar spit, then reached down, grabbing the king by the throat.

"Now," he said as he squeezed his hands around the Jarl's throat. "We'll see who truly is stronger."

A loud blast rang in the distance. The people running from the wolves and the warriors stood frozen, along with the wolves themselves. The faint image grew closer until a red form appeared in the sky, approaching ever quickly. In the distance flew the dragon; in the distance, Emalyn was closing in.

Iago and Nox closed the stone doors behind them as they exited the Crypt of Lyhaal. Nox held the black sword at her side. The sun had risen to the height of noon. Iago took a deep breath, feeling the air of the outside once again.

"Well," she said as she stretched her arms, "that's over with—"

Iago held his hand up, stopping her mid sentence.

"You hear that," he said. "I hear the sound of wails. It's faint, but I can still detect it."

Nox and Iago looked at each other for a moment, then nodded. They knew what they had to do, and they knew that, whatever was going on out there, they needed to be a part of it. At that, both bolted through the door to the palace, moving gracefully as they slipped through the now-empty halls.

"They need our help," Iago said in between breaths.

"You think it's him?" Nox replied, "The one who ruined the dinner?"

"No doubt, and I hear another noise—a roar?" He looked at her.

For once, Nox saw fear in the Elf's eyes.

"The dragon!" Nox exclaimed.

"Dragon?!" Iago exclaimed.

Nox nodded, then picked up her pace.

Emalyn...

Beogar's grip tightened around the Jarl's neck. Agmundr felt it become impossible to breathe.

"See," Beogar laughed, "I should'a been Jarl all of this time. Instead of a weakling like you."

"Why don't we get rid of him for good," Athor said as he grew closer, "Why don't we turn him into a chicken, like he *really* is."

Beogar laughed.

"I think I *love* that idea!"

Agmundr squirmed under his brother's fierce grip. He wouldn't fight—no, he *couldn't* fight—not against his little brother, not against the one who he grew up with, not with the one who once loved him.

A yellow aura surrounded Athor as he reached out his hand to touch Agmundr.

Gladyus Millenio.

Suddenly, a phantom sword sliced through the air, cutting Athor's hand. The wizard screamed in agony as he held his bleeding arm.

"Athor?!" Beogar said loudly as another sword came, slicing his arm as well. Beogar shrieked and writhed as his wound began to bleed profusely.

Agmundr fell to the ground, coughing and gasping.

"Who—?!" Beogar screamed as he turned to see Iago standing with five blades dancing around him.

"That man has been good to me," Iago said. "I can't let you hurt him."

"You—!" Beogar said as he approached the Elf. The Giant felt a tap on his shoulder. He only turned halfway before the huge fist of Agmundr collided with his jaw with incredible force. Beogar flew from his feet; his limp body fell limp to the ground.

"Beogar!" Athor said in horror as he rushed to the fallen warrior.

"So," Iago said as he approached the old man. "You're the wizard?"

"Athor looked up, terrified.

"Yes," he said with a vain intimidation, "I'll turn you into a slug! Doesn't it scare you?"

"Actually," Iago laughed, "it gets my *blood* boiling!"

Suddenly, hundreds of phantom swords surrounded Athor.

"W-what?" the mage said, hyperventilating. "I—"

He never finished before he hit the ground. Whether it was from blood loss or fear, Iago didn't know. He also didn't care.

Agmundr turned to the Elf and nodded.

"You have my thanks."

A blast came as the dragon dropped to the ground, the force from its large body creating a tremor that knocked the Giants to the ground.

Agmundr stood, walking toward the large beast.

"Emalyn!" he exclaimed, his voice cracking.

"My Jarl!" the warriors yelled, but he didn't hear them.

Suddenly, Agmundr felt a hand on his leg. He looked down to see the small Nox, wielding a black sword. His eyes widened in shock.

"That sword!"

Nox looked up at him and smiled. Agmundr felt the weakness in his legs as his knees buckled and he fell.

"Emalyn!" Nox yelled as she approached the immense red dragon.

Agmundr watched the black sword.

The Sword of the Black Moon...the Black Blade of Lyhaal...

The Jarl knew exactly what it was.

"Emalyn!" Nox held out her hand, "I know you're in pain!"

Nightbringer!

The dragon roared; the powerful wind from it's breath caused Nox to stumble.

Nox pointed the black sword to the transformed Emalyn.

"I want to do something about the pain inside of you." Nox closed her eyes.

All became quiet; a purple flame engulfed the sword, then spread to Nox's whole body.

"My Jarl!" Caedmon yelled worriedly. "She'll kill it if she—!"

"Silence!" the Jarl hushed the Thane.

Nox opened her eye.

"I will sever your shackles! I *will* set you free!" a bright beam shot from the tip of the blade, piercing the dragon. The beast cried as the purple flame exploded from it. Slowly, the large form of the dragon melted smaller and smaller. Finally, after a moment, the form of a woman became visible.

"Emalyn!" Agmundr cried as he caught his precious wife and embraced her in his arms. "Oh, Emalyn!" Rivers formed from his eyes as the warriors watched him. The wolves turned back into harmless chickens.

The woman moved slightly, then her eyes opened.

"Agmundr?" she questioned through a cracking voice. "Where am I?"

"You're home!" the Jarl weeped. "You're finally home!"

XXXIX

A Distant Wind

Nox and Iago stood before Jarl Agmundr in the throne room. Their clothes were adorned in rich hides, with leather pauldrons and breastplates. Nox felt giddy as she examined her new, solid black armor; Iago couldn't care less.

Agmundr stood to face them from atop the stairs, the beautiful Emalyn at his right side. Nox looked at her in wonder. The slim Giant was so peaceful, her long, blue hair falling to the middle of her back.

"Nox of Zerlina. Iago of the Thousand Swords," the king began. "You have aided me—you have aided *us* immensely. We of Hawkhaven are in your debt." The king knelt to one knee. Nox and Iago watched as all of the warriors which aligned the walls knelt as well.

"We," the Jarl said with a bowed head, "will forever give you our gratitude."

Nox smiled.

"Rise, my Jarl," she said softly. "We helped you because it was the right thing to do. You owe me nothing."

Agmundr stood.

"Young Nox," he laughed, "I do indeed owe you something. I at least owe you the help of finding your friend."

"Y-you" she stuttered with bright, bewildered eyes, "You will?"

"You have retrieved the *Nightbringer* and used its power. You have proved yourself as Lunae." He put his fist to his heart. "I am honored to have you as a warrior in my court."

Nox paused a moment in deep thought.

"Agmundr," she said. "I learned something in the crypt."

The Jarl raised an eyebrow.

"When we fought the beast that lived there, I was able to tap into some sort of magic.

"Magic?"

"Yeah! It taught me something," she continued. "It taught me that I'm nowhere near strong enough to protect the ones who are dear to me—even if I do have the power of *Nightbringer.*"

The large king looked at his wife, who nodded in return.

"I...do not understand, little one?"

"I guess what I'm saying is that..." she paused. "I want the Soothsayer to teach me how to control my magic! Now that I know that I have magical power—Lunae or not—I know that I can become powerful enough to shield the ones I love!"

"I..."

"It is true..." A familiar voice entered the room. "Lunae is correct in what she says."

Everyone turned to see the old mystic, who was adorned in beautiful furs.

"I felt her power in the cards, yet she has much to learn."

The Jarl and his men looked at each other blankly.

"I believe the girl is right, Mundr," Emalyn giggled.

The Jarl turned to her and smiled.

"I see."

"Then it is as such," the mystic said.

Agmundr turned to Nox.

"And where will you go afterward?"

"I guess..." she said. "I guess I'll go back to Zerlina. I want to find out what happened there. It'll also be retracing my steps. Maybe *they* know where Lukas is."

He smiled, then sat upon his throne.

"As you wish, little Nox," the Jarl said. He motioned his hand, and servants entered at his beckon, carrying superfluous amounts of foods. "Tonight, however, we feast!"

All of the warriors took their seats at the table and began to eat.

Nox and Iago sat once again at the Jarl's left side. For that moment—at least to Nox—it felt that things were finally looking up.

Eldric was busy with papers upon his desk, though his thoughts were distracted elsewhere. It had been a week since the disappearance of Lukas and Blake. There was truly no way of knowing if they were alive or their whereabouts. But, what truly perturbed him was the silence of action from the enigmatic man he, Snow, and Prince Reethkilt encountered back at Avelle's Brook. He knew that one of the man's objectives was to rescue Valter Rivyra. That was a goal that he also achieved. But, Eldric couldn't figure out why he didn't just stop there. He could have simply used his companion's spacial magic to rescue Valter without anyone knowing, like he did with Iago of the Thousand Swords. But no. Instead, he sent letters; he passive-aggressively notified the Master Inquisitor himself. It wasn't an invitation; it was more exactly a *challenge*. And as to why the man went so far as to destroy the Sky Prison Tower was also a mystery. It was as if the man wanted to flaunt his power.

He was showing off.

"My, my, such a messy office. You know, a clean room eases the mind."

Eldric froze; his gut wrenched.

That voice.

The Inquisitor looked up. Suddenly, his body went rigid. Before his very eyes, sitting in the chair across from him, the man from Avelle's Brook sat in his office.

"I actually thought you'd be happy to see me, dear Inquisitor." He sat comfortably, as if he were in the presence of an old friend.

Eldric sat, utterly frozen, his voice locked deep within his paralyzed body.

The man held up his finger, a radiant emerald flamed kindled on his fingertip. He pointed the flame at the papers on the desk. The papers levitated in the air as if folded into the forms of swans.

"I am Zurriel, by the way," Zurriel said, putting his hand to his head carelessly with a chuckle, "I can't remember if I made introductions in our last meeting or not," he paused. "You know, Eldric, I have spent many years of my life as a storyteller." He pointed to his eye. Eldric watched as the piercing blue eye faded into a deep red. "The story of the Philosopher King was always one of my favorites. Truly, I believe he existed. Our old boy Lukas is proof of that." Zurriel sighed. "I really liked that boy, to be truthful. He was a good kid, but...I guess what's gone is gone— unless he finds he finds his way back, in which I'd have to kill him," Zurriel laughed. "I didn't come to ramble, however, my dear Inquisitor."

"...Y-you..." Eldric's words came out as a mere forced whisper.

"You know," Zurriel continued, "one of my favorite stories was about the Wind Stitch of Aestriana—you know the one—it sits above the throne of the King of the Four Winds. Legend actually says that it is where Lythia and the Nihilo become closest."

Zurriel paused. "Nihilo, the Boundary between Worlds. You know, Eldric, they say that there are monstrous fiends that dwell there, just beyond the thin veil. They are the ones who lost their souls—the 'Ex Nihilo.' As a matter of fact, your Devil's Blood is a curse that came from the *first* Ex Nihilo, but that is neither here nor there."

He looked into Eldric's white eyes. He could see the fear; he *reveled* in it.

"You know, Eldric, we are a lot alike. We both want what is best for the world. We both want the *greater* good."

"What are you trying to say?" Eldric murmured.

"The Wind Stitch is a strange thing. It is a unique strand in the fabric of space and time, a rift created by the Cosmic Sword, *Exillio*, three thousand years ago. It's like a crack within a stone wall, you see." He twirled his finger, and the paper swans flapped their wings as they flew around the room, "I've always wondered what would happen if someone were to make it go...*boom!*" the swans suddenly fell from the sky and unfolded themselves. "But no one has ever tried it," he shrugged. "Oh well..."

Eldric could feel his palms sweat; he felt himself shaking. The very man who destroyed a city now sat in front of him, and the Inquisitor had nowhere to run.

Zurriel laughed.

"I just thought I'd share my curiosity with you. Anyway, I best be off."

Zurriel snapped his finger, creating a small, bright, spark. Eldric flinched. When he opened his eyes, the man was gone.

The old man sighed, feeling as if his heart had started beating once again. He knew what Zurriel was going to do now; he knew exactly what.

He's going to open the Wind Stitch.

Snow held her claymore, *Silvershear,* with one hand, the sterling blade glinting in the light of the half moon above. The other knights had already left the training grounds to retire to the barracks. Personally, she loved this time. The large courtyard seemed endless under the light of the moon.

She practiced her form, trying new techniques and rehearsing old ones. Her mind escaped in combat. It was all she knew. Slowly, as the blade danced, she slipped into her zone. The life of a half-Elf was one of hardship and denial. In the Kingdom of Mirea, the Elves of the ruling class looked down upon those born outside of the blood; however, through all of her pain, she had never blamed her parents—but that was mainly because she never knew them. As far as she was concerned, it was Eldric who was *real* her father.

What's your name?

I'm Snow.

Well, Snow, you'll find that being different is more a blessing than first appears.

"Snow!" the voice of Eldric finally reached her.

She turned.

Eldric smiled.

"I knew I'd find you here," he laughed. "You're quite the ascetic warrior."

She blushed, then shook her head to hide the redness.

"What's wrong, Inquisitor?"

His face hardened.

"Prepare yourself and head to the *Orca*. I've already notified the captain and crew. I'm headed to meet with the Archbishop to hopefully acquire his help, as well."

Snow could detect the seriousness in the Inquisitor's voice. She straightened herself.

"I understand. I'll prepare right away."

"We'll be heading to Crown City, so pack accordingly."

Snow saluted, then walked away without another word.

Eldric smiled and continued to Marven's office.

Prime Minister Eizen Zilheim sat at his mahogany desk, his back straightened as he impatiently inspected his pocket watch.

Suddenly, there was a knock at the door.

"You may enter," he called.

The door opened to reveal a tall, Elven soldier, standing at salute.

"Your Honor, may I speak?"

"Granted," Zilheim said, his eyes still fixated upon his watch.

"Your guest has arrived."

The Prime Minister stood promptly, his desk chair scraping the floor as it was pushed backwards.

"About time," he gruffed as he walked quickly by the soldier and down the hall.

Marko Jharres sat at a table in a small white room. Paintings of rulers from times past decorated the walls, along with extravagant blades and shields. Some of the blades, fashioned in such exquisite design, incited his candid astonishment.

"You're late," an irritated Prime Minister said as he stepped into the room, closing and locking the door behind him.

"I'm late, yet you've just arrived?" Marko laughed. "Please, spare me."

"I'm still waiting to know why you arranged this asinine encounter."

"How is the king?"

"Bah!" Zilheim scoffed as he waved his hand dismissively, "That old fool? He's dead. He's been dead for quite a while. Time to move on, if you ask me."

"Someone is cranky." Marko laughed as he pulled tarot cards from his sleeve and began to stack them, making a house.

"My patience is thin, Jharres." The Prime Minister's eyes were cold and obdurate.

"The End is upon us." Marko didn't look up from his house of cards, which was now two stories high. "It's time for your little conquest."

"He's ready, you say?" Zilheim stepped backwards and checked his watch. "That was quite soon."

"My pieces are set upon the board, so now it's time for you to take a turn."

"Attacking Aestriana isn't necessarily an easy task—"

"Blah, blah, blah." Marko waved his hands. "C'mon, Eizen. The guy is practically a god at this point. He even has the *Eye of Lunae.*"

Zilheim felt his hair stand on end. A Cheshire grin strung out across his face.

"The Eye itself?"

"Yeah. It's an 'Aeonic Object'—a piece of the gods themselves. With that, he's unstoppable. And, don't worry about the siege of Crown City. I'm the nephew to the almighty King Reethkilt, the King of Winds or whatever they say." He waved his hands to get back on subject. "Anyway, all I have to do is order the door to open and," he said, motioning his hands as if they were doors opening, "BOOM. You're in. Easy."

The Prime Minister took a seat.

"You have men on the inside, don't you?"

Marko began a fourth story to his house of cards, which had become so large that he had to stand to complete it.

"That's not all I have," he said without looking, "trust me. You've nothing to worry about. *Because I can hear it now.*"

"You mean...?"

Jharres suddenly swung his arm with great force, sending the cards flying everywhere. With a snap of his fingers, the cards immediately froze in midair. Zilheim smiled as he watched a wind surround Marko as he sat back down.

"You see," Marko said as he sat. The cards began to fly around him and quickly came to his hand, creating a neat and orderly deck. "I have powers of my own. My stupid cousin can't hear the Wind, but I can. As a matter of fact, the Voices of *all* Four Winds are at my command. Aestriana will be yours before you know it!"

Marko put the deck in his pocket.

"Good." Zilheim checked his watch.

"You got somewhere to be?"

"As a matter of fact, I do."

Marko smirked.

"Best not keep *him* waiting."

Eldric walked to Archbishop Marven's office and knocked on the door.

"Come in," the muffled voice answered.

Eldric entered.

"May I sit?"

"Of course."

Eldric slowly stabilized himself on his cedar cane, then sat on the cramped wooden chair.

"I received the results of the tests that I had the labs run. The ones on the sample that Snowbird recovered at Ildar, I mean," he paused. "This stone, whatever it is, is crystallized zellinium. But, it's mixed with some other substance that we have no record of."

Marven stopped writing and dropped his pen.

"An unknown substance?"

"Right," Eldric lit his pipe, "I said that as well."

"Crystalized zellinium is harmless without being bound to a soul, isn't it?"

"Not this kind," Eldric puffed his pipe, "It's been refined by some unknown means and is highly volatile."

"Do you think that the man that destroyed Avelle's Brook is behind this?"

Eldric blew out a large cloud of smoke.

"I have no doubt in my mind."

"What would he possibly hope to gain by refining zellinium?"

"Well," Eldric said, "I wondered as well." He inhaled from his pipe once more. "But he told me himself." He blew out another plume of white smoke.

"*What?!*" Marven froze.

"The 'Wind Stitch' is the treasure of Aestriana—the mysterious phenomena that takes place in the throne room of King Reethkilt. As you know, it's the place where Lythia and Nihilo are closest."

A look of eldritch horror crossed the Archbishop's face.

"You mean—?"

"If he were to set off enough of those stones, it would blow the Wind Stitch wide open, therefore releasing the onslaught of the Ex Nihilo into Lythia."

"By the One!" Marven shrieked, "What do we—"

"We go to Crown City. Immediately. We can't allow that man to bring those stones anywhere near the Wind Stitch."

"Immediately?"

"Yes." Eldric hobbled to a stand. "I have the *Orca* ready, and Snow is ready as well."

"We need Inquisitors and knights to Crown City!"

"Yes." Eldric smiled. "And we need the Red Ravens."

Prince Reethkilt walked briskly down the hallways that led to the open courtyard. Once outside, he walked along the vibrant mixture of yellow and red tulips and down the elaborate stone walkway, which was covered in a mosaic of blues, reds, and purples. The door at the end of the path led to the throne room, a large room consisting of high wooden buttresses and colorful stained glass windows, depicting the kings of times past.

Inside, he walked toward the feeble King Reethkilt, now an old man of eighty-three years. Behind his majesty's throne, high in the air, hung the mysterious Wind Stitch. Clement hated it; to be honest, it made him nervous. He looked at it as he approached his father, the soldiers saluting him as he walked past them. The Stitch was merely a small area above the throne where the air became thin, and looked almost like a refracted diamond.

"Clement," the king's hoarse voice almost had no echo.

The prince knelt to one knee.

"Yes, father."

The king held his hand to his head as he bent over in pain. Clement suddenly rushed to his side.

"The winds of Lythia are loud, yet the Wind Stitch shrieks."

"Shrieks?"

"I hear them; I hear the ones of Nihilo crying. The winds are fast. The winds of destruction come to us, my son."

The thought of the mysterious man flashed through his mind.

"I will protect you with all of my being, father."

"My son," the king's voice was quiet. "In the midst of the maelstrom, I can see it. It is there, a vague wind, a distant gale. There is little hope in his wake."

Clement looked from his father to the Wind Stitch, its ominous gales refracting the light that touched it.

"This distant wind will not stop me. I swear I will protect you."

The king looked back at his son's face, then bowed his head, as if to pray.

"May One save us all."

XL

The Old Man

Lukas slept dreamlessly upon a cot as Blake watched him with a conflicted desire to wake him or let him sleep. She always felt he slept so quietly; he slept as if nothing were wrong in the world.

Suddenly, a ladle flew from behind her and hit him on the head. Blake jumped, turning to the one behind her.

"Was that really necessary?" she asked, half-spooked.

"He needs to wake up already! It's been two days!" the mysterious man behind her said as he stirred a small stone cauldron in the middle of the small, adobe hut.

Blake turned to see Lukas rise from his cot, holding his temple.

"Blake?" he groaned, "I have a headache..."

Blake picked up the ladle and turned to the man.

"I wonder why..." she glared.

The old man laughed.

Lukas looked at him, realizing that *he* had saved them. For a moment, Lukas just stared at him. The old man was rather tall, his dark blue skin and clearly Abdian features seemed to have rusted with age. His hands and skin looked rough and calloused, and he merely dressed in rags.

"Who are you?" Lukas sounded hoarse. "Where are we?"

"He saved us," Blake interjected.

"You are in the Miljinn Desert," the calloused old man laughed. "Smack in the middle of it, too. The closest city is Dhul, and it's about a day's travel from here."

"And I've been asleep for *two days*?" Lukas asked with

astonishment.

"Maybe two." The old man picked up the ladle, dusted it then went back to stirring the soup. "Maybe four. Who knows?"

Lukas stared at the old man, an irritated visage cast over his face. He looked at Blake, who merely sighed with a shrug of her shoulders.

"Hey—uh—sir?" Lukas' words came out a bit more awkwardly than he had intended. "Who are you?"

The old man stopped stirring his pot and lifted the ladle to taste the soup.

"No one special," he said as he reached over for a small urn, then rolled it in Lukas' direction. "It's too thick. It needs more water."

"What do you mean 'no one special?'" Lukas' voice slightly hinted at his irritation toward the elder's cryptic answers.

"I mean what I say." The old man motioned with his hand. "Now go get some water from the well, boy!"

"Can you at least tell me your name?"

"No." Now *he* sounded irritated. "I don't have one. Never have."

Lukas and Blake looked at each other, their faces equally bewildered.

"Water. I need water."

Lukas sighed, picked up the urn, and stepped outside. He looked around for a moment, but, as the old man had said, there was only sand. The air was dry. He looked to his right and saw the well.

"What do you mean? You have no name?" Blake asked calmly. "Did your parents not give you one?"

"They did," he cackled. "I just forgot it."

Blake looked at him, befuddled.

Lukas pushed the curtain back as he came through the entrance, the urn now filled with water.

"Good!" the old man said as he took the urn and began to pour it into the cauldron. "Now, what are *your* names?"

"I'm Blake," she spoke up, pointing to herself, then to Lukas, "and he's Lukas."

"That is a pretty sword, Lukas!"

Lukas looked at the sword Durandal strapped to his back.

"It's so unusual," he laughed. "It's pretty!"

"Thank y—"

"Let's eat!" the old man suddenly burst into loud excitement.

He took the three clay bowls and filled them, then handed them out. Blake looked down at the soup she'd just received. The concoction was white and quite watery, all but some chunks of a mysterious meat. She looked over at Lukas, who was already helping himself.

"Eat! Eat!" the old man laughed as he slurped, his lips on the edge of the bowl.

"It's actually really good," Lukas laughed.

Blake looked at the old man, then at Lukas.

Well he certainly cheered up.

"Scorpion soup is my favorite!" the old man said as he poured himself another bowl. "Always has been!"

"It's really not that bad, Blake!"

Slowly, Blake dipped her spoon in the soup and ate a bite. She was surprised by the sweetness.

"See!" the old man laughed.

"It's great!" she exclaimed in surprise.

They both ate a few bowls, or at least till all was depleted from the pot.

The old man wiped his face with his dark, worn, arm, then burped.

"My favorite..."

Lukas laughed, then cleared his throat.

"Sir," he began. "We need to get to the nearest city."

"Yeah! We do." Blake concurred.

The old man contorted his face, as if in deep concentration for a moment.

"You wish to go to Dhul?"

Lukas nodded.

"Yeah! We got separated from our allies, and we need to find them."

The old man nodded, then stood.

"Okay," he said with a smile, then walked outside, waving his hand for them to come, too.

Outside, the sun bore down upon Lukas and Blake's bare skin, yet didn't seem to bother the rugged old man. They stood for a moment, looking around.

"Over here." The old man pointed to a small wooden caravan. "We'll take it to Dhul."

Lukas and Blake looked at each other.

"How?" Blake said slowly, her eyebrow raised.

The old man turned and held up a worn finger.

"You'll see!" he made a beckoning motion, "Get on. Get on."

Once on board, they took seats underneath the small cart's shade—a withering cloth, suspended by four thin, equally withering, posts.

Lukas unstrapped Durandal and placed it beside himself. The old man sat at the driver's seat and picked up a stick, almost a twig, with a simple string that went into the ground. The two passengers looked at each other anxiously.

"H-how will we get there?" Blake stuttered.

The old man laughed.

"How indeed!"

"What do you—?"

Lukas barely got the words out of his mouth when the old man yanked the string. Suddenly, the ground began to shift and shake as a giant worm burst from the sand, rattling the two passengers as they desperately held onto their seats.

"Gary!" the old man exclaimed.

"*Gary?!*" Blake blurted out, "What kind of name is that for a *sand worm*?!"

The old man merely smirked.

"Get, get!" the old man said as he pulled the rope, which was attached to a giant leather ring, wrapped around the beast. Without another moment, the giant worm dove into the sands and began to slither forward, leaving only the rope visible.

A long moment followed, with only the whirring of the sands as Gary slipped through them seamlessly. Lukas looked around at the environment that surrounded him. Never in his entire life would he have imagined that such a barren place could have possibly existed. He looked at the old man. This man had saved him from certain death, yet, he still knew nothing about him at all.

The ride was silent, all but the sounds of the old man, who was humming a tune and singing under his breath.

Lukas sat silently as his eyes locked on the shadow of the city of Dhul, tucked behind the waves of heat that radiated from the hot sands. As the city grew closer, he could determine the bright colors that decorated the strangely shaped buildings. Curiosity enveloped him, wide-eyed, and he felt giddy to get there.

The worm swiftly carried the modest caravan to the eastern gate of the desert oasis of Dhul, slithering easily under the warm sands beneath them, unnoticeable all but from the string that leashed it. Lukas watched as the once distant and hazily vague walls became increasingly gargantuan, and, now that he saw them up close, he believed they were even more ornate than the artwork painted upon the ceilings of the monastery at Zerlina. Along the towering walls were painted brilliant mosaics depicting men hammering steel and holding up blades.

"You don't get out much, do you, young man?" The old man poked Lukas in the head with the stick. Lukas felt his face turn red as he realized he had spaced out again. "Dhul is known as the 'City of Smiths.'" He laughed. "Legend says that even the famed Durandal was forged here. It's quite an interesting story, ain't it?"

Durandal? Here?

Lukas and Blake hopped off of the cart and looked toward the entrance. Through the stone archway, they could see the bustling city, full of life and color. Lukas began walking towards the entrance; Blake followed after she'd turned and waved.

"Young man!" the old man called out from behind them. Lukas turned to see the old man pick up the Sword Durandal by the hilt and lower it to him. "You forgot your sword."

He—?

Lukas stood, baffled. Blake stood beside him, similarly stunned.

"It's a pretty sword," the old man said with a friendly smile. "I would hate to see you lose it."

Lukas and Blake looked at each other, speechless glances cast over their faces. Lukas looked back at the old man, who was now riding away.

How did you—?

Only one question swirled in Lukas' mind as his frozen body watched the man zip off into the vast sand before him.

How did you lift it...?

High Priestess Marise Myi Kefnir sat upon her throne, terrified, as her soldiers stood with their backs toward her. Prime Minister Eizen Zilheim and Agnon stood before them, unhindered by the tips of the soldiers' blades that surrounded them. All along the courtroom, Elven soldiers held blades to the backs of the Abdian army.

At the forefront of the troop stood a decorated man, clad in an elaborate orange robe, with many piercings along his face and red tattoos surrounding his eyes that extended to what appeared to be an image of the sun upon his forehead.

Zilheim stared into his eyes. "Now, my dear Kefnir, have you considered my proposal?"

The queen sat up in her chair, her blue skin in contrast to her pale green eyes and ghost-white hair, which was adorned in jewels.

"Proposal?!" she scoffed. "You come into my country, full force, and coerce my people into submission. And you ask me to abdicate *my* throne?!"

Zilheim opened his mouth to speak.

She cut off whatever he was going to say.

"What sort of fool do you take me for, you dreaded Elf?!" she pointed her scepter at Agnon. "And who is this Abdian you have brought with you?"

Agnon remained silent, his pale green eyes locked onto hers. Zilheim checked his pocket watch.

"We really ought not to waste so much time." He pointed at the hands on the clock. As he did so, the soldiers dropped into fighting stances. "It's quite simple really: You give me your throne, and I will spare your people from what might be a..." He snapped his fingers as if fishing for the right word. "Difficult transition."

High Priestess Kefnir slammed the butt of her scepter against the ground as she rose from her throne. "You dare come into *my* throne room and actually have the nerve to ask me to abdicate *my throne*!"

Zilheim checked his watch once more.

"My dearest High Priestess, I'm afraid you're wasting my valuable time, and, if you do not wish to stand down peacefully, then I'm afraid I have no choice but to *remove* you. I'll give you about ten seconds to decide."

The Priestess stepped back as if someone had pushed her, simply dumbfounded by the Elven commander's audacity.

"Ten. Nine. Eight. Seven..."

"Ginrah!" she commanded the tattooed man with a strike of her scepter upon the ground. "Everyone! Kill them!"

"Five. Four..."

The tattooed man yelled to the others. Suddenly, all of the men converged upon Agnon and the Prime Minister, blades raised high.

Zilheim looked up from his watch. "Dearest Kefnir, it appears we're out of *time*."

Chronn Valda.

Kefnir's scepter dropped to the ground, creating a clanging echo throughout her large, mosaic, court. As she watched, the soldiers—her finest men—were moving slowly, as if held back by a great weight, with the Elven commander in the center of them, seemingly unhindered.

"Magic user!" the queen growled.

Zilheim put his hands behind his back and straightened his posture. "Agnon."

The large Agnon moved his cloak to reveal a long dagger. *Nuun Gravikka.*

He waved his left hand, and small, black, clouds began to form around him. He waved again and more appeared at the necks of the sluggishly moving soldiers. He drew his dagger, and with several lightning fast motions, he swished the dagger through each of the clouds. The Abdian leader watched in horror as the blade sliced through each of her soldiers' necks, dyeing their bright orange robes in the warm, deep, red of their own blood.

The soldiers fell.

"You—" She fell to her chair as the large, muscular, figure of Agnon approached her, "You would defy the gods by practicing magic?" Her pale eyes turned dark under the shadow of the large wizard, as he lifted her by her throat. "You would kill your own queen—" Her breaths struggled under his grip, causing irregular gasps. "You would kill your own kinsmen?"

She looked into his eyes, yet there was nothing there; all that seemed to be in those pale, green was hate—a cold, blank glare, devoid of all empathy.

Agnon raised the queen higher.

"I have no kinsmen," he said.

Zilheim turned away. All he heard was the crunching sound, then the Priestess' body fell.

XLI

The Black Lotus

Enlil walked down the streets of Dhul at a casual pace, however, despite her apparent demeanor, she remained vigilant of the Elven soldiers as they marched to and fro around the city.

They probably think their armor makes them look tough. They're just cowards hiding behind Elven steel.

She walked down the main street and into the market district, her eyes scanning the soldiers in search of an advantageous situation.

Found one! she sang in her thoughts as she maneuvered through the crowd seamlessly.

Two Elven soldiers were in the middle of what seemed to be a transaction. At a distance, Enlil sat upon a bench; she closed her eyes and exhaled fully.

Okay. Remember what the Lioness said.

Enlil had mastered her psychic abilities at a young age, yet she still reiterated her mistress' lessons in her mind, mainly because it gave her comfort at this point.

Focus on the light inside. Feel it extend, and think beyond yourself. Now, touch the earth, its vibrations, its mind.

Enlil felt herself fall, as if in a deep chasm. She inhaled, then opened her eyes. Instead of seeing the masses, all she saw was a deep abyss. The people were gone; the world was silent. She exhaled again, her breaths seemingly echoing like a gong. She turned once again to the soldiers and the butcher.

"The goat leg is twenty sylvr," the butcher's voice shook

slightly.

She could see his posture; he was slumped forward slightly, his hands clasped together as if begging.

"Twenty?!" the first soldier laughed, his visor raised to reveal his Elven features.

"Tell me," the other leaned in close, taking the merchant by the collar, "You know what happened to those beastfolk back in Mirea?" He released him, shoving him backwards in doing so. "They would pull this crap, too, but eventually they submitted."

Enlil stood.

The soldier took meat off the counter and the two walked away laughing. Suddenly, a small force caused one of the soldiers to stumble.

"Sorry!" Enlil exclaimed as she ran down the street.

"Stupid—!" he cursed.

The man felt his pockets and panicked; his face turned pale as he burst into a sprint. "Hey! Thief!"

Lukas entered the city of Dhul through the large, decorated, archway, Blake following close behind him.

"Everything is so pretty!" Lukas exclaimed unknowingly.

"It's what you call an 'oasis,'" Blake said dryly. "It's basically a fertile place in the middle of the desert. You know, where trees grow and stuff."

Lukas looked around at the marvelous greenery. The palms swayed under the light desert breeze, which wasn't as harsh than the one they'd experienced when out with the old hermit. Lukas' gaze fixed on the white flowers that grew at the base of the palm as he bent down to see them closer.

"You've never seen a Abdian Lotus before, have you?" Blake asked as she walked to his side. "It's a sacred flower to the nation's religion. The white lotus is the symbol of Obsidian, Aeon of Death."

She paused.

"But...what I want to know...is why the Mirean army is in this city."

"Mirea is here?"

Blake pointed to the soldiers, the entirety of their bodies covered in slick, golden, armor with no skin visible.

Lukas caught on instantly.

"If they're here, does that mean there was an invasion while we were gone?"

"I'm not sure," Blake said, her finger to her chin. "If there has been, could that mean that they're headed for Aestriana next?" she slipped away into thought, muttering to herself. "Would Zilheim do this?"

Lukas simply watched her mind process, a confused look on his face.

Blake looked at him and sighed, realizing that he understood nothing of what she had just said.

"He's the Prime Minister of Mirea. Ever since the king has been out of commission and the prince dead, he's taken over the political decisions." She switched back to muttering, "Would he...?"

"I think we should just ask!"

Blake's eyes quickly locked onto her partner's, a look of sheer astonishment.

"Ask?! Ask who?"

Lukas smiled and pointed at a big building with a sign that read *Livya Cantyna.*

"The Abdians, duh!"

Blake sighed as she watched him run off in that direction.

It's always so simple for him...

Enlil made her way through the crowd of customers in the Livya Cantyna. She was looking for her big brother, and she knew he was gambling. She knew he loved to play poker. To be honest, she never saw the appeal, but he was older, so she figured it was a grown-up thing. Really, he would win all of his money playing the game, but she was sure he used his psychic powers to cheat.

He sure is smart. The thought brought a smile to her face, and, she knew that one day, she'd be even better than him. *But now, I need to get one over on those two Elves.*

Enlil shifted around the people, her eyes set on finding her brother's table. The crowds seemed to completely fill the tavern. She made her way to the other door, looking for a chance opening where she could disappear. As she approached the door, it abruptly opened, causing her to stumble. She braced her hands for the ground when she felt a hand grab her arm.

"Hey! Enlil?" a voice began.

Enlil looked upward to see Lukas. Briefly, their eyes met. She knew him instantly.

"I can't talk, Luke!" she said as she put her hand on his arm as if shaking it. "They're after me! I have to go!"

"Hey—!" Lukas watched her plunge into the crowd as the doors opened once more and two soldiers entered the room, shoving Lukas and Blake out of their way.

The room stopped; all eyes were on the two Elves.

"There!" one of them pointed, raising his blade as he forced his way through the crowd. The other followed, storming through the customers. The two made their way to one of the tables in the middle; all of the customers stood well out of the soldiers' way. Lukas looked at Blake, his heart pounding at the sight of the Elven knights; he turned his gaze to the table.

At the table, Lukas could see a fine, white tablecloth draped over its large, circular frame. Only one man, a young Abdian man, sat at the table, drinking. Lukas studied him. His lean build seemed relaxed even as the two soldiers in full body armor approached him. Even his pale green eyes seemed at ease.

"Give up the thief!" one of the soldiers commanded, the edge of the silver sword resting perfectly above the Abdian's head.

The man took a sip of his dark, caramel-colored drink. "Thief? I ain't seen no thief."

The soldier nudged the man's head with the hilt of his sword. "Don't be clever! I saw the thief sneak under your table."

"Oh, you did, did you?" the man laughed, then waved his hand dismissively. "I'm trying to play a game here, and, if you can't tell, I'm winning. So can you go thief-chasing somewhere else?"

"That's it!" the soldier shoved the man's head harder this time.

The man closed his eyes, then sighed. Abruptly, a blast of psychic energy swept through the room. For a moment, the soldiers stood, looking around the room as if they had suddenly become dizzy. Without warning, the Abdian's body moved quicker than Lukas' mind could process. It was as if one moment he sat at the table, then the next, the first Elf was on the ground, writhing in pain.

"He broke his arms!" one of the Abdians yelled in astonishment.

"Zhin'sai!" another exclaimed. Everyone in the room looked at each other for a moment.

Lukas turned to Blake.

"Is his name Zhin'sai?"

"I have no clue who he is," Blake whispered back. "Zhin'sai is the martial art of the White Lotus priests, but..." she paused, "there's no way he's a priest, right?"

"You son of a bitch!" the other soldier said as he raised his blade to the man. "You'll die—!"

With the same lightning-fast swiftness, the Abdian's foot swung upward, sending the blade flying and lodging it into the wooden ceiling. The man's foot came back around, heel-first, and collided into the Elf's helmet, the force of which dented the visor.

The Abdian walked over to his seat and sat back down.

"You boys up for another round?" he yawned.

"You really outdid yourself, Ayize!" Enlil laughed as she crawled out from under the table. "These guys had *armor*!"

"Yeah, yeah," he groaned. "You got their wallets, right?" He pointed to the bar. "Get me some more of the dark stuff, you know which one."

Enlil smiled, then laughed. The Abdians looked at each other for a moment, then laughed as well. Lukas and Blake watched in amazement as the tavern returned to normal.

The sounds of merriment returned as if all had been well from the start. Lukas and Blake meandered through the crowd, making their way to Enlil, who sat on a stool in the far corner as she swung her legs back and forth, obviously bored.

"Hey! Enlil!" Lukas said with a smile once he had pushed his way past what seemed like countless tables and drinkers.

"*Lukas!*" a large smile cast her dark blue face.

"Yeah!" he laughed.

She pointed at Blake. "And you were the girl Damasko had all wrapped up!"

Blake stopped.

"You mean you were that girl back at Ildar?"

"Yup! And it seems fate has us together again!" she laughed. "So why are you two all the way out here?"

"Well," Lukas said, "to be honest, it all happened so quickly. One moment we were in Avelle's Brook, and the next moment we wound up here." He sighed, "It's sorta a long story."

Enlil looked dumbfounded. "You two survived Avelle's Brook?!"

"Sur—" Blake stuttered as horror filled her eyes. "Survived?"

"Yeah! It was obliterated." The small girl held her hands out wide. "Only a few people survived! The entire Sky Prison Tower was blown up!"

Zurriel! Lukas looked at Blake. He caught on instantly; he could see the fear in her eyes. The pain. The terror.

"Then Cilli, Ralf? The Master Inquisitor too?"

Enlil spoke up. "Nope, Eldie's alive! That's why me and Ayize are going to Crown City! The Archbishop and Master Inquisitor are going there!" She smiled. Lukas could see an innocence in it, like the glee of a child gone to play. "We're gonna pillage the *whole castle* while the security is focused elsewhere!"

Blake gasped. "Pillage?!"

Enlil looked at Blake and smiled. "Of course! I'm a Black Rose!"

"Enlil!" Lukas ignored his partner's reaction. "We need you to take us with you to Crown City!"

Blake sighed. "I won't hold your occupation against you, Enlil. As much as I don't want to ally myself with criminals, Lukas is right."

Lukas looked in his partner's pale blue eyes. In that moment, he saw in the same flame he'd seen periodically throughout his travels with her; in those eyes, he saw indignation.

"Right!" Lukas said as he placed his fist to his heart. "Zurriel is going to want a show. What better place to perform than in a court full of leaders. Enlil." He took her hand. The little girl flinched, surprised once again by his forwardness. "You were my lucky charm once already! Will you be that again? Can we go with you to Crown City?"

He's so strange, she thought with a chuckle.

"Okay!" Enlil laughed.

"Okay!" Lukas nodded.

Blake's face went blank.

That was easy...

They followed the thief as she squeezed her way through the multitude over to her partner's table.

"Ayize!"

Ayize finished talking to whoever he was gambling with, then turned his head and spoke gruffly.

"What?"

She motioned to Lukas and Blake. "I have a couple friends who would like a ride to Crown—."

"No." He cut her off with a dismissive wave.

Lukas sighed, and the three of them walked away.

"Thanks anyway, Enlil." Lukas began. "We'll try and find another way there."

She grabbed his arm as he turned away. "What are you talking about?"

Confusion washed over the travelers' faces.

Enlil smiled with a clever wink. "We'll just have to sneak you on board!"

Lukas looked at his partner. Blake's face had shifted from confusion to uneasiness. He looked back at Ayize, who was busy with the card game, then looked at Enlil and smiled.

"Alright!"

XLII

A Friend Like You

The aerodock was wildly alive, with all sorts of people coming from all over Lythia. As he followed Enlil and Blake, Lukas looked around in amazement at all of the different types of airships that were docked there. In his mind, he held the images of the lavish harbors in Zerlina and Avelle's Brook. This one, however, was *much* different. Outside, the vessels were merely anchored to the ground. Lukas noted how small these crafts were compared to the massive Airship *Orca*.

Enlil led them to a black, medium-sized, cruiser. Blake looked it over, the sleekness of the metal appeared to be in good condition.

"Enlil," Lukas said, "This ship is cool!"

Enlil laughed.

"She's the *Prometheus*! I think she's more ratty than cool though," she said as she clumsily opened the landing ramp to reveal a door locked by a keypad.

Lukas looked at Blake, who met his glance.

"Do you...?" Blake began.

"Know the code to get in?" Lukas finished just as the door opened.

"We gotta find a place to hide you!" Enlil sang as she skipped through the doorway.

Blake turned to Lukas, a mix of confusion and anxiety across her face. Lukas shrugged as he walked on board; Blake sighed as she followed.

Here we go...

Inside, the *Prometheus* was lavishly decorated. Lukas scanned the room, making note of the couch and chairs made of fine cloth.

"You can hide here!" Lukas looked in Enlil's direction to see her holding open the door to a storage closet.

"Isn't it a bit cramped?" Blake said. Lukas could hear her voice shaking slightly. She was scared without the use of her magic, he could tell, and after Ayize's show back at the tavern, he understood why.

Enlil put her finger to her chin. "I guess so, but it's the best choice!"

"I know you're scared, Blake," Lukas said, but we *have* to do this. We *have* to get to Crown City."

She jumped as Lukas took her hand.

"I'll protect you. No matter what!"

Blake could feel her face grow hot; she smiled in return.

"You going in the closet or what?" Enlil yawned.

Blake looked at Lukas once more. She saw that light in his eyes. It was the same one that had remained since she met him. No matter the trial or torture, she had always returned to see that hope.

He's right.

She nodded; he returned the gesture.

"By the way, Enlil," Blake said as she and Lukas stuffed themselves inside of the cluttered closet, "how do you know that your partner won't find us?"

Enlil gave a big smile. "Oh, he probably will!"

Blake suddenly became alert. "What—?!"

Enlil whistled as she shut the door.

The room was dark, all but a lamp by the window which cast light upon the droplets of rainwater upon the glass. Eizen Zilheim sat in his desk chair, watching the rain outside aimlessly, the low light of the lamp casting shadows about the room.

He sat, waiting.

He checked his watch, now for the third time.

In a bright flash, green flames erupted from the floor, forming a bright column, yet no heat. The flames quickly subsided to reveal Zurriel wrapped in his cloak of wolf fur.

"You're late," the Prime Minister said, checking his watch a fourth time.

"Late?" Zurriel's deep laughter filled the small, dark room. "What exactly is 'late' but a mere concept? Why, perhaps you are merely early?" He lifted his finger; a small tongue of green flame danced on his fingertip. "Time is so subjective, Minister, and who can truly claim it even exists with certainty?"

Zilheim watched the small ember flicker upon the tip of his guest's index finger. He had heard terrible things about this flame; truly, he feared it. He exhaled and checked his watch; he rubbed his clammy hands on his blue dress pants.

"Oh, dear Prime Minister, what ever shall I do with you?" Zurriel said as he nonchalantly took a seat by the lamp.

Zilheim looked at him in the dim light. The yellow light cast over his face, glistening off of his red eye.

It's true. He has it.

Zurriel waved his hand in the direction of the desk. Green flames surrounded the pens inside the cup that held them. Zilheim watched eerily as the pens spilled out of the cup and gently floated to his guest.

"Do I scare you, Zilheim?" Zurriel narrowed his eyes and smiled wolfishly as the pens began to swim in the air around him. "I don't wish to. Really, I don't." He took one of the pens and spun it along his fingers. "I simply wish to set right all of the wrong in the world." With a flick of his wrist, the pens formed a circle in the air and began to spin like a wheel. "You wish that as well, don't you, Eizen Zilheim?"

Zilheim's gaze was locked onto the crimson eye. He noticed his breath had become steady. Regardless, his palms still sweat.

"The eye?" Zurriel smiled. "It was a gift from the Aeon herself. With it, I could rule all of Lythia." He held out his hand, the pens gathering above his palm. The Prime Minister watched in awe as the pens mutated and molded into a small, glass, globe depicting the world in vibrant color. "But that is what *you* want, isn't it?"

Zilheim froze, his eyes peering into Zurriel's red eye.

"Yes," he replied louder than he had intended.

"The Eyes of Lunae do not lie. The power they hold allows me to read your heart like a book."

Zilheim straightened his posture. "Conquering Abdiah was an easy feat. They're such a primitive people, and without Elven technology, they crumpled almost instantly." He cleared his throat. "Along with your comrade, Agnon, we subdued the entire country within a matter of days. However..."

Zurriel made the globe spin as it levitated just above his finger. Zilheim watched the green flames. Right now, he knew more than ever that he feared the brilliant, yet chaotic, tongues.

"You will weaken Aestriana for me?" The commander's question came out more like a plea than he had hoped or intended.

"Of course," Zurriel laughed. "Anything for you, Prime Minister."

"Why are you helping me? What is in it for you?"

"I've already said." The globe floated toward Zilheim, who slightly flinched when it was closer than he would have liked. "I simply wish to right the wrongs in this world."

"But, you're not an Elf? Why would you fight for an Elven regime?"

Suddenly, the globe mutated into a small, thin, knife. Zilheim went cold, the touch of the steel pressed slightly against his neck daunted him.

"You're right, Prime Minister. I am no Elf." He pointed to his red eye. "I am something *far* greater."

The nighttime air was wet with fog as the Airship *Orca* cruised carefully over the forests of Aestriana, bound for Crown City. Inside, Eldric sat on his bed, peering through the window to see the darkness outside. He reclined back, his head softly hitting his pillow. It had all happened so quickly. In all of the many years as his being the Master of the Inquisition, he had never once encountered a problem—no, an enemy—so problematic as this. He closed his eyes.

There was a knock at his door.

"Enter." Eldric said promptly.

"Eldric," Snow said as she opened the door, closing it behind her.

"Snow?" Eldric said quizzically as he sat up with mild struggle, "You aren't asleep? It's quite late."

"I can't sleep," she said as she sat in his desk chair. "I keep...thinking."

"You're troubled?"

"That man—" She stopped suddenly, averting her eyes from him. "Zurriel. What does he want? What does he *really* want?"

Eldric sighed.

"I have no idea. I'm sorry."

"You felt it too, didn't you?" She turned her eyes to the old Inquisitor. "When he called upon his Word of Heart—his presence—it was so extreme, I..."

"It's okay, Snow," the old man said calmly. "I did feel it, as well. The extent of that man's power was immense. I owe you for your quick actions."

"No. I was merely doing my duty." She smiled. "You took me in when no one else would, Eldric. You fathered me, and for that, there is no possible way you could be in my debt."

"Don't be silly," Eldric laughed as he took off his shoe, revealing his clubbed foot. "I took you in because we were quite the same. A half-Elf is seen just as deformed as a cripple." He paused and reclined once more. "You should return to your room, Snow. You need to sleep. We will be at Crown City soon.

Snow nodded in agreement as she rose.

"Thank you, father."

Eldric chuckled as she closed the door behind her on exiting.

The moon illuminated the dark blue sky above Crown City. Clement stood upon the balcony, stargazing as if lost in the seemingly endless abyss above him. He could feel the light mountain breeze caress his face. The wind had always been something he cherished, though he could not hear its voice like his father could.

"Up here all alone, at this time of night?" A voice approached. "Even the Prince of Aestriana needs to sleep."

Clement turned and smiled. He knew that voice; he'd never forget it.

"I should ask you the same thing, Marko."

"Ah." Marko shrugged. "Can't sleep. Tried to, but couldn't."

"I feel the same..." the prince replied as he returned his gaze to the night sky.

Marko sat on one of the ornate stone benches by the wall. He took in a deep breath of mountain air.

"It saying anything?"

Clement breathed deeply as well, feeling the wind sift through his short brown hair.

"The wind?" he laughed, "No. The wind does not speak to me as it does my father."

Marko laughed as well. "King Alexander Clement zel Reethkilt. It's got a ring to it." He reached into his pocket and pulled out the deck of tarot cards. "I'd be a bit happier if I were the next King of Four Winds. I mean, you're technically a demigod, right?"

"No. No such title is mine. I am merely a servant of the people of Aestriana." Clement turned and smiled. "I am just as much a man as the beggar on the streets."

Marco laughed as he fanned the deck open. "You always have been a good man, cousin."

"You still have your father's deck?"

Marco began to shuffle the deck. "Yeah, I do. That old bastard."

"He served my aunt well."

"Maybe so." Marko put the deck back in his pocket, then leaned against the back of the bench, trying his best to sit comfortably upon the stone. "To you, that is. The man was a failure—I suppose the only thing he was good for was to be my mother's husband." He laughed under his breath. "Better be glad your father didn't end up like him."

"Well, I am thankful for my father, and I am thankful for *you, cousin.*"

"Gosh." Marko rolled his eyes playfully. "You're such a sap."

Clement returned to stargazing; the air was silent for a moment. "Something on your mind?"

The prince looked off of the balcony. Below him, he could see the city in spots, illuminated merely by street lamps and lights along every tavern; he could see the people walking beneath the faint glows; he could see the vague movements of automobiles.

"My father," he said. "He's been on edge as of late. I believe it has something to do with *The End.*"

"The 'End of the World' thing? Listen, I'm sure there's nothing to worry about."

The prince looked upon the horizon. Atop the hills, he could the vast, mountainous expanse that was Aestriana. He watched longingly as the light of the half-moon lowered beneath the earth. Above the city, he could see merchant ships and civilian cruisers zipping about.

"Marko," he finally said after a moment, "What if the world really is ending? What if the events of Avelle's Brook are simply a harbinger of a greater catastrophe?"

"I think you're obsessing, Clement."

"Perhaps. Perhaps not." He turned to his cousin and smiled, "If the world should end, at least it shall end in the company of a friend like you."

Marco smiled.

"You're a sappy fool, cousin."

The desert sun had vanished below the horizon a few hours ago. Ayize collected his winnings from his card game and paid his bill before leaving.

Outside, the dry air had cooled under the light of the half moon. Ayize cautiously watched the Elven soldiers which patrolled the alleyways, always in groups of two. The lanterns lit the dirt streets in an orange luminescence, causing to them appear almost bronze.

Along his way, he looked around. People, both citizen and

soldier, went along their ways, whether it be a patrolman on round, a man trying to walk home from work, or someone searching for a place to get drunk.

"*No!*" He heard loudly enough to catch his attention. "Go bother someone else, old man!"

Ayize looked to his right to see a passerby kick up dust with his foot. There, in the cloud of dust, sat an old man. His unkempt white hair looked as if it had not been washed in ages—ages that seemed to be defined by the callouses and deep wrinkles on his face.

The old man held his hand out, his fingers contorted into a clubbed wrist. The deformity extended all the way to shoulder. His arm was bent unnaturally, making it slightly hard to look at.

"Sir—" he called out to the man as he walked away.

The beggar slumped himself against the wall and sighed as he tried to make himself comfortable given what he had. Suddenly, a bag of tokens fell beside him, the noise of which caused him to flinch. The old man looked up just as Ayize sat beside him.

"They treat you like a disease, don't they?"

The old man picked up the bag with his good hand. It was heavy.

"But they don't understand that you're just as much a part of the world as they are." Ayize took a swig from his nearly empty bottle of ale.

"Is this...for me, young man?"

"'May your charity be as pure as the Lotus,'" Ayize recited. "I keep my vow of charity, at least."

"The Lotus?" the old man laughed, "Priests should not be gambling tokens."

Ayize smiled and laughed as he pulled the collar of his shirt to reveal the tattoo of a black lotus.

"Well, I ain't a priest." He offered him the rest of the ale. "Besides." He reached into his shirt and pulled out the medallion of a black rose that was hung around his neck. "I like the *other* Obsidian better anyway."

"You're the Black Lotus?"

"Yeah," he yawned.

The old man suddenly became a bit uneasy. "Why are you telling me this?"

"Because." He smiled as he took off the medallion and handed it to the man. "I didn't want you to think I was a priest. I didn't want you to think I was trying to get some blessing outta my charity." He stood up and looked at the old man. "I wanted you to know that I helped you because you're a person. Just like me and everyone here."

The beggar looked at the medallion, then looked up at Ayize. Ayize looked into his pale green eyes.

"What's your name?"

"Salyr."

"Salyr." Ayize smiled. "Go to the Livya Cantyna and order a drink called 'Obsidian's Kiss.' They'll lead you to the back and you'll talk to a man named Fallior. Tell him Ayize sent you. If he bitches about it, stand your ground and show him the medallion."

The old man inspected the medallion.

"The Black Rose?"

"The symbol of the *other* Obsidian, the Aeon of Love." The Black Lotus waved as he walked down the street. "I hope the best for you, Salyr."

Ayize smiled as if lost in memory, then walked toward the aerodock.

It was cramped in the small closet. Lukas and Blake were not comfortable at all, and the thought of an entire flight in this position was daunting to say the least. Neck-to-neck, the two of them were squished between a mixture of clothing and boxes— boxes with sharp edges.

Ayize walked up the landing deck and reached the door. He noticed that there were footprints on the steps that had not been there before.

Yep. All three of them. He sighed. *When will that child learn?*

He entered the code into the panel, and the door opened.

Inside, Enlil sat in a chair, her feet propped up against a table.

"En!" He exclaimed. "Get off the table!"

"I know! I know!" Enlil groaned.

"If you knew, then you wouldn't," Ayize snapped back. "Now where are they?"

He knows! Blake thought from within the closet.

"Oh, they're in the closet!" Enlil laughed giddily.

She told him! Blake felt her blood turn cold.

Suddenly, the closet door swung open, and Lukas and Blake fell to the floor.

"En!" Ayize yelled over his shoulder. "I told you I'm not a taxi!" He turned to the other two, "*Get. Off. My. Ship.*"

"*Ayize!*" Enlil walked over to her partner with her hands on her hips. She put her finger in his face, almost as if reprimanding a child. "They helped me escape back at Ildar!"

Ayize's face contorted into a grimace of utter confusion. "*These two?*"

"Yep! And you know the tenets!"

"Don't—" Ayize groaned.

"'Always repay kindness.'" Enlil dragged out her sentence to give it full effect.

Ayize exhaled a long frustrated sigh as he sat in the driver's seat.

"Whatever..." he finally said, "you guys just shut the hell up, alright?"

Lukas and Blake looked at Enlil, still fully taking in what just happened. She returned the glance, then winked.

XLIII

The End in Progress

The mountain air outside was chilly, with swift breezes occasionally bringing showers from the gray fabric of clouds above that seemed to extend forever, as if blanketing the world. The drizzles were just enough to coat the red and yellow tulips of Castle Aestriana with tiny beads of water.

Inside the throne room, the Archbishop, the Master Inquisitor, and his knight, Snow, stood in the audience of the king. At His Majesty's side, Prince Reethkilt stood, listening intently.

"What brings both the Archbishop and the Master of the Inquisition to my court in such a rushed fashion?" King Reethkilt's weary voice barely echoed in the large sanctuary.

Eldric stepped forward. "Your Majesty," he said leaning against his cane for support, "I am sure news of Mirea's campaign against Abdiah has reached you; and I know that you are aware of the destruction of Avelle's Brook."

"Yes," the king replied, "I am aware that Zilheim conquered Abdiah. It appears that he is acting upon his own will. I have known King Mirea for the entirety of my life, and he is not the man to do something like that."

"Well. I believe that Zilheim's military action and the destruction of Avelle's Brook are linked. And I believe that it involves the man that I witnessed destroy the Sky Prison Tower, the man the one you knew as 'The End of the World.'"

"The End of the World...?" Reethkilt muttered to himself, then looked at Eldric. "How so?"

"The man's name is 'Zurriel,' and he possesses magic of a magnitude I've never seen before. He single-handedly destroyed the Sky Prison Tower, and he also killed the Butcher like he was a small bug. The man has been plotting in the shadows, however, for some reason, he has been leading me along with every step he takes. I don't know why, but as of two days ago, the man himself appeared in my office. He spoke what seemed to be nonsense— but I think I know what he'll do next, and it's terrifying." Eldric nodded to the king. "*That* is why we're here."

The king turned his face to the archbishop. "Marven, is what he says true?"

Marven bowed and then straightened his posture.

"Yes, Your Majesty. About a month ago, I sent one of our Inquisitors to investigate the reports of a Vampire Lord working in Ildar, along with the boy who drew the sword Durandal from its stone. It was supposed to be a training experience for who we thought was the Heart of Hearts. The situation escalated, and we retrieved a mysterious stone that was being used to shroud the entire town in darkness." He bowed once more. "I apologize, Your Majesty, for not telling you at the Conference. We simply were not ready."

"The substance was Zellinium, but refined into a form which is extremely volatile to magic energies," Eldric spoke up.

King Reethkilt tried to push his weak body upright in the chair, but had to be aided by Clement and Marko, who stood on either side of him. He whispered to them his gratitude.

"What does this have to do with me, Master Inquisitor?" The king placed his hands in his lap.

"I believe he wants to open the Wind Stitch."

The room silenced. Everyone looked above the throne. The Wind Stitch levitated in the air above them. The air flowed erratically inside of it, strangely disrupting the light. It looked like a giant mirror above them.

Clement looked at his father upon the throne.

So that's why he said the wind screams.

"Your majesty!" Havell Maro ran into the throne room in a

huffing panic.

Everyone turned to him, alerted.

"Elven airships to the south! The *Golden Gavel* is among them!"

"The Golden Gavel?" Marven exclaimed in astonishment.

"So," Reethkilt said under his breath, "Zilheim himself is paying us a visit?"

The king turned to Commander Clement and they simultaneously nodded to each other.

Zilheim stood, his back straightened upright, his hands behind his back. He felt he could fear no one, yet was feared greatly by many. All around him, soldiers and technicians sat at their posts, performing the necessary operations that were required to pilot the equally feared airship *Golden Gavel*.

He turned to Zurriel, who stood beside him, and Agnon, who stood behind the terrifying wizard. "I assume you will remain true to our promise?"

Zurriel kept his gaze forward, watching Crown City grow ever closer. "I told you I would give you Aestriana in one day, and I will do that."

His smile adequately reflected his cavalier attitude, and Zilheim wondered if the man had ever experienced fear in his entire life. "You, however, must merely keep them busy while I do my work."

Zilheim checked his watch. "That shall be easy enough," he said, his voice unwavering.

Zurriel turned to the Prime Minister and smiled as he put his hand upon the Elf's shoulder. Zilheim looked into the wizard's eyes; in those eyes—in that fearful sanguine eye—he saw nothing but frigid winter.

"Do not you or any of your men dare enter the throne room while I am at work." He chuckled slightly as he stared the commander in the eyes. "If you do, I will kill *you*, and everything you love."

Zilheim was silent; his body froze. Perhaps thoughts—replies and rebuttals—came to his mind, but in the ghastly presence of Zurriel, he remained silent.

The sorcerer turned and motioned to the Agnon, who appeared just as brooding underneath his thick black hood. Agnon whispered beneath his breath and summoned a dark cloud. The two stepped into it—Zurriel first—then vanished with the mist.

At the command of Clement, the throne room of the King of the Four Winds filled with the Red Ravens' most elite warriors, all of them lining the walls with one strategy in mind.

Defend the Wind Stitch, *no matter the cost.*

Havell Maro had been sent to command the defense of the city —a fitting role for the man who was often deemed Aestriana's greatest fighter pilot.

A great black mist formed in the middle of the room.

"So he comes..." the king said in a soft, tired voice. "And the winds shriek."

Clement turned to the soldiers as one of them brought him a long, blue spear which seemed to reflect the light around it like a mirror. The soldiers suddenly stood at attention.

"Well," Zurriel laughed as he stepped out of the cloud, followed by Agnon, "It's good to see you again, Your Majesty."

The mist dissipated, then was gone.

"So," King Reethkilt said as he raised his head, "the Master Inquisitor was right. I wouldn't so soon forget that voice! It was you. It was you who appeared to me that night. You're—"

"The End of the World, yes." Zurriel grinned, showing his teeth and squinting his eyes. "How kind of you to remember."

Clement raised his brilliant lance without another word. His soldiers reacted almost instantly. All around the room, the sounds of swords leaving their sheathes sounded.

Zurriel looked around the court to see an army of blades pointed in his direction.

"How sad..."

"Charge!"

Immediately, soldier after soldier barreled forward. The screams deafened the room; Eldric and the others watched as each soldier's blade sifted through the wizard without affect.

"Is that any way to greet a guess, dear Commander?"

Clement watched in horror as Zurriel stood in the middle of the room. Places—holes where the blades had pierced simply caused the man to ripple like water.

The prince broke into a cold sweat.

Is this man a god?

Zurriel looked around the room as he dusted off his clothes.

"Truly I did not wish to kill you all so horrifically," he laughed as he held up his hand. Suddenly a green flame engulfed it. "But I just as much did not expect such a rude welcome. It's truly too bad."

Zurriel snapped his fingers, and a great green flame exploded around him. The prince flinched. After a moment, he opened his eyes to see a great blue ward encircling him and the others. Outside, he saw his men covered in green flames. For a moment, they writhed in pain; some of them stabbed themselves with their blades. Some clawed their eyes out.

In front of their leader, all of them died.

Clement turned to see Archbishop Marven covered in a blue aura.

"Archbishop," he called, his voice suddenly gruff.

Marven returned the glance, his eyes concentrating on the prince's. "Protect me, and ward my spear!"

The prince pointed his blue spear at Zurriel as he walked out of the ward. The Archbishop spoke softly, weaving another to cover the prince.

"You know I'll kill you." Zurriel raised an eyebrow. "Why do you still resist, Prince Reethkilt?"

"I am just as much the Commander of the Red Ravens as I am the Prince of Winds. If it means defending my people, I would endure a thousand deaths!"

Zurriel laughed as a green flame lit his hand. "Why don't we test those words?"

With a quick flick of the wrist, a bolt of green flame shot from his fingertips. Clement did not flinch this time, raising the butt of the spear upward just in time. The force from the parry volleyed the green blaze into the wall, causing the stone work to explode.

Clement straightened his fighting stance again, his eyes like that of a hawk with prey determined.

"Oh?" Zurriel's looked at the Archbishop. "So your wards do work against my magic."

The prince broke his stillness, rushing spear-first toward his enemy.

"How bothersome." Zurriel raised his hand. The stone floor obeyed its master and rose, creating a wall.

Clement quickly broke for the left, spinning along the wall, preparing to spear Zurriel on the flank. Quickly, Zurriel snapped his fingers just as Clement came into sight, commanding the wall to jab the prince in the ribs, throwing onto the ground, his armor dented, holding his side.

"The Eye says I broke four ribs," Zurriel laughed as he raised his hands. Two columns of stone wrapped around the commander's arms, and brought him to a stand, arms extended to each side—his armored chest exposed. "How shameful to die like this, Commander. Truly, I will do your honor no justice." Zurriel raised his free hand toward the dead soldiers. "Now, tell me. Which one of your soldiers' blades shall I pierce you with?"

"You would dishonor their deaths by bathing their blades in the blood of their leader?" he coughed.

Zurriel was silent for a moment, then turned and chuckled. "Marko was right. You really are a righteous fool."

Marko?!

A green flame appeared on one of the soldier's swords. It quickly floated over to the dark one.

"What do you mean!?" the prince spat, "How do you know Marko?"

Zurriel twisted his wrist; suddenly, Clement and everyone had eyes on Marco. Clement's eyes opened in horror.

King Reethkilt froze as he felt the chilling steel of the knife pressed gently against his throat.

"You really are dumb, cousin," Marko scoffed almost in a huff. "I've wanted to do this for a while. All my life, I've watched your stupid chivalry; all my life, I've watched you gain honor and glory. You're so vain, it's pathetic! For my entire life, I've watched your sickening righteousness, and now," he paused, then laughed. "I finally get to see your precious world burn!"

Prince Reethkilt watched helplessly as the dagger slid along the throat of the King of Winds, a deep crimson bathing it in regicide.

"Marko..." Clement's words were a mere whimper. "My cousin...? My brother...?"

The prince froze as he watched his father's blood drip from the blade. For a moment, he stared at Marko's smiling face.

"Marko, you slithering bastard!"

"And, now," Zurriel said as he motioned his wrist with a whirl. The broadsword swished in the air and stopped right at the prince's chest. "You die."

The prince closed his eyes as indignation flooded his heart. The blade rose, then swept rapidly toward the prince.

Rex Ynfernim!

The prince opened his eyes as soon as a giant black explosion erupted all around him, the force of which sent his rock tomb flying apart. Clement dropped to the ground; the force of the fall caused him to yell in pain.

Zurriel began clapping as he turned to the front of the room once more. There, Eldric stood, arm extended to the fingers, a brilliant black blaze lit at his fingertips.

"If the prince shall fight, then I will defend him with my all!" Eldric yelled, his deep, raspy, voice almost a roar.

"And I as well!" Snow said as she stood by the inquisitor, her tall, lithe, figure covered in ornate armor, both the *Silvershear* and *Silversong* drawn, one in each hand.

Clement coughed as he forced his now weary body to a stand. He picked up his lance once more, then pointed it at Marko.

"Commander!" Snow said as she stood beside him, her silver blades pointed at Zurriel. She turned and gave an affirming nod. "Take your revenge."

The Heart of Hearts

"I plan to."

Suddenly, he burst into a sprint, hurdling himself toward the king-slayer. Marko drew his tarot deck and calmly threw the cards in the air, causing them to disperse.

"That's another thing, *cousin.*"

One by one, the cards shot toward the prince, whistling as they sliced the air. Clement raised his spear. The cards created scraping sounds against his armor. He raised his spear high, light glinting off of the sleek blade, and hurled to toss it. Just as he began his stroke, two cards spun around him. The prince fell to the ground, shrieking as he held his bleeding eyes.

"Such an idiot," Marko said as he walked over to the commander. The cards returned to him; he spun his finger in a circle, and the blood spun off of them, sprinkling the white tile in red. "You would dare so blindly challenge the Lord of the Four Winds?"

"The Four Winds!?" Clement roared as he squirmed, his back hunched in pain as blood ran from his face, covering his hands.

"Yes!" Marko laughed. "I can hear the Wind's voice! Something that even the noble *prince* couldn't do!" He put his foot on Clement's shoulder and kicked him onto his back and spit on his armor. "You really are an idiot. You can't even see an enemy right in front of you."

"You wish to take my life?"

"Nah." Marko smiled. "I think blinding you is enough. Sorta poetic, really. You couldn't see an enemy right under your nose, and now you can't see anything at all."

The prince rolled over and felt around for his lance. It was true; he couldn't see anything. All was dark, all but the sounds of war around him.

The battle over Crown City grew ever apparent as the *Prometheus* appeared upon the horizon.

"The *Golden Gavel*?" Blake's question floated in the air. "Crown City is surrounded!"

"We have to get around to the castle," Ayize said. "There's an aqueduct on the far side where we could enter into the castle easily."

"But we can sneak around them, no? You know, just go around to the back?"

"They probably already have us on their radar!" Enlil said serendipitously.

"They probably knew we were here when we broke the horizon," Ayize yawned.

Enlil smiled. "Trust us, we do this all the time!"

"But are you fast enough to outrun those airships?" Lukas asked nervously.

"Outrun 'em?" Ayize laughed. "Why would I do that?"

"Silly, Luke!" Enlil laughed as she pressed a button on the dash.

Suddenly, the lights within the cockpit went dark.

"We don't need to outrun anyone if they can't detect us."

"Yeah!" Enlil said as she slumped in her chair. "The *Prometheus* can go invisible!"

Lukas and Blake looked at each other and shrugged. They looked outside, and it was true.

They had become a phantom within the battlefield.

XLIV

The Roar of Hope

Eldric and Snow stood before the dark wizard, Zurriel, the blue aura of Marven's ward defending them from his manic, emerald flames.

"Master Inquisitor," Zurriel laughed, "Eldric of the Black Flame. You know you cannot beat me."

"Silence," Eldric commanded as a black flame flickered on the tips of his outstretched fingers.

Zurriel turned his gaze to Snow. "And who have we here? The famed blue-haired maiden that defends you?"

Snow made no effort to reply. Instead, she kept her eyes locked on the dark one's figure, her Elven eyes vigilant for any sudden weakness in his stance. She remained on guard, her claymore in one hand and short sword in the other.

"You must be quite strong, blade." Zurriel smirked. "To wield that great blade in one hand so easily."

"Shut up," Snow said blankly as she rushed toward her adversary. She was sure she could strike him. She was sure her calculation was correct.

The ward is on my blades, she thought, *I might be able to cut him!*

The wizard scoffed as he raised his hands. The stone floor answered. Pillars of stone rose from the ground and shot toward the knight. Snow's Elven eyes reacted with superhuman speed. Her blades arced as she charged, slicing through the quickly-advancing pillars.

Zurriel watched as the knight destroyed the stone. "So! Those are not normal blades." he clapped his hands, applauding the show. "Are they made of orichalcum, hm?

"Forget something?" Eldric exclaimed, now off to Zurriel's right with his arm outstretched to the points of his fingers.

Rex Ynfernim!

A blast of black flame burst from Eldric's fingertips. Zurriel stood still as he was engulfed by the ebony inferno.

Snow sighed in relief as the stone pillars crumbled to the ground. She turned to Eldric.

The flames that burn the very soul...

"Burn!" the Master Inquisitor exclaimed as he flipped his hand, palm upward, and balled his fist. The dark fires heeded their master's commands and began to swirl, creating a massive, flaming whirlwind.

Snow's eyes opened wide. She had seen the blazes many times in her history of working with the old Inquisitor, but never had she seen a ferocity such as the present one.

"I rend you of body and soul!" Eldric commanded as he raised his hand into the air, his body resting on the cedar cane. His hands moved slowly, as if being held back by some restraint.

Snow knew the toll this immense power had on his body.

This is it!

"*Perish!*" Eldric extended one finger, then brought it down and swiped left, creating the image of a cross. The hiss of the dark flames deafened the room. Snow held her Elven ears to avoid total loss of hearing. The black whirlwind suddenly imploded, then exploded; the force of the winds shattered the windows of the throne room, momentarily blocking out the sun. The room sat in vivid darkness, lit merely by the scarce embers of the hellfire that lingered in the air.

"You definitely live up to your name, 'King of Hell.'"

Eldric and Snow felt their blood freeze. Eldric watched in sheer horror—a feeling he rarely held, a feeling others felt toward *him*.

This.

This was fear.

He's still alive?!

Zurriel stood upright. Unharmed. Untouched.

"I haven't forgotten you, Inquisitor," Zurriel laughed. "However, I believe *you* are the one who has forgotten."

Suddenly, the blue auras surrounding Eldric, Snow, and Clement exploded into bright blue shards. Eldric felt his heart stop...

He'd made a terrible miscalculation.

He turned to Snow.

"Where is Agnon?!"

An agonizing wail filled the room. Eldric whipped around, almost losing balance. "*Marven!*" he felt his heart sink; his blood began to boil. Before him, Marven stood, arched backwards. Agnon stood behind him, one arm wrapped around his neck, the other stabbing him straight through the back with a long dagger.

Eldric dropped his cane and fell to his knees.

His friend...

...his childhood friend...

...his brother!

Lost on *his*

folly...

Black fire, huh? That's pretty cool!

You really think so?! Even if I'm a cripple? You still think I'm cool?

Of course! Cripple or not, you've really got a gift!

"*Marven!!!*" Eldric wailed as tears flooded his eyes.

Agnon released, and Marven fell onto the floor.

Enlil, followed by Lukas and then Blake, and finally by Ayize, exited the *Prometheus* that had managed to elude the dogfighting to land in the forest areas behind the castle—the place where the aqueducts pumped water from the lakes and into the city.

"Wasn't that fun!?" Enlil sang as she clicked her heels together in a giddy dance. "You really gave them the slip, Ayize!"

"Ah, keep it down, will you?" Ayize turned to the *Prometheus*, reached into his pocket and pulled out a small object, then pressed the button on it.

Lukas and Blake watched in amazement as the *Prometheus* cloaked itself and became invisible once again.

The Castle of the Sky King seemed to extend high into the sky, the gray stones of its foundation rose upward to the white marble of the castle's actual exterior. Lukas had seen many things in his life outside of the Zerlina Monastery, but never had he seen anything with such a luster as this one building.

"That castle is *huge!*" Lukas exclaimed, not really meaning to voice his thoughts.

"Yeah," Ayize laughed. "Of course it is. It's the Palace of the Sky King."

Lukas stared straight up the castle's length. He could see why they'd call it the Palace of the Sky King. The pearl-colored spires seemed to extend into the clouds, each of them wrapped in elegant white staircases. Lukas wondered how long it would take to climb it, and he wished Nox could be here to share this with him.

"You know, kid," Ayize said. "If I had to make a guess, I'd say you don't get out much, right?"

Lukas scratched his head and smiled. "You have no clue!"

"The aqueduct is rather dark, but there are some lights here and there," Enlil laughed as she skipped ahead of them. "Ya know, in case they have to fix it up or something."

Lukas laughed in excitement as he followed after the young thief.

Blake sighed.

Gotta be nice to be that carefree...

She turned to Ayize, who was left behind along with her. "You two seem to really know your way around this place."

"Yeah," Ayize said, "didn't you hear Enlil when she said we do this all the time?"

"You steal from the treasury of the Sky Palace," she paused, "all the time?"

"Well...mainly just when security is lazy, like in times like this. The treasury isn't well hidden, and we know of a secret chamber that leads right to it." He yawned. "Basically, we just look around."

Blake looked at him, astonished at his inconsiderate demeanor.

After a short moment of awkward silence, Ayize, yawning, waved his hand dismissively in her direction.

"What?" he said, "We're the Black Roses. We're the world's shadow, the dark hands of Obsidian, the Aeon of Death and Love."

Ayize made no eye contact, his gaze fixed forward. Blake could sense a certain nonchalant tone in his voice. In the short time she had known the Shade, he seemed to be either austere or lackadaisical, with no real in between. He was a strange man, for sure.

"H-hey, Ayize," Blake said after a moment, her voice almost timid. "By the way, you know Zhin'sai. Are you a White Lotus?"

Ayize pulled his collar to reveal the tattoo of a black lotus. "I *was.*"

"You're!?" Blake exclaimed before covering her mouth. "*You're* the Black Lotus? You're one of the most wanted men in the world!"

"You've come this far, and *now* you act surprised?" he chuckled under his breath. "'Black Lotus' is just what they call me. I wouldn't think too much of it. I know *I* don't."

Ahead, Lukas stared into the mouth of a giant stone cavern.

"*This* is the aqueduct?"

"Yep..." Enlil said flatly.

"The path diverges a little bit further from here," Ayize said as he approached, Blake following close behind. "If you want to reach the throne room, just keep going forward."

"It was nice to see you again, Luke!" Enlil smiled.

"You mean you won't be going with us?" Lukas asked.

"Nope! We gotta go the other way to the secret chamber!"

"Yeah," Ayize yawned as he and Enlil walked past them and disappeared into the shadows, "best of luck, though!"

Agnon stood over Marven. The Archbishop's sanguine blood dripped from the wet blade in the large wizard's hand; Eldric beheld the Archbishop's limp body before him.

"Marven?!"

No. The thoughts spiraled through his mind.

"Marven!?"

Please, oh One, no! No!

"So, Master," Marko said as he kicked Clement in the side, then walked past him, "You want us to kill 'em now?"

"It would be rather easy, Master," Agnon said as he looked down at Eldric, who was lost in the moment of his comrade's death.

"No," Zurriel said matter-of-factly. "I wish for them to be around for the surprise."

"Alright..." Marko groaned.

"Surprise?" Snow separated her swords, one pointing at Agnon, the other at Zurriel. "What do you mean—?!"

"*Silence!*" Zurriel held his hand up and looked out the corner of his eye.

He paused. He could hear it this time, he knew what it mean. He could hear the faint pulse, the distant sound of a heartbeat—the one he had heard ever since he took the eye.

He smiled wolfishly.

He's here.

"Agnon!" He pointed at the large Abdian. "It seems we have some guests coming our way. Block the waterway."

Without saying a word, the muscular wizard waved his hand and summoned the dark cloud, stepped into it, and was gone.

Eldric crawled to his dying friend, his face a ghastly shade filled with fear and despair. All around him, the world was crumbling; all around him, he only feared one thing; he only feared the one certain factor in his life: Marven would die.

"Marven!" he said as he took his friend into his arms, out of breath, "Marven, no!"

"El...dric...?" The weakness in the Archbishop's voice sent chills up Eldric's spine. "Am I...still strong?"

Eldric felt Marven's body go cold. He stared into his blank, open eyes. Eldric's breath became choked as tears welled up behind his eyes. He felt himself shake. It was true, and knowing that preemptively held no avail against the pain. He knew this was reality.

Marven was dead.

Zilheim watched the dogfights and infantry battles from his perch inside the Airship *Golden Gavel*. He was sure of himself as he could see the foot soldiers like ants below his feet. He enjoyed the thought, mainly because it was true. He could see the Mirean air force scattered the remaining Red Ravens. He smiled.

"Vondell." He turned to the captain beside him and motioned to the destruction outside. "It seems even Aestriana is no match for the might of the Elves."

Outside, Havell Maro found himself cornered, with three cruisers tailing him. He could see them in the rear mirrors as he swerved and dipped in a vain attempt to outmaneuver the onslaught. His mind raced as he felt the bullets push their way into his cruiser's metal.

Dammit! The thought was his last as he plummeted into the trees of a park.

He closed his eyes. Sharp pain when through his left arm as his forearm collided with the yoke. His craft began to fume. The sirens were sounding. He knew one thing: he had to escape before the flames reached the aether reservoir.

His arm limp, Maro unwound his belts. He tried lifting the harness, but to no avail. He pushed upward with his working right arm, yet the brace held. He looked at the release—the button to his right. His arm was limp past his elbow, but this was no time. Quickly, the injured soldier raised his arm, crying out at the pain. His heavy hand lay limp in the air. He placed his hand over the release, then, in an excruciating gesture, applied pressure to it. Suddenly, he heard the click of the lock. Immediately, he raised the harness with panicky might. The windshield was cracked. He placed his greaves on the breaking point and pushed, breaking it easily.

Once outside the craft, he broke into a manic sprint, ducking behind a stone wall. The flames reached the aether tank, and Maro felt the tremor of the blast even from afar.

He sighed.

"Well, look here, men!"

Maro turned frantically to find a bayonet at his chin. Anxiety gripped him like a punch. All around him, Elven soldiers stood, swords ready. He knew there was no fighting left to do. He knew what this meant.

He'd been caught.

The aqueduct, as Enlil had said, was indeed dark, lit dimly by vague blue lanterns.

"So do we just go straight?" Lukas said as he and Blake passed multiple corridors.

Blake pointed to the large flow of water beside the sidewalk in which they traveled. "I'm only guessing, but given the size, this flow must be the main one." She pointed into the darkness. "And we can't afford to get lost in here if we take one of them. Besides, I trust Ayize, if he truly does sneak into the castle often, like Enlil said."

They walked silently after that, both simply focusing on the path ahead. Rats scurried beneath their feet, and many times, Blake had scared Lukas by screaming when one brushed by her feet. After the first time she had apologized and explained her fear of rats. But even with the apology, it still made him jump every time.

Lukas watched the shadowy hallways. The water seemed to create a small breeze, which Lukas found chilling rather than comfortable. The hissing of the currents resounded off of the sleek stonework around them. He felt cramped slightly, so he followed Blake in a single-file fashion.

They traversed for what seemed to Lukas a while before they saw the light of the entrance to the castle's interior. They hastened their steps up the ramp, when, suddenly, Blake stopped, frozen.

Lukas looked over her shoulder; chills went up his spine.

Before them, a large, dark, shadow stood at the entrance.

It's him. Lukas thought. He extended his hand; with a flash of light, the sword Durandal moved from its sheath to his right hand.

"You won't send us away this time!" Blake growled.

"No, I will not." The figure extended his hand. A dark cloud formed. He reached into his cloak and removed a long, bloodstained dagger. "I'm going to kill you both here. That is the will of my Master."

"*Zurriel!*" Lukas roared. "So he is here! I was right!"

"You are, yet too late." He stepped into the cloud and was gone.

Nix Celshior. Blake exclaimed. Lukas felt the air cool to a freezing temperature. Mist wafted off of frost that laced her skin, and he saw it cover her eyes in the low light.

Suddenly, a dark cloud formed behind Lukas. He barely recognized what happened when suddenly Blake pushed him into the wall. The large man stood in the cloud, a knife extended from within it. Lukas could hear his heart in his throat.

"Agnon, was it?" Blake said as she stood in her fighting stance.

"So, you are the Snowbird?" he responded as he stepped out of the void.

Lukas caught a quick glance at both of them. All he could see in the darkness was how massive the Abdian was compared to Blake.

Blake turned to Lukas. "Go!"

Lukas nodded, regaining focus, then bolted for the exit. Agnon waved his hand once more, then disappeared. The dark cloud quickly formed in front of Lukas as the muscular wizard burst from it.

It was all a flash. Lukas flinched. Suddenly, an icicle shot out from the wall with amazing force, slamming Agnon into the wall. The Abdian reacted, forming a cloud and disappearing before he submerged in the rushing waters.

"Go, Lukas!" Blake exclaimed. "I've got this one."

Lukas gulped and nodded, then exited the aqueduct.

Enlil skipped by Ayize. Ayize looked at the soldiers in the

hallways with abhorrent disgust.

"They're all dead...?" he muttered to himself as he beheld the mass of dead soldiers surrounding him.

"Doesn't look like they've been shot or stabbed or anything, either." Enlil scratched her head. "So weird..."

"Magic?" Ayize said as they continued walking down the halls.

"Maybe it was the person Luke and Icy were looking for?"

Ayize walked around the corpses, "But to kill at *this* magnitude. I mean, the *whole* castle is dead."

"Scared?" Enlil giggled.

"Please," he scoffed with a shrug. "Just get our loot and get out."

"Sounds like a plan!"

Lukas sprinted out of the aqueduct in a mixture of haste and panic. When he reached what he thought was a safe distance from the fray behind him, he stopped. All around him were cadavers, the bodies of soldiers littered the palace. He inspected further as he grew closer to them. No scars. No wounds. Just dead.

Lukas clenched his fist. This was the moment he'd anticipated and feared equally; this was the moment that would define all that happened before. This was the final battle, the fight with the man who wrought so much misery upon the world, the man who lied. In that moment, Lukas felt his indignation skyrocket as he saw the death surrounding him.

He took a deep breath.

ZURRIEL!!! he roared as loud as he could. *I'M COMING FOR YOU!!!*

The sounds reverberated throughout the halls. Further down in the throne room, Eldric, Snow, and the blinded Clement could hear it perfectly.

That voice! The thought shot through Eldric's mind as he raised his tear-ridden face.

"Lukas..." Snow whispered in disbelief.

The two of them looked at one another.

Suddenly, Zurriel broke into a manic laughter, a cackle which filled the battle-scarred court. He threw his hands up in the air theatrically, as if addressing a grand crowd.

"So!" he announced. "It appears the hero has *risen* to the stage!"

XLV

The End, Realized

Zurriel stood before the crippled Eldric and the injured Snow and Clement. His laughter filled the sanctuary.

The Heartbeat.

He could hear it as it grew closer. The heart beat in his ears.

"Oh Heart of Hearts!" he exclaimed, "Come to me—!"

Suddenly, the doors exploded, catapulting them off of their hinges. All eyes looked in that direction.

Lucyn Rejiis!

Lukas swung the green Durandal, sending bright blasts of light in Zurriel's direction.

Quickly, the sorcerer summoned a dead soldier's sword to his hand. Green flame snaked upward along the blade. Zurriel raised his sword and, with one blinking moment, redirected the surge. As the magics collided, their forces rippled the stone floors as if water disrupted by a stone, causing Zurriel's coat of wolf fur to ruffle in the blistering gales they created.

Eldric held his hands over his face to avoid debris from the blast as Snow rushed over to him. He looked at Lukas.

Is this really...the boy from before?

"So," Zurriel said, a smirk dancing on his lips. "You've grown since we last met. You've learned your Word of Heart?"

"Where is Nox, you bastard!?" Lukas yelled back, ignoring the wizard's inquiry.

"Oh ho!" He laughed back at the young Lukas. "She's no longer with us!" He pointed at his crimson eye, "I'd say she's floating somewhere in the North Sea!"

"Her eye!?" Lukas raged. "You—"

"Yes!" Zurriel pointed his blade. "I see your heart! Your Heart of Hearts! It burns with anger! Hate, no?" He waved his left hand, and all of the soldiers' blades responded. Lukas watched as hundreds swirled around the dark master. He smiled wolfishly. "Why don't you *share* some of that rage with me?"

Lukas pointed his blade at Zurriel.

It's just like with Iago. GO!

Lukas burst into a wild sprint, headed straight for the dark mage.

Zurriel pointed, and the flurry of swords all rushed at once, speeding rapidly toward Lukas. Lukas reacted by shifting his weight into his upper body swinging the Sword Durandal in a grand arc. A radiant white slice spun off of the fabled blade, hissing as it severed the air with amazing speed. Zurriel watched as his wall of swords shattered under the might of the young man's powers.

"You're strong, Lukas! Surely, I will kill you this time. I've made my mind up on that."

"Well then." Lukas pointed the shining Durandal at his enemy. "At least we're on the same page."

Zurriel smiled, almost joyfully. Never, in all of his life, had he met someone he wished to slay more than this man—this boy. Despite his age, the Eye allowed him to see Lukas for who he really was. And the sight of such a light enraged him.

Agnon towered over Blake, a mammoth compared to her petite figure. The once cool air of the flowing currents had become a biting chill. Blake could see that the freezing air was impacting him; he was indifferent mentally, but all she cared about was his body's physical condition.

Without a word, the large man opened a small cloud and stabbed it with the dagger in his right hand. Blake dropped her knees just as the blade thrust over her head.

He was aiming for the neck.

Quickly, she reached upward, her misty hand wrapping only halfway around the man's thick wrist. Agnon shrieked in pain as he dropped the dagger into the river. He retracted his arm from the cloud and held it with his free hand.

Blake looked at the redness of his arm. She smiled cleverly.

"What? Does the ice *burn?*" She dropped into her fighting stance, hands open, covered in frost, and ready to grab any punch or kick. "If you don't treat it soon, it will be full-blown frostbite."

Agnon reached into his cloak and pulled out another dagger, just as long and menacing as the first.

"I see your strategy," the brooding mage said. "You lower your body temperature as a defense mechanism." He opened a cloud. "But that will not save you."

Quickly, Agnon threw the blade directly at Blake. The chilly mage reacted by summoning a large icicle to shield herself. A cloud formed behind her and she dodged the hand that reached out of the void by sidestepping. Another cloud formed at her feet as she put her weight on the ground and the large dark hand grabbed her and pulled. Blake fell to the ground with a screech.

"So it's true." Agnon's thunderous voice filled the frigid corridor. He stood over her, one hand in the dark cloud that gripped her leg. Blake looked up at her assailant; his body was blackened from exposure to the temperature of the room. Blake swished her hand. A great wall of ice suddenly encased the large wizard.

"You lower your body temperature to evade the contact of an enemy."

His growling voice echoed throughout the corridor.

What...?

She looked at the frozen sepulcher she had created. Her heart stopped. Agnon was visible inside the icicle, but she saw the black clouds fill his silhouette. The cloud formed outside of it, and the giant man was free once more.

"As I was saying," he continued. The large man pinned her arm to the ground with his foot. Blake winced at the sharp, shooting, pain. "You lower your body's temperature, but it also makes your bones more brittle, doesn't it?"

He put more pressure on her foot. "Like this." The gloomy mage put his gargantuan weight on Blake's small arm. Blake screamed in bitter pain as she heard her arm crunch. "Snowbird, I will clip your wings."

Blake cried out as she raised her free arm to summon another icy coffin. Agnon held his hand out. With a flick of his wrist, an immense cloud formed around them. Blake felt a sudden warmth, then a bright light. She shielded her eyes.

"Open your eyes."

Blake saw the desert. All around her was sand, and all above her was the clear, hot, desert sky.

"You're useless here, correct?" Blake watched in horror as she saw the frozen burns on Agnon's flesh begin to return to a natural color. She ground her teeth at the pain of her broken arm. Agnon lifted her from the ground by her neck. He watched the frost on her body begin to melt. He smiled and opened a portal.

"I win."

The treasury was quite organized, as it usually had been for the many times that Enlil had seen it. Ayize sifted through some of the pure-golden trinkets and amulets, while Enlil eyed the ornate suits of armor. There was a quaking in the ground. Ayize and Enlil both stopped and turned to each other.

"What the hell?"

"Something is happening," Enlil said, her head lowered anxiously.

Ayize sighed and turned away. "The answer's no, En."

"But, we have to!"

Ayize purposely didn't turn in an attempt to avoid any eye contact. "I gave them a ride here. *That* was our deal."

The ground shook once more. The two thieves watched the lights flicker under the force.

"Something *bad* is happening up there, Ayize!"

"The answer is *no,* Enlil."

Enlil put her hands on her hips. "Ayize!" she exclaimed. "What about the Tenets?"

"We've already repaid the kindness, Enlil."

"But there's another one," she demanded.

"No."

"Tenet number three: 'Always repay kindness!' By Lukas and his friends being here, they've made it super-duper easy for us to steal things. So, really they did us a kindness to repay!"

There was silence. Ayize could feel Enlil's expectant yet reprimanding glare boring into his back. He knew how she was. Behind those ditzy eyes was a person of compassion and generosity. Probably the wrong traits for a thief or assassin to embody, but, regardless, those two things were the exact reasons Ayize wished to work with her, and it was for those reasons that he respected her as a person.

He sighed, then turned around. "Is *that* the only Tenet you know?"

She smiled cheerfully.

"Nope! It's just my favorite!"

Lukas panted, Durandal ready to strike; Zurriel stood calmly, his flame-wrapped blade pointing at the Heart of Hearts menacingly.

"You truly have resilience, young Heart of Hearts!" he laughed. "But you and I know just as well that you cannot beat me, even in your present state. Besides..." A dark cloud opened beside him, and Agnon appeared, holding the defeated Blake in his large hands. "You wouldn't want anything to become of your dearest partner, would you?"

"Snowbird!" Eldric exclaimed. He could see the film over her eyes, the bruises on her body where she'd been beaten severely.

"Blake...?" Lukas stared in a mixture of frustration and fear. Ever since he'd met Blake, he'd seen her as someone who always overcame. Never...never had he seen—or wanted to see—her so humiliated.

"Drop her." Zurriel snapped his fingers. Agnon released Blake, who hit the ground with a loud thud followed by gasps and cries of pain.

"What did you do to her!?" Lukas growled as he raised his blade.

"Well," Zurriel said as he turned to Blake. The dark one put his foot on her shoulder and kicked her onto her back. "I'd say it was a broken arm? Or maybe a beating?" He smirked. "Maybe both?" He looked at Agnon, who stood in stoic demeanor. He put his foot on her chest. Blake yelled in inhuman pain. "Yes, I'd probably say both."

"Zurriel! Leave her alone!" Lukas roared as he burst forward, sword swinging at the sorcerer. The wizard raised his blade and parried Lukas' left swing to the right. Quickly, Lukas shifted weight to lower his chest just as Zurriel swung for the neck, barely evading. Lukas spun and struck in a lightning-fast thrust. Lukas felt the jolt as his blade penetrated flesh.

Zurriel stopped and let out a ghastly shriek.

"I told you I'd kill you," Lukas hissed as he drove the blade deeper into the dark wizard's abdomen. Lukas could feel the warmth of the blood running down the blade and covering his hands. He looked into the madman's eyes and saw only hopelessness and a void.

Lukas thrust the blade even deeper. He could feel a fire within him—something he'd never felt to this degree before—a raging torment of hatred upon his heart. He looked into Zurriel's eyes.

"Lu...kas..."

Lukas opened his eyes wide as an eerie dread sank his heart lower than he thought possible. The mouth of Zurriel had spoken, but it was not his voice that came out.

Lukas' hands became sweaty, and he could feel himself shaking.

"B-blake?" He watched as the illusion of Zurriel slowly melted to reveal Blake. Lukas looked down at his hands. Durandal had lodged into her belly almost to the hilt.

He heard clapping. "Very good, Lukas!" Zurriel laughed. "But, not good enough."

Lukas dropped Durandal and embraced Blake's limp body as he placed her on the ground.

"Lu...kas..." She coughed as blood filled her mouth. "I don't...want to die..."

"Blake!" Lukas shouted frantically. "You aren't going to die! We'll—" He looked around the room at the surrounding death and destruction. He turned his eyes to Eldric, who merely returned his own glance. "We'll get you out of here..." This time, not a shout, but a meager whimper. She *was* going to die. He knew this. She knew this. He knew she knew, and he loathed himself for it.

"Lukas...I'm...cold."

"No no no no!" he cried; he could see into her eyes, her low, lifeless blue eyes.

Blake was dead.

The room fell silent, a maddening, deafening, gut-wrenching silence. Lukas merely looked at his friend—his dear, dear friend. Suddenly, all of the experiences they shared rushed behind his eyes. Lukas felt the flood of tears before he realized he was crying. This was awful; this was madness; this—he knew—*this* was *evil*.

"Even in death," The voice of Zurriel came from behind him. "Her heart made her weak. Such is its way. It fools itself with virtue, kindness, and love, yet, in the end, it returns to its madness, its hate, its evil."

"You..." Lukas whispered under his breath.

Eldric sat the best way he could, Clement beside him, wounded. Snow stood, doing her best to protect. In that moment, the air became thin. Incredibly thin. Eldric reached for his throat, gasping. The three turned to Lukas. Surrounding the young man, a raging white inferno engulfed him. Eldric's sat in shock as he watched the boy change before his eyes.

Suddenly, Snow fell to her knees as he gripped her chest.

"Snow!" Eldric exclaimed.

"My blood!" she yelled as he contorted her face. "It feels like it's *boiling*!"

The rocks on the ground began to lift into the sky as if carried by a great gale.

"So." Zurriel smiled as he watched the Lukas burn with white flames. "You *can* manifest the Starblood. Even though the Heart is not your own, you can still wield it?"

"I'm going to *kill* you!" Lukas growled as he whipped around to attack Zurriel. The young man extended his arm, and, with a flash of light, the bloodied Durandal returned to its master. Lukas charged violently at the wizard, blasting forward with inhuman speed.

"I've told you once, Lukas," Zurriel said as he raised his hand. Stones reached up to grab the Heart of Hearts' feet, wrapping themselves around his limbs as he charged. Zurriel watched calmly. Lukas was captured. Stones encased his body, just as the tip of the sword Durandal was about to pierce the Dark Lord's throat. "You are no match for me, even if you *are* Starborn."

Lukas could feel the stones constricting him. Zurriel stepped back and admired the blade Durandal.

"Lukas!" Eldric cried anxiously.

"Ah, yes!" He smiled. "The Sword Durandal, sword of the Great Philosopher King!" He threw up his hands as if addressing a large audience. "The myth of the grand king who gave up his precious Heart of Hearts for an all-seeing eye, only to be scorned and rejected by the Goddess and the people he so loved!" He bent down to Lukas' face. "I've spent many years of my life as a storyteller, wandering Lythia and hearing and collecting fable, myths, and folktales from all types of peoples. But the story of the Philospher King is the only tale *I did not have to learn.*" Zurriel held his hand over his blue eye. Lukas could see the red of Nox's eye staring back at him. "Do you know why that is?" he laughed. "I'll tell you." He removed his hand. Lukas watched in horror as the once blue eye was now just as crimson as the other. "I know that story *because I am that very king!*"

Fear engulfed everyone in the room. All had heard it.

"By the Aeons!" Eldric exclaimed, looking at Zurriel's red eyes.

"That's impossible!" Lukas yelled back, "That was a thousand years ago!"

Zurriel grabbed the collar of his shirt and laughed as he ripped it in half. Horrific awe gripped everyone...

In Zurriel's chest was simply a hole where the heart would go.

"Young Lukas," he said. "You would be surprised by the longevity of one without a heart."

"No...heart...?" Lukas almost whispered.

"Yes," Zurriel said as he extended his arm, palm facing Lukas. "And now you've seen too much." Suddenly, bright green flames danced on his fingertips. "Goodbye, Heart of Hearts."

Nyhilo Zurriel.

At his command, a giant blast of green flame engulfed Lukas, Durandal, and their stone prison. The explosion sent a giant rush of wind throughout the sanctuary. In the next instant, the wind came back as the blast imploded. Then, there was nothing. No Lukas. No Durandal. No stone.

Zurriel turned to the others. "Now, for the real show!"

Eldric stared into the hole in Zurriel's chest.

He really must be...

"I'm sure you know of my little zellinium experiment going on."

The Philosopher King...

Zurriel raised one finger into the air, then snapped. With a quick, green flash, a luminescent stone appeared above him, then floated toward the Wind Stitch. The enigmatic gusts surrounding the Wind Stitch seemed to hiss as the stone grew closer.

Eldric looked at Snow, who had now mysteriously recovered and managed to carry Clement from Marko.

"You know, Inquisitor," Zurriel said as his finger followed the stone to the large gusts of the Wind Stitch. "They say that the Wind Stitch is the one area in this plane of existence in which this world and the realm of Nihilo are closest." The stone moved beside the Wind Stitch and stopped.

The hissing stopped. There was only silence. Eldric watched the phenomena above him as he listened to his own heart beat anxiously in the deathly quietness.

"Not much is known about Nihilo, save that it is a place of darkness and nothingness." Zurriel said, "But there is not *nothing* there, no. There is much to see there." He smiled. "Much that you will see if you survive the blast."

Suddenly a bolt of emerald flame shot from Zurriel's fingertip and blasted the antithicite stone.

"Snow, Clement! Come!" Eldric shouted. Red lightning exploded from the stone.

Rex Ynfernim!

As the blast was upon them, Eldric raised his hands, palm up. The black flames heeded his call and rose around them in a whirlwind just as the gargantuan wave exploded. Wind coursed against the wall of flames and Eldric held himself at full power for longer than he would have ever known.

There was a moment of grim stillness as the walls of flame came down. Eldric fell to the ground, weary. Snow rushed to him pick him up. She put him on her back, then looked in awe at the open Wind Stitch.

Above them was a black void, a nothingness. They turned to the other three in the room. Zurriel stood there, and Agnon and Marko stepped out of the cloud and joined him.

"Snow..." Eldric huffed.

"Don't speak, Father." Snow said, "We're going to get out of here. This war can't be won."

"Clever of him," Zurriel laughed. "To think he would use his flames defensively! How exciting! I do hope he's okay."

Snow and Eldric stared at the hole in the sky. Snow saw it before Eldric, her Elven eyes perceptive. She felt her heart start to race.

What...is that?

"Like I said before, there are things that live the in abysmal realm of Nihilo. Things *I* have the power to control."

Suddenly, a multitude of claws the size of a bear's gripped the rim of the hole. Snow watched as black beasts the height of a man began to pour from the void.

Zurriel laughed. "The *Ex Nihilo*..."

"We're running!" Snow exclaimed.

"Running?!" Clement shouted back, still holding his eyes. "I can't see anything!"

He felt a hand take his.

"Do not worry, Commander." He knew it was Snow's voice. It was quieter than normal, tender and smooth. "I will be your eyes."

With one strong motion, Snow raised him, then bolted, leading him by his hand.

Marko watched them leave then turned to Zurriel. "Master, shall I kill them?"

Zurriel laughed. "No reason to kill mice when there are cats on the loose."

Snow raced frantically down the desecrated halls of the Castle of the Sky King. Clement by the hand, she ran aimlessly, her mind racing for an answer.

"Hey! Blue!" A young girl's voice caught Snow's attention. Swiftly, she turned. Before her, stood a little Abdian girl. For a moment, she felt like she'd met her before.

"You're the girl who took my pipe, aren't you? What was your name?" Eldric said with a weakening smile.

"You remembered!" the young girl said in a giddy tone. "I'm Enlil! I'm Luke's friend. Where's he at?"

Snow looked down at the ground mournfully.

Enlil gulped and nodded. "Um, oh. Well...follow me."

Snow sighed as the girl bolted off, then followed. The halls were littered with the corpses of dead soldiers, the bodies of which were already creating a foul odor. Snow did her best to keep the prince from falling. She followed the young Enlil down into a dark hallway, the sounds of the otherworldly beasts' roars behind them.

"It's the aqueduct! We came in this way!"

Snow simply nodded, then followed the girl's lead once more. The roars were becoming very close, and the darkness of the aqueduct grew ever never-ending. Snow turned to see the large, red eyes almost at arm's length of Clement when suddenly she saw a light ahead. The four of them raced outside into the green clearing. Snow turned just in time to pull him away from one of the Ex Nihilo's snarling jaws. Before she knew it, one of them jumped high in the air. She readied *Silvershear* as the beast came down, she swung with all of her might, slicing its head clean off. But there were more. Many, many more.

Snow stopped.

"So," a male's voice said, "we dyin' today or what?"

Snow turned to see an Abdian man, an adult, she could tell, and a black airship—one that had not been there before.

"Get on!" he commanded. "Beacause I'll leave with *or* without you."

Snow nodded as she sliced through one of the beasts. Quickly, she grabbed Clement by the hand and the three of them and Enlil rushed onto the ship.

"You're *late,* Ayize!" Enlil said in a pouty voice.

"Just be glad that I'm here at all," Ayize snapped back as he turned and hit the accelerator.

"Hold on—" Enlil almost said as the *Prometheus* shot off and cruised into the sky smoothly.

"We kept the engine on while I went to go find Luke. What happened to him?"

Snow placed Eldric on a couch that Enlil had showed her to. "I don't know."

"Wherever he is..." Enlil smiled. "I just know I'll meet him again."

Snow turned to Eldric. "Are you alright?"

"Of course," Eldric smiled. Snow could see the warmth in his eyes once more, "I'm only tired. Let me sleep, and I'll be good as new."

Clement sat in a chair as Enlil wrapped his head.

"Snow," Clement said. "What does it look like outside?"

Outside the window, Snow watched in the distance the *Golden Gavel* in a completed siege of Crown City.

"Well, my friend," she said. "It looks as if it is truly as your father said."

"So..." the prince said, almost a whisper, "it's the end of the world..."

XLVI

The One Who Waits

Lukas lay on his back in the pure white snow of the forest, no longer aflame, holding his head as he screamed in anguish. All around him were stones and rubble from the castle.

In his mind, he could see it. He could see Blake dying over and over again.

I could've stopped! Why didn't I stop! I could've seen through it!

His blood-stained hands wrapped tightly around his neck as he wailed out into the dark forest around him, and amid his screams, he failed to hear the footsteps approaching him.

They were quiet, but just loud enough to hear between gasps.

The Old Man from the desert watched Lukas lie on the ground. Casually, he reached down and picked up the sword Durandal.

What a fool.

Without a word, he took Durandal and lodged its blade into the ground between them.

Lukas awoke to see the Old Man standing over him in the dim first lights of dawn.

"You!" Lukas exclaimed with frosty breath. "You're that old man! You can wield Durandal, too?"

He laughed. "Of course I can. I'm the one who *forged* it."

Lukas raised to his knees, his voice raspy from wailing. "Okay! Who are you?! Who are you *really?!*"

A wintry breeze began to blow. The wind whistled between them as they silently stared at each other.

"I am the one who waits." Lukas looked into his eyes. He was no longer the delirious old hermit.

These eyes were cold.

"I am the one who watches the bleak horizon patiently hoping for the brilliant light of dawn." He pointed to Lukas. "And I have been waiting quite a time for *you*, Heart of Hearts."

"Me?"

"Yes. You were not ready when we first met, but you have seen his true face now."

"You mean Zurriel?"

"Yes. You know him as Zurriel. I knew him once as 'Lucyn of Zerlina,' the Heart of Hearts." The old man paused. "The heart that *you* now possess."

"Me?" Lukas said through his tears.

Then, it dawned on him—the memories of Nox.

"Yes, you know now what I mean. You know now the truth about the one who gave it to you."

"Nox..." Lukas bowed his head in pain, "Just like Blake—! She's—"

"She's what?! *You* tell *me!*" The old man cut him off.

"He said that she was dead, but—" Lukas coughed as his tears began to flow once more. "But for some reason, I don't think it's true. Just...a certain...warmth in my chest."

"You know she's alive, Heart of Hearts. From the moment that Lunae gave you the Heart, you were inextricably bound to one another."

There was a moment of silence as the dawn sun brought a sparkle to the crystalline ice around them.

"*Zurriel*," the old man finally said. "In the ancient tongue, it means 'Shadow.'"

Lukas balled his fist and hit the ground. "What does he even want?! All of this madness...for *what?!*"

"The Answer to Evil!" the old man roared. "It's what he's *always* wanted. And I believe he has finally found his answer..."

Lukas looked up at the old Abdian, staring into his cold, pale green eyes.

"But I do not know what it is," the old man began, "or why he is seeking the eyes. But if he finds them, then I fear—"

"But he already has *both* eyes!" Lukas retorted, "What can we do—"

The old man held up three fingers. "He has two, but there are *three!*"

"Old man!" Lukas said through tearful gasps. "I cannot rise to this destiny? How could I stop this madness?!"

"Fool!" The old man said flatly. "Have you truly come this far, yet still understand nothing? Heroes do not rise to meet destiny; heroes rise to meet *opportunity*."

The old man held out his hand.

"Heart of Hearts, your opportunity lies within this solemn moment. So tell me, are you truly prepared to rise to meet it?"

The light of dawn cast rays through the tall fir trees. A light wind blew flakes of snow about like dust in the air. Lukas buried his face in the icy ground, his tears still fresh.

"I..." he gasped.

He raised his head. He peered into Durandal, his reflection on its sterling blade. In that moment, he could feel the times he had up until this point. He remembered Eldric, Snow, even Clement, and Havell. He knew that, wherever they were, they needed him. He knew that Nox needed him, and so did the world. As he stared into that mirror-like blade, as he watched his tears stream down his face in the first lights of dawn, he knew that he couldn't let Blake's death be in vain.

He knew he *must* persist.

"*I am!*"

To be continued...

Book two coming soon!

Like the story?

*Sign up for my **email list** for more content and information about my upcoming works at:*

williamfburk.com

Or connect with me on socials:

Twitter: @burkwill

Facebook: @burkwillwrites

Instagram: williamf.burk4

Thanks for reading! :)

About the Author

William F. Burk was born and raised in rural Northwest Georgia, where he spent much of his childhood exploring forests and pretending to go on all types of adventures. Exposed to fantasy at a young age through *The Legend of Zelda,* he began to constantly think up new ideas and slowly surrendered to his wild imagination. Now, he spends most of his time writing and giving into the muses that captivate him. *The Heart of Hearts* is his first novel, and will be the beginning of a grander chronicle known as *A Tale of Gods and Men.*